HOW TO KILL YOUR FAMILY

Bella Mackie has written for the *Guardian*, *Vogue* and *Vice*. She is the author of the *Sunday Times* bestseller *Jog On*. This is her first novel.

ALSO BY BELLA MACKIE

Jog On: How Running Saved My Life
Jog On Journal: A Practical Guide to Getting Up and Running

HOW TO KILL YOUR FAMILY

BELLA MACKIE

THE BOROUGH PRESS

The Borough Press
An imprint of HarperCollins*Publishers* Ltd
1 London Bridge Street
London SE1 9GF

www.harpercollins.co.uk

HarperCollins*Publishers*
1st Floor, Watermarque Building, Ringsend Road,
Dublin 4, Ireland

This is paperback edition 2022
11

First published by HarperCollins*Publishers* 2021

A catalogue record for this book is
available from the British Library

ISBN: 978-0-00-836594-3

Set in Adobe Garamond by Palimpsest Book Production Limited,
Falkirk, Stirlingshire

Printed and bound in the UK using 100% Renewable Electricity
by CPI Group (UK) Ltd

MIX
Paper from
responsible sources
FSC™ C007454

This book is produced from independently certified FSC™ paper
to ensure responsible forest management.

For more information visit: www.harpercollins.co.uk/green

For my dad, who read me a hundred murderous bedtime stories.
For my mum, who read me a hundred uplifting ones.
I promise never to kill either of you.

Unsex me here, And fill me from the crown to the toe top-full of direst cruelty. Make thick my blood.

William Shakespeare, *Macbeth*

PROLOGUE

Limehouse prison is, as you might imagine, horrible. Except maybe you can't imagine it, not really. There are no games consoles and flat-screen TVs, as you have surely read about in the newspapers. There's no friendly communal vibe, no sisterly tribe – the atmosphere is usually frantic, hideously loud, and it often feels as though a fight will break out at any moment. From the beginning, I've tried to keep my head down. I stay in my cell as much as possible, in between meals that could optimistically be described as occasionally digestible, and attempt to avoid my roommate, as she tiresomely likes to be called.

Kelly is a woman who likes to 'chat'. On my first day here fourteen long months ago, she sat on my bunk, squeezed my knee with her horribly long fingernails and told me that she knew what I'd done, and thought it was fantastic. Such praise was a pleasant surprise, given that I expected an onslaught of violence as I approached the looming gates of this shabby place. Ah, the innocence of someone who only knows about prison from watching one fairly low-budget TV drama. From this initial introduction,

Kelly decided that I was her new best friend, and worse, a trophy cellmate. At breakfast, she will bustle up to me, linking arms and whispering to me as if we are in the middle of a confidential discussion. I've heard her talking to other prisoners, her voice dropping to a stage whisper, as she intimates that I've confessed all the details of my crime to her. She wants leverage and respect from the other girls, and if anyone can provide her with it, the Morton murderer can. It is *immensely* tiresome.

I know I say that Kelly professes to know all about my crime, but perhaps that diminishes my deeds somewhat. To me, the word crime sounds shabby, inelegant and commonplace. Shoplifters commit crimes. When you go at 35 mph in a 20-mph zone in order to get a tepid latte before you start another dull day at the office, you're committing a crime. I did something much more ambitious. I conceived and carried out a complex and careful plan, the origins of which were set in motion long before the unpleasant circumstances surrounding my birth. And given that I have so little to do in this ugly and uninspiring cage (one misguided therapist suggested I attend a spoken word class, and I was gratified when my mere expression ensured that she never made such an offer again), I have decided to tell my story. This is no easy task, given that I have no state-of-the-art laptop such as I am used to. When my lawyer recently presented me with some tentative light at the end of this tunnel, I felt like I should mark the time I've spent here and write down some of what I've done. A trip to the canteen provided me with a thin notepad and a tired biro – taking £5 off my weekly spend of £15.50. Forget magazine articles breezily suggesting you save money by scrimping on takeout coffee, if you really want to learn to budget properly, spend some time at Limehouse. The writing might be pointless, but I must do something to ease the stultifying boredom of this place, and I'm hopeful that

Kelly and her interminable group of 'ladies', as she insists on calling them, will stop asking if I want to watch reality TV in the rec room with them if I seem intent on a task. 'Sorry, Kelly,' I will say, 'I'm writing important case notes up for my appeal, let's talk later.' I am confident that the merest hint that I might tell her some juicy nugget about my story will have her tapping her nose like a ludicrous character in a Dick Francis novel and leave me to it.

Of course, my story is not for Kelly. I doubt she'd have the capacity to understand what motivated me to do as I did. My story is just that – mine – though I know readers would lap it up if I ever published it – not that I ever could. But it's nice to know that people would pore over it nonetheless. It would be a bestseller, and the masses would rush to the shops, hoping to know more about the attractive and tragic young woman who could commit such a terrible act. The tabloids have been running pieces on me for months now, the public doesn't seem to tire of the two-bit psychologists willing to diagnose me from a distance, or the occasional contrarian who will defend my actions to outrage on Twitter. The general public are so enthralled by my actions that they are even willing to watch a hastily cobbled together Channel 5 documentary about me, which included a fat astronomer explaining that my star sign predicted my case. He got my star sign wrong.

So I know that people would fall on my words. Without any attempt on my part at an accurate explanation, my case has already become a notorious one. And ironically, that is without anyone knowing about my real crimes. The justice system in this country is a joke, and there is nothing which illustrates that more than this one sentence: I have killed several people (some brutally, others calmly) and yet I currently languish in jail for a murder I did *not* commit.

The crimes I did orchestrate, if known about, would ensure that

I was remembered for decades, perhaps even centuries – if the human race manages to hold on for that long. Dr Crippen, Fred West, Ted Bundy, Lizzie Borden and me, Grace Bernard. Actually that displeases me somewhat. I'm not an amateur or an imbecile. I'm someone who, if you saw me in the street, you'd gaze at admiringly. Perhaps that's why Kelly clings to me instead of punching the living daylights out of me as I expected. Even in here, I retain a certain elegance, and a froideur that those weaker than I desperately wish to break through. Despite my crimes, I'm told I've received letters by the sackful, professing love, admiration, asking me where I bought the dress I wore on the first day of my trial (Roksanda, if you're interested. That terrible Prime Minister's wife wore something very similar just a month later, unfortunately). Often hate mail. Sometimes mad shit, where the writer thinks I've been sending them messages through the air. People seem to really wish to know me, to impress me, to emulate me, if not in my actions then at least in my sartorial choices. It matters not, since I don't ever read any of it. My lawyer scoops it all up and takes it away. I've no interest really in what I represent to strangers sad enough to put pen to paper and write to me.

Perhaps I'm being too kind to the general public, ascribing to them a more complex set of emotions than they deserve. Maybe the reason for such sustained and frenzied interest in my case is best ascribed to Occam's Razor – the theory that the simplest answer is usually the correct one. In which case, my name will live on long after I am dead for the most prosaic reason of all – merely because the idea of a love triangle seems so dramatic and grubby. But when I think about what I *actually* did, I feel somewhat sad that nobody will ever know about the complex operation that I undertook. Getting away with it is highly preferable, of course, but perhaps when I'm long gone, someone will open an old safe and find this confession.

The public would reel. After all, almost nobody else in the world can possibly understand how someone, by the tender age of 28, can have calmly killed six members of her family. And then happily carried on with the rest of her life, never to regret a thing.

CHAPTER ONE

I step off the plane and encounter that glorious blast of hot air that British people always dramatically exclaim at when they land somewhere hot and remember that much of the rest of the world enjoys a climate which doesn't just veer between grey and cold. I'm adept at moving through airports quickly, and today that's especially true, since I'm keen to avoid the man I had the misfortune of sitting next to during the flight. Amir introduced himself the moment I'd finished putting my seatbelt on. A guy in his mid-thirties, he was wearing a shirt which was stretched desperately over his almost comical pectoral muscles, and he'd inexplicably paired it with shiny tracksuit bottoms. The worst part of his outfit, the cherry on the whole mess, was the pair of sliders he had on instead of shoes. Gucci pool shoes, with matching socks. Jesus. I considered asking the hostess if I could sit somewhere else, but she was nowhere to be found and I was already trapped between the embellished he-man and the window as the plane started to taxi.

Amir was on his way to Puerto Banús, as was I, although I would never have told him so. He was 38, did something with nightclubs, and was fond of saying that he liked to 'go large'. I closed my eyes as he bored on about the Marbella lifestyle, and told me about the challenges of having his favourite cars shipped over for the summer season. Despite my body language, my aisle mate didn't let up, forcing me to finally engage. I was going to visit my best friend, I told him. No, she wasn't in Puerto Banús, but further inland, and we were unlikely to venture into town to experience the delights of the 'Glitter' nightclub.

'Do you need a car?' the man-mountain asked me. 'I could give you a sick one to ride around in, just let me know and I'll sort you out with a nice Merc for your holidays.' As politely as I could, I declined, before firmly announcing that I needed to get some work done before we landed.

As we started our descent, Amir saw his opportunity and reminded me to shut my laptop. Once again, I was drawn into conversation, remembering to be careful not to mention my name or give him any personal information. I was furious at this attention, having deliberately dressed in black trousers, a shirt, and no makeup for the flight so as to draw as little notice as possible. No jewellery, no personal touches, nothing that might stand out in a person's mind were they to be questioned. Not that they would be, I'm just a young girl going on holiday in Marbella, like so many others this summer.

The flight was all Amir can have of me, and even that was taken not given. So now I'm squeezing past people, flashing smiles as I push to the front of the passport queue and head straight for baggage reclaim. I position myself behind a pillar as the room fills up, and look down at my phone. A few minutes later, I see my bag and grab it, before turning on my heels and walking purposefully towards the exit. And then I have a thought and stop in my tracks.

I'm leaning by the railings outside the airport when Amir emerges. His face brightens as he sucks his stomach in and puffs up his chest.

'I was looking for you!' he says, and I note the bright gold watch as he gesticulates.

'Yeah, sorry, I'm in such a rush to get to my friend in time for lunch, but I couldn't leave without saying goodbye,' I reply.

'Well let's have that night out, gimme your digits, and we'll link.' Absolutely not a chance, but I have to keep him sweet if I'm to get what I want from this.

'I've got a new phone, Amir, can't remember the number for the life of me. Tell you what, you give me yours and I'll be in touch,' I smile and touch his arm lightly. After I've stored it and declined his offer of a lift, I wave goodbye.

'Amir,' I call, as he walks away, 'that offer of a car, is it still on?'

* * *

I arrive at my rented apartment just under two hours later, a fairly pain-free drive from the airport in my hire car. I found it on Airbnb and arranged to pay the landlady in cash so as not to have a record under my name. She was fine with a private booking when I said I'd pay double. It's painfully expensive, especially in the high season, but I only have this week booked off work and I'm keen to get on with my plan, so I'm throwing money at the problem. The flat is tiny and stifling, the aesthetic is very much reminiscent of an Eighties cosmetic clinic but with added china dolls. I'm desperate to see the ocean and stretch my legs, but I have a limited time here, and there's work to be done.

I've done my research, as much as you can do on two old bigots who have an inconsiderately minimal online presence, and I've got a good idea where they'll be tonight. It seems, from the little I could glean from Kathleen's Facebook page (the poor love has a public account, blessings be that old people do not understand privacy settings), that between feeling angry at the amount of Spanish people living in Spain, the Artemis seniors spend most of their time shuffling between a restaurant called Villa Bianca, which is right on the waterfront, and a casino called Dinero just outside of town. I've booked a table at the restaurant for dinner.

Let me be clear here. I have no idea what I am doing. I'm 24, I've been thinking about how to best avenge my mother for many years now, and this is the biggest step I've taken so far. Mostly, I've been working my way up the career ladder, saving money, researching the family and trying to get myself into a position where I can get closer to them. It's been helpful, but mundane. Of course, I'm willing to make these sacrifices in order to get nearer to my end goals, but my God it's hard to pretend I care about customer surveys and participate in the optional (read mandatory) team-bonding drinks on Fridays. If I'd known I'd have to drink Jägerbombs with people who willingly work in marketing, I'd have given myself more time to research trepanation first. Maybe that's why I'm rushing this big move, desperate to prove to myself that I've made inroads and can do what I've been saying I will since I was 13. And yet, I am woefully underprepared. I envisaged that by the time I got to Marbella, I'd have a firm plan in place, carefully plotted my route, the timings, and have invested in an incredible disguise. Instead, I am holed up in a flat which smells like your family hamster died underneath a wardrobe and your mother didn't know what the smell was and has been going mad with the bleach for six months. I have a plan in my mind, but no idea whether I'll be able to pull it off. I have a wig that I bought at a cosmetics shop in Finsbury Park, which looked convincing enough under the store strip lighting, but appears worryingly flammable in the Spanish sun. Despite this free-floating anxiety about my lack of preparation, excitement spreads through me. As I fix my wig and apply my makeup, I feel as though I'm getting ready for a brilliant date, and not at all like I'm on the way to kill my grandparents.

* * *

That was overly dramatic of course. I'm not going to kill them tonight, that would be foolish. I need to see them, listen to their conversation, see if they drop any hints about their plans this week. I need to drive the route to their villa a few times, and importantly, I need to pick up the promised car from Amir. That car is either a sign that I am stupidly chaotic and should postpone my plans, or it was a little gift from some unknown deity. Let's see which!

I decided long ago that Kathleen and Jeremy Artemis would be the first to leave us. This was for several reasons really, the first being that they're old so it doesn't matter as much. Old people who do nothing but drain their pensions and stultify in their favourite armchairs isn't a brilliant advertisement for humanity in my opinion. Great that we've worked out how to make people live longer with medical intervention and healthier lifestyles, unfortunately they will become useless bed blockers who get more and more mean-spirited until they are nothing more than bigoted beasts of burden living in the room you wanted to make a study.

Don't be shocked, I know you think it too. Enjoy your life and shuffle off this coil around 70, only the very boring would want to live to be 100 – the only reward an impersonal and brief letter from the Queen. So really I'm doing everyone a favour. They are old and disposable, and they live staggeringly useless lives. Wine at lunch, naps, a trip to the boutiques in town to buy hideous jewellery and gaudy watches. He golfs, she spends a lot of her time getting things injected into her face, which has had the strange effect of making her look like a very old toddler. A waste of life, and that's all before I tell you just how racist they are. Oh fuck it, you can imagine. They live in Marbella and yet they speak no Spanish, there you go. No more explanation needed.

Of course, I have skin in this game. I'm not Harold Shipman, merrily going around killing off as many geriatrics as I can. I only want to kill two of them, the rest are safe to keep watching *Emmerdale* and buying terrible presents for grandchildren who resent their boring visits. These people are technically my grandparents, though I've never met them and they have never bought me as much as a Toblerone. But they *do* know about me.

Let me explain. I wasn't aware of this for many years, imagining that my father Simon had successfully kept me a secret, but my mother's friend Helene was in London for a visit recently, and over a bottle of wine, she confessed that she'd paid them a visit shortly before she left for Paris all those years ago. She felt like she was letting my beautiful mother down by leaving me. Poor dead Marie. Helene did the only thing she could think to do to ameliorate the guilt. She looked them up online, and found their London address on Companies House. I was almost climbing across the table to hear what they'd said to her, to commit this new information to memory. I'd been to their house before many times of course, before they'd moved to Spain full-time. I'd spent hours outside, watching, waiting, occasionally following their chauffeur-driven car when they went out. But speaking to them was a whole new level, and I was half impressed with Helene, and half furious that she'd never told me about this meeting before.

She was clearly reluctant to tell me just how bad the encounter was, not meeting my eyes when she explained they initially slammed the door shut when she told them who she was. She didn't leave though, and eventually they let her in and coldly disclosed that they knew all about me and my 'ghastly' mother. My ears started to buzz as I let that sink in, and I scratched at my neck, waiting for the lump in my throat I knew would appear any second. They knew about me from the start, Helene explained, when their 'poor' son turned up unexpectedly late one night and, pacing the living room, confessed that he'd got into some trouble. According to Jeremy, who did most of the talking while Kathleen sat rigidly on the sofa sipping a large gin and tonic, Simon had asked how he should tell his wife, Janine, and told his father that some financial provision would have to be made for me.

'So he did want to do the right thing in some way,' Helene said, almost apologetically, as she drunk her wine and fiddled with her hair. I ignored the comment, and told her to carry on. I had no interest in entertaining that man's pathetic attempts to salve his conscience.

Jeremy proudly told Helene that he and his wife had spent several hours shutting this idea down, making him see that Marie had done it deliberately for money, warning him that Janine would never recover. 'Simon made a foolish mistake, as many young men do,' he had told Helene, 'and I'm sorry that this young girl has to grow up without parents, but many people have faced worse. I myself lost my mother at a young age, and I didn't go around looking for handouts from strangers.' Helene said that she argued back, shouting that Marie had not gone out to trap their son, and trying to explain that she had not known how wealthy he was, or that he was married for that matter, until much later. But they would hear none of it. 'That girl tried to ruin my son for money,' shouted Kathleen, suddenly rising from her seat. 'If you think your friend's daughter is going to start all this nonsense up again, you're as foolish as she was.' And that was pretty much that. According to Helene, who had downed her wine and was now gesticulating furiously, Kathleen had suddenly started sobbing and hitting her husband on the chest. He had grabbed her hands and forcefully pushed her back down onto the sofa, before turning back to Helene, who was standing, slightly stunned, by the door. 'You've upset my wife and ruined our evening. I want you out of my house, and don't even *think* about trying this crap with my son. We'll have lawyers on you so fast you'll be fucking homeless before you've seen us in court.'

'I was shaking a bit by then,' said Helene, 'because he suddenly looked mad. His eyes were bulging and his carefully combed silver hair was flying about. And the weirdest thing was that his accent had completely changed. When he first spoke to me, he sounded like a proper English gentleman, but by the time I left, his voice was rough and hard and he reminded me of the market traders I used to know in the town where I grew up. I'm sorry. I tried, but I thought his parents might be nicer, more sympathetic. I thought they'd want to know their beautiful granddaughter, for God's sake! But no. They've done well for themselves, but underneath it all, Grace, they are thugs.'

So they're old, they're mean and they take up precious space in the world. And all of this would be reason enough to help them meet their end in a more unpleasant way than might have originally been on the cards. But if I'm totally honest, it's mainly because they knew. They knew about my mother. They knew about me. And they didn't just flap their hands and do nothing, they actively lobbied their son, blaming Marie, Helene, the clubs, his friends who led him astray. They blamed everyone but Simon. He shirked his responsibilities as a father and his family helped him do it. I thought they were living their lives unaware that their son had rejected his child and left her mother struggling. But they wanted it that way. And in the end, that's what swung the decision. They die first.

* * *

I get to the beach restaurant at 6 p.m., assuming that like most old people, my grandparents eat early. I've asked for a spot on the terrace, but it turns out that the restaurant is much bigger than it looked online, and I'm anxious that I'll be too far away from them to glean anything useful. I order a glass of white wine (I like my wine; the Latimers always made sure they drank the good stuff, I chose a Rioja), and force myself to open up the book I've brought with me so it won't look too obvious when I start eavesdropping. I'd chosen *The Count of Monte Cristo*, which was far too on the nose, but I'd thought it funny when I was packing. I don't have to wait long for the Artemis party to arrive. Barely past page one, I see activity out of the corner of my eye. Two waiters are escorting four elderly people past the bar and towards the terrace. I stay still, not allowing myself to look up, but sensing that they are coming closer. A loud female voice: 'No, not that table, Andreas, it's in direct sunlight. Put us over there.' The party turns and moves to the other end of the space. Fuck you, Kathleen.

Once they're settled in their seats and have ordered drinks, all of which takes an age, with complaints about the wind, and a dither about what to choose, I permit myself a quick scan of the scene. The ageing Artemises are facing me, their friends opposite them. Kathleen has had a blowdry that would leave Joan Collins spitting blood. Her hair is pale blonde, and has a structure, not a style, set so rigidly that the wind she worried about won't dare to touch it. The cosmetic work on her face is visible from some distance, and her eyes have been deliberately given a slightly startled look which I think is meant to be coquettish but makes her look demented. She's wearing a beige tunic over beige trousers, with her obscenely large Chanel bag resting on the table. Her neck is adorned with a large string of . . . I can't make out the stone but I can safely assume they aren't cubic zirconia. I have the luxury of a little staring, since they're all engrossed in the menu. I'm wondering if there's anything of me in this dissatisfied-looking woman when she lifts her hands up and clasps them together and I see her nails. Pointed, painted in a classic pillar box red. There we are, Kathleen. My hands, holding my forgotten book, are long and slim, unlike hers. But my nails, my nails are bright red and pointed too.

After a few minutes pretending to be immersed in my book, I call the waiter over and ask to move out of the direct sunshine. Not a moment too soon, since I have a sneaking suspicion that this wig could melt at any moment. The terrace is busy, but not full, and I'm taken to a table just behind that of my targets. Much better. I want to hear what they're talking about. I won't learn anything insightful or interesting about their characters, they're too closed-minded for that, but I might get an idea of their plans for the week. I'm only here for five more days, all the holiday I could take, so time is tight. I order another glass of wine, and some assorted tapas, and open my book up again. Jeremy is looking at me, in a way that all women recognise. The old goat is sizing me up, appreciating my youth, not realising for a second just how pathetic he looks. I smile for a brief moment, in part because it's amusing to see my grandfather checking me out, and partly to make him think I'm charmed. The moment is interrupted by waiters bringing their food. No order was taken, but upon seeing the dishes I'm not surprised. Steak and fries for the whole party. It must be the only thing on the menu they go for. Steak and fries, never straying into foreign territory, never doing anything different, being small, turning nasty. And I got all of that just from steak, imagine what I could learn from their bookshelves. I'm kidding, they won't have any books in their house.

They drone on about friends at the golf club, discussing someone called Brian who disgraced himself at the recent charity auction (poor Brian, imagine the shame of being cast out by the elderly ex-pat community). Kathleen and the other woman dining, who looks a lot like Kathleen but with more girth and a smaller Chanel, move on to slagging off a hairdresser who takes too long and couldn't fit her friend in last Monday. My attention is wandering. I want to learn everything I can, but by God these people don't make it easy.

Can I have one more glass of wine, or will that sabotage this fact-finding mission? Fuck it. Glass of wine ordered, I pick at the remnants of my tapas. Perhaps the group I'm watching had the right idea when it came to the steak. The food I ordered is confusingly rubbery, and looks less like it came from the sea and more like it was grown in a warehouse off a motorway. The group in front of me have ordered coffee, and Kathleen is fussing over a stain on Jeremy's tie, which looks as though it's a club tie of some sort. I bet Jeremy is a Freemason, it would just *fit*. Fat friend's husband is asking when they will next be at the casino, and mentions a drinks event this coming Thursday.

'Yes we'll be there,' says Jeremy sharply, brushing Kathleen's proffered napkin away. 'We're having dinner with the Beresfords at 7.30, and we'll drop in on the way back.'

WHERE ARE YOU HAVING DINNER, I want to scream, but they don't elaborate. Instead, Jeremy asks for the bill by brusquely beckoning the waiter. The other man at the table grabs the saucer the moment it comes, and does a nod towards my grandparents.

'We must get this, I'm sure it's our turn – no please, I insist.' A gold card is thrown down, and Jeremy barely responds, instead looking over at me again. This time I look away. I don't want him to mark me, or know my face too well. I'm not worried, I assume he spends a lot of time looking at women young enough to be his granddaughter. Perhaps fewer who actually are, but with Simon's track record, who could ever be sure?

As they leave, I notice Jeremy's tie properly. I was wrong, not Freemasons. A print in green and yellow, with the letters 'RC'. A quick google tells me it's the official tie for the Regency Club, a private members' establishment in Mayfair, opened in 1788 for men, royal, and wealthy, to consort without their wives. I almost laugh. I know where you started life, Jeremy. In a two-room dwelling in Bethnal Green, with a seamstress mother and a father who fucked off and ended up who knows where before you were five. Simon has talked about it in interviews with pride, as a sign of how hard your family has worked to rise in the world. So here you are in your tie, imagining it shows your pedigree – the one you bought for yourself. Admirable to some, perhaps. Even to me, since I'm trying to do the same thing – climb out of poverty, get away from my starting offer in life. But I know you. I know your hatred of your roots, whatever the story you've spun since. You saw it in me, and when asked to help your own flesh and blood out of a similar situation, you ran. Helene was right. You're just a thug, and your private clubs and your expensive clothes don't do much to conceal that. But wear your tie. Thursday isn't far away.

I walk back to my rooms, taking in the main promenade in Puerto Banús as I go. The boutiques are filled with women holding up embellished dresses in the mirror and chatting to their friends. Teenage girls stroll past engrossed in a discussion about their tans. I wonder if I'd have been one of these empty shells had I grown up within the folds of the Artemis family. I read books, I follow world affairs, I have opinions on more than just shoes and golf clubs. I am better than these people, that's not in doubt. But they look happy despite their ignorance. Perhaps *because* of it. What is there to worry about? None of these idiots are thinking about climate change, they're wondering what to wear on the yacht tomorrow. But it's fascinating to watch, and I only have a short time to see it. Once I've done my job, I won't be coming back to this playground for the diamanté class. Perhaps I should buy a memento. I look at the shop windows, with their overpriced tat. I have neither the money nor the desire to buy a fur-cuffed kaftan, even as a silly joke. Besides, I think I know what my keepsake will be, and it won't cost me a thing.

The next day, after a quick run along the beach, I drive to their house. It's a large villa in a secure complex, hidden away from the unwashed masses and guarded by big gates and a bored security officer in a hut, who I imagine is supposed to check who visitors are, but lets me through with a wave when I say I'm here from the boutique Afterdark to drop off a dress for Mrs Lyle at number 8. I guessed that there would be a fairly steady stream of deliveries for the bored ladies alone in their pristine villas, always ordering a new outfit, or demanding a nail technician visit at short notice. I didn't say I was going to the Artemis household. I don't want there to be an obvious link, just in case questions are asked later.

Their house, number 9, is almost identical to numbers 8 and 10. White stucco, terracotta tiles leading up to the door. Palm trees on either side of the porch. Perfect green lawn, even in this scorching heat. I guess hosepipe bans don't apply when you live in a compound away from normal society. I take my foot off the pedal and roll by, but there's nothing to see really. There's nobody in sight on these wide avenues, not a dog walker or a mother and buggy. All this money, and it can only buy silence. I appreciate silence, by the way. You don't grow up on a main road in London and not dream of the day you might live in a home without hearing your neighbours alternately having angry sex and or sobbing to the soundtrack of *Les Misérables*. But this calm is artificial – it feels flat and dull, as though made for people who wanted to create an environment which completely denied the loud reality of human life. The Artemises choice of house only tells me about them in so far as it tells me nothing. It's a house which was built for rich people who don't care about design but really value security and status. Did Lynn and Brian buy a house in this compound? Well then let's buy a bigger one. That's it. There's no nod to personality, there's no activity – only sanitised conformity. I leave feeling rather depressed. I share DNA with these people, will I too one day hanker after beige carpets and a maid I can mistreat? I guess a maid would be nice, but I think I'd find their inevitable sadness a bit oppressive. I imagine it's a bonus for Kathleen though. Someone who is more miserable than her, in full view every day.

From the compound, I travel to the casino, which is about a thirty-minute drive along a fairly hairy road. A cliff edge on one side heads down towards a . . . gorge? A ravine? I don't know. As I said, I grew up on a main road and I've always had what I feel is a healthy suspicion of big open spaces. The countryside baffles me, and anywhere that takes thirty minutes by car isn't somewhere I'd waste my time going if I was at home. Sometimes I get the urge to have a quick meeting with a man (I mean sex, lower your eyebrows), or just waste my time mindlessly scrolling on dating apps. I flick through chancers posing in front of BMWs, as if that's a sign that they've 'made it' instead of a clear indication that they are stupid enough to think that hire purchase makes good financial sense. But a tacky car and a V-neck T-shirt aren't necessarily complete no-nos. I'm not going to be spending my life with these men, after all. I don't even care enough to commit their names to memory. But I do have a firm line in the sand. If you're more than a couple of kilometres away, it's not happening. My mood is fleeting, and I'm not waiting for you to change at King's Cross, or text to say the Overground has been replaced by a fleet of buses because of essential repairs. So the Spanish countryside is an alien world to me, and fuck it, the cliff leads to a ravine. Whatever you'd call it, it's a long drop and the cliffside is covered in gnarly-looking bushes. Plus there isn't a soul to be seen on this route. Perfect. The sun is out, and the warm breeze hits my arm as I balance it on the door while I drive. I turn on the radio, and the local station is playing the Beach Boys. 'God Only Knows' fills the little rental car, as I slowly hug the road and make my way towards the casino. I don't believe in God, obviously. We live in a time of science and the Kardashians, so I think I'm safely in the sane camp there. But also, any god with real clout wouldn't have paired me with these people and given me such a calling. So no God. But I do feel like someone is smiling down on me today.

While I'm on God, there's a story in the Bible (I mean, it's not in the Bible, I heard it in a film and it involves modern technology), which goes something like this: A man lives in a little house very happily for years, until one day, the emergency services knock on his door and say, 'Sir, there's a storm coming, we need to evacuate.' And the man says, 'Thank you, gentlemen, but I'm religious, I have faith. God will save me.' The men leave and the storm comes. The waters rise around his house, and a boat comes past. 'Sir,' says the captain, 'come with us, the water will only rise.' But the man says 'Thank you, gentlemen, but I'm religious, I have faith. God will save me.' Later on, the man has to climb to his roof as the house floods. A helicopter hovers overhead. 'Sir, climb up this ladder, we can get you to safety.' The man waves them away. 'Thank you, gentlemen, but I'm religious, I have faith. God will save me.' Later on, the man drowns. When he gets to heaven, he meets God, and says, 'Father, I had faith, I believed in you, I stayed true. Why did you let me drown?' And God looks exasperated (and why wouldn't he, this man is an idiot), and says, 'David, I sent you the emergency services, a boat, and a helicopter. Why are you here??'

Someone has sent me big, stupid Amir with his powerful cars, a definite date when my grandparents will be out late at night, and a windy dangerous road. And unlike that stupid man in the fable, I fully intend to take advantage of them all.

* * *

I have a little over thirty-six hours before I carry out my plans. I could spend the time following the couple around to learn more about them, but honestly, they're just not interesting enough to make it worthwhile. So I go to the beach for the rest of the afternoon, splashing out on a sunbed at a private beach, and drinking rosé as I read a book about a woman who kills her husband after years of gas-lighting and emotional abuse. I couldn't get on with *The Count of Monte Cristo* – too close to the bone, I expect. I did flick to the back though. A terrible habit for sure, but my cheating nature was nevertheless rewarded with this line: 'All human wisdom is contained in these two words, "Wait and Hope".'

Wait and hope. I've been living this line since I was a teenager now, and finally the waiting part is coming to an end. I put my hands on my hot chest, and try to feel if my heart is pounding faster than usual. But no, I'm breathing as normal, as if today is just another day and I'm not about to commit a terrible crime. How strange. My mind is going over and over the plan, and the anticipation is rising like steam ready to burst out of my ears and yet here I lie, shielded by dark glasses, heart refusing to betray me by bursting out of my chest. My body is ready, even if my mind is behaving like a teenager getting ready for a first date.

Later that evening, before I get into bed, I send Amir a text from my newly acquired burner phone. That's what Edward Snowden called a phone that you buy to try and stay untraceable. A little grand in my case, given that I am not aware of any state secrets. But a good tip nonetheless, and a twenty-minute trip to a less salubrious part of London plus sixty quid in cash got me this rather quaint old flip phone, which I added credit to so that I could text. It won't make its way back to England but it's serving a useful purpose. I ask Amir if he's around tomorrow and whether he could sort me a car for a couple of days. I've told him that I'm travelling further into the countryside for the night and would feel safer in a bigger car, which is sort of true, I suppose. The best lies have a kernel of truth, making it easier to stick to your story and less likely to get caught up in different versions. My friend Jimmy has a terrible lying face, the corners of his mouth automatically turn up in a smirk when he fibs. It's sort of endearing, but it makes it impossible to trust him with anything, given his tendency to get caught out when confronted.

When I wake up, I check my phone immediately. As I suspected, Amir replied in the early hours of the morning. A big night out at Glitter, I imagine. I text right back, thanking him for his offer of a night out but explaining again that I'll be leaving this afternoon. I know I'm not getting away with just a straight key handover, so I suggest meeting at an ice cream parlour on the Calle Ribera at 2 p.m. I know I won't hear from him until at least midday, given the amount of champagne I imagine he imbibed last night, so I hop in the tiny shower and throw on a sundress I hope makes me look slightly dowdy in Amir's eyes. Certainly it's devoid of any shimmer or stretch, and so is practically a boiler suit in comparison to what most of the women in this place choose to wear. In my short time here, it has come to feel as though a mix of sequins, gold buttons, and animal prints form some kind of unofficial uniform. Well that, and the blow-up, rubbery lips that make these women look as though they're in the midst of a terrible allergic reaction to the iced coffee they sip on as they sunbathe.

I don't plan on coming back to this apartment, though I've booked it out until Saturday. I might be being too optimistic, but I don't want to allow doubt to creep in at this crucial moment. I tidy up, throw the bedsheets in the washing machine and wipe down the surfaces. I pack up my small bag, and then lay out what I'll need for the rest of the day. In my crossbody bag (it's Gucci, one of the first things I bought when I started my new job, and even the ladies of Marbella would be impressed), I place my burner phone, wig, euros, folded-up plimsolls, a torch, latex gloves, a travel-size perfume bottle of liquid and a box of matches. Everything else goes in the holdall, including my real phone, passport, and credit cards.

I lock the apartment and take the key – just in case. In a fit of paranoia, I wipe down the door handle with my sleeve and realise I need to be better at this. If I'm going to carry on without being caught, a quick wipe down of random surfaces isn't going to cut it. Ah well. This is the test balloon. The car is parked a good thirty-minute walk away, far away from the bustle on the main drag. I didn't want it to be recorded in a car park, and this was the closest I could get to the apartment without risking it being towed away within seconds.

It's boiling already, and sweat is running down my chest and pooling underneath my bra. I dump the holdall under the driver's seat and check it's not visible from all angles. Then I walk back into town, taking a different route by mistake and ending up by the sea. After a couple of hours whiling away the time at a café where a coffee seems to cost five euros, Amir finally texts. *Hi bbz, I'm steaming off of last nite, you missed a proper big one! Will be at the Oceania club from 3 to get on it again, meet me their 4 a drink and I'll sort you out! :)*

His reply almost makes me rethink. I cannot engage with a grown-up who seems not to possess the ability to use basic English, even in text. It's just bad manners, and on top of that, it implies a level of ignorance that you might forgive in a teenager but is appalling in an adult. You can only blame a poor education for so much. My secondary school was hardly Hogwarts but I still took the time to learn the difference between their and there. I doubt Amir did even that. Not for the first time, I wonder what he does to earn so much money, I doubt it's entirely kosher, but who am I to lecture on morality? I consider using my little rental, and decide to stick with Amir's offer. I'll just have to be stern, shut down all offers of alcohol, and leave as soon as I get the car keys. Ugh. I resent having to rely on a man (and worse, a man who wears wrap-around shades) for help in a matter that really should be done by me and me alone, but

I have to be realistic. And Amir won't be getting anything good from this interaction. If it all goes to plan, he'll be none the wiser. If it goes tits up, he'll be in a world of trouble. This cheers me up a little, and I drain my coffee.

I arrive at the Oceania club just before 3 p.m. The place is enormous, a palace of vacuous frivolity. I assume it's mainly one big bar, but souped up, on steroids. The driveway is littered with sports cars in lurid colours, each being dealt with by harassed-looking valets in white jackets. A Rolls Royce parked haphazardly in front of the entrance displays the number plate 'BO55 BO1'. I wait at reception while a girl with a tan which the sun would reject outright as being beyond its powers speaks on the phone in estuary English. Eventually she turns her attention on me. I imagine she's unimpressed by my brown hair, sans extensions, and my flat sandals. I'm wearing red lipstick, which I always wear when I feel like I need a shield of sorts, but apart from that, I look fairly plain. I like plain. I have a somewhat beautiful face and I don't feel arrogant saying it. Women always backpedal when they slip up and admit they think they're attractive, a lifetime of being told by men not to be 'up ourselves'. Be as beautiful as possible but make sure it seems effortless and, crucially, never acknowledge it. Run away from any man who says that you're beautiful but you don't know it. The same men want you to be constantly up for sex but never take charge of your own enjoyment. I am pretty nice looking. Not tall, but slim and in proportion. Dark hair, symmetrical features, a nice full mouth without being too pouty. I like looking at my reflection but I'm not obsessed with it. I know my appearance helps me out in life but I'm not my mother, too reliant on her beauty and left to flounder when it's not enough. My look is probably incredibly disappointing to the men in Marbella compared to the peacocks you see around here. Coco Chanel supposedly once said that you should take off one accessory before you leave the house.

These girls would scratch old Coco's eyes out with their acrylic nails before they did that. I tell Miss Tan that I'm meeting Amir, and her face changes. Clearly, he's a valued customer, as I'm whisked through marble hallways and past a library bar stuffed with fake books and objects which look old but I'm willing to bet are bulk-bought from a supplier who churns out this crap for those wanting to *look* authentic but care nothing for true provenance.

We emerge outside, into the blinding sun and what looks like a theme park for adults. There are several linking pools, each with a bar in the middle, where people have swum up and are enjoying cocktails underneath straw parasols. House music blares and waiters walk briskly between loungers, topping up drinks. Some people have whole beds, laid out under canopies, where several people lie around smoking and chatting. Nobody is sporting anything more than swimwear, apart from me and I have no intention of joining them. I spy an actual belly chain of all things. Jewellery for the waist, for when you run out of places to flaunt your diamonds. Coco Chanel would die.

'Mr Amir is not here yet, please relax and have a drink.' I'm almost pushed down onto a large white lounger, where I am conspicuous only in my solitude. I order a tonic water, in the hope that Amir will think I'm 'already on it', and wait. My new friend is only forty-five minutes late, time I spend watching the bronzed girls rolling down their already tiny bikinis to get more sun, and staring at the men with their shaved chests and mini bum bags preening and showing off – mainly it seems, to each other.

I spot Amir as he walks through the sun loungers. He'd be hard to miss, dressed as he is, in neon orange shorts and surrounded by a posse of lads – all of whom seem to signal that their main aim in life is to look as much like their leader as possible. Waiters appear from all sides, bringing towels, glasses, ice buckets and, bizarrely, a coconut.

Amir reaches the lounger where I'm sitting, and peers down at me over his sunglasses. 'Hello, gorgeous! This is Stevie, JJ, Fatlad, Cooper, and Nige.' He gestures to the posse, all of whom nod uninterestedly, already looking at the bikini girls next to us. I wonder why 'Fatlad' has been given such a harsh moniker, given that his body fat percentage looks to hover in the single digits. I can only see muscles, more than a person should rightly have unless they have a physical job and I rather doubt that Fatlad has a job of any kind.

Amir grabs the coconut and throws it to the gentleman he called Nige, who bounces it hard against his head to loud roars of appreciation. Not satisfied, Nige tries again, and the fruit breaks open. He climbs onto the sun lounger and holds the pieces high in the air, as bikini girls and muscle boys alike holler excitedly.

'It's his best trick,' says Amir proudly. 'He practised that for eight summers in a row until he managed it. We're trying to get him on that talent show where dogs do magic.' I feel a slight sense of panic spreading through my veins, as I envisage an entire afternoon spent watching these people practise their mating rituals around a tiny swimming pool presumably contaminated by oil, fake tan, and fag ash. I must be sterner in my mission and not allow Amir to dictate my day.

With this new resolve, I reach over and hold his wrist until he turns and focuses his full attention on me. 'I'm really sorry, but you guys were a bit late, and I only have another hour before the next part of my journey. Did you bring the car here? Only I don't have masses of time.'

He looks at me for a minute and then throws his head back and laughs. The beefy posse behind him echo his snorts, despite not being near enough to have heard what I said. I guess whoever pays for the drinks commands a full-time rapturous audience.

'Babes, I don't even know your name! Calm down speedy. I have a car for you here, but let's hang for a bit, get into it, mix it up yeah?' I suppress the shudder I experience upon hearing such nonsensical bollocks, and allow my shoulders to drop slightly.

'My name's Amy,' I say smiling, 'and I'd definitely be up for mixing it up for a while.'

I end up spending nearly two hours with Amir and his growing group. I try to lean into it, but it's not easy. Champagne is sprayed, girls are lured over, music is turned up on request. Amir's attention span is limited, to put it mildly, and I have to wait patiently as he jumps up and down several times, often just to shout 'Tuuuuuune' to nobody in particular.

I tell him that I work in corporate events, and emphasise that I just broke up with my boyfriend so I'm not looking for anything romantic. Luckily, Amir seems to be genuinely uninterested in anything like that. He's clearly a guy who collects friends and chases a good time. Perhaps there's not much else to it. Makes a change. I check my watch several times, and when I can't stand it anymore, I tell him I've run out of time and really have to go. It's the truth, I don't have too long before I need to be in position at Dinero.

He rolls his eyes, but gets up and signals to JJ, who scurries over, practically knocking a bikini-clad lovely into the pool in his haste. 'Get the Hummer brought round, mate,' Amir orders, and takes a sip of champagne. 'You're a funny one, Amy. I didn't think you was into our chat on the plane, didn't think I'd hear from you again. But nobody can resist Amir in the end, haha.' He puts his arm on my back, and steers me towards the building, where we walk through as waiters back against walls. 'This car is a sweet ride, darling, but it's powerful. It's a beast, will you be OK with that, can you handle the ride?' I assure him that I've got loads of experience with big cars, which is a total lie, and I don't ask what a Hummer is, which is a wise decision. We wait outside for the car to be driven round, and Amir tells me to enjoy it, and not to worry about bringing it back until Sunday. It'll be back well before that, but I just smile and thank him.

A tank appears on cue. The noise is startling, and I flinch momentarily. Amir laughs at this, and high fives JJ as he hands over the keys. This car is enormous. Tinted windows and matt black alloys. He makes me practise on the driveway with him a few times, pointing out the chrome finish and the triple suspension, or something. I clutch the steering wheel and hover my foot cautiously over the brake, wondering whether this is a good idea after all. But when I dare to put my foot down, I realise the power in this machine will serve me well. I tell Amir how great this will be for my little trip, and gush over how my friend will love the drive.

'Girls love big cars, innit. Look proper sexy in them. Just don't mess my baby up, I want to take it to the South of France next week.' I feel momentarily guilty that I'm almost certainly going to, if not total his baby, then at least inflict some serious cosmetic damage on it. Still, nothing that a wad of cash can't fix, and from what I've seen today, Amir has no problems on that front.

He tells me to drop the car at the club whenever I'm ready, and with that, he winks, gives me a bear hug and walks back inside. I sit in the car for a minute, enveloped in the lingering smell of his woody aftershave, marvelling at my luck. A man who knows nothing about me has given me a car without quibbling about insurance, proof of ID, or even a guarantee I know how to drive. My little hire car is safely tucked away in a side street and I am free to carry out my plan with even less of a footprint than I imagined. I wonder if it's a trap, but since nobody knows my plans, I shake that thought off.

It's now 6.30 p.m. Time flies when alcohol is being sprayed all over you. I know that Jeremy said that they would head to the casino after dinner, so I guess they will get there around 9.30. I'm not going to follow them around all evening – for one thing, I don't want anyone to clock the car – so I drive very slowly towards Marbella, hoping to find some food that isn't chicken goujons or soggy chips.

As I sip a bowl of soup, I breathe slowly and force my foot to stop tapping. Marie used to ask me to list the top five moments of the day, 'To remember how lucky we are.' I haven't done this since she died, but today seems like a good time to take stock. Today, as terminally earnest people like to say, is the first day of the rest of my life. Perhaps it's the day my life properly begins. So much of it has been focused on getting here. My childhood was brief, my teenage years a frustrating waiting room on the way to adulthood. My twenties have been functional – a means to an end. I've not felt that lucky, sorry, Marie. You left me too early and fortune never smiled that brightly as a result. So I might not manage to list five top moments. But maybe one is enough for now? Let's start small and see what happens.

At 8.45 p.m., I pay my bill and head back to the enormous wagon parked across the road from the restaurant. I wonder if there's an inverse correlation between money and taste – Amir's predilection for chrome seems to suggest there might be. As does Jeremy and Kathleen's house, for that matter. But these people are new money, or 'nouveau riche' as Jimmy's mum was guiltily fond of saying. Perhaps the older your cash, the better your eye. If I pull this off, I'll be richer than Croesus, but thoroughly nouveau. Perhaps I'll develop an eye for bronze and beige and bling, but I doubt it. That probably means taste is more to do with whether you're ghastly or not. The Artemis family would certainly back that up.

I don't put my destination in the satnav, just in case Amir looks, or the police do find the car. Instead, I have a little map which I bought at the airport for six euros. I've checked out the route many times now, and I've got plenty of time if I do get lost. I pull the wig out of my bag and wince at how bedraggled it looks from just one wear. Buy cheap, pay dear, as Jimmy's mum says. Next time I'll invest some proper money in a disguise. I drive up winding dark roads in silence, never going above 30 kph. There's barely a car on the road, but I wonder whether the casino visitors will change that as I get closer. I'll only get one chance at this, and if there's any sign of another car, I just can't risk it. Fuck. It has to work. It *has* to.

The casino is in the middle of nowhere, but surrounded by a strange little cluster of restaurants and bars, which means I can park in the car park with no fear of sticking out like a sore thumb. I do a quick stroll around it to ensure that the Artemises' Mercedes isn't yet here, and then I head over to the entrance. I'm not going in – for one thing I'm not a member and for another, I don't want to be picked up on the casino CCTV. Instead, I hover in the darkness between the club and a bar called Rays. This place looks like an out-of-town shopping centre and I half expect to see a Homebase. It's hardly glamorous – I'm surprised that my grandparents deign to visit. Then again, they choose to spend their old age in a gated community in Marbella, a place which makes Florida look like Renaissance Italy in terms of culture.

I'm angry that I've given myself so much time. I'd bet on my grandparents being the kind of people who worry if they're not home by 11 p.m., but what if they're secret night owls? I can hardly hang around the car park with a few sparse bushes for cover. I lose my nerve and head back to my car, to regroup and go over the route again. As I'm walking, a silver saloon creeps up the drive, hogging the middle of the road, headlights on full beam. I hold my breath, squinting at the number plate, but it's unnecessary. I see Mrs Artemis, her miserable expression and the resplendent blowdry which frames it in the glass. I hear a giggle, and quickly retreat between two cars until I realise that the sound came from me. I'm clearly more excited than I'd thought. At least part of me is looking forward to this.

The elderly couple get out of the car slowly, Jeremy throwing the keys to the valet and barely glancing at his wife, who's gingerly stepping onto the pavement, clutching her Chanel like a child holds onto a teddy bear. They head into the casino without a word to the valet or the doorman, just silent statues there to show respect to the great and the good, I suppose. Still, statues can't wipe their arse on your leather seats like a valet can (and hopefully does).

For the next two and a half hours I sit in my car. I eat a disgusting cheeseburger and resolve to give up meat when I get home. I smoke three cigarettes and vow to quit back in London. I listen to some terrible Spanish radio and veer between manically tapping my feet and obsessively checking my mirrors to see whether the Artemises have emerged yet. A younger crowd is pulling up, it seems the casino gets livelier as the night goes on. I'm guessing that this probably means the olds push off earlier, and I'm right. The steps are soon busy with women swathed in Hermès scarves and men waving car tickets. They are all wearing expressions which signal a mix of wealth and angry entitlement. Bang, there they are. Kathleen with a gift bag, stumbling just a little. Jeremy with a cigar. Must have been a fun night. I'm glad. I'm not a monster. It's nice that they're leaving the world on a high note. It's more than Marie was given, but I must be the better person here. I'm going to decimate their entire family, the least I can allow them is a goody bag and a spin at the roulette table.

They head down the steps and Jeremy gives the valet their ticket. This is my cue. I turn on the engine and head out of the car park. I've told you I haven't planned this, and I'm not being falsely modest. I have a vague idea, which seemed pretty solid back in London, but now I'm here, I'm not in any way confident that I'll even get the chance to try it out. But I'm here, driving fast down the windy roads below the casino, following the route that the Artemis seniors will hopefully take to their villa. After a few minutes I turn onto the cliff road, darker and more bumpy. I estimate that I'm about ten minutes ahead of the couple if they drive cautiously, and I need to find the right spot – I marked it the other day, but in the dark the road seems to want to conceal it.

I'm going too fast, and I can feel the lump in my throat taking up its usual place, threatening to overwhelm me. WHERE IS THIS FUCKING SPOT? I breathe through my nose, and talk to myself out loud, 'You'll find it, you've got time, Grace. It's OK.'

I drive past and brake, just like they teach you to do in lessons, as if anyone ever does a perfect emergency stop in real life without causing a pile-up. But the road is dead, and all I can hear is cicadas. I do a U-turn, which takes a few goes in this ridiculous vehicle, and pull into the lay-by, letting my breathing return to normal, waiting for the lump to go. I've got a clear view of the road from here, and if I'd missed this spot, I wouldn't have had another before they arrived home. I wait, drinking in the silence.

Headlights. A car dipping in and out of view as it winds down towards me. I've got two minutes. I rev the engine, as if this tank needs some extra persuasion, and drive, holding the steering wheel with locked arms. The car comes into view – they are slow, cautious, taking their time. As I abruptly spin the wheel and accelerate towards them, I see Kathleen's mouth form a perfect O, before she covers her head and the lights blind me. The impact of my swerve forces me back into my seat and I brake fast. The car almost bucks from the command, as if annoyed by the interruption. As I rub my head and look up, all I can see is dust from the road and a satisfyingly large gap in the stubby bushes on the side of the cliff.

I pull the car over, tuck it into the other side of the road and turn off the lights. I've got a little time before I have to head back, leaving

Amir's car at the club before I retrieve my hire car and go to the airport. I grab my torch and shakily pull on the latex gloves, breaking the thumb portion on my left hand. The matches and little perfume bottle go in my pocket. I cross the road and hover on the cliff edge. My plimsolls aren't up for a big scramble and I can't quite see how far the car has travelled until a scan with the torch shows it about 15 metres down and upside down, cradled by a bush.

I should really turn back, get to the airport, leave the scene clean. Whatever happens now, I can get away. But where would the fun be in my grandparents dying without ever knowing my role in it all? It's vanity really, and I'm inexperienced in the art of murder – next time I won't allow myself this indulgence. But I climb down the cliff, holding onto bits of scrubby plants and crouching low so I don't tumble towards the darkness. I reach the car. It's hard to tell what's happening inside, since branches seem to crisscross the doors. I shuffle up the car on the driver's side and twist my head upside down, shining my torch into the glass. Jeremy is suspended, his head hanging over the seatbelt. He looks uninjured, apart from being very definitely unconscious and upside down. Kathleen is clearly dead, no forensic expertise needed here, since you definitely need your head to be attached to your body to stay alive, and a tree branch has considerately removed that requirement for me.

I yank at Jeremy's door, but nothing happens. So I try the door behind his seat, and it opens enough for me to be able to squeeze my head in – just behind his seat rest. I stroke his haughty face, now thin and bleeding, and listen to his ragged breathing. I get as close as I can, which is difficult as he's upside down and I'm twisting like a pretzel, and whisper his name. His eyes open a crack and he whimpers as I begin to speak.

'Kathleen is dead, Jeremy, I'm so sorry. I don't think you're going to make it either, but you're not alone. Do you recognise me? I'm

Grace – your granddaughter. Simon's daughter.' He twitches ever so slightly. 'Yes, Marie's child. I'm so sorry that we never met before, well, this sad day. But then you made sure of that, didn't you? You didn't want me anywhere near your family. That's all right, Jeremy, I don't think we'd have got along really. But it wasn't kind, was it? And so now you have to go, I'm afraid. Not for me, you see, but for my mother. Family first – I know you understand that. Oh, and it's not just you and your wife, Jeremy. That's the really good bit.'

Pulling out the perfume bottle, I turn his head towards me as gently as I can, and look into a single grey eye. 'I'm going to kill your whole family.' As I say it, I yank his tie towards me, and he slumps. I pull it from his collar, carefully roll it up and stuff it into my pocket. My little Spanish souvenir. Then I open the bottle, and strike a match.

CHAPTER TWO

The guards bang on our cells at 8 a.m., before handing over breakfast on a tray and departing. Obviously it's not poached eggs and fresh coffee. We are given teabags, milk, and two slices of white bread made so cheaply that I held a slice back last month just to see what would happen to it. Nothing, as it turned out. It curled up at the corners slightly, but other than that was worryingly unaffected. It reminded me of a story we were told at school, about how the poor in the nineteenth century were sold bread which was made with chalk and other inedible substances to pack it out. Prisons, mostly now run by private companies with ridiculous made-up names designed to sound commanding, would probably admire such methods and rue the day food standards were imposed. I don't have much of an appetite in here as it happens. The prison diet could surely be marketed to those vain Instagrammers who shill appetite suppressants and dubious vitamins. Just eat bland dough three times a day, and trade anything left over for cigarettes – your standard-issue tracksuit will be suitably loose in no time.

Kelly asks if I want to talk anything over, tilting her head in what I imagine she thinks is a sympathetic gesture. She knows my final appeal is due any day now, and her recent forays into group therapy seem to have convinced her that she has a bright future in counselling. I have to stifle the urge to explain that the best therapy that Harley Street has to offer wouldn't help me much, so I doubt that Kelly's offer of trying to contact my inner child will suddenly fix whatever she imagines might be wrong with me. Besides the fact that Kelly is an undeniable moron, I think talking is overrated. As my mum used to say 'never complain, never explain'. Although she died inconsiderately early, and left me to rectify the wrongs done to her, which is why I'm here. A bit more complaining might not have been such a bad thing, on balance.

After Kelly takes the hint and wanders off to go and coach someone else, I settle down on my bunk to start writing down my story. I've not got long if I want to set it all out in full – the result of my appeal will be with me shortly, according to the long-faced solicitor I've engaged, who wears the most beautifully tailored suits when he visits, but spoils the entire look by pairing them with garish loafers. I imagine he thinks these add a touch of character but they tell me that actually he has none. Perhaps a younger second wife bought them in the hope of making him seem more youthful. I wish she hadn't. Absurd vanity is not a trait I particularly wish to see in a lawyer attempting to get me out of a life sentence. Especially not if my hefty fees encourage him to buy more of the terrible things.

I was born twenty-eight years ago, at the Whittington hospital, the only daughter of Marie Bernard, a young Frenchwoman who had been living in London for three years before falling pregnant with me. After giving birth alone, she took me back to her studio flat in Holloway where I first experienced the boredom and claustrophobia of a confined space and all the limited joys of a toilet in the bedroom. Studio is such a misleading description when applied to property, conjuring images of an airy and large room where one is bound to be creative and perhaps hold chic gatherings where beautiful people hang over balconies to smoke. Our flat was on the fifth floor of a building which housed a chicken shop at ground level. The landlord, perhaps as part of a complicated social experiment to see how many people he could house in one old Victorian building meant for four, had divided up each floor to make three flats each. My mother and I lived in one room, with a small attic window which did not open (either because of an impressive accumulation of pigeon shit, or because said landlord didn't want us to be tempted to yell at passersby to save us, we never did find out which). This sounds quaintly Dickensian, doesn't it? It was not. Don't forget the chicken shop. My mum slept on the pull-out sofa, and I had the single bed. I still get stabs of guilt when I think of how hard she worked, and how tired she was, and yet still always insisted that she liked the lumpy couch. As a selfish child, I didn't think to offer her the bed. As a grown-up, I splashed out on a king-size memory foam job from John Lewis, but never stopped falling asleep thinking about her on that sofa. It rather ruined the extravagance, if I'm honest.

Marie had come to England because she'd been told she was pretty enough to be a model, and she was. My mother was strikingly beautiful, with olive skin, and shaggy brown hair which she clipped up in a bun no matter how many times I implored her to wear it down. She had that effortless French girl vibe, which every fashion influencer tries to copy now, to varying degrees of success. No bra, ever. Wide slacks and a long gold chain upon which hung a miniature portrait of an old man, his identity lost to time. Before I came along, she'd done a few small campaigns, modelling for high street stores that were long gone by the time I was born. Kookai, she insisted, was the coolest shop of its day, and she kept a rolled-up poster that she'd featured in, which had hung in their shop windows for an autumn campaign. In it, she's crouched on the ground, a brown cardigan draped over her knees, covering a short dress and platform trainers, which I've seen making a regrettable return to high streets recently.

My mother was too short for catwalk modelling, and her career never took off in the way she had dreamt about when she came to London and shared a flat with two other European girls seeking success. But she certainly had fun for a while. The London nightlife in the early Nineties, was, to hear Marie tell it, a golden age. Evenings at Tramp, a private members club which opened in 1969, were almost as glamorous as when Liza Minnelli used to frequent it. At night, when I couldn't sleep, she'd lie next to me on my small bed and tell me about the champagne served with sparklers in it, and the leather banquettes in the restaurant, where she would dine with actors and sports stars and dance until dawn. You could smoke inside, she used to tell me, and the richest women wore fur unapologetically. Her life before me appeared to be one long whirl of parties and castings. A woman blessed with such innate beauty doesn't have to try particularly hard, it's always seemed to me, and Marie never worried too much about money or the future. Someone would always look after the French girl who never wore a bra and wanted to have fun. Someone will always zoom in on the girl who doesn't know her worth.

Besides, my mother had already met the man she would give her whole heart to. The man who would become my father. The man who would promise her the world and shower her with gifts. The man who I would grow up swearing to ruin.

CHAPTER THREE

Even now, just thinking about that man makes me tense up. I force myself to breathe deeply. I am a master of self-control. It hasn't come naturally. As a child, I used to throw tremendous tantrums and dive on the floor if something displeased me, as my mother gazed on in amusement and apologised to those around us. That sense of drama lives on inside me, but I've long learnt to keep it in check. If you're going to execute a plan to, well, execute a bunch of people, you cannot let your emotions run wild. It would all get very messy, and there would be nothing worse than to be found out because you were too self-indulgent to maintain self-control. As when I was a child, I have ended up suffering the indignity of having to use a toilet three feet from my bed. But at least it wasn't because I gave myself away with a foolish flair for the dramatic.

I am breathing normally again within a minute. Did you know that Hillary Clinton practised nostril breathing when she lost the 2016 election to Donald Trump? She relied on wine as well of course, but losing to such an ignoramus required more. Nostril breathing requires you to breathe in heavily through one nostril, and expel the air deeply through the same cavity. You might scoff, but it helps to calm me down quickly, and it helps to have techniques like this in prison, where you can't rely on quality pharmaceuticals, or a decent glass of Merlot at the end of the night. At night, when I cannot sleep and my thoughts invariably turn to my life's work, I often think of Mrs Clinton, up against that flashy orange moron. Whatever her politics, she stood up to a bully who refused to abide by convention or decency. A person like that can drive you to madness without any noticeable exertion, while you employ all the strength you have just to hold the line and maintain a sliver of your humanity. Hillary had one advantage over me. Her opponent was a man she could walk away from in defeat. Mine was my father. OK, perhaps I had the advantage. Clinton couldn't kill Trump, much as she must've wanted to. I wish she'd had the opportunity, I find it relaxes one far more than plain old nostril breathing.

* * *

Marie met my father in 1991. He was gone before I was born. She made sure that I grew up surrounded by love, but by the time I went to primary school, it became clear to me that this love, fulsome as it was, was only coming from one direction. Other children had daddies, I would tell her, as she fussed over my dinner, or washed my hair in lukewarm water over the little sink. In the beginning, my mother would try to distract me, but by the time I was nine, she understood that my wilful nature was only growing stronger, and she sat me down one day after school, and told me about my father. Most of what I know I learnt from digging around later on, since Marie obviously wanted to give me a Disneyfied version of the man who willingly gave up his seed to create me without a thought about the later consequences.

Marie met him at – where else – a nightclub. He had been a little older, she said (later I found out that he was twenty-two years older. How little young women think of themselves), and he had sent champagne to her across the dancefloor. Marie had sent the bemused waiter away, she was having too much fun dancing, with no need for a bucket of Veuve Clicquot. I have been to clubs like this and I have seen men like my father, night after night, as they make themselves comfortable in dark corners, watching young women putting on a show for whomever they think might be watching, waiting to be invited to a table where someone will buy them prohibitively expensive drinks. If my mother had been like all the other girls, there would have been some dancing, a whispered exchange, perhaps even a pleading dinner or two. And that is where it would have fizzled, just another beautiful girl, just another entitled rich man. Except my mother sent back the champagne. And nobody had ever done such a thing to this particular rich man. I conjure up this moment in my mind from time to time. I like to imagine that he couldn't stand to watch her dancing so joyously, throwing off his attempts to impress so easily. I can see him now – reassessing, working his reptilian mind harder than usual to come up with a new plan, a way to command her attention. To bend her to his will.

Two weeks later, she bumped into him outside another club. It was raining, and she was huddled in the queue, holding her coat aloft as she jostled with the other hopefuls trying to gain entry into the exclusive nightspot, all desperate to experience the decadence promised within, or at the very least get out of the rain. As we sat there on the sofa bed, my mother looked into the distance and her voice grew soft, as she described how a blacked-out sports car pulled up outside the club, splashing the pathetic crowd as it screeched to a stop. By the time she told me about my father, he had already treated her with a cruelty that makes my stomach burn, and yet she spoke about him with affection in her voice, and perhaps even awe. 'He got out of that car, and threw his key to the valet who was standing by. I only noticed him because of the awful noise from the car. And when I saw him throw the keys . . . bouf . . . I thought it was a horribly arrogant move, to park a car in the middle of the road like that.'

She looked away, she insisted, as the bouncers unclipped the red velvet ropes to usher him inside, and the crowd pushed forward, angry that they were still stuck in the cold. And then a hand beckoned her towards the rope. A stern-looking woman with a clipboard nodded rapidly as if to say 'yes, you', and Marie weaved through the throng, and presented herself to the doormen. She was directed inside, she explained, and wasn't about to question it, even as the people behind her grumbled and booed. As she got to the bottom of the stairs, she was met by *him,* leaning against the wall, arms crossed, smirking. I've seen that smirk many times in the press. It's almost his signature expression. A powerful combination of arrogance and charm. An infuriating combination too, since you quickly find that with men like that, the arrogance always overcomes the charm and yet by then it's too late, for the initial mix is intoxicating and hard to forget.

'So you don't want my champagne, but you'll accept my hospitality?' he said, looking her up and down. Honestly, I still think poorly of her for not turning around and walking away right then and there. Even aged nine, when she relayed their initial meeting to me, I remember thinking that this was a truly pathetic opener. If I'd ever imagined that my father might have been some mythical figure who we lost to a heroic act of bravery, this is the moment when that unspoken assumption died. My father was a cheesy charlatan in an expensive suit, and my mother ate it up.

I assume she played it cool at first, batting him away with some witheringly French put-down, but even if she did, it still counted for nothing. By the next day, he'd found out her address and turned up in a soft-top filled with flowers. Her flat-mates woke her up screaming with laughter, as Helene told me much later, teasing her about the British man in the flat cap who was tooting the horn and holding up traffic. A week later, he flew her to Venice on a private jet, taking her to St Mark's Square for cocktails (honestly, how tacky), and telling her that he loved her. The extravagant displays of affection continued over the next few months, as they would go out for dinner, to the nightclubs they both loved, to walk in Hyde Park on sunny Monday mornings. Her barriers were demolished, no longer was she cautious and dismissive of London men and their intentions. Marie stopped going to castings as much, preferring to be available if he happened to call. And he did, frequently. But only between Monday to Friday, and he rarely stayed the night with her, crying off with work, or explanations about his elderly mother and her need for him to stay sometimes.

Did your eyes just roll back inside your head so hard it made you wince? Well yes. We can dwell on my mother's stupid decision to place her faith in a man who wore large buckled belts and enjoyed the music of Dire Straits, or we can move on. I don't have enough time in this place to unpack the manipulation on his end or the naivety on hers. Obviously, my father was already spoken for. Not just spoken for, he was married with a baby, and he lived in a house high on a hill in North London which had several live-in staff, two pedigree dogs, a wine cellar, swimming pool, and several acres of grounds. He wasn't just committed, he was embedded.

This bit of the story was left out when I was first told about him. I don't blame Marie for glossing over some of the more delicate details I probably wouldn't have fully understood anyway. Instead, my mother attempted to explain why my father never came to see me, never sent me a birthday present, never turned up at parents' evening. Stroking my arm, Marie told me that he was involved in big and important business deals which affected the lives of thousands of people, and that's why he couldn't see us. He flew around the world, she said. He loved us both very much, and when the time was right, we'd all be together, but right now, we had to let him work hard and prepare for the time when we could live as a family. Did she believe it herself? I've often wondered. Was my smart, kind mother really so, to be blunt, stupid? Maybe. My sex is so often disappointing – I remember once reading about a woman who married a man who convinced her that he was a spy. He persuaded her to sign over her life savings to him, to the tune of £130,000, saying that he was undercover and needed it to tide him over until his handlers could safely make contact. She'd never asked for proof, so desperate was she for this ridiculous charade of a love affair to be real. And to compound her humiliation, she'd willingly posed for photos in a weekly magazine and told her story, looking downtrodden and sad. Was I supposed to feel sorry for this person, a grown-up who dreamt of fairy-tale romance, and didn't question why this man whisked her, a woman in her fifties (who looked every inch of it), off her feet? Marie was a cut above this woman and those like her, but she obviously still had the capacity for similar delusion.

For all the ridiculous promises that Marie made to me about my father and our eventual life together, she was wise enough to only tell me selective information about him. Enough to stop my questions, not giving me anything too concrete. But she did make the mistake of pointing out his house to me after a trip to Hampstead Heath a few months later. We got lost in a wooded area, and it started to rain. My mother grabbed my hand and marched me up a hill, attempting to find a route to the main road where we might get a bus. But when we finally got to the bus stop, she briskly carried on, as I grumbled and pulled my anorak tightly around me. Despite the torrential skies, we walked another ten minutes down a long private road, until she slowed down and finally stopped.

We stood in front of a house and Marie stared up at it silently for a moment, until I yanked on her hand impatiently. I say we were looking at a house, but the enormous iron gates with security cameras attached deliberately obscured most of the actual property. We lived in an attic room on a main road. I had never imagined that a house could be so important it would have to be hidden from view. Without looking down at me, my mother gestured towards the gates, almost reverentially. 'This is your father's house, Grace,' she said, still not looking at me. I didn't know what to say. I felt uncomfortable lingering in front of this grand place, drenched to my skin. Marie must have noticed that I was slowly moving backwards, trying to encourage her to head to the safety of the bus stop and home, so she smiled brightly. 'Such a shame your father isn't in today, but isn't it lovely, Grace? One day you will have your own bedroom there!' I nodded, not knowing what else to do. She took my hand, and we turned around, and headed away, back down the hill to our home. We never mentioned that trip again. But I thought about that bedroom she'd promised would be mine many times growing up. I imagined it, with pink wallpaper and a big double bed, and maybe even a wardrobe full of new clothes, but even when I burrowed down deep into this rabbit hole, I knew that Marie had been lying, and that there would never be a bedroom behind those grand gates for me. And even then, I remember understanding so clearly, that something very wrong had been done to Marie and me.

So that's my dad. Not the one I'd have picked had I been consulted, but there we are. Some people have fathers who beat them, some have fathers who wear Crocs. We all have our crosses to bear. I haven't told you much about his personality or his background, have I? That'll come. But if you really want to understand why I did what I did, I have to go back to my childhood again first. Hopefully it won't sound too self-indulgent, but even if it does, well, it's my story. And I'm currently lying on a bunk bed in a cell which smells like a potent mix of sadness and urine, so I'll take any excuse to escape into my memories.

Here are some early memories: Marie not having enough money for food, electricity, and on one grim occasion, for sanitary products. Getting up at 6 a.m. so that Marie could get to work on time, where I would sit in the backroom of the coffee shop and do my homework. Seeing my mother so tired that she looked yellow and hollowed out day after day. Being cold all through winter because we only used the heating at the beginning of the month when Marie got paid. Being cold instils a raw fear in me to this day. I paid to have extra radiators installed in my flat as a grown-up, much to the bemusement of my landlord, and forked out an obscene amount of money for a, in hindsight, fairly hideous fur throw to blanket my bed, because I needed certainty that I wouldn't wake up shivering, as I had done so often as a child. Fur might be unethical but truly, it feels wonderful next to the naked body.

Marie dealt with our lack of money and support as best she could. Her parents, disapproving of her life choices, as they put it, gave her nothing. Hortense met us for lunch once, on one of her trips to London on which I can only assume she terrorised shop girls and made waiters cry for fun. My mother put me in my best outfit, which consisted of an itchy jumper she'd bought for me at M&S one Christmas (which I hated, but she was proud of, because it was real wool and had a pie-crust collar), and corduroy trousers, which pinched at the stomach and had belonged to another child at my primary school, before being handed on to me. My grandmother said hello to me, then promptly turned to my mother and spoke in French for the rest of the meeting. Marie would answer in English, which served only to make Hortense even more determined. As we left the restaurant, Hortense bent down, pulled my jumper sleeve towards her face and sniffed. She said something to my mother as she gestured back at me, and my mother's eyes sprung with tears. That was the last time I ever saw the old witch. When Marie died, she sent me a letter, which I didn't open, opting instead to flush it, piece by piece, down the toilet at Helene's house. She must be dead by now, but I hope she isn't. I hope she sees the news reports about me. I hope she and her repressed old husband got doorstepped by scummy tabloid journalists during my trial, and I pray that their neighbours view them with suspicion, or worse – faux sympathy.

So we were poor, and Marie had nobody, apart from Helene. Bea, her only other real friend, had fled back to France after a doomed love affair and a mean model agent who suggested in so many words that she should try to develop an eating disorder if she wanted to make any money. Occasionally, my mother would write long letters late at night, as I pretended to be asleep. She'd sit at the kitchen table, tearing up pieces of paper, and starting again and again. In the morning, the letters would be propped up on the table, ready to take to the postbox. I didn't recognise the name until I was older, when I saw a discarded attempt in the bin and fished it out.

My darling, I know we cannot meet again, and I have always respected your decision. You know how much I loved you, and that I would never do anything to hurt you or jeopardise your family. But Grace is growing up, and I wish so much for you to know her – just a little. I do not ask for money, or expect that we can ever experience the closeness we once revelled in. But she needs her father! Sometimes she tilts her head and gives me a little smirk, and she looks just like you, which inflicts such a mixture of pride and pain you could never imagine. Perhaps you could come and meet us one Sunday at the park in Highgate, just for an hour? Please write back to me, I never know if you are reading these letters.

From this letter, I learnt three very important things. First, that snooping will almost always pay off. Second, that my father was married and wanted nothing to do with me, despite Marie's attempts to spin me a different story. And third, and most importantly, I found out the name of the philanderer who broke my mother's heart and left us to live in misery. I already knew his name, it turned out. Most people do. My father is Simon Artemis. And he is one of the richest men in the world. I should say was, back when he was still alive.

That was the bell. I have to go and do laundry. Endless greying sheets to wash and fold. The glamour is sometimes too much to bear.

CHAPTER FOUR

My younger years were not like something out of one of those terrible books you see in airport bookshops, usually called something like 'Daddy Don't', which might be a story of unimaginable suffering, but only sell because people like to read about other people's misery and feel good about themselves afterwards, simply for feeling the merest shred of sympathy or horror. 'I read this and cried my eyes out, such a sad story :(' is the usual review on some online mum book club. Oh, you read about child abuse and constant trauma and found that upsetting did you, Kate1982? (Kate just sounds like the name of someone who'd frequent a site like that.) So glad you could tell us all how it affected *you*.

Anyway, my childhood (the part Marie was alive for anyway) had some good moments. I was very loved, and I knew it – even though it all came from just one person. Mothers are adept at providing love from all angles, so much so that you often don't realise you're missing out on love from other people until much later in life. Marie took the brunt of the hardship and hid it well from me. Of course I knew she was struggling, children always do, don't they? But children are also astonishingly selfish, and as long as she successfully managed to paper over most of the cracks, I was more than happy to go along with it. My mother would save up her wages – from her job as a barista at a coffee shop in the Angel where hot drinks were at least £3 and cake was made without flour for those women who'd recently discovered gluten intolerance, and from her cleaning gig which took her to the homes of the ladies up in Highgate who probably didn't eat cake at all. Every three months she would have just enough to take me on a 'magical mystery tour', which just meant a trip to the *Cutty Sark*, or a Tube ride down to Selfridges to see the Christmas lights. Once she took me to the fair up on Hampstead Heath, where I ate candy floss for the first time and won a fish during a game of hoops. We put the fish in a vase on our kitchen table and called it RIP, which I thought was funny since fairground fish never live very long. Marie thought it was mean, and nurtured that fish, cleaning out its home every week and adding in some green plants and a desultory rock. I lost interest in that fish, but under her early care, RIP ended up living for ten years. He outlived my mother.

Marie and I struggled on. I went to a nice primary school just off Seven Sisters where I made precisely one friend, a boy named Jimmy, whose family lived in a very large house with an excessive number of rugs and cushions and books stacked from floor to ceiling in every room. His mother was a therapist, and his father was a GP, and they easily could have sent their son to a prep school not situated next door to a pawn shop which did a nice side hustle in hard drugs. But they had a big Labour poster in their window and carried a huge amount of liberal guilt about their good fortune, and Jimmy's education was one of the ways they squared it. Jimmy is still in my life. In fact, our relationship has matured somewhat in recent times, I guess you could say.

We might have gone on like this, Marie and me. I went to secondary school down the road (with Jimmy initially, who was mercilessly teased for being posh in Year 7 and so was sent off to a private day school which had goats and did a lot of art – another tortured compromise made by his parents), and I made a few more friends. Perhaps if we'd had longer, Marie might have got a better job, and who knows, maybe met a nice man to take some of her burdens. I might have made it to university, and later earned enough to look after my mother, buy her a flat, get her a car. But if that had been our fate, then I wouldn't be here, writing this, waiting for Kelly to burst into our cell and try to lure me into a conversation about her brassy DIY highlights. Instead, Marie got slower, greyer, and slept more, to the point where I was getting up for school and leaving her in bed. She lost a cleaning job because she didn't wake up until 11 a.m. one morning, and some starch-faced witch in a house which had six bathrooms and no soul fired her by text at 11.30 a.m. Her back ached, she said one night, chatting to Helene on the sofa as I dozed in bed. Helene urged her to see the doctor, but she dismissed it. 'When have I not had aches and pains since we've been in this cold damp country?' she laughed.

Who knows how bad she really felt? Certainly not me. Kids are self-absorbed and parents are supposed to be invincible. That's the deal. But Marie broke it. Two months later, she took me on holiday for the first time, to Cornwall. We stayed in a caravan park on a cliff overlooking the vast sea, and we walked along coastal paths and I ate a lot of ice cream. Marie drank wine on the doorstep of our van as I lay on the grass and asked her questions about her childhood in France, about how I could train to be a photographer when I grew up, about whether I would ever like boys in the way that grown-ups did if they were all as immature as the ones in my class. She laughed at that one. She laughed a lot that holiday.

I had just turned 13 when it became obvious that her aches weren't just a sign of endless work and constant worry. Helene picked me up from school early one day, and took me to the hospital. Marie had collapsed at work, and before I could see her, my mother's only friend sat me down in a visitors' room and told me that my mother had cancer. She'd held off going to the doctor and, like so many women who care for others, she'd neglected her own needs entirely. She didn't want me to know, Helene explained, but I deserved to. I gazed at the strip lighting overhead, and felt my ears hum as Helene asked if I could keep calm and be brave in front of my mother. I felt something switch off in my brain at that moment, as though I were suddenly on standby, not able to function at full capacity. I later learnt that this is called disassociation, when your brain disconnects to protect you from stress or trauma. It's a horrendous feeling but it has served me well in times when, well, I've had to do some pretty unpleasant things. Frankly, when you're surrounded by blood and the sound of someone screaming for their life, it's actually a relief to switch off.

Marie never came home, and six weeks later, my lovely, tired mother was dead. In the brief window between her diagnosis and her death, my mother and Helene had agreed that I should live with her from now on – as if there was anywhere else I could go. My grandparents didn't even come over for the funeral, which was a small affair made up of some former models from my mother's early years in London, a few of her work colleagues and Jimmy's parents John and Sophie. We toasted her at the local café where we used to go for hot chocolate on Saturday mornings when we needed to escape the damp and cold of our flat. And with that, my childhood was pretty much done. I moved to Helene's flat in Kensal Rise, and had my own bedroom for the first time – a small space which used to house her clothes and long since abandoned old exercise equipment. The fish came with me, its bowl dumped on a dressing table. Helene never envisaged a teenager in her life, but to her credit, she did as well as she could by me. There was always food, and she gave me money for travel and clothes. I never said it out loud, in case I was struck down by some vengeful deity, but it was a much better standard of living than the one we had in our depressing bedsit. I moved to a school nearer her flat, and became pretty independent almost immediately. Helene worked at a modelling agency, and was out a lot, so I would walk around the local park for hours after school to pass the time, or go and sit in the local Costa and nurse a tea. Anything rather than go back to the empty flat and think about all that I had lost.

Helene had cleaned out my mother's flat, and although there was nothing of much value to give me, she did make sure to pass on Marie's favourite opal ring, which fitted my thumb perfectly, and which I would rub constantly throughout the day. She also gave me a box of letters, documents, and photos from Marie's younger days, including her prized Kookai poster. I never opened them. Apart from the ring, I'm not hugely one for sentimental relics (of course, I was never immune to keeping a few prized tokens after a murder, but that could hardly be called sentimental). But one day, while foraging around under Helene's bed for her hair straighteners, I found another box. This was unlike the one I had in my room, which was decorated with flowers and hearts. This one was like those I was used to seeing in my head teacher's office – sturdy and formal. And it had something written carefully on the spine in red ink: 'Grace/Simon'.

Obviously I was going to look inside. I didn't even hesitate. I still pay no heed to the supposed privacy of others – if you leave something around me, I will look at it, soak it in, commit it to memory. I expect growing up relying on just one person means that I need more information than a normal person when it comes to trust. Or maybe I just want to get inside your head and gain an advantage over you. It doesn't always work, I've been looking through Kelly's diary since I landed in this prison, but it's hard to gain an insight into someone's innermost thoughts when they're so completely devoid of any original ones.

I slid myself down Helene's door and wedged myself there, just in case she came home. My mother's friend witnessed the whole of my parent's brief relationship, but she'd never given me any information on it, even when Marie died. I know she felt it wouldn't help, that she was protecting me, so I didn't push it. But this box might tell me more than she could anyway. Helene was kind, but she was hardly a great intellect, and had a fairly basic level of insight. Her favourite shows were all on ITV, if that makes it at all clearer.

Inside was a bundle of papers in no discernible order. I saw various newspaper clippings, letters, and photographs all jumbled up, and began sifting them into corresponding piles. Once done, I started looking at the photos properly. A few were of my mother and her girlfriends on nights out at dark clubs around London. Marie and Helene in minidresses, both smoking, mid-dance. Girls I didn't know holding bottles of champagne and spraying it around. As I flicked through them, the girls slowly vanished, moving blurrily to the edges of the pictures, as Simon stepped onto the stage. There were photos of Simon with other men, all in white shirts and expensively distressed jeans, big gold buckles on their belts. They had their arms round each other's shoulders, just like the boys at school, but chomping on cigars, holding shot glasses, leering at the camera. Then there were photos of just my mum and Simon, him twirling her around, her polka-dot skirt blurring but her expression perfectly clear. She was rapt, twisting her head around to maintain a direct look at my father. He wasn't looking at her though – he was smirking at the camera. He wasn't looking at her in any of the pictures, instead he was grinning at his mates, who all seemed to desperately gaze up at him like Marie had, or mugging for the camera, slamming shots, dancing on a table while people cheered, and putting a harassed-looking waiter in a jokey headlock as the crowd around him creased their faces and applauded.

It's strange to realise that you loathe your father before you ever have a chance to meet him. Of course I knew that he had treated my mother badly, but there was more to it. Just from a few photos, he made my skin crawl. His tanned, shiny face spoke to a vanity I'd not encountered before. His obvious need to grab all attention available was pathetic. He took up other people's space – women were pushed out to the margins, only featured as beautiful props for Simon Artemis. His gang of friends looked about as shifty as you can imagine – certainly the kind who would be wise to keep their heads down in a post #MeToo era. Everything I saw made me feel slightly ill. This man, with his horrible flashy clothes and his clear need to advertise his testosterone levels with every pose, this man shared and contributed to my DNA, my character, my existence. Again, I wondered whether Marie had successfully hidden some major personality defect from me – how else to explain this man, this choice. How could she have made such a huge mistake?

I was 13 when I first saw these photos. I didn't know much about the relationships between men and women, the concept of patriarchy, the idea of emotional manipulation or even just the facts about basic sexual attraction. I just saw this disgusting man openly displaying all his worst qualities for the camera, as my beloved mother stared at him. And I hated her in that moment too.

As I shoved the pictures back in the box, I noticed that my fist was curled into a ball, and that the muscles in my neck were beginning to burn slightly, always the precursor to a headache, but I knew that if I didn't plough on, I might not have the chance again for a while. Who knows what Helene planned to do with the files?

Next up were the newspaper clippings, musty and fading. The

headlines were a mixture of business and personal news. 'Simon Artemis buys teen fashion chain Sassy Girl', 'Artemis criticised for "sweatshop" conditions', 'Simon and Janine show off their perfect new daughter', 'Simon Artemis, OBE? Rumours of an honour for the CEO of Artemis Holdings'. The last one was from a glossy magazine and had photos of Simon and his wife (who I now knew to be Janine), surrounded by fluffy dogs, fluffy carpet, and flanked by an enormous Christmas tree, the height of the room. In his arms, he held their daughter, who I noted was called Bryony. She looked to be about three. I checked the date on the article. The neck muscles were getting hotter. I was 13 months younger than her. My sister was a baby when Simon was in those clubs, wooing my mother, promising her who knows what. The photos showed the same house my mother had walked me past that wet day in Hampstead. It looked, even to my young eyes, fucking hideous. Janine (I assume it was Janine, given that men so often still assume it's the job of women to keep the house nice), clearly had an overwhelming passion for grey and silver. Have you ever seen a silver mantelpiece? I'm not talking metal, or paint, I mean real silver. Imported from Vienna, I learnt many years later, when I was very briefly allowed into their house for a staff party. Janine was a gracious hostess, speaking to everyone for a few moments as though she were the queen, and I asked many questions about her, let's say, unique take on interior design. She probably wouldn't have been so nice had she known my plans for her and her nearest and dearest, but she was so proud of that appalling fireplace it's actually hard to be sure.

The clippings showed me a little of what Simon did. He owned, amongst other things, Sassy Girl, the budget airline Sportus, and about 1,800 properties across the South East, the state of which had earned him the mildly amusing moniker 'The scum landlord'. He also owned a few hotels, and a couple of yachts which could be rented out by the week if you felt a five-star hotel was a little too down-market for your holidays. In what was the very definition of a vanity project in 1998, Simon and Janine also had a vineyard, and produced wine which I assume was only bought by their friends and cronies. It was bottled under the name 'Chic Chablis'. As if anything could tell you more about a person.

The last thing in the box was a thick, cream envelope. Inside were two pieces of paper. The first one I opened was a letter from Simon himself. It was a hasty scrawl, written in black ink, the words almost ripping through the paper.

> *Marie, thank you for your letter. I am sorry to hear that you are ill, but what you suggest is impossible. As I have told you <u>many</u> times before, your decision to have your child was yours alone. You had no right to imagine that I'd risk my family and reputation for the product of a six-week fling. Instead, you chose to have the baby (which I have no proof is mine anyway), and then try to entice me into seeing her. This delusion has to stop. Your daughter is not, nor ever will be, a part of my family. I have a wife, Marie! I have a daughter. I may possibly be due a peerage in next year's Honours list. You must stop trying to impress upon my life. I have enclosed a cheque for £5000, which is more than generous, but given your health problems feels like the right thing to do. In return, I demand that you cease all contact. Simon.*

The other letter in the envelope was the letter my mother had sent which provoked this nightmarish screed. I didn't want to read her pleas, see the vulnerability and sadness in her own handwriting. It was too embarrassing to see how weak my mother was in the face of this man. She was weak, but I was strong. So I would read it and reinforce the rage in my stomach, fortify it with steel and keep it there. I opened it.

Dearest Simon,

I know you have asked me not to write, and I have tried to respect your decision, though it makes me sad. But I must tell you that I am not well. I will not live too long, according to the good doctors at the Whittington Hospital (it is not far from you). I am resigned to it, not because I wish to die but because I'm tired. I'm tired and I have felt unwell for many years now, and life since I had Grace has been hard and it does not seem to be getting any easier. But do not for one second think that I blame Grace. She has been a light through it all. I wish so much that you had met her as a baby, as a toddler, when she was six and insisted on being called 'Crystal'. I wish you had been there for her frog phase, when she ribbited instead of speaking for a week, or when she won the drawing prize at school. You have missed so much, but you do not have to miss the rest. I will. I will miss it all, and it makes me so anxious that I cannot sleep, though truthfully the monitor and the ward noise don't help. Simon, you must take her. You must tell your wife about her – she will forgive you for something which happened so many years ago. Surely as a mother she would not let a child go without both her parents? I have little money to ensure her coming teenage years will be smooth, and my parents have never stopped being angry with me for my choices – I will not let her blossoming spirit be squashed by them. My friend Helene has offered to take her in, but it would not be as wonderful as having her own family around her. I do not want to beg, but I will, for our daughter's sake. Please do the right thing, I know you are a good man and that you would not leave your own child alone in the world. I will not be going home, so please write to me at the hospital, Floor 4, the Hummingbird Ward.

All my love and affection,
Marie

I shut the file, pushed it back under the bed and checked the floor for any loose paper which might give me away to Helene. After that, I must have walked straight out of the flat, because I found myself in the local park, where I sat down on a bench and tried to slow my heart down. I stroked the palm of my hand with my other one, and tugged at the bottom of my throat, trying to loosen the lump which had suddenly taken up residence there. I knew more about my father than ever before. I knew he was rich beyond comprehension. I knew he had a family, a home, a horrible mantelpiece. He owned businesses I had heard of – Sassy Girl, was a label the girls at school wore. He was a public figure. My mother had asked him for help as she was dying (and humiliated me by doing so). And he had rejected her, berated her, and knocked her down. I wanted to run to his house and jump on him, hit him, push my fingers into his eyes and force his head against his hideous marble floor. I breathed slowly, trying to focus on the see-saw in the children's play area. But the rage stayed. I knew it wouldn't fade now, no matter how calm I could make myself feel outwardly. In life my mother had ably shielded me from the rejection, from the callous and cold detachment of this man. And I had been safe with her warmth to surround me. But in dying, she could not absorb this hurt for me anymore. I knew I couldn't really go to his house, ring the bell, and demand that he pay some vague price for what he had done. I'd get as far as the bronze gates outside and be turned away. The Artemis family were clearly used to putting up walls and dismissing those who inconvenienced them – debtors, fans, beggars, and unwanted children. I would have to wait, I realised, sit it out and come up with a plan for when I was older and more able to make contact. This thought comforted me. I had five years until I was 18. Five years to think up a way to make the Artemis family suffer. I still remember this moment vividly, and

I've thought of it many times since, always with a smile. Because even at 13 (and though I was too nice back then to let myself think it explicitly), I comforted myself with the knowledge that I would grow up and make them know, really know, the pain that we had suffered.

CHAPTER FIVE

I didn't much want to kill Andrew Artemis. It had to be done, of course, I knew that and held firm, but I wasn't prepared for one of them to be so, well, nice. The research I'd done on his relatives had been thorough, meticulous, I suppose one could argue obsessive. And from that, I'd come to know just how morally rotten this family was. It made it easier to focus on the task at hand, knowing that I wasn't taking anything decent away from the world. In my head, I had even begun to explain away my wholly personal pursuit as a public good. The Artemis family were the embodiment of toxic capitalism, a vacuum of morality, a totem of greed. God, I was insufferably young.

The ease with which I offed Jeremy and Kathleen emboldened me. It was luck really – one dramatic swerve of a wheel and they whooshed off a cliff, not even a scratch left on Amir's car to cause suspicion. So many things could've gone wrong, so many things that make me wince when I look back on it. And if anything had gone differently, I might have lost my nerve, reassessed my plans, or worse – been caught. But I wasn't. I had a full house that night. Frankly, the considerate way my grandparents died so fast meant that I carried on. I can thank them for something at least.

Andrew was the son of Simon's brother Lee and possibly the hardest to glean any reliable information about. He wasn't present at any of the grotesque family parties, where waitresses dressed up like peacocks (thank you gossip columns for that titbit) and neat lines of cocaine laid out on silver platters were offered about by dwarves in top hats. He wasn't on the family yacht come summer, oiled up and lying out on the deck with Bryony and her thin, bronzed friends. He didn't even have a token job at Artemis HQ, the looming building off Great Portland Street where an immaculate grey Bentley idled outside whenever Simon was at the office, the nouveau version of raising the flag whenever the queen is at home. Even Tina, my Artemis informant – someone I'd begrudgingly befriended when I worked there (I'll get to that) – couldn't help me much when I cast around for information about him, vaguely saying that she thought Andrew 'might have followed his own path' when I texted her to ask why he wasn't mentioned in the magazine coverage of the annual Artemis charity ball. As usual, I couldn't push her too far on these matters. I had to let her lead, so as not to raise any red flags, and my cousin clearly didn't interest her at all.

I knew something was really up when Andrew was a no-show at his grandparents' funeral (that was a deliciously strange event to witness from a respectful distance). I persevered. When Facebook failed to locate him, I set up a Google alert on my young cousin and waited patiently. Eventually I found a mention of him in a local online freesheet, a profile of the work some old crusty was doing on marsh frogs in an area of wetlands in East London. Once I'd boned up on what exactly a wetland was, I realised that Andrew, perhaps more than me, had strayed far and away from the family Artemis. Saying something, when you consider that my very existence had been denied since birth.

Andrew wasn't trying to bulldoze the wetland and build a factory for small children to make flammable polyester clothes, nor was he intent on rounding up the marsh frogs to use their skin for designer handbags like most in his family would have suggested if the profit margins were good enough. No, he was *volunteering*, helping to observe mating behaviour, ensuring that these hideous creatures had a place to live and thrive. And for next to no money. Honestly, if I'd not driven his grandparents off that dusty Marbella road, I think they'd have done it themselves upon hearing what their grandson was doing with his life.

It quickly became clear that the work I'd put in at the Artemis company would count for nothing if I wanted to try to get close to Andrew. In fact, I suspected it would actively count against me. From the casual enquiries I had made when I worked at Artemis HQ (depressingly few given my decidedly junior role), it seemed that my cousin had cut himself off from the family some years ago, barely speaking to his parents from year to year. Ironic really, in the Alanis Morissette definition (who really understands what irony is anyway?), that I'd spent so long trying to smuggle my way into the Artemis inner circle and my cousin had broken out just as determinedly.

But despite his obvious intentions to lead a different life, he was still one of them. Still likely to be welcomed back with open arms if he got bored of helping disgusting frogs gentrify East London – which, let's face it, seemed likely. And crucially, still a potential beneficiary when the rest of the family died (and as you know, I was helpfully hastening that day along). So I did what I had to do. I researched frogs, bought a hideous windbreaker and signed up to a volunteer scheme at the Walthamstow marsh project.

I once watched one of those 'based on a true story' movies on Channel 5 late one Sunday night. It was about a high-flying city woman who packed it all in to live the simple life tending to goats in the hills. She renounced her designer bags and (the obviously male director's eye played heavy here) her vapid life. She saw the purity in earth, in nature, in getting back to the land. It was glossy and the leading lady wore pristine overalls and the sun shone – and for a brief minute I was seduced (before I remembered my pressing family extermination goals). My tenuous point is, the Walthamstow marsh project will never be the setting for anything remotely similar. Nobody is coming away from this particular section of nature with an inspirational tale. Nobody will ever learn that the greatest love in life is loving yourself while wearing a hairnet and rubber gloves, so as not to contaminate the sacred frog area.

The volunteer induction took place on a sticky May Day, and I travelled by train from King's Cross, wearing clear lens glasses, sensible shoes, a parka and a bucket hat. I felt completely invisible, which was disconcerting and interesting at the same time. Nobody glanced at me, no man smiled my way. I even brought a packed lunch with me, something I've always thought was a warning sign in a person over eight years old. According to Google Maps, the marshes were nowhere near a familiar coffee shop, and I wasn't going to risk food which might have been cross-contaminated by anything remotely both wild *and* in Zone 4.

The visitors' centre was a bleak affair. That description is already grandiose – don't imagine a brightly lit complex with friendly signs or a working loo. It was a hut with a corrugated iron roof and, inside, childish posters displaying scribbled weeds and the occasional abstract bird. Roger, the man who ran the marsh project, was there to welcome the two of us who'd turned up. I was slightly shocked that someone else was voluntarily coming to work in a bog without the motivation of murder. But here one was. Lucy, she told Roger and me, was a 30-year-old woman who worked in IT but had always had a yearning to spend more time in nature. She had the look of someone who wasn't exposed to vitamin D on a regular basis, pallid and drawn in the face. I fought to keep my expression neutral, seeing Roger's eyes light up as he nodded enthusiastically in agreement with her every word.

'You've come to the right place, Lucy!' he said. 'We might not be a UNESCO world heritage site but I always like to say that these marshes are the real eighth wonder of the world!' His eyes disappeared into the crinkled skin which surrounded them as he laughed. I imagined he told someone that line at least once a day and idly wondered if he had a wife who'd dearly like me to dispose of him too.

My cagoule was pitch-perfect. Lucy wore a similar one, and Roger seemed to have taken it one step further and was decked out in what I can only describe as a waterproof onesie. A thermos of tea was proffered, as Roger leant against the reception desk and described what our duties would be. Though there were repeated assurances that we'd be entering the exciting world of conservation, our duties seemed really to boil down to just weeding. This was very important, according to Roger, to maintain the delicate ecological balance of the site. From reception, we were taken on a tour of the marshes, which only took us twenty-five minutes in total. Perhaps marsh singular might have been more appropriate.

It was a sorry affair, with little in the way of great beauty. A forlorn heron stood some way off, and a host of flies buzzed around the reeds, but aside from that, it wasn't singing with wildlife. It also wasn't exactly heaving with visitors. At one point, Roger muttered something about the local leisure centre and how funding was terribly weighted, his face darkening. Imagine a leisure centre being your nemesis.

Lucy seemed genuinely interested in the induction, asking detailed questions about netting and composting. I stayed quiet, nodding along, all the while searching for a man who could be Andrew. From the few photos that showed him at a younger stage, he was a tall, slim guy, with sandy hair and unnervingly symmetrical teeth. Moderately handsome, might get a second glance at a bar, standard enough London level handsome. But apart from Roger and an old lady, who reminded me somewhat of Alan Bennett's old lady in the van, ripping up some unidentifiable plants, there was nobody around.

Amusingly, Roger wouldn't let us actually do anything practical on the day, telling us that the job was very sensitive and insisting we spend an hour in the hut going over health and safety requirements instead. This mainly consisted of repeated warnings about the ponds, a few measly looking puddles, I'd thought, but Roger told us sternly that they were much deeper than we could imagine, their size concealed by reeds. We must be very careful when we worked near them, as one misstep could mean trouble. Even Lucy didn't look very convinced at this.

As the induction wrapped up, Roger paused reverently, looking to the sky as if seeking permission before he spoke. 'And now for the moment I'm sure you've been waiting for,' he grinned. 'The FROGS.'

'There are,' Roger said with a smile, 'only two native species of frogs in this country – the common frog and the pool frog. They are commonly found in shallow water and gardens. But we have a more exotic customer here. Oh yes, we have the MARSH FROG.' He waited for a murmur of approval, which Lucy duly gave, and continued. 'The marsh frog is a special kind of fellow. A chap called Edward Percy Smith brought twelve of them back from Hungary in 1935, and they duly escaped the confines of his garden and multiplied. Clever buggers,' he nodded, as though the frogs had some kind of master plan to colonise the British Isles.

We were guided down to the banks of the main pond, and instructed to stay quiet. Roger must have weighed sixteen stone at least and yet he moved with the skill of a practised cat burglar.

'Mustn't frighten them,' he mouthed, as he surveyed the scene. As we stood there, I wondered whether this was really the best approach to finding Andrew. I envisaged weekends spent with Roger silently waiting on these creatures, mud seeping into my boots, rain chilling my bones, and felt somewhat defeated. But I had no better options. Andrew was the next person on my list and I don't like to deviate when I have a plan, it unsettles everything.

After about fifteen minutes of awkward silence, as Roger prowled around on the lookout and Lucy stood stock-still, her body almost humming with anticipation, there was movement. The old man flicked a hand at us, and bent a finger in command. We tiptoed through the reeds, straining to get a look at the promised animal. From the description, I half imagined we'd see some giant multicoloured thing, with glittery skin, hopping about with joyous abandon. Instead, we looked down to see a small sludge green speck, the only embellishment a few light green lines on its back. It was just about the most overrated thing I'd ever seen, and Jimmy's mum, Sophie, once made us watch *Life Is Beautiful*.

The frog scuttled (can a frog scuttle?) back into the reeds the moment we approached, and Roger gave us a look of deep disappointment, as though we'd tried to spear it with arrows.

'Ah well, you've not learnt the ways yet. Next week you might see a mating! Tis the season for it.' Resolving never to learn the ways of a basic-looking frog, I trailed Roger and Lucy back to the visitors' centre to collect my things. As we departed, I spied a notice board with photos of staff and volunteers pinned up, with notes typed in Comic Sans explaining who was who. Not caring what Roger or Lucy thought, I made a beeline for it. And there he was. It took me a minute, my eyes searching for the clean-cut prince I'd seen in photos. But in this photo, he had a ponytail and . . . a large earring made out of a shell. Even Camden Market doesn't sell hippy tat like that anymore. What terrible thing had befallen Andrew, for him to make such a life choice? He'd doubled down on his decision though, with an ear tunnel on the other side, and a wooden necklace that suggested a gap year had been taken and decisively wasted.

I stared at the photo for longer than was probably acceptable, before trying to casually ask Roger about his colleagues.

'There's Linda, who you might've seen outside weeding.' He lowered his voice, 'She's lonely, poor love, caring for her husband with dementia.'

I wondered whether weeding out a frog's habitat was preferable and came to the conclusion that it probably was. Rather that than helping the man you used to fancy go to the toilet.

'Then there's Phyllis – Phil, we call her. A bit of a battleaxe but very good with school visitors. And then we have young Andrew. Does research on the wildlife and is very knowledgeable about conservation. We're lucky to have him – he did his degree in ecology at Brighton and he's got a grant to go and ID undocumented species in Australia next year. They have 240 known types there already,' he said wistfully.

'Is he around?' I asked offhandedly.

'Not today – he's at a seminar on fungus in the general population.' I must have looked alarmed, because he quickly added, 'In FROGS that is!' and laughed uproariously.

Finally released from the trial day, I gathered up my things, pleading an engagement and saying I had to rush. I was worried that Lucy would want to head back with me, and dreaded the idea of forty-five minutes on a train going over the day's events with someone who'd set the bar so low for a new hobby. But strangely she had lingered, and Roger seemed thrilled about it, offering her another cup of tea and asking what she knew about newts. I hoped that wasn't Roger's idea of a chat-up line and fled.

So that was that. Every Saturday, I headed off to serve Roger in his tiny dull kingdom. Every Saturday I pulled weeds, cleaned pathways, and tried not to feel insulted that Lucy was working closely with Roger on frog maintenance, while I did manual labour. Their heads close together, I'd hear snatched words and occasional laughter as he showed her how to trap and mark the frogs, for what I will never know. I've since learned that the marsh frog is in no way special, endangered, or prized. There were no amphibians that needed Roger's tender care, these mongrels of the marsh world would have been just fine without the watchful eye of a 50-year-old man wearing what looked suspiciously like Hush Puppies.

The only thing that stopped me from deliberately braining some of these animals and leaving the centre for good was Andrew. On my first proper shift, I spied him immediately, cleaning the pathway down to the ponds, humming along to music (what genre I didn't learn, since his enormous headphones blocked it off, but I'm guessing it was something like UB40). I waited for the inevitable introduction and sure enough, at break time, Roger brought him over to meet us. As we said our hellos and Lucy droned on about how interesting the work was, I drank him in. The long hair, almost down to his shoulders, was badly cared for and straggly. He wore khaki trousers and an ancient grey vest, and his fingernails were encrusted in dirt and grime. But he was broad and fit, with muscles clearly made by manual labour and not in a fancy gym. If he'd cleaned up, I could easily see how my cousin fitted into the Artemis family. His face was kind, but his eyes had the same fleck of grey that my father's had, and when he turned to the side, I saw that he had the same profile as Jeremy. Was there the same arrogance? Hard to tell.

I gave him the same vague story I'd told Roger and Lucy. I was Lara, an estate agent in North London, had just broken up with my long-term boyfriend, was looking for a new challenge and I'd had a fascination with conservation and rewilding since uni. I'd deliberately given myself his mother's name to see if it unnerved him but he didn't blink. Instead, he nodded eagerly and told me that he'd also come to develop this particular interest at university. Off to a good start at least.

That first day, Andrew was busy repairing a fence which had slipped, while the odd couple Lucy and Roger busied themselves with frogs and I cleaned the visitors' centre. I must just note that I'd not seen a visitor as yet, but Roger was full of anticipation for a school trip on Monday. 'Just what our young people need – the great outdoors – none of this leisure centre drudgery.'

I watched Andrew work, effortlessly rebuilding the fence, engrossed in his work. If he hadn't looked so like his grandfather, I'd have been convinced I'd got the wrong person. This man was carefree, simple, hardworking. I'd wager nobody in the Artemis family had done a day's physical labour since about 1963, unless you count stepping on other people to get what they want as hard work.

I had to think up a reason to talk to him, and as asking advice on how to properly clean the minuscule kitchen wasn't really going to cut it, I waited until everybody stopped for lunch and took my sandwiches over to where he sat, eyes closed, soaking up the spring sun.

'It's so lovely to work outside,' I ventured, 'I'm so tired of working in an office just chasing profits and cynically duping clients.' OK it was a bit too on the nose, but it got the right reaction. People so often just want you to hold up a mirror for their own opinions. This is especially true of men, and Andrew might have presented himself as a woke eco-warrior but he wasn't immune.

'God, that's so TRUE,' he said, turning towards me and smiling. 'This place is my sanctuary. I can't bear the way we, as a society, have been tricked by those with everything into chasing impossible gains, just so that big corporations can make more off their labour.'

OK, so this was going to be easier than I thought. After fifteen minutes of chat about capitalism and the evils of the empire, I told him a bit about 'my' family, the Latimers. Of course, I didn't use their real names or explain that Sophie and John weren't my real parents, but I hedged that, telling him about my liberal family who marched against climate change and voted Labour might get him to open up about his own relatives.

'I guess your family was the same growing up?' I said, as I helped myself to his Waitrose olive pot. His body slightly shifted, and he scratched at his neck with his pinky finger.

'No, actually. I figured all this stuff out by myself. My parents didn't bestow me with much in the way of ideological direction. Too busy enjoying themselves, making money – well, spending money, I guess. I had the best private education, lovely nannies, a good home, and for a while, I guess I drifted down that road – interned at a wealth fund at 16, enjoyed all the nice things that my family had. But uni changed me – it made me see proper inequality for the first time. People think that Brighton's wealthy you know? But it's got really poor pockets and the other students . . . well, they were all so engaged and connected to the real world y'know? It made me ashamed of myself, you know?'

I charitably assumed the constant 'you knows' were a nervous tic and tried to see beyond them.

'Good on you,' I said and squeezed his arm. 'Takes guts to really open your eyes.' Well, not really, if there's a multi-million-pound trust fund to fall back on when you get tired of living like the common people, but he seemed to appreciate it, absent-mindedly rubbing the spot I'd just touched.

From then on, I was in. It took a couple more weeks of weeding to suggest a drink after work, but he was keen. Unfortunately so was Lucy. And, even worse, Roger. We ended up in a dismal pub near the centre which I guess could've been nice if a roundabout hadn't encircled it at some point in the recent past (and, let's be honest, if the clientele had been completely different and the wine list had offered more than a lukewarm chardonnay from Australia). The talk was mainly about fucking frogs, with Andrew keen to tell us about his own private collection.

Roger rolled his eyes. 'This chap thinks the local ones aren't interesting enough, don't you, fella? Always looking for something a bit more . . . exotic.' He said it as though a foreign frog was dangerous, enticing Andrew away from the decent hardworking types found in the marshes. Roger definitely voted to leave the EU. I feigned interest, and encouraged my cousin to say more, while Roger turned to Lucy and attempted to engage her on the topic of topsoil. Andrew lowered his voice and tilted his head towards me slightly.

'The centre is a lovely place, and Roger means well. But he's right, I *am* interested in the more "exotic" ones, just as he says. It might sound mad . . .' he trailed off as I looked at him with interest, 'but I've been researching what frogs can do for depression. Have you heard of Kambo?'

No, Andrew, of course I fucking haven't. Normal people don't think about frogs and depression. Normal people don't spend their days in dingy marshes off a dual carriageway waiting for visitors who never come. But then, normal people don't try to annihilate their entire families so I really should learn to judge less and listen more. I opened my eyes wide.

'It's a secretion from a type of frog and there's a ton of research on how it helps to cure depression and addiction. We're all so dependent on western medicine pushed on us by big pharma, but it's becoming so clear that nature offers us better ways to tackle our human struggles. Kambo, man . . .' he paused. 'It's worked miracles on so many people.' He glanced over at Roger to make sure he wasn't listening and turned back to me. 'That's why I've got these frogs at home. I'm trying to perfect the dosage. Too much and you vomit uncontrollably. It's a tricky process. And I'm breeding them so that I can increase my supply and help more people.'

I didn't need to fake interest by now. What a weird path for Andrew to take, doping himself up with frog juice. Surely there must be a nice Harley Street therapist available to deal with his issues in a less bonkers way? Then again, rich kids have always tried to forge their own path, stymied by a lack of drive and comfort levels that make hard work seem unnecessary. Some become club promoters. Some weed-smoking artists. Why not a frog dealer?

I bombarded him with questions, and told him I thought he was brave. I'm not ashamed to say I opened up about my own personal struggle with depression and made myself vulnerable in front of him. Didn't matter that it was all tosh and that despite having very good reason to experience deep sadness, I had been lucky enough to swerve it. Men like women being vulnerable. They like to feel that we might need help, despite any surface-level confidence.

By the time we left the pub, I felt like I'd cracked him. And yet my shoulders were tense and my hands were balled up into fists as I walked to the station. He was a nice man, I thought, though fairly clueless. I didn't feel the acid burning in my throat when I thought about him like I did when I conjured him as an image of his father or grandfather. And that feeling, the ever stoked anger which made my ears feel as though they were on fire, that's what made it easy to kill Jeremy and Kathleen. That's what made it fun. I didn't feel that corrosive sensation in my windpipe for weeks afterwards. How would I enjoy this new challenge if I couldn't summon the acid?

By the next shift, we'd swapped numbers (one of the perils of a burner phone is never knowing your own number off by heart) and would text each other during the week with links to research papers we thought the other would enjoy. I didn't read anything he suggested, but it was easy to react appropriately with a quick skim of the conclusion. God bless these pointless academics who spend years doing some mind-numbing survey that nobody will read but helpfully tack on a footnote which summarises it all in two minutes. Texting might sound like there was flirting going on, but thankfully I think Andrew really just enjoyed someone who was willing to indulge his niche interest in amphibians and hallucinogens. The alternative would've added a hideous dimension to what I hoped would be a fairly straightforward catch and kill.

Four weeks in and we were firm friends. I knew where he lived (Tottenham in a houseshare with four other guys, all doing PhDs), what his favourite novel was (something by William Boyd, but I forget), and that he was a strict vegan. We started going to the dreary pub after work on Saturday, where we'd get pretty drunk and I'd make jokes about Roger until he'd tell me off. By now, I knew how I'd kill him. Much like with my grandparents, the plan was vague in form and had the potential to fail, but I was confident after my first foray, and Andrew was trusting to a fault. After the pub one Saturday, I mooted going back to the centre and bringing a bottle of wine with us. It was a balmy night, and the stars were out, a rarity in this smog-draped city. He was game, if a little nervous.

'Roger would go mad,' he laughed, 'but I guess there's no harm done.' Not much of a rule breaker, my cousin, despite his much-vaunted radical beliefs. I guess that's what fourteen years of private education does well. Parents don't cough up close to £250k in the hope that their child wilfully breaks the unspoken rules of British society.

Security at the marsh centre was . . . nothing. There was no security. No CCTV (what would you steal? Some minnows?), no barbed wire. Andrew just used his key and we were in. We went down to the main pond and sat on a small section of decking Roger had installed so that he could observe the frogs more easily. I cracked open the wine and sipped from the bottle. As we passed it between us, I broached the subject that had been turning over in my head.

'Can I try the frog drug, Andrew? You've talked about it so much, and it sounds like an adventure I'd kick myself to miss.' There was a silence, and then I heard him breathe in and then breathe out in quick succession.

'I don't think so, Lara. I'm no expert yet, and I'm still trying to perfect the dosage. Last week I took too much and passed out cold for fifteen minutes. It's so imprecise – I don't want to use you as a guinea pig.'

I nodded, and made reassuring noises. 'I totally understand. I don't want to put pressure on you in any way. I just thought maybe it might help with my panic attacks in some small way . . .' I trailed off, hoping to capitalise on his English built-in awkwardness. He sighed again.

'I didn't know you get panic attacks. I do too, ever since I was a little kid. I used to tell my mother I couldn't breathe. But I couldn't explain it properly. They came back with a vengeance recently.' He looked at me with understanding and rubbed my thumb clumsily.

'What happened?' I asked, looking at him with a suitable amount of concern. Men like to be stared at intensely, I've found. It shows them you're really absorbed in what they're saying.

'My grandparents were in an accident . . .' He looked down and dropped my hand. I didn't push it, instead taking the wine again and dipping my fingers into the pond.

'Hey, how deep is this water? Roger always acts as though the Loch Ness Monster could be hiding in here.'

He laughed, and pushed his hair away from his face, making the hideous shell earring tinkle. The tension dissipated. 'This place is his life. He just likes to imagine that everything here is bigger and bolder than it perhaps is. The ponds are all pretty shallow, though this one I've waded through and been caught out by how deep it is in the middle – probably up to your waist. And you don't want to let Roger catch you – consider the frogs, Lara,' he said in a faux outraged tone. We finished the bottle and I said I'd better call a cab. Andrew helped me up – I was drunker than I'd thought – and we stumbled back to the front gate, giggling and shushing each other. I offered to drop him home, but he said he wanted the air and I poured myself into a Toyota Prius, driven by a man listening to a strange medley of acoustic show tunes. A few minutes before we pulled up outside my flat, I heard my phone beep in my pocket. Clumsily, I unlocked the screen and peered down.

OK, let's do it. Next Saturday, after work. You bring the wine – I think rosé would go nicely. But it's TOP SECRET. Nobody knows that I do this.

Despite the terrible interpretation of 'All that Jazz' being played as we arrived at our destination, I managed a smile. Gotcha.

* * *

The following week is hard. I find it difficult to sleep, to work, to do much of anything except think about what is going to happen come Saturday. I remember a moment, aged 17, when Jimmy and I had been invited to a kid at school's birthday party at a nightclub in Finsbury Park. Oh, the glamour! We'd spent weeks organising fake IDs, and consulting each other on what we'd be wearing. We'd come up with an eloquent lie to tell Sophie, and practised the details so that we wouldn't get caught out in the run-up like so many idiotic teenagers do. This was all on me by the way, Jim would've been sprung in an instant. Terrible lying face. By the Monday before, we were so hopped up with anticipation that I couldn't sleep. My stomach would flip and adrenaline would seep into my limbs, and I'd toss and turn worrying about whether or not our plan would work – if we'd get to the club and have the night we'd envisaged. It was miserable. We made it, and everything went like clockwork in the end, but the party was a huge letdown and we got stuck waiting for the bus at 1 a.m. in an icy downpour, Jimmy trying not to be sick, me trying not to go near him in case he was. All that worry and anticipation for not very much. This feeling is similar, except the stakes are much higher and I refuse to take night buses anymore.

Prep for Saturday is less about what dress to wear, and more about making sure the wine I buy is in a screw-top bottle and that I have some discreet gloves. Both of which I procure by Monday. Then I endure five days of jittery feet, racing thoughts and an image of a smiling Andrew inserting itself into my brain at inopportune moments. Honestly, I don't remember Patrick Bateman ever having fleeting moments of guilt or a gnawing feeling of moral transgression. It's much harder to carry out this plan with a truly blithe spirit than I thought it would be.

Nevertheless, Saturday comes, and instead of taking the train to the centre as I normally do, I walk the entire way, hoping to calm my nerves with the rhythm of my feet. It works fairly well actually, and I arrive with a smile, able to start work on painting the accessible toilet door as Roger had directed. Andrew arrives late, and for a stressful thirty minutes, I worry that he isn't going to show. But then there he is, hair tied up with a strip of old T-shirt, and wearing a pair of patchwork shorts which look suspiciously like they're made of old flannels. His father would have an account at a tailor on Jermyn Street, I think, wincing. What a tragic waste. I wave at him, but don't stop painting. No need to be too eager, especially if he's feeling uneasy about later. As the day wears on, it gets hotter. Roger,

Lucy, and the old lady who is escaping her decrepit vegetable of a husband sit in the equally decrepit deckchairs just outside the welcome centre and write names of plants on sticks to put in the earth, as if we were at a National Trust property. Thank God for the sun. Rain would surely keep us indoors, and the plan I have in mind would crumble.

I don't think I've ever worked as hard as I did today. Two coats of weatherproof paint and a good scrub down of the internal walls to boot. Nothing like the promise of a murder to boost one's productivity, it turns out. At 5 p.m., Roger brews tea, and we all down tools and drink it on the deck. It feels nice actually. Like I'm part of something. Something mundane and totally pointless, but that's not nothing when you've never really experienced it. There have been a few moments like that on my journey – times when I've wondered if God is telling me to get off this road and embrace a different life. But then I remember that I don't believe in God and that if he does exist, then he gave me this life to begin with. What would he know?

We head off to the pub at 6 p.m., Roger and Lucy tagging along. Lucy has really come out of herself in the time we've been at the centre. Gone is the slightly nervy rabbit vibe. Today she wears a bandana and dungarees, her face brown from the outdoor work. Is Roger a father figure to her? I can't quite work it out. Given the alternative, I fervently hope so.

The pub is fairly quiet, just a few tables of misfits, and one young man sipping a pint alone with a book, looking faintly out of place. This is not really the kind of establishment you come to to read and ponder. Andrew and I down a bottle of rancid white, while Lucy and Roger sip shandies. Talk is stilted. It's not a natural group at the best of times, especially not now we're counting down the clock like lovers desperate to get home and to bed. Eager to push on, I order another bottle and make a show of saying that I need Dutch courage for a date I have later on. Roger is tickled by this, telling me to 'make the chap pay' and offering advice on conversation starters. One of which, and I kid you not, is to ask which board game was the best.

'My favourite is . . . and it's controversial . . . Monopoly!' Nobody asks why it's controversial, and his look of disappointment is a reward in itself.

Andrew starts tapping his feet and I begin to worry he'll back out if we linger here for too long. So I decide to be bold. Draining my glass, I stand up and smile brightly.

'Well wish me luck. I've got to be in Angel at 8.30, let's hope he's worth it.' I sling my bag over my shoulder and clap Andrew on the back with gusto. Roger lifts his glass to me and Lucy waves half-heartedly. I walk out of the pub and turn off the main road and back towards the centre. I decide not to text him, allowing him the chance to take the reins himself. Instead, I sit on the kerb, drinking from a flask of wine I've brought with me.

I don't tend to drink out of a vessel which so obviously screams 'cry for help', but I have to carry my own wine separately. The stuff I've chosen for Andrew is now heavily fortified with vodka and I need a clear head. Now you see why I need the screw-top bottle, no tampering with trusty corks. One third of the bottle went into my flask, and I topped up the rest with the finest spirit I could find. Not that he'll have a hangover tomorrow, but it just feels more respectful not to give him the complete paint stripper variety. Last meal and all that. Although apparently America doesn't give last meals anymore. One guy ordered hundreds of pounds' worth of food and then refused to eat any of it. The guards were so furious at this display of independence that nobody gets that final treat now. His fellow prisoners will curse his name, but I admire that man's determination to piss off everyone to the last.

After what I estimate to be half a glass, I see a figure lurching down the road towards me. Some men walk with such an air of dishevelment that they look like they've been drawn by a toddler. Andrew is such a man. If there is any doubt, the silhouette of the hair tells me it's him. The slight swaying suggests he finished that second bottle of wine. I stand up and laugh, waving at him with my free hand.

'Fuck you for leaving me there,' he says, punching me lightly on the shoulder. 'Roger kept on about council recycling schedules and Lucy does nothing to stop him. She seems to almost find it charming?'

He drops his rucksack and fumbles for his keys. Once we're in, he dumps his bag on the main desk and I go to the kitchen to find some cups. Can't let him see we will be drinking different things after all. By the time I find them, he's gone outside and started setting up. With a flicker of amusement, I note that he seems to be wearing vinyl gloves. We're both taking precautions tonight then.

'I'm going to give you the liquid from a dropper, OK? Didn't think you'd actually want to lick a frog.' He laughs, but I can see he's still anxious.

'Don't worry about that now – line it up and then let's have another drink. We can take it later,' I say with a smile, handing him a mug with 'Frogtastic!' embossed on the side. He takes it gratefully and swigs. I tense up, wondering if he'll notice the unusual strength, but he just takes another gulp and sits it down on the deck beside him.

As he decants the frog paste, we talk about his fieldwork and the places he wants to go after Australia. Figuring I have nothing to lose, I ask if his parents are supportive of his ambitions.

'We don't speak,' he says bluntly. 'Haven't done for a few years now. It's for the best. My family is toxic.' Ain't that the truth, I think and rub his arm.

'What happened?'

'Oh, nothing. Everything. I was just born to the wrong people. I used to joke that I'd been swapped at birth and that my parents' real son was driving down some beach in a Bentley. They're not bad people . . . well, Mum's not. She's lovely actually. But the expectations they had for me all centred around money and my uncle's business and it was just terrible and vicious. I kept in touch for a while after I'd told them I wouldn't be working for the family, but it got too hard. They'd push it, telling me I was making a stupid decision and that I was behaving like a spoilt child.' He swigs more wine. Everyone should drink wine from a mug. Really makes you overdo it.

Andrew opens up to me as he relaxes. As I top up his vodka-infused wine, he explains how his father was consumed by jealousy of his older brother, how his mother was emotionally neglected and his sister had died at nine months old, making him always feel as though he had to live for both of them. I play the silent yet supportive friend, while inwardly thanking the universe that I only have to deal with the one cousin. By now, I've switched to drinking water, but Andrew is so drunk he'd never notice. He's too far into confessional mode, thinking that he can trust me with his deepest and most complex thoughts. Therapists earn every penny. I don't want to rush him, but the family talk isn't detailed enough to help me much and any pointed questions I ask are being met with slurred and vague replies. Time for the frog slime, before he is too drunk to function and I have to wait another week. I really can't face another pub evening with Roger.

Thankfully, the private school politeness that's been pummelled into him doesn't seem to fade with alcohol, and when I remind Andrew of the original plan, he's all hands on deck. The pre-prepared droppers are brought out, and Andrew explains that he will have to make a small burn on my skin in order to allow the serum to enter the body more easily.

'Where do you want to be marked?' he asks. 'Most people choose somewhere easily covered.' I settle on the foot, since I don't want to have to remember to cover up or explain away a mark on my body. I pull off my trainers and roll up my socks, putting them into my shoes. I scan the deck, making sure none of my things are lying around. I won't have a lot of time to linger after we finish. After he's finished. The rosé bottle is empty, and I place it near my bag, stuffing the mug into a side pocket to take back to the kitchen.

'You have to do it with me, Andrew,' I remind him. 'I'm too much of a wuss to go it alone. Do it at the same time. We'll jump together.' He waggles his finger in my face and smiles, pushing a lone dreadlock behind his ear.

'Don't worry, Lara, I'm used to it. I'll guide you through the journey.' Ugh. Journey. It's not a journey unless you're going from physical place A to physical place B. Which I guess he is, in a way.

He chooses to use a spot on his arm, underneath a tattoo of what looks suspiciously like a dream catcher. I guess be grateful it's not a Chinese symbol? Matches are produced, and he lights two, holding them against the sole of my left foot. The sensation is hot but not painful – clearly a sign that I'm in need of a proper pedicure. Then he applies the liquid.

'Lie down,' he instructs. 'Wait a few minutes and breathe.' I gaze up at the night sky, watching him burn his own skin out of the corner of one eye. I hear him exhale and he lies down next to me. 'If you need to be sick, just tell me and I'll roll you over. Good thing there's a lake.' Then he laughs for what seems like an age, before falling silent. We stay there in the dark, and wait. I don't know how long we're lying there like that. I feel warmth creeping over me, a sense of comfort seeping through my body, as though I'm being embraced by my surroundings, held by the wind.

'I feel it,' I whisper, and turn towards him. Andrew has his eyes closed and he's moaning softly. I decide I don't want to move. I don't want to stop the connection I feel to everything around me. The constant chatter in my head goes silent and only my heartbeat can be heard. I wonder if Andrew can hear it too. Slow and steady. Pulsing through my skin. I feel an animal brush past my fingers and look down. It's his hand, linking with mine. Solidarity. A kind of kinship. And it feels nice.

NO.

I roll over and use the power of our entwined hands to push him into the water. His body is limp from relaxation and I barely have to apply force, which is handy because I feel woozy as hell. As he moves through the air, his body uncurling, our eyes lock onto each other and he comes out of his reverie for a second. His face twists into surprise and his mouth opens wide as if he's about to cry out. But it isn't enough. The wine and the frog juice have done their work and he falls head first into the pond. I sit up on the deck and kick my foot into the water, pushing his head down as I hold onto the edge of the wood to apply pressure. I can see my toenails glint in the moonlight. Though his own feet kick for a brief moment, there's remarkably little splashing before he goes limp and the water becomes calm again. I don't know how long it takes but it feels like I'm watching it from a distance so I bend over and stare down at the body in the water, looking for any sign of life. It's probably not advisable to commit murder whilst under the influence of an untested amphibian drug. Sloppy really. But you work with what you have in this life.

When I'm sure he isn't going to burst out of the water, as is law in most horror movies, I lean into the pond and run my hand around his neck. I splash my face and then I stand up, put my shoes back on, pull a towel out of my bag and wipe down the deck, leaving the bottle and one vial of the serum. The rest of the detritus goes into a plastic bag. I grab his phone, which I'd seen him unlock with his code being his birthday (even hippies have iPhones), and delete our most recent messages. I'd been careful not to be specific about our plans over text, but he'd mentioned our meet-up and I don't want any questions. I survey the scene, as Andrew floats behind me, using the torch device on my phone and I'm satisfied it all looks good. It looks accidental. It looks tragic but not suspicious, the perfect balance.

I take my mug back to the kitchen, clumsily wash and dry it and put it back in the cupboard. Then I slip out of the centre, pull my hoodie over my head and walk purposefully towards the main road where an Uber is waiting for me. I stop for a second on the road and look round, with an eerie feeling that someone is behind me. But the drugs are making me sense things which might not be there, and I shake the feeling off. The car weaves through the quiet back streets before it hits the main roads full of Saturday-night revellers out in force, the figures spinning and blurring as we go. The whole way back, I breathe deeply out of the window to steady myself, and twist the beads on the necklace I'd removed from Andrew's neck as he lay in the water. Another keepsake, I suppose. It was an affectation really, something taken from movies about serial killers. But they were mainly lonely men doing it for sexual kicks and I am doing this with an end in mind. And not one that ends with my mugshot flashed across a Channel 5 show about sexy murderers.

I get out of the cab a good ten minutes away from my flat and dump the bag with the towels and gloves in a bin. I pause and hold my breath for a second, feeling like I can't get enough air in my lungs, before deciding that I'd allow myself the rest of the walk back to feel sad. For precisely nine minutes I let tears stream down my face, and endure the regret which floods my thoughts. As I turn the key in my door, I rub my eyes with my sleeve and shake my head. Enough. A glass of wine and two episodes of *Golden Girls* later, I feel as if the drug has subsided enough for me to be able to sleep. The regret I'd felt on my walk home passes through my system in a considerately hasty fashion, and my last thought before I sleep is not about my sweet cousin, now face down in a muddy pond. As I tuck the bottom of the duvet under my feet and prop a pillow under one thigh at a very specific angle in order to get comfy, my second to last thought is that I'd take myself out for a nice brunch the next day. I drop off deciding whether I'd follow that with a pedicure, just to get rid of any frog paste remnants. Self-care is the latest consumerist trend pushed at women wrapped up as empowerment. But that doesn't mean it's not nice. And after all, it's important to look after yourself after a hard week at work.

CHAPTER SIX

The worst thing about prison isn't the hours of waiting around in your cell, or the food, or the austerity cuts and privatisation which have led to incompetent fools in cheap uniforms put in charge of serious criminals. It's not the old, freezing buildings where rats are as prevalent as I assume they were in the Marshalsea. I honestly could stick all of these things out, with the hope that one day I'll be freed and never forced to sleep below a woman who dots her i's with hearts. The worst thing about prison is that, on occasion, a governor or a politician will decide that we captives need something to enrich our souls, to better ourselves, to stop being quite so rough and terrifying. From that sudden thought, a plan will emerge. This usually involves some lefty sap (you never get a Tory wanting to show us how ceramics can quash our rage problems) volunteering to run a class (which is always compulsory) where we're encouraged to paint our feelings or some such nonsense.

They invariably only come for one class, and then either they're too overwhelmed to come back, or they feel like they've done enough to virtue-signal about it for the rest of the year. If they're really enterprising, they write a piece for the *Guardian* about how prisoners just need respect and education, as though they've been working in jails for four years rather than for one hour in a quiet work period.

Today we all filed down to the classroom wing, where we suffered through an hour-long class on spoon making. Truly, even one murder wouldn't warrant such a punishment. The only highlight was getting my hands on a proper knife for the first time in a while. It's a pity they count them back in so carefully. Kelly is extremely jealous that I was part of the group forced into such nonsense, and gushes over the wooden spoon I produced. She would've loved today's class, she says, when I bump into her afterwards, and 'What a fab Christmas present that spoon would make for your mum.' I look at her blankly, wondering how long it'll take her to remember that my mother is dead, but there is no such realisation. So instead, I toss her the spoon, and tell her to pretend she made it and to give to her own mum. She's delighted, and I wonder, not for the first time, what kind of woman Kelly's mother is. To be thrilled with a wonky spoon made in a jail by your grown-up convict daughter, you must have some uniquely low expectations. Her mother can add it to the cross-stitched bird she got at Easter, and the dismal sugar bowl made out of something akin to playdough she was gifted on her birthday. The only difference with the spoon is that it has some special marks on it. They look a bit like hieroglyphics, but they're actually the initials of every person I murdered, though nobody would look that closely. Not a particularly sophisticated move, but I was finished whittling long before the other idiots in the class, and I didn't want to waste my time with the blade. I wonder if Kelly's mum will appreciate them?

Back in my cell, I take out the paper and pen from inside a pair of rolled-up socks. There is no privacy here, especially with a cellmate like mine. Everyone here tries to get hold of everyone else's possessions, tries to gain their secrets as leverage, wants to know their stories. Kelly doesn't even bother to hide her diary – that woman would tell you everything about her life if you were stupid or bored enough to ask. Once you ask Kelly a question, you'd likely never make the mistake of doing it again. Did I mention why she's in here? Not for violence or theft, like some of us. Kelly was a blackmailer. She had a nice line in getting married men to send her photos, photos which their wives might not like too much. She started small, on dating apps, and got bolder when she discovered Twitter and targeted men with higher profiles. She's attractive, is Kelly. Big pouty lips, which I suspect are the results of cheap filler but look all right from a distance, and lots of red hair. Sadly, her limited intelligence meant she was easy to find when a man finally plucked up the courage to stop sending her money and contacted the police. She'd had the money sent to her boyfriend's account, the stupid cow, and has wound up doing an eighteen-month stretch as a result. Not an elegant crime, I grant you, but I have no sympathy for her victims either. If you are delusional enough to believe that anyone wants to see a grainy iPhone picture of your flaccid little friend, you deserve to get bled for it.

My paper uncurled, I settle down to write for a bit before dinner. I didn't know whether I'd enjoy revisiting my past, but it turns out I'm quite happy to go over it all again. If anything, writing it down makes me feel proud. I remember the urgency of my youthful emotions, and the strong need to right a wrong. In the years since, I've not felt much of anything really, the task in hand demanded too much discipline.

To a casual observer, not much happened between the death of my mother and the moment I put my plan into action. A person who ran into me in that decade or so would've come away thinking that I was a fairly mediocre millennial. In some ways, I was. I lived on with Helene for a year or so, which was good, since she was away a lot and I had loads of time to myself. It was testament to her fundamental unsuitability at being a guardian that she thought it was OK to leave a recently bereaved teenager alone so often, but I never complained. I like being by myself, other people so often enrage or annoy with their inane small talk and fumbled attempts at meaningful connection. When I was 14, Helene told me that she'd been offered a job in Paris and felt like it was time to go home. She held my hand and insisted that she would stay if I wanted her to, but that Jimmy's parents had offered me a room and were delighted to have me. She looked genuinely distressed, and I felt it would be unseemly to jump at the chance and start packing up my stuff then and there, so I squeezed out a tear and looked at the floor while I told her that she must take the job. I would miss her, I said, but I couldn't live with the guilt if I stopped her from a new opportunity. In truth, Helene was a nice enough lady, and I cherished the link she gave me to my mother, but I was itching to get on with life and start working towards my plan, and Helene, with her limited connections and resources, would not be able to assist me in any meaningful way. Jimmy's parents, for all their discomfort with their own privilege, lived in a world where doors could open if you knew the right people. I felt confident that they could help me in some way. I had nothing to lose at least, knowing nobody of any importance and having no advantages of my own.

A month later and my bags were packed. The fish and I took a taxi over to Jimmy's house. Helene was in the midst of packing up her life for the move back to France and fairly frantic, so I took the opportunity to grab the box she'd hidden under the bed. I assumed she wouldn't miss it, but I wasn't too concerned if she did. The files were about me and my family, and I doubted she'd want to cause a scene – by the time she realised, she'd be across the Channel and immersed in a new life. Jimmy and Sophie welcomed me at the door, their dog Angus nearly knocking RIP out of my hands as he jumped up to lick my face.

'We've made you a welcome dinner, Grace. Vegetable lasagne, and Annabelle has made dessert.' Jimmy rolled his eyes at his mother.

'Can she at least see her room before she's made to sit down and eat that mess of a cake?' He grabbed my bags and leapt the stairs, two at a time, as I thanked Sophie and waved at Annabelle, busy in the kitchen with a piping bag. His little sister was a spindly and nervy 11-year-old. I hadn't seen her recently, but Jimmy had informed me that she was already in analysis. Sophie was very keen on juvenile therapy, unsurprisingly. I sincerely hoped she wasn't going to suggest it to me, and made a note to pretend that the school was already providing a counsellor if she did.

My bedroom was on the top floor, under the eaves and across from Annabelle. Jimmy was on the floor below (this was the first place I had lived with floors and the climb from the kitchen to the bedroom already seemed tiresome), which he explained was no accident. Annabelle and he had swapped rooms the week before after Sophie and John had panicked about Jimmy and me sleeping on the same floor. Although nothing was said explicitly, I could imagine them getting in a lather over a bottle of red wine one night, discussing things like consent and hormones and whether their home would be a comfortable environment for a vulnerable girl. They needn't have worried, though I thought Jimmy was a nice boy and valued his friendship immensely, I'd always thought he looked a bit like a potato from some angles (the root vegetable likeness mostly dissipated later in life, thankfully). And anyway, normal teenage distractions like sex and alcohol didn't appeal to me. I wasn't going to be one of those skunk smoking layabouts who dithered about university and went backpacking to delay having to deal with adult choices. I wanted to get on with it all.

After I'd dumped my bags and caught up with Jimmy, we went down to eat. John had just got home, and was pouring a glass of red wine with one hand and absent-mindedly pulling off his tie with the other. He turned to greet me, kissing me on the forehead and rubbing my shoulder before Sophie handed him a stack of plates for the table. The embrace left me feeling slightly odd. Jimmy's family were so affectionate with each other, his mum and dad were always hugging, or holding hands, and nobody seemed to find it invasive or annoying. There was always someone around in this house, something cooking, the constant noise of daily life. I didn't mind John's embrace, in fact it felt nice, warm, gentle. But it niggled, perhaps because I realised that I'd missed out on this stuff. That thought angered me. Normal – I wasn't used to normal, however much Marie had tried to give me some semblance of it. I wondered if this family set-up was something I'd learn to love, whether I too would hug and kiss without a thought, whether I'd forget the time I spent with my mother and lean into this new life. The idea had appeal, but I'd have to guard against going soft. The Latimers are lovely people, and I was glad to be living there, but if I embraced their way of life too enthusiastically I'd risk ending up reading the *Guardian*, working in the arts, and buying people organic British wine for Christmas. A lovely warm bath of a life, apart from the embedded guilt and the glaring hypocrisy that Sophie exhibits so well, but totally pointless.

Despite being fearful of letting myself relax too much, I settled into life with the Latimers quickly. Sophie spent a lot of time trying to make me comfortable.

'Sit anywhere you like, darling girl. Please eat whatever you fancy.'

The constant emphasis on making me feel like part of the family served to show me that I wasn't, but I understood that this was the only way Sophie knew how to Be A Good Person. I returned to my old school, and worked towards my GCSEs, eventually getting straight As and earning a commendation from the head teacher for my success 'in the face of particular hardship'. The head tilt of sympathy I got from her as she presented me with a sad piece of paper with my name written in badly done calligraphy was only mildly aggravating. I still threw the certificate in the bin on the way home from school.

Jimmy and I spent nearly all of our free time together. I got on with the other kids at school, but wasn't concerned with having a clique, spending my life joined at the hip with girls who enjoyed spending hours forensically examining what a boy's greeting meant *really*. Jimmy had always had a group of boys he'd hung about with since primary school – they played football in the local park and had game nights on weekends – but when I moved in, these mates were demoted to bit-part players. Sophie worried about this, I could tell. She would suggest a game of tennis, or offer to host a pizza night for 'all our friends', which really just meant Jimmy's friends. But he'd just roll his eyes and tell her maybe another time. I couldn't share her anxiety. Jimmy's friends were monosyllabic, unless they were taking the piss out of each other, and not one of them would make eye contact with me when spoken to, as though making eye contact with someone of the opposite sex would signify a serious commitment of some sort and they'd be forced to hand over their Xbox in the inevitable break-up. Besides, Jimmy and I got on – we didn't really need anyone else. We enjoyed talking for hours, lounging around in silence, and even doing our homework together. Jimmy never pushed me on my grief, but I knew he understood it when he looked at me. No head tilts necessary.

I got into a routine at the Latimers'. Sophie and John managed to treat me almost like a daughter, only sometimes triumphantly wheeling me out in front of friends, as though I were a refugee they'd heroically taken in. Although I suppose in a way, I was. This was the bargain, it emerged. I was cheerful, helpful, and made Jimmy happy, and the Latimers fed me, clothed me, showed me kindness and we both agreed to ignore any awkward questions we might have had about how long my membership of the family was good for. Despite my protests, they insisted on paying for me to see a therapist friend of theirs called Elsa, a dumpy woman who wore very large black-rimmed glasses and wooden beaded necklaces and who barely spoke at all. I repeatedly told her I was excited about the future and she signed me off after six weeks.

Within a year or two, I fully understood the wealth that the Latimers had. It was not the flashy loot of my father, it was unspoken but obvious in every way. Food came in huge deliveries from upmarket delis. Flowers were found on every table in the house, big bunches of artfully arranged stems you'd never see in the local supermarket. Sophie could spend hundreds of pounds on scatter cushions from the Iranian interiors shop in Crouch End and call them a bargain with absolutely no sarcasm. They talked about how important it was to live in 'real London', but they were insulated from anything remotely real. I didn't even know what they meant by real. I don't think they knew. The Artemis mansion was protected by enormous gates. The Latimers would have thought this awful, but they were no different really. I recognised how absurd their life was but it was hard not to enjoy it. Aged 15, I found myself using Sophie's expensive face creams and seriously considering three different shades of green Farrow & Ball paint for my walls. I had never known I might have expensive tastes before. I'd never had the chance to know. But I was fast finding out.

The summer before sixth form started, Jimmy and I were allowed to go on holiday alone for the first time. We went to Greece with his friend Alex and his girlfriend Lucy, who went to private school in West London and delighted in exclaiming in shock whenever I admitted to not having experienced something. It was a CRIME that I had never been to Greece before, how could I not have had a Macchiato in my WHOLE LIFE, oh honestly it was TOO FUNNY that I'd never been swimming in the sea. It was a huge relief when she came down with food poisoning on day two of the trip and didn't trouble us again until day six, just before we were due to return home. Well, I say food poisoning, but it was decidedly less random than that really. A few doses of Ipecac syrup given with breakfast (which I insisted on making for this very reason) did the trick. I don't think anyone would blame me, there's only so much time you can spend with someone who goes shooting on weekends and calls her mother 'Mummy' with a straight face. Alex seemed to perk up in her absence too, and the holiday was brilliant. Lucy was subdued on the flight home, and only gave a tiny shudder when I passed my hand over her leg to pick up my bag. Nobody else noticed. They broke up a few weeks later, which just felt best for everyone under the circumstances.

Back in London, I had chosen my A levels, settling on English, French, and Business Studies. Jimmy spent a lot of time going over university prospectuses with his parents, and discussing the merits of different Oxbridge colleges over dinner as Annabelle and I made a great performance of rolling our eyes and sighing loudly. I wasn't going to uni, much to the dismay of John and Sophie, who seemed not to understand that there was any other option. In their eyes, finishing education at 18 would fast-track you towards a job packing boxes in warehouses, pregnant, on drugs, or possibly worse – it might mean you had to move out of London and live miles away from an artisanal cheese shop. But I wasn't wasting three more years on rigid learning, getting into debt, and wasting time with other students, who I assumed would spend their free time talking earnestly about safe spaces and organising ineffective marches on rainy days. I had things to do.

CHAPTER SEVEN

Unsurprisingly, most prison activities are compulsory. Some of it is set up as though you might have a choice, 'There's a quiz night tonight in the TV room, we'll need you ladies to pair up!' but when you politely opt out, a guard will drop the forced smile and say, 'Six p.m., Grace, I expect to see you there with a partner.' And then Kelly will grab my hand and announce loudly that we'll be playing together and I will unsuccessfully try to disassociate from my body. Today there is a non-optional lecture on how to be a boss. All morning, Kelly has been singing 'Who run the world? GIRLS!' at the top of her lungs as though the seminar will be the first step towards managing a FTSE 500 company and not an exercise in platitudes designed to tick a box on a government target form somewhere. 'Empower these women,' some young wonk in a short-sleeved shirt has said, 'we need to encourage them to channel their specific skills into more mainstream work opportunities!' As if Kelly and all the other women on my wing will be shown how to make their blackmail, theft, fraud, and other assorted crimes work in a more respectable way. To be fair to some of these girls, in another life they would have made great bankers. But even for bankers, a line in murder might be frowned upon. I have a few hours before the ghastly talk so I shall get back to writing.

When I left school and refused to go to university, so upsetting John and Sophie, I got work in the Sassy Girl shop in Camden. An obvious plotline for our heroine I hear you say, but I was 18, had to start somewhere and I naively imagined that working for one of Simon's businesses would give me an advantage. I started in the stockroom, unboxing deliveries and affixing price tags, and graduated to the tills shortly after. The days were long and frantic. Stock flew off the shelves. The brand knew exactly how to appeal to teenagers back then, selling whatever had been on the hottest celebrity mere days ago. This process was a mystery to me – I remember imagining that the in-house designers must have had their finger so on the pulse that their clothes matched up with the latest couture completely. I later understood the reality: Artemis Holdings had grim-faced women in head office subtly altering said couture designs and running the amendments past the legal department. Once greenlit, the garments would be made up in any kind of synthetic fabric they had at the ready. The teenagers didn't give a shit. Glittery jean shorts as seen on their favourite singer for £15, who cares that they smell faintly of rubber?

I surprised myself by enjoying my time on the shop floor. I didn't have a minute to stop and think, I just worked really hard and did whatever was asked of me. Folding up stained and crumpled polyester after it had been discarded in the changing rooms put me off cheap clothes for life, but my diligence got the attention of my boss, a slightly scrawny woman who I thought was ancient but was probably under 30. She put me forward for the Artemis trainee manager scheme, a grand title which just meant I could be entrusted with handling the day's profits. Aged 19, I was a titled employee with a badge and a lanyard and the power to discipline new backroom staff.

Jimmy was off to uni, along with most of our year group. There were a few who made it to Oxbridge, but mainly they flocked to Sussex, where it was said that drugs and parties were most plentiful, and Manchester, which gave cosseted North London kids some delusional idea that they were really roughing it. Sophie, bless her, managed to spin Jimmy's rejection from Oxford as a sort of moral triumph.

'Well, Oxbridge is just too stuffy really, Sussex is *such* a vibrant campus and so progressive. The kids really learn so much more about the world than we did at St Hilda's. Lucky Jim!'

I stayed on at the Latimers' house for eight months, which was a thoroughly awkward experience for everyone except Annabelle, who I suspect liked having someone in the house who wasn't a Latimer. With Jimmy gone and Sophie realising that she was one child closer to an empty nest, her need to try to nurture grew more intolerable. Every day she would make Annabelle a flaxseed smoothie for breakfast ('Dear girl, there's nothing of her, she still doesn't need a bra!') and she became fixated on trying to get her daughter to meditate with her at every opportunity. For a therapist, she was remarkably obtuse about the root of her neurotic daughter's problems. But perhaps the children of other therapists would say that was pretty standard.

It was clear to all of us that the uneasy bargain we'd made when the family took me in was on its last legs. I'd come to their house too late in life to really be one of them, and Jimmy had been the glue which held us together. Without him, our interactions dwindled rapidly, and I took to spending more time out of the house or in my room. Earning my own money for the first time meant I felt less inclined to follow Sophie's unspoken rules to the letter. I eschewed home-cooked food for McDonald's and chopped all my hair off into a severe bob which even I will concede was a mistake. I don't have the jaw for it. If I didn't eat dinner with the family at night, Sophie would tell me that she was worried about me. She was never cross, an emotion that she would have found too base. She just expressed concern endlessly. About my hair, about my ambition, about my lack of friends. She was right about the lack of friends. Jimmy was the glue there too. I had never found it easy to forge relationships. Partly it seemed like a skill I didn't possess but mainly because I had decided early on that teenagers were terrible. I wanted to skip ahead to adulthood where I could be on my own as much as I required. I like to be on my own, and have never understood what weakness exists in people who crave the company of others all the time. Perhaps that was partly why Sophie and I never really connected. John was like me, he could hide away in his study or work late hours every night of the week. But she wanted everyone around her, that would show that she was a successful person with a family who saw her as the vital lynchpin.

So I moved out. They protested, which was understood by both sides to be the standard polite thing to do, and then John paid for me to hire a van and to buy a mattress. They also subsidised some of my rent, which I found uncomfortable at the beginning but grew to accept. After all, people like John and Sophie need to offset their guilt. Sponsoring a child you'll never meet in another country is base level. Fostering a (semi) orphan is big league. I'd played my part, so why not let them help long term? I found a one-bedroom flat in Hornsey, barely a fifteen-minute walk away from the attic room I'd shared with Marie, and I endured one final meal with the Latimers. Jimmy came back from uni for it, Sophie was insistent, and after a desultory moussaka (the woman could never cook something if she didn't find its provenance exotic in some way), he came back to my new flat with me and produced a bottle of wine smuggled out of the family home. We slept together that night, which was a strange but inevitable event. Sex was a form of intimacy we'd been growing more and more curious about as we got older, as we got closer. It was a way of binding us together even further – something nobody else could claim. Perhaps there was a control element for me too, opening up another part of me to him and only him in the knowledge that he would prize our relationship even more fiercely. It wasn't just a calculated act on my part. I have spent years now wavering between loving Jim like a brother and wanting him like a partner. Sometimes he's just a comfort blanket I take for granted. But he's also the only person I know who could break my heart. I find it all confusing really, always pushing him away and pulling him towards me. It's not surprising that I didn't let him stay over that night. I didn't want to find him there when I woke up in my new home. I wanted it to be mine and mine alone. But I still opened my eyes that morning expecting to see him lying next to me.

I worked and I ran and sometimes I would meet up with a schoolmate who'd come back home from uni for a few days. I cooked a lot, something I'd never really done before. I studied books about making your way in retail, some of the most boring words a person can ever have the misfortune of having to read. But they were helpful, if only because the bullshit jargon it used gave me a language that has helped me to this day. If you introduce a few choice phrases, you're understood to be competent. 'The PC will love this deal' tells a retail manager you understand what the price-conscious customer is and also makes you want to walk into a door.

I walked up to the Artemis house most weeks, for no other reason than to remind myself of my ultimate aim. That aim felt like it was getting closer when I was asked by head office to apply for a job on the marketing team. I'd been working at Sassy Girl for nearly a year, and I had no real business working in head office, but I had pestered my manager near constantly to let me know if anything came up away from the shop and she must have taken pity on me. She recommended me for my hard work and interest in learning about the brand, and commended me on my window displays, which must've swung it. Who knew that pairing a pleather parka with a day-glo bum bag would count as experience? It was a bottom of the ladder job, but it was a *rung* on the fucking ladder. And it would mean working in the same building as Simon. Five floors and a world of marble away but still, a connection that meant something to me back then.

I lasted precisely thirteen months. The work was simultaneously stultifying and embarrassing. I had no interest in 'getting the creative juices whizzing' at roundtable meetings where we discussed shopfront displays and hearing about 'merch to make the client wet themselves' made me feel like I was living in a bad simulation. I got three good things out of the experience. The first one was that I earned great money for a 20-year-old and I saved it obsessively. The second was that I got to visit Simon's house when he threw his annual party for head office staff. I would have given all I had to get a glimpse into that mansion on the hill and here he was, welcoming me in. A proverbial viper, slithering into the bosom of the family.

We got the invites at random. It was said that they invited people by drawing names out of a hat each year so that the system wouldn't favour anybody over anyone else. So it must have been a coincidence that the party was full of senior management and pretty young girls working at a much more junior level. Gary, the obese website designer who sat three desks down from me had never been one of the lucky ones. Then again, his appearance and his vague 'given up on life' aura wasn't one I'd want at a party either. The man ate instant soup with the same plastic spoon every day for a year. There were many other spoons available in the communal kitchen. Baffling.

The Artemis staff party was a fairly tepid two-hour garden event with canapés and warm sparkling wine passed round by bored-looking students. There was a candyfloss machine set up next to a mini maze, and a few people had made the mistake of accepting the floral hair crowns being woven by an earthy-looking woman who was completely out of place in this palace to greed. Turns out a slightly sweaty man in a grey suit jauntily wearing a flower crown is exactly what a loss of dignity looks like. Even with the dismal activities on offer, you could see that the event was a tick-box exercise – keep staff morale up by pretending to value them enough to allow them into your home. We weren't valued enough to be allowed access to indoor toilets though, and a stern-looking housekeeper stood on the staircase should anyone think of going upstairs for a nosy. But for me, it was completely fascinating. This house that my mother took me to, that I stood outside of, knowing in my bones that I wasn't ever going to be invited into. I was here. I was ushered in with a glass and a lukewarm smile. I spent a good twenty minutes just watching a maid discreetly follow people around and then sanitising anything they happened to touch. It was riveting.

Bryony clearly had more sense than to mingle with the employees and was nowhere to be seen. Simon stayed in one corner with the male members of the senior management, cigar smoke forming an orb around their heads. He did not interact with his wife once as far as I could tell. Occasionally a young female member of staff would be beckoned over and a roar of laughter could be heard across the lawn. One could only hazard a guess as to how many HR offences were being committed in the spirit of 'banter' by a bunch of men in tan loafers and open-necked shirts. I wandered around, drink in one hand, as though I was vaguely looking for someone, and headed through the French doors of the sitting room. Janine wafted around the doors seconds later, her hair blow-dried into a helmet, her gold jewellery clinking like body armour. I assume she was on high alert, the idea of anyone pilfering her lot-bought high-end knick-knacks too much for her nerves to bear.

I turned my head away and pretended to be looking at a gaudy painting of flamenco dancers and she strode past me, into the kitchen, followed by an anxious-looking woman in an apron and white gloves. Obviously she didn't see me; people like Janine don't have normal vision. They are blind to people they deem irrelevant. I don't begrudge it, it's a talent I admire. Why waste time on people who offer no value? The corridor was empty, so I continued walking, reaching a wide spiral staircase which would take you upstairs and to their more private space. I hovered, wondering what would happen if I was caught rummaging through the marital bedroom. Would I be thrown out and fired? Would they do a background check on me? Probably not worth the risk, as much as I was tempted.

Instead, I spontaneously tried the door to the right of the stairs and stepped into what was clearly a study. Bookshelves lined the walls, stuffed with leather-bound volumes bought for show. I doubted anyone in this family had read the complete works of Dickens, let alone a volume by Derrida. Oh God, alphabetised. On the mahogany desk sat a fountain pen, a stack of thick cream paper and a large silver heart ornament I recognised as classic Tiffany. There were two gilt frames, both showing the Artemis trio: one which showed Bryony at her christening; the other was more recent, and peering more closely, showed the family at a Buckingham Palace garden party. Janine's enormous hat couldn't completely obscure the building behind them. They must have milked this moment to the max, as though it was a private meet up of mates and not a thousand-person gathering for people the Royal family would find appalling were they able to speak frankly and shrug off their duties. I picked up the photograph, and dropped it on the floor. Thick cream carpet cushioned the fall, of course. So I trod on it with my heel until I heard a quiet crack, and then put it back on the desk. The broken glass had come loose, and I used a shard to lightly scratch across Simon's face. Then I cautiously crept back into the hallway.

I didn't want to rush back outside, so I lingered in the main living room, nursing my glass. Janine came back out of the kitchen and I felt ready to make eye contact. Her face had such a sour expression – permanent rich-lady dissatisfaction etched into her skin. But she clearly felt obliged to come over, or perhaps she just wanted to make sure I wasn't trying to steal the silver. As she approached me, I had a moment of panic. Sophie often commented on how my face never betrays any emotion. She seems almost offended that I don't want to give away all my deepest thoughts with a look. But in that split second, I imagined that Janine could see my intentions plastered all over my face. I started talking about her home, using adjectives to describe her style, in a way which didn't actually convey that I liked it. We had a brief chat about her mantelpiece, the only thing I could think of to focus on. Her posture relaxed a little as I asked questions about the wide array of different marbles in use in the living room, but her smile remained tight. That might have been because of the extensive work she'd had done, freezing her face to a point which made spontaneous expression difficult, but it was hard to say. She talked about how hard it was to style a house of this size, and told me that her most beloved ornaments were kept at her home in Monaco, as though I would understand the trials of losing track of where my best gilt candlesticks were.

'Have you always lived here?' I asked, as I trailed my hand across the mantelpiece, deliberately leaving a vaguely smudged handprint. Her hand twitched in reaction, and I could tell that it was taking every shred of willpower and breeding not to smack my arm away.

'Yes, we moved in shortly before Bryony was born, since we knew we'd need a bigger place for children.' It was strange to hear her talking about children plural. Since I assumed she didn't mean for his illegitimate offspring, of which there could be many, it suggested they expected to have more kids. I weighed up asking about that against the prospect of getting escorted out of the house by one of the many burly security guards dotted around, and decided to hold my tongue.

'Well it was so nice to meet you. I'm sure Simon's kids are lucky to have a father so able to provide for them,' I said, as I walked past her and back into the garden. I heard her calling for the housekeeper before I even got to the French doors.

I left that party feeling like I was finally getting somewhere. I had been in their midst. It wasn't just a distant dream anymore. Until now, my interactions with Simon had been precisely zero, unless you counted my pathetic trips past his gates once in a while and the one time I saw him in the lobby of the office. And even I, keen as I was to press on, couldn't really call them encounters.

The third benefit of working at Artemis Holdings was meeting my beloved informant Tina. Beloved isn't exactly the right word, since I'd never have given her a second of my time if she'd had nothing to offer me but friendship, but I prized her for her information and that was more valuable to me than any mate. Tina was the PA to the deputy CEO, Graham Linton, a close friend and henchman to Simon. A man who wore grey suits with a slight sheen, like the type you see in those shops which always say they're having a closing down sale. I got chatting to her accidentally on a fag break one day, several months into my job at head office. The office manager was very strict about people smoking anywhere near the front door of the office. There was a smoking terrace for the top brass on the fourth floor, cigar smoke would waft through the offices for hours when Graham, Simon or his brother Lee decided to indulge, but everyone else had to go around the back to the goods entrance. One day Tina mentioned that she liked my scarf and I gave her a half-hearted smile, which was more than enough for her to come and sit next to me. She was the friendliest woman I'd ever met, and that alone was sufficient reason for me to quit smoking and avoid the area. I would have done too, had she not mentioned who she worked for just as I was hastily stubbing out my cigarette. It's horrible having to do a U-turn when you realise that you can get something out of someone, isn't it? Suddenly having to flatter and praise a potential donor who's been leering at you all night, or laughing at the jokes of a guy who will pay for every round of drinks? You feel slightly dirty. But really, everything in life is a trade. And I thought Tina might tell me things about the family I wouldn't be able to find out by myself, so I sucked it up and played nice. Super nice. Getting her coffee, messaging her little cheery hellos on our office chat system, having lunch with her and pretending that she was losing weight when she asked. It was a good trade though. Tina was a loyal employee when it came to Graham (who was often called a creep by women in the office and not just because he wore an extremely unconvincing toupee), but she'd sing like a canary when it came to the Artemis family. Nothing she ever told me was itself the silver bullet in my arsenal, but knowing more about these people who I'd watched from afar for so long was endlessly fascinating. And because almost nothing she told me ever painted them in any light other than *fucking terrible*, it was a reminder that I hadn't built them up in my head as monsters with nothing to back it up. Yes, Tina was a gift, even if I had to fuck up my lungs even more to spend time with her.

But working at Artemis Holdings wasn't actually getting me any closer to my father, despite my naive expectations. I had somehow envisaged working my way up to be his closest aide within a few years, gaining his trust, worming my way into his life before doing a dramatic reveal and killing him as he gasped at the betrayal. But the man employed thousands of people and he was no more going to invite me into his inner sanctum than he was going to read a book which wasn't about crushing it in business. So, when I was headhunted by another fashion PR and marketing company, I left. My resolve was as strong as ever, but I would be earning nearly double my old salary and, more importantly – I had come to realise that murdering an entire family while working for their firm might not be the smartest of moves. I allow the initial misstep because I was young.

This was when the fog that I had always felt swirled around me started to lift and my life became clearer. I got to a place where I felt safe and in control, and I was able to look to the future with more focus. In some ways, it meant slowing down and becoming familiar with the art of patience. I've worked at the same company ever since. I have stayed in the same flat, which I still rent from the ancient Turkish man who lives above me and has not raised the rent since I first moved in, much to the chagrin of his son. I have saved money, kept a low profile and lived life on a small scale, all the while waiting for the moment when I would kick-start my plan and begin a new chapter. It's not a time about which great tales will be written, but so many people live like that every day and don't seek a next chapter at all. They are content with their small and banal lives, their basic requirements met and 'ooh a nice bottle of prosecco' as a treat once in a while. So I don't find it especially odd or disappointing that I spent those years living dull. The best years of your life are said to be those which whizz by in your early twenties when you can drink and party and live spontaneously. Mine were not like that. Instead, those years were followed by a thrilling hurtle through time as I carried out my plan, and now I anticipate many years to come which will be as large and as exciting as I wish them to be.

I don't mean to imply that I lived like a puritan. There were little luxuries now and then. I do seem to appreciate the slightly nicer things in life, a predilection which I imagine I inherited from both my mother and father in some ways, and unleashed by living at the Latimers with their penchant for organic wines and exorbitant interiors. It's why my small flat has one wall dedicated to shoes, the most basic starter drug when women look to treat themselves. As I got a little older, I took wonderful solo holidays to places I could barely have imagined when I was growing up with Marie. And every time I sat and drank a glass of wine on a terrace somewhere, I squashed the thought that perhaps my life had turned out better than it might have had Marie lived. Sure, I suffered a huge trauma in the loss of my mother and the Latimers were never my family, but gaining instant entry to the affluent upper middle class and harbouring a vicious and long-standing grudge had worked out somewhat well for me. I pushed the thought away most of the time.

The alarm has gone off again. It's probably just the weird girl three cells down who won't stop screaming but I have to go line up. More later.

CHAPTER EIGHT

I felt bouncy as I walked to work that sunny Friday morning. A dull week of slogan brainstorming had slowed time down to a crawl, and I'd been taking late-night runs around the city just to burn off some of the boredom. But that weekend I'd cleared my schedule, I'd made sure I had good wine and nice candles in the flat. I'd booked a massage for Saturday with my favourite masochist masquerading as a masseur and I was going to a sex party in the evening. Spare me any shock. Don't be horrified, or worse, excited. This isn't a random swerve into my particular proclivities. I went for research.

It had been nine months since I'd watched Andrew Artemis float away to be with his beloved frogs and I'd been keeping my head down, working hard and resisting all urges to jump back into my plan. I knew before I started that the pacing had to be strict, despite the constant yearning I had to get rid of them all in a week and take the consequences. The initial, and let's face it, more irrelevant murders had to be well spaced out so as not to cause suspicion early on. 'Tragic accidents' was what I wanted people to say. This could then grow to 'an unlucky run for the family', before ramping up to 'curse on the Artemis clan'. At a push, the last murder might make a few people mutter about foul play, but by then the whole family would be dead and buried and too many others would stand to benefit. I felt confident that nobody would be rushing to avenge them.

So I'd let the dust settle after Andrew. And I'd felt little joy when I looked back on it, unlike the euphoria I'd had when Kathleen and Jeremy rolled off that cliff, so I'd been happy to step back for a bit. I knew Andrew's funeral had been well attended, by earnest people in cagoules and red-faced private school chums alike. I had read that his mother Lara had been utterly devastated by her only son's death, making no public comment but pulling back from her work as Artemis Holdings Vice President and establishing a charity for wildlife preservation in Andrew's name. I wondered whether the incident had caused her to break from the family as well as the brand. The society pages still constantly featured Lee, but Lara seemed to have retreated from London entirely, staying mostly at their farmhouse in Oxfordshire. I've seen the property on Rightmove. The main house is entirely painted in shades of muted grey, and there are a wide variety of tasteful Persian rugs throughout, but then there's also a driving range in the grounds and it has the biggest hot tub I've ever seen overlooking the herb garden. It's not hard to see who chose what there. If it helps you guess, Lee wears cowboy boots and calls them 'his signature'.

From what I had read, Lara seemed totally unsuited to Artemis life. Perhaps that's why I initially assumed Lee couldn't be as nightmarish as he came across, despite all the signs pointing to him being exactly that. She was smart, a first from Cambridge and an MBA from an Ivy League college. He was a chancer, steeped in privilege and greed. The Artemis family might be canny, but I was confident that Lara was rarely stimulated by intelligent conversation at the family dinner table. According to Tina, who continued to gossip her head off to me long after I'd left the office, there was still much bafflement about Lara's choice of partner. 'He was handsome, everyone thought so. Don't roll your eyes! That's not nothing when you're young. And he was good at adapting his behaviour to mirror those he was around. He'd get these big inspired eyes when she talked, and tell everyone how clever she was. She was shy, but you could tell she was flattered by the attention. This lovely looking young girl, awkward as hell but just so smart. She wasn't prepared for a man like Lee and by the time she understood who he was, it was too late. Of course, his parents didn't like that she was mixed race. They didn't say it explicitly, but it was obvious. And he shut them down completely. He did love her, I think. In his own way.' It was a weak explanation and it didn't seem enough for Lara. Aged 18 you might get fooled by a man like that, but you learn. You learn fast or you end up trapped.

By the time I met Lara's husband, Tina's rationale seemed even more flimsy. Lee was Simon's younger brother by three years. If old copies of *Hello!* were anything to go by (and I had bought six years' worth of them on eBay to search for mentions of the Artemis name, which also gave me a good education in the various scandals of minor European royals), then Simon might have been the ultimate playboy back in his Nineties heyday, but Lee was his enthusiastic shadow. He was similarly good looking for the time (in a way that conveyed heartless sociopath – why was that considered attractive back then?), with a permanently bronzed face, and jet-black hair, slicked down. It sort of worked for him, when he was slim and unlined. Photos show him surrounded by women, often with a magnum of champagne in hand. But twenty years later and the same aesthetic was somewhat marred by the tiny white circles around his eyes showing you that the tan was now from a sunbed shop in the suburbs, and the slightly smudgy ring around his collars which appeared when he got sweaty, revealing that he probably didn't tip his colourist enough.

Lee was never a complete black sheep. No serious addiction problems, though he definitely dabbled. No bankruptcies, though he'd been listed as CEO of no less than twenty-seven different companies at Companies House, all of which were closed within months. One venture, GoGoGirl Pictures, was shut down in sixty-three days. The name didn't exactly suggest he'd hoped to make Art House movies. Perhaps his pearl-clutching mother got wind and put her foot down on that one.

Kathleen and Jeremy had Simon to hold up the family name. He was a success story, the guy who bought his way into royal dinners and pressed the flesh with the Mayor, the Prime Minister, and anyone else who was easily swayed by his money, which was most people. Even decent people go mad when faced with the uber-wealthy. They might have strong views on the wealth imbalance, and think that the rich unfairly run a system in which they accrue even more to the detriment of all others in society, but give them a glass of champagne and ask them to pose with a millionaire who might give them a job or write their organisation a cheque and they simper like the best of them.

Before the various scandals surrounding the Artemis company, there was even talk of giving Simon an OBE, which was insane since the most he ever did for anyone else was show up at a few annual charity dinners and bid on stupid prizes offered up by other rich people. He once hit the headlines for buying a painting of a horse by a controversial but popular artist who sold his crap for millions. It couldn't just be a nice lifelike painting though, nothing as simple as a George Stubbs picture which took practice and skill. The horse would have the face of the buyer. It went for 300 grand. And now somewhere in the Artemis mansion proudly hangs a giant centaur. That was one part of the inheritance I would politely decline.

Anyway, the OBE idea was quietly shelved but Simon remained respectable – held up as an icon of British business. And as a result, Lee got to play the stereotype of the slightly hopeless younger brother with no real ramifications. He was rescued when he fucked up (once sneaking up to the viewing platform at St Paul's Cathedral after a football match while drunk and making a video of his mates chanting as they mooned over the side of the rails. Someone made a call, and after a fulsome apology to the Church of England, the matter was considered closed) and given jobs by the family which he didn't need to do much for when his own career ideas went off the rails. In fact, I imagine he was very much encouraged not to take his role in the company too seriously, for fear he might fuck things up.

Aged 29, he met Lara through her work at Artemis Holdings, and married her eight months later with a three-day wedding extravaganza on a Greek island. One of the Bee Gees played, and one tabloid sent a reporter out who infiltrated the party dressed as a waiter. The write-up gleefully commented on the yobbish behaviour of various glitterati guests, including one model who got so drunk that she fell into the pool in a pearl-encrusted couture dress that she'd borrowed for the event. As per Tina, who wasn't there but who always did her homework, Lara had somewhat cold feet before the wedding, but had been assured that the big affair was just a one-off for family and friends before they settled down. He promised that the party days were over, talking about creating a future where she could be the boss in the family. How little men promise. How much we grasp at it.

His family had bought them a large stuccoed house in Chelsea, just off the Kings Road, and they had Andrew fairly soon after moving in. Lara worked her way up the ladder and seemed to spend the rest of her time either organising charity lunches for worthy groups or lobbying the government on behalf of vulnerable children. The family must have tolerated Lara's charitable nature, recognising that it lent them an air of respectability, but I imagine that her husband drew the line at ever having these do-gooders step foot in his house. In his own life, Lee clung onto the excesses of his twenties, pictured out at nightclubs in social diaries, cruising the Kings Road in his latest supercar, occasionally being named as a partner in new bars and restaurants which popped up only to shut down six months later when the real owner realised that slim margins and long hours weren't as glamorous as the opening night may have suggested.

I suspected that Lee liked more than a couple of drinks and a flirt when he went out. His face, once firm and sharp, was now puffy, and his eyes always looked slightly glazed in paparazzi photos.

More often than not, he was driven around town in a lurid green Bentley when he went out at night, an early drink-driving charge (tossed out after a good lawyer argued that his cold medication had interfered with another, more private medication – the papers had a lot of fun with that delicate phrasing) had meant that a permanent chauffeur was a prudent investment. This meant it was easy to figure out where he was if you happened to be in town of an evening, the car would double-park on even the narrowest of London streets, starting off at the most upmarket bars that Mayfair could offer, then heading for the private members clubs, and by 3 a.m., when most of the revellers were starting to disperse, weaving down towards Chinatown, towards the slightly seedier venues which weren't keen on fully advertising what they did exactly.

I knew this because I'd followed the Bentley on several nights around town. It was the easiest way to do research on Lee. He wasn't on social media, apart from a scarcely used Facebook account which seemed to peter out sometime in 2010 but which gave me some early amusement with his penchant for doing quizzes about which animal he'd be and what superhero power he'd most likely have (meerkat, laser eyes). He rarely left the townhouse until about 3 p.m. for a workout, and then he'd invariably grab a coffee in Knightsbridge where he met other men in Gucci loafers for a catch-up at a café which served drinks in gold-plated cups. They would all keep their phones on the table, as if they were running the country and might have to leave any minute. I'd sat next to their table once or twice, and listened to them talk about the stocks they should invest in, the next Vegas trip they could take, all while they occasionally threw in some casual misogyny just to keep the conversation light. Men of state they were not.

But night-time was the best time to find my wayward uncle. The more I saw of his twilight world, the more I wondered if he ever made Andrew accompany him on one of these jaunts. It would explain a lot about why my cousin fled for the frogs. After a few nights following the car but never actually going into the establishments that Lee frequented, I took the plunge. I never attempted to get into the VIP sections of the clubs he visited, it seemed too degrading to tart myself up and try to beguile a bouncer. But the bars were easier, and the Chinatown dives a breeze. I could end up nursing a drink right next to his posse, watching, listening.

The main object was just to be seen, as far as I could tell. Champagne was bought by the bottle, air kisses were showered on young women, men grabbed each other in wrist-wrapping handshakes, jewelled watches throwing patterns on the ceiling. Thirty minutes later, with new people picked up and others discarded, Lee and his crew would head out and on to the next venue. By about 12 a.m., trips to the bathroom would become more frequent, and Lee would start to get lively, insisting loudly that people 'party', and trapping his burly mates in headlocks. By the time it hit 3 a.m., I was deathly bored and drinking water. None of them noticed me, I wasn't a girl that would turn their heads. Not young enough. Not displaying the goods. I would always wear a black trouser suit and a T-shirt, some red lipstick for effort and a pair of heels. The heels were my only concession. If you tried to wear sensible flats to bars like the ones Lee frequented, they'd assume you were some kind of undercover police officer and view you with suspicion.

I spoke to Uncle Lee on my third scouting mission. I hadn't planned to – nothing rested on getting to know him better – but I figured it would be more fun than watching him down shots and try to dance badly enough that one young model type actually winced and shrugged his arm off her shoulder.

Lee and his posse had gone to a private members club off Berkeley Square in Mayfair, and I headed to the bar opposite, knowing not to try and blag my way into an establishment with red ropes around the door and an old man in a top hat standing guard. I sat at the window nursing a glass of rosé, waiting for the moment the Bentley was brought round, which would signal the next move. The club must have been quiet that night, because the car pulled up outside at 1 a.m. I hurried out of the bar and flagged down a cab, telling the driver to follow my friends who were travelling ahead. The explanation sounded weak, and I cringed internally, but he didn't bat an eyelid. As expected, we went straight for Chinatown, pulling up outside a venue I'd not seen before. In fairness, it wasn't obviously a bar. It wasn't obviously anything. It was a tiny door with no sign or menu, squished between two dim sum restaurants, a place you'd walk past a million times and never notice. I watched Lee and two burly mates buzz on an intercom and push the old door open. Just before the door slammed shut, I got my foot over the threshold and slid behind it. I let their footsteps recede before I followed them, not wanting to bump straight into them on the narrow stairs. The place was dingy, with dark red wallpaper and faded carpet. Everything about it screamed brothel to me, except for the loud house music I could hear coming from above. That gave me the confidence to at least try to gain access. Silence and I would've left immediately.

I waited a couple of minutes on the stairwell and then made my way up. The door that met me was a big black fire door, and I pushed it open tentatively. Behind it was a small room, presumably the old reception area for an office, with black lace blinds over the window. Two attractive women of about my age sat on raised stools behind a table upon which were champagne glasses and a bowl of condoms. The women were smiling at me.

'Hi there,' said the one with a blunt bob and eyeliner winged up to her brows. 'Welcome to the Pleasure Parade. Do you have your invitation?'

I have always been able to think fast, without stammering or avoiding eye contact. The trick is to smile and not over explain. This was clearly a sex party. I'd never been to one, but I've read enough articles in women's magazines about the rise of private parties where beautiful people meet up and shag to recognise what was happening here. *Vogue* had endorsed these gatherings. Why be bashful?

'I'm so sorry,' I said, putting my hand on the table, 'I've been out in Soho and remembered that this was happening tonight, but stupidly forgot to bring it. I hope it doesn't matter – Flick said it would be OK.'

The other woman, wearing a headband made of green silk and large gold hoop earrings, looked me up and down and flashed a glance at bob girl.

'Well, as you know, these events rely on exclusivity and . . . discretion,' she put a finger to her lips. 'But if Flick vouched for you then it should be fine. Can you just sign the form here and put your phone in this box?'

I thanked God for the magic word. Flick, the posh white-girl name guaranteed to open doors in certain situations. There's always a Flick – she might be a party PR girl, or a gallerist or just a friend of a friend. Mention her and you've signalled that you're OK, on the inside, that you probably know Floss and India too.

I signed the form, which basically told me that I am not to talk of the Pleasure Parade to others, nor mention the names of any high-profile guests. I am not to take photos or record anything. I must pledge to keep things 'safe and fun' at all times, and respect the boundaries of others.

I handed over my phone and headband girl gave me a condom with a wink. 'Remember that the blue room is for kink play. And if anyone gives you hassle, Marco is in the bar.'

'Oh sure, I'm all set,' I said, as I handed her my coat and went through the door behind their perch with more confidence than I felt.

I like sex. I'm not squeamish or repressed about it. It's a fun stress-busting activity, even when it's done poorly, which is a lot of the time when you're shagging men raised on porn who think that women need minimal foreplay and desire a lot of flexible positioning. Orgasms are a wonderful thing, especially when received alone and followed by silence and not the desperate need to get a strange man out of your house immediately. But I'm not enamoured of the rampant sex positivity we get bombarded with. Women who want to tell you all about their sexual journey as if enjoying sex is a character trait. Couples who put up photos of themselves entwined in bed sheets on social media, pretending that their post-coital bragging is art. Terrible essays and amateur poetry about fucking. Do it, don't go on about it.

Sex parties always seemed to me like a way for boring people to show others that there's a more interesting side to them. Perhaps there would be if you suddenly kicked off an orgy in a supermarket on the local high street, but a fancy invite-only gathering in the West End where girls wear Alice bands doesn't scream alternative to me. It's like a luxury gym where the smoothies cost £9 and the shower gel is designer and everyone there is showing off their bodies in high-end leggings, barely concentrating on the fitness element. It's all performative.

Entering the party that night did nothing to disabuse me of that preconception. The first room was the bar, where fully clothed people stood around drinking out of crystal glasses. The lighting was dim, but I could make out a Gucci bag, the flash of a diamond ring, the heady mix of too many Tom Ford perfumes blending together. It was rich and banal, and the fact that bodily fluids were being exchanged in nearby rooms didn't make it any less so.

The music was cranked up, perhaps to mask the sounds of ecstasy coming from elsewhere, and I made my way over to the bar, trying to spot Lee in the gloom and hoping that he hadn't already headed into a sex room, mainly because then this would be pointless but also because I desperately didn't want to catch a glimpse of my uncle naked. I was ambitious in my revenge plans, but I had to draw a line and it turned out that the line was having to watch a relative sweating away over a woman I assumed would be at least twenty years younger than he was. Not where I thought my squeamish level was after killing three people, but there we were.

As the bartender fixed me a Martini (I hate cocktails but I felt like playing a role), I studied the people around me. A good-looking couple in their early thirties – him in a blue shirt and chinos, her in a green silk dress with pink high heels and a slightly apprehensive look – were next to me at the bar. He was holding her hand and looking back at me with a smile. I returned it, but looked away sharpish. I didn't want to get bogged down in conversation. From her frequent whispers, and his comforting back rubs, it was obvious she was only here to please him. I hoped they didn't peg me as the ideal choice for their first unhappy threesome.

Towards the other end of the room I could make out two women, both as thin as greyhounds and just as elegantly nervy, sitting together on a plush velvet sofa as a slightly stocky man crouched down at their feet and talked at them. From his gesticulating hands, he was clearly trying hard to be entertaining, but their polite smiles and wandering eyes screamed boredom. It certainly didn't look as though they were desperate to climb the guy like a tree. In fact, there was very little sexual energy vibrating off anyone around me. The room felt muted and slightly awkward, as though everyone was waiting for someone else to take the lead and kick things off. Perhaps nobody had yet had enough alcohol.

A sharp prod knocked my arm off the bar and took my drink with it. I looked around and saw that one of Lee's mates had made room for himself at the bar, not troubling to see that the space he now occupied had been taken up by another person just a few seconds before. Men often do that, spreading out their legs on the Tube as though they have an innate need to fill any space that isn't filled, walking down the middle of a narrow pavement and being almost surprised when they career into you, nudging too close in a coffee shop queue as though you'll give way. They don't even notice what they're doing. They are important, their needs are important. You are not as important. You are not important at all. Unless you're attractive to them. Then your space will be occupied in other ways. Men will stand in front of you and block your path to get your attention. They will slow their car down so that you feel uncomfortable as you walk down the street. They will hover over you in bars, touching your arm, grabbing your hand. If you're lucky, it'll just be your hand.

I did not move another inch. Instead I fixed my eyes on the sweaty man's profile as he tried to get the barman's eye. If someone stares at you long enough, you eventually have to return the gaze. It took the guy a minute, but he finally looked at me.

'You just knocked my drink out of my hand,' I said, not moving my face, not moving any part of my body. Not blinking.

'I'm trying to get a drink, love, give me a break,' he said, and turned away again. I felt fury build up, my face getting hot.

'You spilled my drink. What are you going to do about that?' The man turned towards me again, clenching his fist on the bar.

'You're not getting free drinks off me. I'm not an idiot.' He gestured to his mate, a dismissive shrug. Just as I was about to explode with rage, Lee appeared between us. He blocked my view of his burly mate and put his hands together as if in prayer.

'I'm so sorry about my friend, darling, he's no gentleman but I can see that he's cost you a nice glass of wine and I'd very much like to buy you another one to make up for it.' He grinned at me, clasping his hands around my own and bringing them up to rest on the bar, signalling to the waiter to bring me a new drink.

And that is how I got chatting to my uncle. He was charming, in the way that my mother used to say that Simon was. All gab and smiles. The confidence to take control and take liberties without any real offence. I allowed him to order me wine. I didn't tell him I was having a Martini. I didn't object when he picked one I didn't much like, and I didn't flinch when he touched my hands without asking. There was nothing likeable or interesting in his behaviour, it was more that he'd grown up confident that he was an all-powerful man and acted as though everyone else knew it too. Men like that get away with an unbelievable amount. Even if you hate that kind of attitude, it's hard to push back against it sometimes. And then later, you hate yourself for enabling it.

Lee made his friend, who he called 'Scotty dog', apologise to me, before releasing him back into the bar where he promptly headed towards a door to the left of the bar.

'Doesn't waste time does Scott,' winked Lee. 'So what brings a girl like you to a place like this then?'

I told him my friend had recommended these gatherings as a good place to start if you were thinking about getting involved in the scene. Lee nodded. 'It's a vanilla crowd, nothing too raunchy happens here, bit of shagging, some nice girl-on-girl stuff. Less hardcore than I like but it'll do for a rainy Thursday.'

'What do you like then?' I asked, feeling increasingly aware that this sounded very much like flirting and having to quash the slight nausea that I could sense rising up. Hard not to sound like you're flirting at a sex party though, even a discussion about council tax would end up coming across as suggestive when you're fifteen feet away from people having sex with strangers.

He tilted his head and smiled at me. I could see he was only now looking at my face properly, taking the time to actually pay attention. He was sizing me up, either as a proposition or as an oddity. I sipped my drink and tried not to look coquettish. If he wanted to tell me about his sexual proclivities that was one thing, but I wouldn't try and seduce them out of him.

'That's bold, considering we've still got our clothes on, missy.' Lee smirked and checked his watch, a big silver Rolex dotted with diamonds which flung a glittery reflection onto the bar top. 'It's not stuff good girls like you want to know about, trust me. Try this place out for starters, then we'll talk.'

The fresh-faced ingénue approach wasn't working. I was boring him already.

'What, you like being humiliated, is that your thing? Big rich guy, never told no, gets treated like a prince but really wants someone to reflect his own sneaking sense of failure back at him? Or maybe you like being hit. Really smacked about. Or is it that you want to get fucked? You're not gay, oh no heaven forbid, but you want someone to push you down and dominate you? It's not that interesting, honestly. You think your fetishes are unique or different? They're not, mate, I assure you.'

That made him laugh. Men often laugh with surprise when they find women funny, as though it's a skill we're not expected to possess. Lee was engaged again now, I'd won him back. My dignity took huge knocks while I tried to rid the world of this awful family. The end result would be worth it, of that I had no doubt, but hanging out in Marbella, digging up weeds at a nature centre and now talking about sex with my uncle . . . it was certainly a trial. In a funny way it reminded me of a line from *Sense and Sensibility:* 'The rent here may be low but I believe we have it on very hard terms.'

'Hard to impress, aren't you?' He looked around, as though he were preparing to divulge state secrets. 'OK, Miss Seen-It-All, I like a bit of choking. Belts, scarves, whatever works. Losing your breath as you edge towards glory. It's fucking wild, I tell you. I've always liked it. I guess some big-brained psychiatrist would say it's because I nearly drowned in the family pool when I was ten or some nonsense, but who the fuck knows.'

I looked down at his hand pointedly. 'Does your wife indulge?' I said, smiling at his wedding ring. 'I assume she'd like to choke you occasionally.'

To his dubious credit, Lee didn't even try to look ashamed. 'My wife is . . . she's classy. She ignores some of my pastimes and I let her get on with redesigning our kitchen for the eighteenth time. She acts like an old lady half the time now. I get it, she's got a good life out of me, that's the deal with marriage. But men and women are different species, you know? I've still got desires. If she doesn't want to help me with them, she can't really be too surprised when I look elsewhere.'

At that moment, Lee's other mate barrelled towards us, spilling his drink and bumping into a group of people standing nearby.

'Oh Christ, that's Benj done for the night,' said Lee. 'Nice to meet you, love, don't do anything I wouldn't do.' I swallowed down the need to visibly wince and waved goodbye with one hand as he took command of his friend and steered him out of the bar.

I gave it five more minutes to be sure that they'd gone, finished my horrible wine, and made an exit, giving a wide berth to the nervous couple who were now arguing by the door, mascara pooling below the wife's eyes. The girls in reception gave me a cheery wave as I left, not surprised by how short my stay was. Perhaps a lot of people nip in to sex parties?

I spent my cab ride home with all sorts of interesting ideas forming. What a generous man my uncle was. In just twenty minutes, he'd given me a free drink, and a lead on how to kill him. Who says the ultra-rich don't help the needy?

* * *

I fell asleep during my massage, despite the harsh pressure the therapist applied, and then had a long bath, re-reading my battered old copy of *The Second Sex* before shaving my legs and giving my hair a deep condition. I began reading feminist literature aged 16, when Jimmy's mum became concerned at how much time I was spending with Jimmy and his mates. I think she thought that a lack of female role models might lead me down a path where I would be completely unprepared to deal with the disadvantages that my sex would throw up. This was typically well intentioned of Sophie, but it also showed just how privileged she was. A wealthy white woman, insulated from actual discrimination in just about every way possible but very keen to talk about it in general outraged terms. The Latimers and their friends were masters of this – shaking their heads about the local corner shop closing, when they always sailed past it to go to the next-door deli, talking loudly about giving their cleaner sick pay at a dinner party but getting rid of her when she could no longer work Wednesdays. 'Very disappointing, she's been with us for ten years and Tuesday just doesn't work as well for us.'

Did she think that I had no understanding of the way the world treated women? I understood how the system was stacked against women long before I ever knew the words to describe how we are marginalised, discarded, belittled. I saw it chip away at my mother day by day. Brought up by strict parents who had rigid views about how girls should behave (who spurned her when she decided to live her life a different way), prized for her looks until one day she wasn't, used by a man for fun until he got bored. Working hard in a series of low-paid jobs where she was never appreciated. Raising a child alone without it counting for a thing.

But the feminist literature introduction was a revelation, and I'll always be grateful to Sophie for it. Perhaps I was spending too much time with boys, adapting my behaviour to fit in with them. Without a crash course in the works of Wollstonecraft, De Beauvoir, and Plath, I might have quashed the early flickers of rage I felt, tried to live small, as women are wordlessly taught to do from birth. But reading about other angry women made me bolder, allowed me to nurture my anger, see it as a worthy and righteous thing. Of course, I do not mean to make these women shoulder any small part of my eventual deeds, though I'm sure that the tabloids would salivate over constructing a 'vicious feminist' narrative should my story ever become public.

There was one book that made me see wicked vengeance in a more positive light though: *The Bloody Chamber* by Angela Carter. This wasn't a book given to me by Sophie, but one I came across in a bookshop in Soho on a rainy autumn afternoon just after my seventeenth birthday, when I'd spent the day in town on my own. Its cover jumped out at me from a pile, the swirls of black and red seemed to complement what was going on in my teenage head. I scanned the blurb quickly, took it to the till and read it in one go at a dingy tourist café off Tottenham Court Road. Her dark fairy tales, where women plot and deceive, opened a door in my mind. I saw that, just as we did not have to be small and quiet and weak, women did not have to be good or strong, virtuous but ultimately sacrificed. We could be underhanded, out for ourselves, led by desires we dared not voice. I finished the book, and walked out onto the street with a sense of new possibility. I gave Annabelle a copy the next Christmas, thinking that the nervy kid could use a shot in the arm, but Sophie pursed her lips as she watched her daughter unwrap the book, and took me aside after lunch to tell me that Annabelle was far too sensitive for such gory stories.

'Honestly, Grace, I know you're a tough girl, but Belle suffers horribly with her worries and I really think you could have thought about that. She looks up to you and obviously now she'll be dying to read this book. I'll have to be the one to put her off until she's a bit older. Could you exchange it for Primo Levi? She'll be studying the Second World War next term.' I just stared at her until she hurried off to stir the gravy. I replaced a book of fairy tales with a real-life scream of pain about the worst thing that humanity has ever done. Annabelle had nightmares for three days after she'd finished reading *If This Is a Man*. Sophie was full of pride for how empathetic her daughter was.

When my bath went cold, I carefully dried my hair, loosely curling it so that it rolled down my back in soft ropes. I painted my nails bright orange and carefully inched new tights up my legs so as not to ladder them immediately. The dress I selected to wear that night was a short black one, with long sleeves and a high ruffle neck. It made me look stern but enjoyably so. After my first brief foray into the world of sex clubs, where my uncle so generously planted the idea for his murder, I went online and did my research. There are dozens in the capital, traversing a sliding scale between 'a masked ball full of models' to 'expect a slick of sadness and bring suitable antibacterial wipes'. But it was easy to figure out which ones to avoid – 'the venue is a three-minute walk from the drive-thru McDonald's' or 'bring your own booze, no tins' get ticked off immediately. Lee was hardly likely to frequent a sex party held on a ring road somewhere near Wembley. And I was happy to do research, but not anywhere near an industrial estate. I've had enough sadness in my life already.

After looking at a lot of generic sex-party sites, where the word 'fun' is thrown around as though you're going to a theme park, I found three high-end clubs which encouraged choking, BDSM, and domination play, and signed up to their mailing lists. They weren't as relaxed as the Chinatown dive. You were asked for a photo, and a small paragraph about yourself before you could attend an event. I sent in a picture of a semi-famous Instagrammer who looked enough like me as not to raise questions on the door and three lines of fluff about how I was a PR girl looking for new experiences with sexy strangers. It's not hard to get into these places if you're a fairly attractive woman, the organisers are much stricter with lone men who will likely stand around creeping people out.

I also, and this is ridiculous in retrospect, took a first aid class. Somehow, I decided that if I was going to strangle someone to death, it might be good to see what experts looked for when trying to save someone from such a fate. I wanted to know what the tipping point was, when the bloodshot eyes and loss of consciousness became irreversible. Unfortunately, this meant enduring two hours in a community centre in Peckham one dull Tuesday evening, while a busy woman called Deirdre stood around showing us how to perform CPR on dummies that looked to be as old as her. It's not easy to ask about strangulation casually, but I did learn that though people normally lose consciousness within seconds, it can take four minutes to actually die, despite it looking like the person has already pegged it. On balance, it wasn't worth having to wrap bandages around the hand of a rather sweaty man called Anthony who stared at me the entire time to learn this snippet when I could have just googled it, but there we were. Now I know that cling film is handy for minor burns, thank you, Deirdre.

Once I was fully made-up, I drank a glass of wine while standing at the kitchen sink. These kind of parties don't start until late, and I didn't think being stone-cold sober would be comfortable. The event I went to is run by the son of a peer of the realm. He's been in the papers many times, promoting his debauched club nights, but he is much more low key about this side of his work. I only knew he was involved because it's held in the same building tucked behind Regent Street which his company is registered to. It makes sense. Entertain the rich and beautiful at your parties, and watch them. Find the ones who still seek more, whose eyes glaze over at the dancing and the champagne on tap. They have everything they want but they want more. A discreet black calling card, with a website address embossed on it, handed to them with the enormous bill. Exclusive, the card signals. For those who require something extra. It's a good spin-off for the Hon Felix Forth. He knows those clients. He is one himself. I'd submitted my application and waited for three weeks for a reply.

When I finally got one, it was simply a pop-up invitation with the date and the venue. Nothing else, no welcome or instructions. I guessed I wasn't supposed to email back asking whether to bring my own ball gag, so I did what any millennial would do, and googled it. From the three places I'd looked into, this one was the most exclusive. The reviews on a site called Sleeksexperts spoke smugly of how hard it was to get an invite (I think I'd proved that wrong), how opulent the venue was and how 'dark' things could get. Everything was vague and infuriating, but it was clear that if I was looking for a place where serious kink was encouraged, then I was on the right track. More than one person said that they'd never been able to indulge in such serious depravity before, which came across as strangely mundane on a review site modelled to look like a TripAdvisor knock-off.

I had no way of knowing whether Lee would be there, but it didn't matter much. I was mainly going to see what the limits were at these gatherings. He liked choking, he told me. But was that a brag, designed to make him seem more edgy than he really was, or did he truly indulge in walking that precarious line between life and death? And if so, did these parties allow him to do it, or did he have to carry out his practices in discreet hotel rooms where nobody could ever interrupt or disapprove?

I took the Tube to Tottenham Court Road and walked the rest of the way. I've always liked walking around the city. When I was younger and the Latimer house got too much for me, I'd tramp around Hampstead Heath for hours with their old dog Angus, letting my thoughts float around, moving in and out of my head with each step. Nothing can stick in my brain when I'm moving. That's why I love running. I can get away from my obsessional thoughts, disconnect from the plans I've made, quieten down the urge to hurry and get on with it all. If I didn't have that time, I think I'd have been weighed down to the point of inertia by the business of my brain.

I got to the venue at 11.45 p.m. Late enough not to look unduly keen and be prey for the prompt and the sleazy, early enough not to walk in and confront sex within seconds. If the Chinatown bar was the last-minute budget airline ticket of erotic parties, then this was a private flight. Complete with free drinks. And free nuts obviously. The vast double doors were opened from the inside by a woman wearing a dress which looked suspiciously like something Chanel sent down the runway last season. I stepped onto marble floor, and ahead of me a grand iron staircase split in the middle, sending you up to a palatial entrance room where a man in a tuxedo and a black mask covering his eyes silently offered champagne from a salver. He held up an identical eye mask made of flimsy black silk, which I assumed was mandatory. Once on, I smoothed down my hair and went into the main room, which was already teeming with bodies, the vast windows behind them giving a view over the shop lights of Regent Street. I briefly wondered how sexy it was to be able to see the Apple store as you came to orgasm before I realised rich people are exactly who would find that erotic.

I drained my glass and took another one from a woman dressed like she was going to a black-tie charity ball, and walked the perimeter of the room. There were three people stroking each other's arms to my left. I saw one woman kissing another as a man in a bowtie inched towards their faces, keen to join. The carpet was so thick my heels sunk low into it with each step. The stroking and kissing was boring. The masks were slightly cheesy. If I was going to be out this late, I might as well see some action.

I went towards a door draped in black fabric, which took me into a hallway with several other doors leading off it. The rooms had names, which I could just about see in the dim light. They must have been offices for virtuous Victorians at some point. Now they had signs which told you that you were entering 'The Playroom'. Still, we don't have consumption anymore, so that's progress, I guess.

I respected myself too much to go into that room, so I walked on and stopped outside 'The Dark Room'. I'd heard about dark rooms from my research. They'd sprung up in gay bars during the Seventies, but were now commonplace at these kinds of parties. It could be as innocuous as a room with low light, but it might also be a place for those looking for slightly more transgressive activities. I opened the door slowly, careful to remember that the room might be in use and visitors not always welcome.

Inside, there was a low blue light snaking round the skirting boards. The door closed silently behind me and I stood with my back to it, letting my eyes adjust. I could hear someone wincing, taking gulping breaths, sucking up the air as another sound took over – the sound of chains. Slowly, my eyes took in the scene in front of me. A woman was suspended on a wall, like a rough approximation of Leonardo da Vinci's *Vitruvian Man*. Next to her, a guy in just his trousers and mask was holding up a heavy chain and preparing to hit her with it. I held my breath, waiting to see what would happen.

The man drew his arm back, and then raised it fast. The chain shot out of his hand and landed across her abdomen. She screamed briefly, before clamping her mouth shut and closing her eyes. He went over to her and kissed her shoulder, while I watched her manage her breathing. Even in the darkness, I could see a welt forming on her stomach. I guess the rule here was only to mark places on the body which would be easily concealed when back at the office on Monday. Despite what I've been doing recently, I don't get excited by acts of violence, even ones which are done with consent. It's almost a prerequisite for serial killers to have spent their childhoods torturing animals before moving onto other people, exploring the rush they get when they see others in pain.

That kind of senseless act baffles me. This woman and her bleeding stomach baffle me. Violence and punishment are necessary in certain situations, but I can't fathom inflicting pain or terror because you find joy in the immediate practice. You find joy in the retribution, in correcting a wrong or in punishing someone who truly deserves it. I am strengthened by what I do. But I'm not doing it because I get off on seeing someone in pain. Yes, watching my grizzled old grandfather getting weaker by the second as his dead, decapitated wife lay beside him held some small reward for me, but that was dwarfed by the chain of events I was setting off. I was eliminating a toxic group of people from society. A family who'd done nothing but take what they could get for themselves, and treat other people with disdain.

My mind had wandered so far away from this dark room that I started when I heard the chain crack again. This time, the woman let out the word 'mighty!' and the man dropped the metal rope and picked up a water bottle, raising it to her lips and stroking her hair. Elegant safe word, I thought, as I backed out through the door. The couple had barely glanced my way while I'd been standing there watching them perform. There was tenderness and trust between them. An understanding that whatever went on, it was done as a partnership. I was beginning to see that the sex party community ran on these unspoken guidelines. That you could transgress, and discard the sense of shame that might normally accompany such acts. You could inflict harm and comfort someone immediately afterwards. And you could walk out the door five minutes later, without ever knowing the name of your victim. And sure, shame *was* suspended within the four walls of this palatial building. But outside? It would be there waiting. If Lee was to die in a place like this, I knew that the Artemis family would do their utmost to conceal and obfuscate. Nobody would strive to understand what Lee sought in these dark rooms. Nobody would look for answers.

I peeked into a couple of other rooms – a couple experimenting with a rubber suit and a group of people awkwardly attempting an orgy but being slightly stymied by the physical logistics of it – but my heart wasn't in it. And neither were theirs by the looks of it. If Lee was here, I wasn't likely to spot him in the gloomy rooms, and I didn't want to look too hard for a glimpse of my masked and possibly naked uncle.

Back in the bar, I struck up a conversation with another woman standing alone. I was drawn to her because I admired her suit, a sharp black tux I'd agonised over buying myself just days before. Standing in a crowded sex party, interested only in tailoring. That was *my* transgression. I asked how her night was going and she flicked her masked eyes towards me, before shrugging her shoulders.

'If I wanted to fuck a coked-up banker I'd hang around Liverpool Street station on a Thursday night,' she said.

That made me laugh and as I got the bartender's attention, I gestured to her to order a drink. 'So where would you go,' I said. 'I mean . . . for more than this. It feels as though everyone brags about how hardcore they are, but these parties all look like a glossy advertorial for gin or something.' She nodded in recognition, paused for a second and then looked around the bar, which was emptying out as people headed for the private rooms.

'Honestly, this place is good only because it's central and the wine doesn't leave you with a hangover you'll regret. But it's so *safe*. They promise depravity but for most of these men that just means telling them that they're losers then they cum. That's what counts as dark for rich men. But what is it that you really want?'

She was truly beautiful this woman, even with a mask covering half her face. Cheekbones which didn't vanish when her smile did. Dimples which made her look a fraction less threatening than such a face would normally be. A mouth which was pleasingly plump but not stuffed with fillers like half the women I'd seen that night. I wondered what her deal was, if she came to these nights to meet the rich guys or whether she was really searching for sexual gratification in a way that I didn't understand. Whatever she was, she clearly favoured the direct approach. So I took it.

'I want to tie someone up and make him completely helpless. Then I want to choke him so hard he passes out. Sexy for him, part of the healing process for me. Do you know anywhere which might host such a situation?'

On the way home, I opened the browser on my phone and searched for the name of the club she'd mentioned. 'Well you only want one place, darling, you're wasting your time with all this,' she'd gestured to the palatial space around us. 'But I've got to say, if you're here then you're an amateur, and I'm telling you about a place where your learner plates will do you no good. Don't go unless you really want it.' She didn't know how much I wanted it, and she didn't push any further, slinking off with her drink towards the Playroom. As she'd said, there was very little online about her recommended spot, just a map of the location – Mile End – and a mobile number. Maybe now I was finally on the right track. I just needed Lee to come with me. Getting him to acquiesce to being choked by a stranger didn't seem like the hard part. I was more worried about asking him to go to the East End.

* * *

Finally I got lucky. One Tuesday night I got corralled into drinks with colleagues, although admittedly that wasn't the lucky part. Thirty minutes at the pub was all I could manage in the end. The table was made up of seven women and Gavin, the sweetly camp digital guy who wore cardigans more than he should, and that is being kind because the correct amount is never. The shrieks of laughter were audible from the bar, where I ordered myself a large glass of Brunello because there was no conceivable world in which these people had chosen anything but a bottle of the house white. When I eventually came around to where they were sitting, I saw that my instinct was spot on. My only mistake had been to imagine they'd only got one bottle. Three stood on the table, and only one had any liquid left in it. Exclamations of welcome were made, a chair proffered.

'We're talking about which Hemsworth brother is hotter, Grace,' slurred Jenny, who never spoke to me in the office but smiled a lot when I happened to glance her way.

'Oh sorry,' I said as I took my scarf off, 'I don't know who they are.' I did know of course, I think wilful ignorance of pop culture is pathetic, but I didn't want them to think that I was the kind of person who enjoyed this type of conversation. It would be a slippery slope where suddenly I'd be expected to join in at work more. Not that I was planning a long career at the company. The moment the plan was all wrapped up, I'd be out of there without so much as a courtesy email.

The conversation continued around me, and a phone was produced to show me the important key differences between the brothers Hemsworth. I listened along, rejecting any attempts to have one-on-one conversations, and took my opportunity to leave when Christie went to the toilet and Gavin went to get another round in. I tried to stay cheery in the face of entreaties for me to stay, but I'm afraid I went slightly too far when Jenny grabbed me by the hand and tried to take my scarf off. I reciprocated the pressure she was putting on my palm, and then dug my nails hard into her fingers as I released myself from her grasp with some force. She winced and looked down at her hand, rubbing it as I said goodnight to the group. As I walked towards the door, I looked back at the table. Everyone was listening to Magda as she told some story which involved miming fellatio on an empty wine bottle. Everyone that was, except Jenny. She was still staring at me with a look of complete shock, her hand tucked under her armpit as though she were trying to soothe herself. It took all I had in me not to wink at her as I turned and headed out the door.

I wasn't ready to go home, so I paused for a cigarette, bothered only once by someone borrowing my lighter – so tedious. The man was handsome in a somewhat generic way, and obviously keen to strike up conversation, but I could already see that he was on the turn. The hair will go first I imagine, and then the jowls will set in. I didn't have the inclination to invest even a minute on that trajectory. I walked around Soho for a bit, looking in shop windows and weighing up whether to have some dinner. It was only 8 p.m., so I headed for my favourite Italian spot, which has counter seating and doesn't make you feel strange for dining alone. It is one of life's great pleasures to eat without anyone talking to you. What could be worse than a bad date with good food? How can you appreciate what you're eating when someone is telling you about how they really don't understand the fun in reading. Or worse, telling you that their favourite film is *Goodfellas*. Liking *Goodfellas* over all other films means the man has never bothered to cultivate a personality.

After a bowl of cacio e pepe, another glass of wine and a macchiato, I looked at my watch and saw that it was already past 10 p.m. Funny how thirty minutes with colleagues can feel like an eternity and two happy hours with just your own thoughts can pass by in a flash. I think I'd known the whole time I was sitting having dinner that I could drop into the Chinatown dive that Lee frequented. Perhaps that's why I'd lingered so long. I'd not been thinking it consciously, but as I paid up and walked into the street, I knew that it had been lurking in my mind. It was still a little early for my uncle, and I didn't even know if the bar was open on a Tuesday. But sex isn't solely for Saturday nights, and Lee didn't seem to stay in very much – if ever, so I thought I'd chance it. Besides, I was keen to push on with the next part of the plan, and I had to be more assertive from now on. I had to persuade Lee to come with me to Mile End. This might have seemed impossible, given that we barely knew each other, but I suspected that his need to seek out risk and his low tolerance for boredom meant that he'd go for it. Men like Lee don't require the levels of trust that other people do. Simon would never take up an offer like the one I was going to give Lee. But Lee had the perfect combination of not being smart, and very much thinking that he is. It's a heady mix, one which made me pretty confident that he'd be up for the offer. I just needed to pin him down.

I walked to the bar. I wasn't dressed for a sex party, in my work clothes and woollen scarf and hat, but it was a Tuesday night, and this establishment could hardly demand sartorial excellence when it seemed to imagine that an abundance of red carpet gave off an air of opulence.

The place was fairly empty, which was unsurprising. A few couples sat having drinks in low velvet chairs, while a slightly too drunk man in a leather jacket stood at the bar and perked up when he clapped eyes on me.

'Can I . . .' he said as I took my scarf off.

'Absolutely not, no,' I replied and stared straight ahead. Never be kind to men who seek to engage you in conversation. Even a polite brush-off comes off as a challenge. Especially in a sex club.

I gave myself an hour. If Lee wasn't there by 11, then I was going home. I very much subscribe to the adage that nothing good happens after 2 a.m., and in this place, it was prudent to knock a few hours off the rule.

Eager not to give the man next to me any further opportunities to talk to me, I took my drink and went for a wander. In a room just next door to the accessible toilets (did Westminster council enforce these rules in sex clubs as strictly as they did in Starbucks?) I found two men and one woman having a threesome. This many people trying to pleasure each other has always seemed like one too many to me. How can you concentrate on your own orgasm when you're having to think about whether someone else is being neglected? In this situation, there was a clear difference in the levels of attractiveness of the two men, which I imagine they all knew but could not address. One man had a gym-honed body, in that vain way that suggests he spent a lot of time creating the appearance of strength but likely meant he had very little. He looked as though he could chop wood with his bare hands, but his manicured fingers suggested the idea would appal him. The other guy had a sizeable belly on him, and back hair, which I refuse to accept is attractive to anyone in the modern age. You don't get points for keeping yourself warm. The worst thing about him was his bottom, which had a pretty serious case of acne. Even the forgiving lighting couldn't conceal it. Grant me the confidence of a man who can go to a sex club with a spotty arse. Truly, it was body positivity in the unsightly flesh.

Not that the woman seemed to mind too much. At least he was putting the effort in, his head between her legs as she leant back and serviced the weak handsome one. The effect was a little like dominoes, and the contortions were surely giving her a lower back ache. Handsome man was absolutely enjoying the performative aspect to it all, I could practically see him flexing his abdominal muscles as he looked over to me and ushered me to join them. I let out a small laugh, which caused the woman to look up and frown, and I felt rather unsisterly in taking her away from her ecstasy. Surely these people didn't think I would want to join in with this. Absurd. But then I was the one wearing a winter coat and watching three strangers getting each other off, so maybe my laughter was misplaced.

I left the room and went back to the bar, where leather-jacket man had found another woman to bore, and I ordered myself a drink.

While I was waiting for it, the door swung open and a very beautiful woman walked in. Behind her was Lee, cowboy boots and all. My heart leapt and then plummeted immediately. Because he put his hand on the small of her back, and I knew that getting him alone would be difficult when this woman, who was decidedly not his wife, was commanding all of his attention. Even I was finding it hard to look anywhere else. Lee was 54 years old. He might be trying to slough off some of those years with the hair dye and the regular gym sessions, but the fact remained. And remained inescapable when he stood next to this woman, who was really just a girl. A girl with five inches on me and lips which looked like they'd been sculpted by God himself but a girl nonetheless. It has always amazed me that older men would be comfortable with the visuals when people see them out with women this young. Do they not see how people laugh, and make their friends guess whether they're with their daughter or their mistress? Or worse, how we think that they've coerced the girl, be it through financial power or emotional experience. But I'm a woman. Perhaps other men of a similar age really do look on with a mixture of envy and admiration. I feel quite often that it's good not to know what goes on in the male mind. If we did, I suspect we would spend a lot of our lives in fearful despair.

The girl who was young enough to be his daughter said something to him and headed towards a side door. Lee was left holding her tiny Chanel bag as he came towards the bar, scrunching it up in his meaty hand as though it were made of paper and didn't cost close to three grand. He was clearly fairly drunk, his eyes slightly glassy, his brow glistening with sweat. He smiled when he saw me, recognising my face. He was adept at greeting people as though they were old friends, an accomplished blagger who never knew your name but made you feel welcome and warm for the fifteen seconds he'd spend on you before moving onto the next person.

'Hello again,' he said as he reached me and air-kissed the space next to the side of my head. 'I thought you were looking for something a bit more hardcore than this?'

'I've found it,' I said. 'I've come here to invite you. But I see you're busy tonight.'

He looked slightly confused and then looked down at the bag he was holding. 'Oh her. She's on the job, if you know what I mean.'

I nodded, not wishing to get into the details of how he was in the habit of hiring a sex worker some thirty years his junior, but he must've imagined I was still in the dark, because he leant forward, his hands slipping on the bar, and lunged at my face.

'Virginie is a tart,' he stage-whispered, breathing whisky fumes into my face. 'A tart who looks like . . . art.' He laughed at his own rhyme, and clicked his fingers at the barman, who narrowed his eyes and ignored him.

'So are you going to try out this new place with me, or are you just going to talk big about all the dark and twisted stuff you like and never go anywhere remotely different? Virginie will do whatever you want, I guess. But that doesn't strike me as very exciting. She's not getting off on it. She's getting her rent.'

He laughed again, but he was too drunk, and I couldn't see how to nail this down before his friend came back to find him.

'You girls are all the same. You put up a big show of being edgy, but you won't do what I need. Paying for it is easy. I don't have to ease this one into it, she'll just get it done for the right price. Scowling bird that she is.'

'Well, I won't waste my time. I've found a place where everything is catered for, no questions asked. It makes this place look like a yoga class for bored housewives. I don't want to go on my own, because where would be the fun in that? I think we could have a good time together. If you get tired of paying by the hour and want to play with someone who'll really put their all into it, give me a call.' I smiled at the barman, who came over immediately. 'I'm sorry this man was so rude earlier. I believe he'd like to apologise. He'll have a whisky on the rocks and whatever you're having. And could I possibly borrow a pen?' The barman delivered a biro and I wrote down my number on a cocktail napkin and put it in Lee's jacket pocket. 'Remember to save that before the maid finds it. Or worse, your wife does. Though I imagine that discovering a woman's mobile number would be fairly unsurprising for her.'

He looked at me, and frowned. 'You're a bitch, you know that?' he said, over-enunciating like all drunks do.

'I do know that, yes,' I said, as I turned to go. 'But that's what you really want, Lee. Isn't it?'

I left the bar and called a taxi. He'd call me. Now I just had to make the final preparations.

* * *

Prep work for killing someone is an odd thing. I wish there was an online group where you could share tips and offer up advice to newbies, telling you which gloves are the most practical and weigh in on whether a shove down the stairs is an effective way to take a life. Mumsnet, but for murders. Actually, I assume there is something like this on the Dark Web somewhere, but I'm not going to seek it out. It's a lonely business, and it involves a lot of waiting around and a fair bit of trial and error.

For Lee, I had two things to do. The first part I'd ticked off already – a visit to the Mile End establishment where he'd be shuffling off this mortal coil. Having seen the place, I almost think his family would be more ashamed that he died in Mile End than that he died of auto-asphyxiation. The venue was off the main stretch of road, below a bridge, the door almost hidden in the arches. There was no glamorous girl with a clipboard here, just two slightly grim-faced men behind a screen, who demanded twenty quid, took my phone and pointed to a staircase which led down below ground. But my God, it was perfect. The place was dark, with sticky floors and no windows. Bodies packed together, loud thumping music almost deafening the moans which came at me from all angles. There was no polite drinking area where you could gingerly inch yourself into the depravity, this place was teeming with people in various states of undress. And they were going for it with really joyous abandon. And it was sort of glorious actually. People of all shapes and sizes writhing around, as though it were a huge Bacchanal orgy and not taking place in a former railway warehouse. I picked my way through the throng, bracing for a stray hand or embrace, but was pleasantly surprised at how well enforced the rules of consent were. I wasn't interested but it's always nice to be asked before the fact.

As with the other clubs I'd been to, there were doorways off the main room, and I'd checked out every single one to size up suitability. Most of them were small and airless, with rudimentary furnishings and different themes. One room was lined with black rubber. One had a huge swing in the middle which was having its weight limit tested by four energetic bodies. But these rooms were gentle and that was no use to me. On and on I went. Further away from the main area, the people thinned out. And then I found the right place. A door painted glossy black took me into a room which looked like an old storage cupboard. There were big silver hooks attached to the brick wall, with ropes attached to each of them. Looking directly at it, I could see more clearly that they were arranged in the shape of a person, with one further hook dangling promisingly from the ceiling. A metal chair was propped up against one wall. I sat down and looked at the room for some time. Since cameras were not allowed in the club, I had to memorise the set-up for later. The chair was integral to the plan, and I could only hope that nobody removed it. Having to go and look around for another one would surely ruin the mood for Lee somewhat.

Someone pushed the door a fraction, and I spoke sternly. 'This is a private session.' The door closed. People were so wonderfully polite at this free for all. Such a typically British respect for the rules. It wouldn't matter too much if we were disturbed since it would look very much like a typical kink session, but I hoped we'd be lucky.

The second thing I had to do was practise. Practice makes perfect after all.

From careful perusal of an old tome called *25 Knots You Need to Know* – discovered by happy coincidence when browsing a second-hand bookshop one day – I learnt that the more knots you tie in a rope, the more you weaken it. So you need one strong knot. God help me, I found this fascinating. I decided that the most suitable knot for me was the scaffold knot. I don't think I need to elaborate on where the tie got its name. This looked like a fairly complicated noose, and my explanation of it will surely be insufficient, but from memory, it went something like this: you form a loop with the rope, wrapping one end through the loop several times before bringing it back to meet its twin. It involved three loops, loosely woven and then pulled tight when finished. I had to practise this many times to get it perfect, because it had to be constructed after it was attached to the hook. I spent an entire Sunday working to get this right, and it took hours of frustration before I finally did it correctly in one go. Even then it had taken me over three minutes of concentration. I wouldn't have three minutes on the day, it would look far too sinister, even for a man who was a willing participant. Within another hour, I'd got the time down to forty-five seconds, which I felt was acceptable.

The other key piece of advice I got from *25 Knots You Need to Know* was that a rope to stop a falling object may be subject to a load many times the object's weight. With this in mind, I plumped for the nylon rope, 10 mm in thickness. It was a little pricier, but you can't put a value on peace of mind, can you?

When women prepare to give birth, they pack a bag to leave in the hallway. I did something similar while waiting for Lee to get in touch. I had a medium-sized Celine tote bag in a lovely chocolate brown which seemed perfect for the job, given that it was roomy and not too flashy. Classic Celine. Inside went my rope, some gloves, which I hoped looked less murderer in a dark alley and more fashion victim, a large-brimmed wool hat which made me look slightly like I was attempting detective cosplay, and some disinfectant wipes. It was needlessly organised to have packed a bag without having a date nailed down, but I was getting to the stage, as I did every time the killing drew nearer, where I was getting impatient and jittery.

I spent ten days doing aimless runs around London, crisscrossing bridges and hauling myself up hills in a bid to get rid of some of the nervous energy. I spent an evening with Jimmy at the pub, where he repeatedly laughed at me for gazing off into the distance. I told him I was waiting for a guy to call, which wasn't exactly a lie. I took to putting my phone on airplane mode for hours at a time, so I couldn't check it constantly for any new messages. It began to be excruciating. And then one Friday morning, I woke up to a text from Uncle. It had been sent at 3.48 a.m., and simply said, *OK, miss smug I'm bored. Let's go out.*

I sat straight up in bed and re-read it. Then I put my phone down and took a long shower, did 100 squats and made coffee. Only then did I return to the phone and compose a reply. Once I'd written it, I decided it was too early to send. I guessed Lee would still be asleep, and I didn't want to look too eager. Only at lunchtime, when I left the office and had space to think, did I check my response and hit send.

I promise what I have in mind won't be boring. Meet me Saturday night at the Tube station. Mile End, midnight. Text me when you're there. Don't be late.

Two hours later, I got a text saying, *Had to look it up on a map. This better be good. CU there.*

I had a date planned for Friday night but I cancelled it. It might have taken the edge off, but I needed the edge. I wanted to feel hopped up. I was so bored of waiting around for these people to get in line with my plans. The immediate run-up was always the delicious bit, knowing that there would soon be another one down, watching the list get smaller, seeking out any reaction from the family that I could find. It could leave me feeling euphoric for days. Of course, this was mixed with a sliver of fear that the plan wouldn't work, that I'd have to start all over again. But that's what made it so heady. If it went well, I could rearrange the date. But he seemed a little drippy, texting that he was disappointed not to see me and adding a sad emoji, so it was unlikely.

On Saturday, I ran from Shadwell to Battersea and then back to St Paul's, my app telling me that I'd scored my fastest 15 km run. Feeling slightly in need of a rest, I sat down on the cathedral steps for a bit just watching the tourists mill about. Another runner did the same, sitting a few steps away and stretching his legs. He smiled at me, and I smiled back without meaning to. He was handsome, in a slightly ruddy way, but with something a little more about the eyes than his posh demeanour initially suggested. I could see he was lingering, and realised with annoyance that he was working himself up to say something, so I got up and headed for the Tube. Shame really. He was potentially not completely terrible, but I didn't have the time or the energy to sit and play romance on the sun-drenched steps of a church. Today was not that day. No day was that day for me actually. At most, we'd have fucked once or twice and then at some point he'd have asked me to go to Putney to meet his friends after rugby and I'd have had to delete his number. Better to opt out of that particular horror sooner rather than later.

* * *

At a quarter to midnight, I wrap my coat tightly around my body and fish my hat out of my bag of supplies. Luckily I have a good head for hats. You either do or you don't, if you look bad in one hat you will look bad in them all. Too many women think that they look cute in bobble hats. They do not. Nobody wearing a bobble hat conveys anything other than a desperate wish to look cute in bobble hats. Those abominations aside, hats suit me fine and this affords me an extra layer of much-needed anonymity. The trusty wig shop in Finsbury Park has done me proud, tonight I am a marvellous jet-black-haired siren. I'm confident that nobody is going to spend too much time looking for someone else in connection to Lee's death, but I also won't be strolling into the place where he dies linking arms with him. A hat and a wig are a nice precaution.

I wait for his text in a nearby pub (genuinely the first and last pub I've seen in East London to have been completely untouched by gentrification – it was refreshing not to see a sad old stag's head on the wall or a pile of tatty board games in the corner), half expecting him to forget or find a better plan. But he texts at five to midnight, saying that he's outside the station.

Great. Meet me on Bushell Street, I text back. Two minutes later, a black Mercedes four-by-four pulls up. I wince slightly, there's no way to hide his arrival in that monstrosity.

The driver opens the door for him, and he emerges into the night. Lee is wrapped up in an enormous sheepskin coat with a large dragon stitched across the back. His black cowboy boots have a snakeskin effect, clearly he's broken out his fanciest pair for the evening. He looks around for me, and I let him waver for a minute as I stand in a doorway just yards away. He's away from his usual stomping ground and he's vulnerable. I want him to know it. To understand I'm in charge here. I am leading the way. So I linger for a few more seconds as he looks increasingly self-conscious, wondering whether he's been stood up, or worse – he might have been set up. I can see him weighing up whether to retreat back to the safety of the car and lock the doors. Just before I can see he's about to cut and run, I step forward and quietly whistle, as though to a lost dog.

Lee looks over and smiles in relief. Coming towards me, he reaches out, grabs my hand and kisses it. 'Thank God, this place is a fucking dump and I thought I'd wasted a journey.' I withdraw my hand as gently as I can and return the smile, forcing my mouth to curl upwards. 'Nice hair, suits you. Makes you look younger. Hop in the car, we don't want to walk around here, babe, I'm wearing a Patek Philippe which would pay for a house in this neighbourhood.'

I tell him that the walk is mere minutes and tease him lightly about being a coward. His frown tells me that he doesn't much like it, but he signals to the driver and the car pulls away.

'How does it work?' I ask as we started walking. 'Does he just wait for you wherever you go, or do you pay him by the hour and sometimes have to get the night bus home with the rest of the masses?'

This makes him throw his head back and roar with laughter. It is always easy to make Lee laugh. It basically just involves saying something about how rich he is. I guess the concept of a night bus *was* funny if you'd never had to actually take it.

'My boy Ke works round the clock for me. I'm a busy man and

time is money, as they say. Nowhere he can't get me in twenty minutes, and for what I pay him, he'd happily wait around in the motor for days. I'll give you a ride home later, if you've been a good girl.' Thankfully, I am very much not about to be a good girl, so the ride home will go unclaimed. We turn the corner and reach the archway which is the entrance to our final destination. Well, his final destination.

'Ta da!' I say, and throw out my hands. Lee looks slightly horrified and stops still in the street.

'I'm not being funny, babes, but what is this? A tunnel or something?' I roll my eyes, and beckon him to hurry up.

'Look I know you're unused to clubs without butlers, but you're also, in your own words, bored. This place will freak the fuck out of you, but I guarantee you'll enjoy it in the end. Just try it, your trusty driver is only round the corner if you need to run back to Chelsea.'

'You better make sure it's as naughty as you say it is,' he mutters as he follows me down the stairs and into the club.

To my relief, it's heaving now, the bar area has a queue three deep and there are already people beginning to get undressed as we wait for a drink. I take off my hat, and subtly feel the front of the wig with one finger for any slippage. Lee has brightened up immensely in seconds, surveying the crowd. It might not be what he's used to, but he knows debauchery when he sees it. His coat is over his arm (he'd refused to check it in, half-jokingly telling the bored cloakroom assistant that it was a one-off Gucci commission and he'd never trust her with it) and he's standing straight, sucking in his stomach a fraction. However much men over 50 hit the gym, there's always a slight thickening around the gut. A nice little reminder every time they try to look down at their dicks that they are losing their youth. I can see his eyes narrowing as he scans the room, already looking for bodies he wants to explore. If I left him right now, he'd have hardly noticed. I grab us double vodkas and steer him further into the room. I'd already decided that I was going to let him play for a bit. He could have his last meal, there was no need to rush it all.

'The main room is tame,' I say, and gesture towards a side door. 'Let's try the private areas.' The man couldn't be more willing, practically jostling me to get on. The first room we go into has a wall of glory holes and Lee makes a face, ushering me back out. 'I'm not into watching women suck cock if it's not mine, you know?'

Holding back the urge to insult him violently, we move on. The next room is more of a success. There's a mock cell with three women inside who are making a big, and frankly overblown, show of trying to get out while a man stands naked, taunting them. I yell to Lee that I need to go find the loo and leave him to it. He barely looks round as I walk away, already striding over to the bars and saying something to one of the women. I give it fifteen minutes, long enough for him to do at least one disgusting thing, but I still prepare to be confronted by the worst when I return. But when I come back to the cell, Lee is gone and there are new people in the room playing sexy prisoners. Pushing down a mild sense of panic, I rush into the next room and find him lying face down on a table where a woman in a balaclava is thrashing him hard with a whip. His jeans are round his ankles, I assume because he didn't want to take his boots off, and his black shirt is rolled-up around his armpits. The whole effect is so absurd that I almost pity him and have to stifle a laugh. Lee has his head turned towards me but his eyes are closed in total bliss, so I don't interrupt. I just stand there, slightly detached from the scene in front of me, watching my uncle getting spanked by a woman who looks like she's just robbed a bank in a budget porn film. Oh Mother, if you could see me now.

Eventually, a few other people come into the room and a subtle tension starts to build. It becomes clear that there's a queue forming for the bench, and one man makes a small coughing noise to alert Lee to it. Queuing. The one peculiar British sensibility that cannot be disregarded, no matter where you might be. He looks up with a grunt when he realises that the whipping has stopped, and reluctantly rolls off and pulls up his trousers. The man impatiently waiting his turn hops up onto the bed and lies there expectantly. No wipe down between sitters, I notice.

'Where next?' Lee asks me, straightening his shirt, grabbing his coat and taking the drink out of my hand. 'This place is wild, you weren't wrong. I'll have to hide those fucking marks from the wife for weeks. Not that she'll take much notice. Unless it involves curtain fabrics or raising money for suckers, she's not too interested in anything these days.'

Is that an oblique reference to the death of their son? I'd not mentioned it to Lee of course, and truth be told, I'd almost completely failed to connect this man to Andrew in any way at all since I'd started zoning in on him. If Lara had felt the loss of her child deeply and agonisingly, Lee seems not to have noticed. People grieve in different ways of course, and I could see that these nocturnal escapes might be the way he coped with it all, but looking at him now, it feels unlikely. I suddenly feel a surge of rage at the way Andrew seemed to have been completely wiped out of his father's life. Completely irrational, given that I was the person who made it happen. But I was not the person who raised him, and even in the brief time I'd known my cousin, I could see what damage his family had wrought.

'Do you have kids?' I ask, as we enter a room where a woman is walking across a man's back wearing dangerously sharp high heels (so many of the rooms were filled with women debasing their male companions).

'Private play!' she barks at us, while continuing to drive her shoe into his buttock. We back out, giggling, and walk on, towards the room I had marked as ours.

'Nope,' says Lee, without looking at me. 'We had two. One died as a baby, poor fucker, and one not so long ago. But he didn't want anything to do with us. Thought we were evil for having money. Didn't stop him enjoying it until he didn't though. Wife hasn't taken it well, but what can you do but carry on, no matter how it breaks you? She's used it as an excuse to hide away, and I've carried on with life.'

We reach the entrance to 'our' room and I pause, not knowing what to say to a man who wrote off his son in just three sentences. Lee and Simon were brothers in every sense.

'What's this then? Is this where we really get going?' he grins, and pushes open the door. That was fucking risky of me. Had he been even 5 per cent less of a monster, he might have been too upset by the question to enjoy the occasion and I'd have lost my chance, probably permanently. Lucky am I, to be dealing with a man capable of discussing his dead son and immediately wanting to carry on seeking his own pleasure. The room is empty, probably only because it was the furthest from the bar. Lee goes to turn on the light, and I see that the stool is still in place. I take a deep breath through my nose and set my bag down on the floor. I put my gloves on, in what I know looks like a commanding way, and speak. 'This is my room now. You're going to do what I want, aren't you?' He smiles again. 'Actually, that wasn't a question. You're going to do exactly what I want. NOW.'

Lee makes a mock salute and I stare at him, not blinking, until he lowers his arm.

'Take off your clothes,' I say, as I get the rope out of my bag and start to make the knot. He does as I say, having some difficulty with his boots as predicted. While he fumbles, I finish the knot and check it for security. With a smaller rope, I loosely tie up his hands, so that he'll have a false sense of security and assume that the knots could be easily relaxed. 'Stand on the chair and let me have a proper look at you.' He's clicked into the role he wants to play now and becomes immediately obedient. I stuff the knotted rope into his mouth and walk around him, noticing the large cobweb tattoo over one bicep. Seeing initials on the side of his arm – KA. His mother. If my mother would be horrified to see me now, I can only imagine how Kathleen would feel. His buttocks are surprisingly firm, I see, with deep tan lines he could only have developed from frequent tanning beds. I force myself to look at his penis, raised as it is in anticipation. To have avoided it would have looked weak. I take the rope out of his mouth and shove it into his hands. 'Safe word?'

He grins again, and tells me that he rather likes saying 'Barbados', which is fine, since I won't be respecting any word he's chosen. 'You could charge for this. You're not the full-on model experience but you're thorough,' he says, looking up at me. I ignore him and put the noose over his head.

'I'm going to tie you up to this hook, and you're going to jerk yourself off as it gets tighter. I'll control the level, and I'm going to watch you getting closer and closer. You're going to squirm and wriggle but you're going to carry on. Don't waste my time with anything less than the full show. And when you've finished, it's my turn.'

I place the end of the rope around the hook and complete another knot, allowing myself a moment of pride in my craftsmanship. I hold the ends of the ropes in my hand and begin to tighten the noose by pulling on them gently. Lee begins to stroke himself, closing his eyes and breathing deeply. I pull harder, and his eyes fly open, but I urge him on with a rough bark. I keep my hand steady and let him get accustomed to the pressure, as his neck bulges slightly and his face grows redder under the perma tan. After thirty seconds, he's groaning as I tell him to go harder. And then, as I lean closely towards his flushed face, I kick the stool out from under his feet. He drops suddenly, and I let go of the rope. My knot holds, and Lee starts to lash out with his feet, writhing and twisting so much that I have to move away fast. His hands are grabbing his neck, clawing at the rope, but I move behind him and pull them down hard. Important not to leave marks. It doesn't take long, you know. Fast but agonising – for him but also for me as I check the door every few seconds. His eyes look like they're almost popping out of his head, and his tongue is hanging swollen between his lips as he desperately tries to get air. I think for a second about telling him who I am, but I can't be bothered. I've never cared about Lee. Killing him is a means to a bigger end and he doesn't warrant an explanation. Within forty seconds he's unconscious and then he's dead. Looking at my watch, I see the whole thing has taken less than four minutes, as Deirdre the first aider in Peckham had so obligingly disclosed. Ta da! Fairly disgusting man dies in a fairly disgusting way. Hardly momentous. Except for him, I suppose.

Once I'm sure he's dead, I get moving fast. Had someone walked in during our little game, I could've told them that this was a couple's room and they'd have left no problem. But this would be harder to explain. I untie his hands and wipe them down with antibacterial wipes. I move the stool a tiny bit closer so that it would appear he'd knocked it over himself and I pack up my stuff carefully, leaving only the rope around his neck. I'd only handled that with gloves, and he'd held it for a minute so hopefully that would be enough. I put my bag over my shoulder and take one last look at the figure behind me, hanging still now. Shame they didn't let you take phones in here, a last photo to remember Uncle Lee might've been nice. Not one to frame though – he looks pretty grotesque. I shut the door behind me, and walk down the corridor, where people are congregating, kissing, flirting. A tall man wearing an animal mask leans against the wall and looks me up and down as I pass him, reaching out for my hand and lightly brushing my fingers. I don't stop walking, wondering which horny stranger will find him. Would it be that girl in the assless trousers, or perhaps the couple in cheap masquerade masks who both could've put in a few more hours at the gym before wearing such unforgiving latex? It's up to the gods now, but I fervently hope that whoever it was had the foresight to go to the tabloids. Hat firmly on, I go back to the cloakroom where I retrieve my phone and head out into the night.

* * *

For all that I found killing Lee to be the most painstaking of the lot, the aftermath was delightful. If the waiting around in posh bars and enduring the sight of naked strangers degrading themselves was a trial, the newspaper coverage of his death more than made up for it. News broke on Monday morning, just as I headed into work. 'Tycoon's brother dies in sex game gone wrong' splashed the *Daily Mail*. 'Kinky Artemis found dead in sex dungeon' was the *Mirror*'s preferred angle. Even the *Guardian* couldn't resist, though their headline needed work. 'Businessman's brother dies in accident' buried the lede a little I thought. Still, I appreciated the word accident, which all the papers seemed to emphasise. Quick work from the Artemis family PR there, calling it a tragic accident and vainly attempting to muddy the waters as to why this billionaire's brother was found dead at a sex club in Mile End. 'It's so inexplicable,' said one unnamed family friend, 'Lee was a happily married man and loved nothing more than weekends in the countryside with close friends. I can only imagine that he was still grieving the devastating death of his son Andrew. We can never know what such a loss can do to a person.' Nicely done, I thought. You can't say anything too critical once someone has invoked a dead kid, can you?

The media coverage trundled on for a few days, but the family machine was in gear, shutting down anyone likely to speak, and the coroner's report didn't give them much else to go on. I did feel a pang of regret for not dressing up the scene a little more. An orange in the mouth, or a choice pair of stilettos would've given the press a few more inches of coverage, but I'd let sense prevail on balance. No need to get cocky with it. I wanted him dead, and I wanted him dead in a way that would be hastily glossed over. I found myself thinking of Lara a lot over the next few weeks. I wondered whether she was secretly, or perhaps not so secretly, relieved. The loss of her son would have been immense. But the loss of a philandering manchild husband who treated her callously for decades probably felt like a gift. Perhaps now she could detach herself fully from the Artemis family and fulfil the potential she had before she came into contact with them all. I was imagining a future for her, which was strange for me, given that she was still on my list. But the more I turned it over in my mind, the more I lost any heart for it. In many ways, she seemed like as much of a victim as my mother, her life swallowed up by a selfish and thoughtless man who cared little for her happiness if it didn't involve his own. And more practically, there would doubtless be an iron-clad prenup involved, exempting her from any claim to Simon's fortune, which meant that I wouldn't have to worry too much about losing out on my final bonus.

My decision was made on the day of the funeral, a private affair which ended up being a total free-for-all, with minor celebrities, a few fashion faces, and a host of burly businessmen all turning up to the Church of St Peter in Kensington to be seen paying their respects. I don't know how much respect there actually was in the congregation, but that wasn't the point for these people. I'd read about it in the morning paper, had taken a long lunch break – saying I had a dentist appointment – and hopped on the Tube to see whether I'd be able to get in. It was too easy really, the silent men in black polo-necks standing outside with earpieces didn't question a young woman smartly dressed in black who walked in with purpose behind a woman wearing a full fur coat and diamonds that even Joan Collins would've found gaudy.

I sat at the back, of course, and studied the programme with my head bowed as the guests poured in. From time to time I looked around, spotting Janine and Bryony at the front. Bryony was looking at her phone as surreptitiously as possible, while Janine talked to a grey-haired man wearing a blue pinstripe suit to her left. When she turned around and saw what her daughter was doing, she grabbed the phone off her and put it in her bag, saying something to Bryony, her mouth pursed hard. Janine was magnificent. Her hair was blow-dried so perfectly that it barely moved as she turned her head, the glossy caramel highlights tucked behind ears which held enormous emerald gobstoppers. She was wearing a cream silk blouse, which I couldn't see enough of to judge, and her nails were painted a deep red. The money she spent was on full display, in a way that she evidently thought was subtle yet unmissable. But her clothes only told one part of the story. Even from the back of the church, I could see the work of the surgeon's knife all over her face. The nose-job was OK, a procedure done many years ago when the gold standard was to remove any suggestion of character and leave just a girlish tip. But there was nothing else subtle here, her skin was pulled taut over the cheekbones, which made her eyes look small and angry. Her mouth had been puffed up so that it was always slightly open. And her skin had a waxy sheen, as though she were wearing a mask of her face over her face. The whole effect was to make her look grotesque. A face which only looked normal if everyone else you knew also looked like that. So I guess living in Monaco worked well for Janine. But under the light streaming in through the lovely ancient windows in the church, she just looked faintly frightening.

The ceremony started very late, perhaps fitting for a man who never needed to be anywhere on time. The last people to come in were Lara, Simon, and a man I didn't recognise, who took Lara's arm when she stepped into the church and rubbed her shoulder reassuringly. Simon frowned slightly, and walked behind them as they made their way to the front where a surprisingly young vicar awaited them.

Lara looked nothing like the broken woman that Lee had made her out to be. She walked with her back straight, in a burgundy trouser suit and bright pink shoes which, on any other day, I'd have been tempted to ask her the origins of. The man who accompanied her towards the altar was almost the opposite of her husband. Tall, slim, wearing a well-cut but slightly crumpled charcoal suit and good shoes. He had brown hair flecked with grey and wore small, rimmed glasses. He wouldn't have stood out anywhere else, but in here the contrast was striking. He looked like a professor in a room full of wheeler-dealers.

The service was boring, traditional, hymns and readings, blah blah. The casket sat at the front, draped in a gold silk scarf, and people stood by it to talk about how Lee was a true character, the life and soul of any party. It was all platitudes, there was nothing said that spoke to his real qualities as a person. When the last hymn was done, the vicar stood up to give a final address, but he faltered and I craned my neck to see what was happening. Lara had stood up, said something to him and walked over to the casket. The vicar sat back down and there was a moment of silence while the congregation waited for Lara to speak. She stood there for a second, and smoothed down her trousers with her hands, looking slightly ill at ease. I began to realise that this wasn't planned, and checked the programme again for any mention of the grieving widow. Nothing. Oh boy.

'Thank you all for coming,' she said quietly. 'My husband would've enjoyed being told how fantastic he was by so many people.' There was muted laughter. 'But he wasn't really though, was he? Sure he was up for a night out. Many nights out actually. Any. But he wasn't a decent human being by anyone's definition. You liked him because he paid the bill at the end of the night, or because he invested in your companies, brought you on holidays, maybe even just because he might do one of those things. But I lived with him, and dealt with his selfishness and his disrespect. Daily. It was daily. For years.' She looked down at the coffin at her side. 'I was young when we met, too young really. And he was charming, but you all know how charming he could be, don't you? How easy it was to ignore his worst instincts. But unchecked, they grew and grew, didn't they? When our daughter died, Lee's reaction was to go on a three-day bender, eventually coming home – high – with a 19-year-old Latvian girl wearing hot pants and asking our housekeeper to make them breakfast. I put it down to grief, stupid as it sounds. But when our son died years later, he did something similar. You've got to give him credit for consistency. It turns out he was a cruel and heartless person with a good front. But I was worse in a way. Because I stayed with him and enabled his behaviour. And now he's dead, by his own hand. Dead through the constant pursuit of his own pleasure. And I can't stand here and listen to his life being totally rewritten. You can't get anything out of him now, so stop. Just stop.'

Lara shook slightly, with adrenaline I thought, not sadness. People were bowing their heads and biting their lips. The awkwardness was all-encompassing. It was wonderful. The tall man in glasses stood up and took her hand, and together they walked down the aisle and out of the church. If I could've clapped, I would have. Instead, I followed them out as the vicar stood up and desperately attempted to regroup. Outside, Lara and the professor type were locked in a tight hug. I heard him shower her with praise, stroking her hair and kissing her cheek. She looked up and gave a small watery smile before they walked down the steps together and got into a waiting Mercedes. I knew then, as I watched the car pull out and drive off, that I would let her be. Enough had been taken from her, by Lee, by me. The women who managed to get themselves ensnared by this family weren't my main target. My own mother was one of them, after all. She might never know it, but Lara saved her own life that day.

CHAPTER NINE

Oscar Wilde wrote *De Profundis* in the last three months of his two-year jail stint. It's much lauded – a love letter (of sorts) to Lord Alfred Douglas in which he alternately rails against and embraces his subject. It's Oscar Wilde, so I daresay it has its merits (his supposed deathbed line, 'This wallpaper and I are fighting a duel to the death. Either it goes or I do,' is undeniably good), but he was also an educated white man, so the bar for genius isn't set impossibly high here.

Wilde slept in a tiny cell on a bed with no mattress. He was given an hour out of his cell to exercise each day and was permanently hungry. By all accounts prison nearly broke him. He died three years after his release.

I know it's easy to envisage me lying on a comfy bunk, seeing a games console that the tabloids seem to insist every prisoner receives immediately upon entering jail. Picturing me in a cosy sweatshirt, watching Netflix on a flatscreen, eating the Mars bar that I bought from the tuck shop with my weekly allowance. So many people imagine themselves to be liberal, open-minded, progressive. The type who might even argue across a dinner table about the merits of not punishing prisoners but instead educating them out of crime, who vaguely mentions the Nordic model without knowing what that means. But inside, in the part of their mind that they won't admit to, they still think that those of us who end up behind bars are scum, even if that word makes them shudder when said out loud. They do. It's the same part of a person that feels secretly sorry for women in hijabs and makes them swerve when they see a staffie in the park. Donate to Amnesty and never tell anyone that they're glad that prison walls are solid and high, or that they executed a tiny, righteous nod when they read that the Tory government voted to extend prison sentences for first-time offenders.

And the worst part of it is, they're not entirely wrong. Prisoners are scum. Well, from my experience of this place they are. These women are missing a few layers of the varnish of civilisation. They have bad teeth, wild eyes, a habit of yelling aggressively, despite the time. Given half the chance, they would ignore every structure put in place by the ruling classes and live by unspoken rules that you do not know. It's fascinating to watch, but I'll be beefing up my home security once I'm released.

Now that I've conceded on this, let me go back to the games consoles and comfort. There the liberal hypocrite would be wrong. Oscar Wilde's cell, despite its lack of mattress, looks pretty similar to mine all these years later. Yes, I have a thin lumpy roll of polyester to lie on, but there's no TV, there's no vending machine and I still have to endure the horror of Wednesday afternoons. Like clockwork, three hours after Kelly has chowed down on the chilli con carne that gets served up on a Wednesday lunchtime (every week in prison you get served the same rota of meals, much like at school only without proper cutlery since the fork stabbing incident of 1996 that still gets talked about), she is to be found on the toilet in our tiny cell, moaning and wheezing for up to half an hour. She does not consider that perhaps chilli con carne does not agree with her. She does not consider that this traumatic performance does not agree with me.

As with Wilde, we too get one official hour for exercise each day. Most of the women here don't bother. I use it. I need it. I set my entire day by it. In my normal life, i.e., the one where I lived in a flat filled with natural light, stocked with good wine you can't buy at Tesco, and stuffed with books that aren't recommended by women's magazines, I ran every day. I ran to get rid of rage, to zone out my constant thoughts, to batter any dark moods and, let's be honest, to stay thin. The women in here aren't too fussed by that last point, as proved by their inexplicable eagerness for chilli con carne, and they seem to think that their rage gives them character, as shown by the regular 5 p.m. scuffles. That seems to be the exact time every day when my compadres realise that they are incarcerated. As though they were doing some mundane 9–5 and readying to go home and slump in front of the telly and then it hits them that there is no going home. That Groundhog Day moment happens every day, with nobody ever learning from experience. It's when the walls really close in here.

I cannot run, since I refuse to do tiny laps in the sports yard like a pathetic hamster, so I do burpees, squats, star jumps, weights – anything to get my heart pumping. Anything to exhaust me enough that I'll sleep through Kelly's snoring. One hour of exercise a day is not enough for me in here. I must do two more in order to stay sane. I continue my regimen back in my cell when Kelly goes out to do one of her classes. Oscar Wilde doesn't strike me as a man who spent much of his time inside wondering how to obtain a six-pack, but I'm not ashamed of my hunger for exercise in here. My arms, once sinewy and lightly toned by the yoga I did to supplement my running, are now gaining bulk. My legs, previously lean from running but without too much strength, now feel heavy and leaden – there's no wobble anymore. The womanly softness is melting away. And I like it. This is none of that Instagram bollocks about 'strong not skinny' which really just hides an eating disorder in an obsessive exercise regimen – a Russian nesting doll of neuroses – I have this growing sensation of hardness, of armour, of being able to physically hurt someone with only my body and not just my wits. Men must feel this from birth. If I'd known how to use my physicality to take out my family, would I have gone a different way? Would it have been easier or more rewarding?

Other than that, I go to the mandated therapy sessions. I endure Kelly and her cohort as best I can. And these last few days, I write. We might not get battered by the guards, or starved half to death (though I would argue that the canteen offerings make deliberate starvation seem like a valid option), but I'm not sure that Oscar Wilde suffered more than he would have now, with Kelly as a cellmate, forced to do pottery workshops, talk about trauma with a group of crying women wearing rubber sandals, and sit in our cells for hours every day while those around us scream and moan because government cuts mean that there aren't enough guards to supervise us.

Mainly, despite the popularity of TV shows about prison in recent years which seem to suggest that every minute is action packed, my stay has been dull. There are lesbian trysts, of course, there are occasional blow-up fights, but mostly it's hours of lying down alone, counting the time in ten-minute increments, crawling towards another week, or month, or in some cases, years. I imagine you could stop counting at some point. But I cannot. To stop marking time would be to allow the possibility that I would be staying here for more of it.

Despite all of this, nobody will compare my work to *De Profundis*. I am not a man for a start, and I'm certainly not delusional enough to think I'm an intellectual. I write no foolish love letters from my cell. I learn no big truths from being stuck in here. But neither will I emerge half broken. I will go on living, thriving, and this period of my life will not mark me.

More than all of this, I believe I hold one further advantage over Wilde. For all that Wilde's writing about prison is held up as the most profound example of the genre, he spends much of it wallowing in despair about a man who has wronged him. Lord Douglas was said to be spoilt, entitled, careless with the feelings of others. He left Wilde's love letters in clothing he gave to male prostitutes. He rejected their relationship and condemned Wilde after his death. Douglas sounds just like my father. Charming, arrogant, centre of the universe. Men who turn their lights full beam on you for a few seconds and leave you chasing that artificial warmth for the rest of your life. It wrecks you and doesn't leave a mark on them. But I learnt that early. Wilde never did. Perhaps then, he could have learnt something from me. Never yearn for the light that some men will shine on you for the briefest of moments. Snuff it out instead.

* * *

Today I ate breakfast, cleaned the kitchens and then went to meet up with Kelly and her friend Nico. I didn't want to, but Kelly had promised to buy me cigarettes from the weekly canteen service and smoking is the best thing you can do in here. In the outside world, it's almost entirely frowned upon now but here, fags are an effective way to make friends, curry favours, and cut through the boredom of prison. So I sat with them as we drank our tepid tea. Nico offered up something she promised was cake. Everything on offer is stodge, stodge, stodge with a side of jam. Everything is brown. It's strange feeling my brain disengage with big picture stuff and obsessively focus on thoughts of meals I'd like to eat, clothes I'd like to wear. I want a bowl of pasta from La Bandita and I want to wear breathable fabric which ripples down my body rather than makes me worry about being anywhere near a naked flame. I think about baths at least ten times a day and I feel panic rising – my fingers scratching my collar-bones – even as I try not to let this stuff overwhelm me. That's leaning into it and I can't let myself do that – I can't get out of here and blink as I emerge into the light. I can't spend time readjusting. I want to hit the ground running, not trying to get my brain back up to speed.

Nico is easier to listen to than Kelly, with a voice that doesn't veer towards the nasal. She's in here for something interesting too – she killed her mother's abusive partner with a hammer last year. I've never asked her directly about it, I know better than to raise someone's crime before they do, but she mentions it often. She talks with pride about how her mum is getting counselling and how she's studying to be a counsellor too now. Nico calls her twice a week, and often cries quietly as she listens to her. I like Nico. I wouldn't go near her on the outside, damaged and wild-eyed as she is, but I respect what she did for her mother. It wasn't as well executed as my revenge plan, but the impulse must have called for speed over design. Unfortunately the lack of thought that went into her actions meant she was still standing next to him when the police turned up ten minutes later. Nico didn't have a hope in hell of a credible alibi, and will be in here for another twelve years. Her mother is 60. By the time Nico gets out the woman will be 72. She's given up her youth for a pensioner. It's love. But it's also patent stupidity.

Today, Nico and Kelly are discussing their boobs. Kelly has ambitious plans for a body revamp when she gets out of prison, and has read up on breast augmentation with all the focus of a research scientist working towards their first Nobel Prize. Turkey is the place to go apparently, half the price and you get a free holiday after the operation. Clint will pay. Or perhaps she'll blackmail some poor fucker more successfully next time and they'll stump up. Nico is worried about general anaesthesia and has heard of a treatment where you can get an extra cup size added on through injections alone. Kelly looks disdainful at this idea. 'Injectables for the face, babe, the tits need a little more work.'

They both turn to look at me. 'What would you get done, Grace?' Nico asks me, as they both assess my face before lowering their eyes to my chest. I've never minded the idea of surgery. I don't want any part of the modern puffed-up plastic face phenomenon, but in general, a few tiny tweaks don't make me outraged. I don't think its mutilation, or an affront to feminism. If you hate something that you have to live with every day, then change it. I like my tits actually. They're small, which means I can wear whatever I like without looking like a school matron from the Fifties. I like most of myself. Not in a desperately empowering millennial way, where stretch marks are rebranded as 'warrior stripes' and cellulite is referred to as 'celluLIT', but I know I'm nice looking. One day I'll be as rough and wrinkled as everyone else, but right now, I have a cosmetic advantage. I use it to full effect. People cut me slack that others don't get, why would I not acknowledge that? Energy spent on examining my every inadequacy would have been such a waste of my time.

And yet having said all that, I hate my nose. It's a good nose by anyone else's standards. I've been complimented by other women for its straight and clean line. But it's an Artemis nose and that's all I can see in the mirror. Marie used to rub it with her thumb when I was being naughty and tell me I had my father's will. The rest of my face is all from her. Sometimes, not long after she'd died, I used to sit in front of the bathroom mirror at Helene's flat, hovering so that I could only see my eyes staring back at me. I felt like I could see my mother in those moments. I would look into them, remembering all the times I'd looked up at her and felt safe. When my legs started to wobble from being bent in a precarious position, I'd have to stand up straight and the rest of my face would hove into view. The little comfort would be snatched away.

Bryony had her mother's nose. Cute, small, tweaked a little bit by a surgeon. Identikit. If I didn't see Simon in the mirror, I'd be grateful for my strong profile, proud to have a nose which didn't adhere so strictly to rigid beauty standards. But as it was, I would have it changed in a second. I've consulted top-class surgeons before, I've seen what I could look like with a few tiny swipes of a blade. Cut the Artemis out entirely. The only reason I haven't done it yet is because I wanted my father to recognise me as I stood over him and told him who I was.

I look up from the mug of tea in front of me, Kelly and Nico having completed their assessment of my face and body and are now waiting to see how my answer lines up with their suggestions. 'Nothing,' I say, taking a swig of the tepid water. 'I don't agree with surgery really.'

My solicitor comes to see me this afternoon, which is a rare chance to see someone other than Kelly or the stodgy, unsmiling guards who, honestly, I'm glad work here and not in one of the caring professions. Some of these women, I imagine, had a fork in the road where they might've become nurses, teachers, or therapists. Given their reaction when faced with mental illness, physical ailments, and even just scared young girls wanting a moment of reassurance, I can only say that they chose well to avoid those areas of expertise. At 11 a.m., I am led into the visitors' room where George Thorpe is already waiting for me. His suit today is typically beautiful. A light navy wool, befitting the recent warmer days, and just a flash of a dull terracotta lining as he stands up. I do not look at his shoes. I, by contrast, am wearing a grey tracksuit. I wonder whether a stranger who walked into this room would pick me out as different, whether my demeanour or my posture would speak of a life so different to that of the other women in here. I have always recognised wealth in others, education in strangers, refinement in deportment. It's a particularly British thing to know exactly where someone falls in the class system without a word being spoken, isn't it? Some people claim not to notice, but they're the same tiresome people who claim not to see race, and that's almost always because they're white and don't ever have cause to. But the grey tracksuit is a great leveller. It's hard to signal that you're not like these others in an outfit made from flammable material that will be rotting in landfill for a hundred years. Even the earth doesn't want it.

Despite George Thorpe being fully aware of my background, and despite the enormous fee I pay him by the hour, I still feel the ridiculous desire to show him that I am not like these other prisoners. That I am better. And I learnt how to do this very easily while working my way up the Artemis ladder. The only way to do it is to treat him like shit.

He stands up to greet me and extends his hand. I ignore it and sit down. 'I know we're already on the clock, George, so why don't you catch me up with what's happening.'

Good manners are drilled into men like George Thorpe. Public school, Oxbridge, their nannies who raise them and leave them with mother complexes that they take out on their wives – all of these structures hammer home the need for politeness, etiquette, and the right way of doing things. I have disturbed the order. He stumbles slightly as he sits, and I make a point of looking impatient as he opens his briefcase and pulls out some notes.

'Right well, um, so . . .' he trails off as he puts his glasses on and I wonder, not for the first time, whether this man is a shark. I want a shark. I *need* a shark. When this shit show started to play out, I researched lawyers obsessively and I was told by almost everyone I cared to ask that he was the real deal, with the added benefit of looking like several members of his family ran the British empire at some point. He's won too many cases to list, he's got people off on appeal (bad people, people who really should be locked up for life and they walk free because he works every technicality, every weakness in an overworked, tired police officer's statement, every wavering jury member who is scared of having to live with putting someone in jail). So he's the best. But this sharkier part of him? Well, he's doing a good job of hiding it and I need for him to taste blood.

George Thorpe goes through the appeal process with me again, reassuring me that we're on track for the final decision next week. There is a reason that those true crime documentaries eke out the crime part and fade away when it comes to the resulting legal process – it's complex, boring, demoralising, and mainly consists of waiting around for months. We filed an appeal on day three of my sentence. We filed for bail pending appeal and that went nowhere, I suspect because of the publicity surrounding my case. So now I've been in this place for over a year, waiting and festering. There wouldn't be much tension for the reader picturing me lying on this bed, desperately trying to avoid more group therapy classes where one person tearfully talks about horrific sexual abuse and then three other women accuse her of taking up all the attention.

I haven't told you much about why I'm in here, have I? That's because I resent having to. It's not the injustice of it that holds me back – it'd be fairly moronic to spend my time railing at the unfairness of it all when what I've got away with is so much worse – no, it's the utter banality of it. The motive ascribed to me was pathetic. The act I allegedly committed is one I'd have had to carry out in a fit of rage, with a lack of planning I'd have hated. I'm not Nico. But you can't use that as a defence, can you? 'Sorry, m'lud, but when I murder people, I do it with a little more precision, you see.' Instead I have had to grit my teeth and get through an entire legal process, dragged out for months and months – at great expense. What's that saying? You make plans and God laughs. I made plans to murder seven people and ended up in jail for the death of someone I didn't even touch. God would be having a hernia.

CHAPTER TEN

When we were 26, Jimmy met a girl. He'd had girlfriends before, nice, quiet, carried jute bags that had independent book shop logos on them, worked for charities, NGOs, small publishing companies – you know the kind of girl I mean. Glasses, small silver hoop earrings, likes a cup of tea intensely. They were all fine. Fine fine fine. But Jim is so laidback, so kind and well-meaning himself, that these relationships had no real drive to them. There was Louise, who obsessively kept an allotment but never showed a similar passion for anything else and faded away within a year. There was Harriet, who made more progress, sharing a house with Jim and some uni friends in Balham for a while. Their break-up was so painless it was barely noted (by me). I'd been working all hours when she moved out, and by the time we caught up for a drink it seemed like he was completely over it and I was relieved that I wouldn't have to spend my precious free evening consoling him over a woman whose face I could no longer quite picture.

His next girlfriend was Simone, and I thought she might have been the one. She was a gallery curator and wore interesting (interesting just means angular) jewellery and brogues in a variety of colours.

She was a serious person, they all were. But she liked my sense of humour and was very relaxed about the long and sometimes blurry friendship I shared with her boyfriend. Importantly, she seemed to really like Jimmy, and talked about their future together with none of those embarrassing caveats some women use in order not to scare a man away. They went on weekends away to Norfolk, and adopted a cat. There was talk of buying a flat together. And I got used to Simone, sharing Jimmy with her was no compromise for me. I might have even watched them grow old together with a sense of satisfaction. But Simone had more ambition than I'd guessed at, and she was offered a curating job at some newly opened gallery in New York just as they'd started viewing flats. I think she'd assumed that Jim would pack up his life and move to Brooklyn no questions asked, but he wavered. He'd just started at the *Guardian*, and couldn't bear to give up a precious staff job at a paper where he'd always wanted to work. He wouldn't be able to work at the same level, he'd protested. He'd flounder around as a freelancer, in a city full of them. Simone listened patiently, she countered his worries with options and emphasised how much this move would mean to her, but he grew more and more mulish. Within a week, he was barely communicating with her at all. They carried on in a muted facsimile of their previous lives while she sorted out her visa, sold her furniture and had a leaving party. Jimmy still hadn't given her a firm no, and I imagine that she thought he might be wavering, just waiting for her absence to become a real, firm thing in his mind before he gave in and followed her to New York. Instead, she flew out on a Saturday, and he sent her a brief email the following Tuesday saying that he couldn't do it, that he loved her, that he was so sorry. I know this because he sent it to me minutes later, with the subject heading 'I hate myself'.

The problem with Jimmy is that he's too comfortable and it's made him a coward. His parents are nice, his family life was stable, loving and safe. He grew up knowing smart people, influential people who made him feel like he would be able to do anything he wanted in the world. He had amazing holidays, speaks fluent German and plays two instruments. All of this equipped him to go out and be king of whatever world he wanted. But it also made him scared to go anywhere else, because where else in the world could he be as confident and established? All of those advantages, all of that privilege and all Jimmy wants to do is live two roads away from his mum and dad and live exactly as they did. And yet, I am tied to him. His familiarity, his smell, his arms which have just enough strength to make me feel safe. It's ridiculous and clichéd and I hate that I feel it. But I do. I've not known anyone as long as I've known Jim. I've not tolerated anyone else like I've tolerated him. And because he's patient and kind, I let myself rely on him, let him know me (most of me), and draw on that old bond which has remained constant. I've never told him about who my father really is, preferring to keep the sides of my life completely separate. But apart from that, he knows me in a way that nobody else ever has nor ever will. And if he doesn't want to be some kind of king of the world, then I'll surge forward myself and learn to be content just to let him be by my side as I go. He used to stroke my arm as I fell asleep, knowing I would get anxious when the day came to an end. He'd lie by my side and trace the freckles on my arm. 'You're so smooth, Gray. Smoooo-oothe!' he'd sing, to the tune of a song we loved. Then I'd be able to sleep.

Simone has her own gallery now. She married a well-known playwright and they have a Doberman, which feels like the height of arrogance when living in a city that really can only accommodate Chihuahuas. I know this because when Jimmy gets drunk he loads up her Instagram and thrusts his phone in my face, trying to show that he's happy for her while also asking me whether the V-neck T-shirt her husband is wearing makes him look like a twat.

Six months after Simone left for New York and Jimmy moved around the corner from his parents, he met someone else. I'd like to say that he shook off some of his cowardice after the breakup and met her whilst on a three-day bender in some ungentrified corner of South London, but he didn't, because he rarely leaves North London at all now except for the odd book launch. He met her at a supper party at his godfather's house in Notting Hill. Horace is some kind of hotshot QC (he put me on to Thorpe, so I guess I'm just as guilty as Jimmy when it comes to celebrating the middle-class connections that his parents gave us) and holds monthly dinners where he invites 'interesting young people' to come and talk about world events. I have never been invited to one of these hideous sounding salons. I have squared this in my mind by reminding myself that Horace is a stuffy old snob and also by taking £50 out of his wallet the last time I saw him at the Latimers.

I didn't see Jimmy for a few weeks after the dinner, because I had bigger things on my mind at that point. I'd just sent Bryony packing – more on this later – and was veering between exaltation at my progress and frustration at failing to come up with a workable way to get to Simon. The whole process had meant I'd not had much time for Jimmy. It was too hard to talk to my closest friend while I was in the middle of it all without being able to talk about even the smallest aspect of my activities. I should have known something was up though, because his texts had petered off until there had been radio silence for eight days. And then he turned up at my flat one Saturday morning unannounced with coffee and croissants. There is nothing that screams 'I have news' quite like ringing someone's doorbell without texting first. It's so self-absorbed that the only excuses would be to inform you of a terrible accident or to bang on about a new love affair. Since I knew from his face that his mother hadn't died in a hideous jet-ski accident, the only real alternative was some new woman. As a result, I tortured him slightly by not asking anything and instead talking endlessly about plans I had for renovating my kitchen. I had no plans to renovate my kitchen. I lived in this flat precisely because it was completely serviceable, and thank God, because people who talk about remodelling plans are insufferable.

Eventually, just as I got going with a particularly monotonous soliloquy about drawer handles, he'd cracked and told me all about Caro. Caro Morton was a young barrister, working at Horace's chambers. They'd been sat next to each other at the grim ideas dinner and Jimmy was, he insisted, set on her within minutes. They'd been on several dates in the weeks since, and discussed moving in together already. Caro, it emerged, was not a woman who played it cool and pretended that she wasn't looking for commitment.

'I want you to meet her, Gray,' he said. 'She's met John and Sophie but she needs to pass your bar.' I was shaken by this. Met his parents? Simone didn't hit that milestone for months. But then, Caro was in the same circle, wasn't she? An associate of Horace, a lawyer who doubtless went to Oxbridge and had a parent that the Latimers either knew or professed to know. Simone, as lovely as she might have been, was not. East London born, daughter of a nurse and a council worker, she never fitted in with Jimmy's family with the ease that one of his own tribe would have. Sophie and John showered her with praise – Sophie once took her to the country house they rented in Oxfordshire for a bonding weekend where she forced them to make marmalade all day – but there would never be a true ease. I should know. Being embraced into that family is not the same as being truly accepted. Someone feeling smug for helping you is not the same as loving you.

Caro. I won't waste time here. I hated her from the moment I met her. Intensely. I imagine you're wondering if this is because her presence threatened to take away my oldest friend, the man I'd relied on since I was a child. To you I say: try harder. We shall have no banal cod psychology here. A month after I'd first heard about the new girlfriend, we were set to meet.

We arranged drinks at a bar in Maida Vale one Wednesday night, something I was silently furious about because I still hadn't made any headway with my grand finale. But it was clearly a three-line whip and I couldn't come up with a good enough reason to postpone again. Jimmy and I downed a bottle of wine as we waited for her. She was so busy with work, he explained, as he scanned his phone for an update on her whereabouts. Ten minutes later, she walked in. I didn't need to be told that it was her – I knew. Caro pushed her way past the group of people waiting to be seated without having to say a word. Phone clamped to her ear, she had long red hair (which looked intensely natural but which I later found out was dyed. Never trust an artificial redhead – their need to be different and interesting marks them out as neither) and wore a cream silk shirt and wide-leg trousers. The only makeup I could discern was a swipe of red lipstick. And it goes without saying that she was beautiful, ethereal, captivating, blah blah. She knew it. Women always know it. And Jimmy would think that he'd discovered some untapped beauty because she didn't wear tight clothes or bother with nail varnish. Men always think that a surface level lack of vanity is a winning trait, as if the amount of effort women like Caro put into their appearance was any different from the dolled-up girls you see on any British street on a Saturday night. It's just a different way of approaching it. And the beauty is still obvious, but men think it's more refined, as if beauty in women is only pure when they pretend not to care about possessing it.

Ah look, I *have* wasted time. But it pays to have a sense of her – even if it's just so that I can congratulate myself on my restraint as I remind myself what eventually happened. She was young – younger than Jimmy and me, but she was remarkably possessed. A lawyer, as I've mentioned, who specialised in complex business takeovers. She explained her job as 'the organiser if Nike wanted to buy Adidas'. I had not asked for an explanation. I think this particularly patronising description was the specific moment when I realised that I hated her. She neither tried to win me over nor did she smother Jimmy to show her ownership. She was cool with him, which of course made him even more frantic in his affection, and she was matter-of-fact with me. We spent a couple of hours circling around each other, but I didn't really give it my best shot because all I could really focus on was how rapt Jim was. How much nervous energy he was emitting. How desperate he was for us to connect, be firm friends, link around him. I felt rising anxiety, feeling my fingers crawl up my neck, desperate to scratch. At 11 p.m., in the middle of a story Jimmy was telling about a family holiday where we ended up climbing a mountain by mistake, Caro put her hand over his and rubbed the skin between his thumb and finger and said that she had to go to bed. And just like that, the evening was over. The bill was requested, Ubers were ordered, and I was dispatched with a bear hug from Jimmy and an air kiss from Caro which did not require her to touch me. Their cab came first, and they drove off, Caro looking down at her phone without a backwards glance. Neither of them had suggested another meet up.

I knew that there was no way to play this and win. Jimmy was completely infatuated with this woman, and any sign of reluctance from me would have propelled him towards her even faster. I've always wondered why people get so defensive about criticism of their partners. If your mother, a person who has known you since you were a screeching potato in a onesie, thinks that the person you're with is a bit off, why the fuck would you discount that? Tell me if the person I've fallen in love with seems like a monster. List the ways. Do a deep dive into it, make graphs. I want all the information. But nobody else ever seems to. And Jimmy was no different. All I could do was be nice and hope that Caro got bored. Her attitude towards him had hardly screamed 'devoted' and I clung to that for a while.

A night at the Latimers' soon slashed that particular dinghy. I had long moved out by then of course but the penance I paid for escaping (middle-class kids stay at home throughout their twenties in London; they might rent a flat somewhere else for a bit, but even then they partially live at home until their parents stump up some deposit for a mortgage and they can actually have their own place for real) was that I had somehow found myself promising Sophie that I'd come for supper at least twice a month. This was a promise I really had no intention of keeping – modern life is 75 per cent cancelling plans and both parties feeling relieved – but I underestimated Sophie's need to stay involved, to always feel as though she played a vital role in the lives of those she knew. I tried to cancel at the beginning – I'd cry off with headaches or late nights at work. Every single time I offered up a plausible excuse that would save us both from the hassle, she'd offer her commiserations and promptly suggest another date instead. And if I cancelled that date, she'd just offer up another. She didn't really want me there, you understand, but it was a good show to keep up with the orphan that she had so selflessly taken in. I fast realised that I'd be better off picking the dates that worked best for me and sucking it up. For years that meant the second and last Sundays in every month. Always at the family home. Always an Ottolenghi recipe that called for spices that even Sophie, who spun out over local grocery shops in the way that others might salivate when they see a shop window full of diamonds, couldn't find. As a result, every meal tasted predominantly of basil, since she could get that at any Waitrose going.

The Sunday when I saw that Caro had burrowed deeper than I'd previously realised was an unusual one, in that neither John nor

Annabelle (nor Jimmy for that matter) were around to join us. Normally we were buffeted along by other people, indulging in pointless talk about how awful it was that the local library was to close, and wasn't austerity finally revealing its true victims. The kind of politics talk that achieves nothing but that a certain type of person perseveres with because it makes them feel like they're doing something about it just by mentioning it. God knows none of the Latimers ever went to the local library in the years I spent with them.

Sophie was completely undeterred by the concentrated chat we would now have to have with each other. Sophie never feels awkward in conversation. The way she views it, she always has something interesting to say, and what on earth could make her feel inadequate when armed with that certainty?

As she poured me a glass of wine and shoved the aged cat off the sofa, she began to gush about Caro. 'Lovely girl – Jimmy said you've met her. She's actually the daughter of Anne Morton – you know, the last foreign sec, and Lionel Ferguson. He writes fabulous books about the British empire. We knew them fairly well from an NCT class we took when I was pregnant with Annabelle – we both had these big bumps and bonded over the ridiculously judgey group leader we had. We saw them at parties over the years but of course Anne had a demanding job and by then they'd moved to Richmond. So remarkable that our boy has ended up dating little Caro.'

Oh God. Of course. That kind of self-assuredness that Caro had didn't come from nowhere. Her father was called fucking LIONEL. Her mother was a politician. And on top of the privilege she'd been born with, she was striking and smart too. I used to flick through the society pages of *Tatler* in the office sometimes, usually to see if Bryony was featured, where the women in the photos were always the daughters of earls or dukes as standard. But it bothered me that they were also ethereal, limby, beautiful. How did the luckiest in society also get to be physically superior? I'd assumed the breeding pool for those kinds of people was so small as to ensure genetic weakness, but here they all were – the Caros floating around looking effortless and perfect, gliding through life with the confidence that they won the birth pool jackpot.

Sophie carried on gushing. Caro had sent her a limited edition of Toni Morrison's essays last week. Caro had cooked for the family round at Jimmy's. The chicken had been perfection. Caro had suggested a weekend in France in the spring. I traced my fingers along the scratch marks the spiteful old cat had made on the arm of the sofa and nodded. Sophie didn't much want me to contribute anything here. And I didn't have anything to contribute that she'd want to hear anyway.

'Yes, it's soon but John and I were only together for a few months before we shacked up in that little flat in the Angel,' I heard her say. I looked up and rewound the conversation. They were moving in together! It had been . . . I cast my mind back . . . a little over two months since they met. What kind of needy lunatic shacks up with someone when they haven't even admitted that their favourite movie is *Die Hard* and not, as they'd said on date two, *Il Postino*? I mean, I don't think Jimmy has even seen *Il Postino*. Maybe he'd say some obvious Tarantino film.

Caro didn't strike me as needy. She didn't give off the desperate vibe that so many high-flying women do who really yearn for a good man and a chance to endlessly look at paint samples for the vintage dresser they bought together. Why was she pushing this? Jimmy might be head over heels but he wouldn't have suggested moving in – he didn't have any get-up-and-go, no drive like that. For Jim, everything plodding along nicely was the ideal state of play.

'Of course, it's very heartbreaking for yours truly that he's moving into hers – Clapham is absolutely miles away – but her flat is divine and much nearer her work, so I do understand.' Sophie looked up from stirring the risotto and smiled at me. 'You'll be a bit unsettled not having him around so much, I think? We'll have to find you your own Caro.'

I *was* unsettled. I wouldn't admit that to Sophie, who has always been slightly nervous about just how close I am with her son. Not that she's ever blatantly discouraged it – nothing so blunt. I think she just found it strange that her son could spend his entire teenage years hanging around with a girl without ever falling for her. Or at least, never saying it outright. Sophie and John don't really have friends of the opposite sex – it's always couples at their dinner parties, or the occasional single pal that they tried to set up with someone, normally in vain. I still suspect that she spent our teenage years hovering outside the den, just waiting to swing the door open and find us naked together. She never did. I think that was even more disconcerting for her than if she had. At least then she'd understand the dynamic.

The thing is, Jimmy has probably always been in love with me. Oh, he's never said it. He's probably not even aware of it on a conscious level. Jimmy isn't one for deep introspection. But I've known it forever. You just know, don't you? And normally, that would be a friendship breaker – at some point, someone confesses, or lunges, or starts acting out. But not Jimmy. He loves me fiercely. I'm a part of him. But it never tipped into anything of note. Well, we wobbled just that once, when we were just on the cusp of adulthood and I didn't want him to pull away completely. But mostly I held the line – never giving him a suggestion of something more, or encouraging him to explore the possibility. No lingering looks, no drunken hugs that feel just a little too intense. I've played it well and kept my friend. I knew that any potential exploration of deeper feelings would break us in ways that we couldn't fix. And why would I fuck it up for some idiotic attempt at a relationship in our teenage years, when nothing meant anything? I always stored it away, thinking that it was something to revisit when we were both older, when the mission that had driven my life was finished. A bond that I'd made over years and years would reward me with a simple and uncomplicated future. But I couldn't think of any of that yet, not while I had such work to do. I'd not even entertained it properly, never imagined the specifics of that life. It was just a vague sense, but one that was strong, and always there. And now I could see that Caro was going to derail it all. You cannot account for the Caros of the world, no matter how tightly you try to control things. People like her take pleasure in striding into your world and taking what they want from it. Not even deliberately, the bonus of your loss is just a nice extra. I might be able to carry out a ruthless line in fairly epic revenge, but I didn't know how to stop love. That felt completely beyond me and it made me feel like I was drowning.

* * *

I have derailed myself. My mother used to do this and it always enraged me. A story about a trip to the supermarket would veer off into some sad tale of the local café owner and her back problems and I would sit there scratching at my arm wanting to bark at her to hurry up. Nobody gives a shit about the stupid café woman, I wanted to say. Stop caring so much for strangers who don't even know your name and figure out a way to get the heating back on. All of this is to say, I could write an entire book about the trials of Caro, but it is not the most interesting story I have to tell, and also, she's dead. So I was the victor. Except I wasn't. Because Caro was never going to let me win with any ease, was she?

The facts are these. Jimmy moved into Caro's immaculate flat in

Clapham. His communication with me crumbled almost immediately. Long chats on the phone late at night were out first. Then impromptu coffees or meet-ups in the pub we'd frequented since we were old enough were next to go – after all, Clapham is another country when you live north of the river. The text chain was not erased entirely, but I was the initiator more often than not, which made me feel pathetic and furious. Worse, whenever I did see Jim, she usually inserted herself into the plans. Drinks (with her friends), dinner at the Latimers' (where she would greet me at the door), occasional parties at their flat, where she would make a great show of introducing me to incredibly dull, ruddy-faced men in chinos and then abandon me and walk off looking amused.

I took it all. I didn't engage in the game. I had bigger things to do – I was gearing up for my final assault on the Artemis family and I was frustrated enough by my lack of a proper plan, I wouldn't compromise that to indulge a bored posh girl who wanted me to care enough that it made Jimmy seem more of a prize. Instead, I watched her. And I learned four things:

Caro had a raging eating disorder
Caro had a not insignificant drug habit
Caro flew into rages with Jim which often became mildly physical (from her side)
Caro was desperately unhappy

What a fucking cliché.

He proposed on her birthday. I don't mean to imply that Jimmy has no spontaneity but people who propose on big meaningful dates lack imagination. I cannot envisage a worse day to get down on one knee than a family Christmas where your dad started on the Buck's Fizz by 11 a.m. Sophie was beside herself with excitement. Even John was beaming at the celebratory lunch. The Morton family were invited, and the old family connections were fast revived over couscous and a nice assortment of Italian white wines that Lionel brought from his cellar. Caro was her usual collected self, wearing a silk jumpsuit and showing off her ring only when requested, nails short and free of varnish. Jimmy smiled a lot at her, but he was quiet, following her around, only really speaking when she asked him a question.

There was one fun little moment at the lunch, when Caro's mother started talking about how shocking the death of Bryony Artemis was. The group collectively leant forward around the table, gossiping like old women about a young woman they'd never met, offering up theories about her demise and talking about how ghastly her family was.

'Gave £50,000 to the government trying to be made a lord, I hear. As if we need more barrow boys in the house. Men like that make a mockery of the entire system.' I sat there quietly, sipping my wine and enjoying the hypocrisy of these people who pretend to be above such salacious stories suddenly finding themselves more animated than they'd been all day. The following conversation about the latest Ian McEwan novel wasn't nearly as lively, I can tell you.

Two days after the lunch, I broke. I had taken my eye off the ball, so consumed with panic about my master plan and the rising impotence I felt about access to Simon. I stupidly assumed I had more time to deal with this lesser problem, but I was gravely mistaken. I asked Jim to meet me at the Southbank, where I greeted him with coffee and we walked along the river. He traced the freckles on my arm absent-mindedly, like he used to when we were teenagers and saw ourselves as a unit of two. Not charged with a frisson of anticipation but warm with the familiar. He called me 'Gray' as he always used to, and teased me about the new shoes I was wearing.

'So flashy, Gray, your footwear doesn't have to look like modern art.'

I retorted that his new silk scarf made him look like an old Italian count, and he had the good sense to look embarrassed. We both knew Caro had chosen it. After a while, I asked about wedding plans, introducing the subject with a light touch which felt obvious. He was vague, talking about Caro's wish to have the dinner at a private club her dad belonged to. Jim didn't sound too keen, and he kept his eyes on the water flowing next to us. A lull in the conversation gave me the push to get to the point.

I told him that her outbursts were concerning me, that I'd seen the scratches on his neck at lunch. I said that Caro had monopolised him, rubbed out all the things that made him him, and that I thought that marrying her would be a bad idea. I'd got it into my head that this was courageous, and that whatever happened, he'd want me to say it. He looked away as I said it, put his cup in a bin, and then walked over to the river barrier and breathed deeply.

'I understand that this is weird for you. Our friendship is intense, wonderfully so. You're my family, my best friend, my surrogate girlfriend, I suppose. For a lot of our life I guess I thought we were bound to be together – but you never let it happen, did you?' I must have flinched because he powered on. 'Grace, you didn't! You kept us at a level you felt safe with. People want to love you and you're repelled by it.' He ran a hand through his hair and exhaled. 'Anyway, fine, you made it clear and I went with it because I know you give what you can. But Caro wants more. I love Caro, and she loves me. And I can't indulge this, Grace. I just can't. I knew you wouldn't be able to just be happy about it – Mum warned me, C warned me. I understand it. But that doesn't mean that you can do this again.'

He looked at me then, with a soft smile, and rubbed my hand. 'We won't change. But you can't talk about her like that anymore. You need to see this for what it is. I'm not abandoning you. I'm not your dad – this is just what happens in life.' He gave me a little hug and walked off towards Waterloo. I didn't say a word. I hated myself for being so weak. I hated that he was right. I hated that I had buckled. I hated them all.

Caro and Jimmy held their official engagement party a month later.

We hadn't spoken much in the intervening weeks, but I went because I was invited and because if I didn't, then it would become *a thing*. And worse, she'd think that I was devastated and she'd enjoy it. I wore a dark bottle green velvet suit with a white silk T-shirt and ignored the slight nausea I felt at how much the whole ensemble had cost. Red lipstick was applied. We dress for other women. It's a banal cliché but it's true. She'd take my meaning from it. That was worth the credit card bill.

I got there at 10 p.m., having had a drink around the corner at a local bar when I judged that I'd arrived too early. Caro's parties usually didn't get going until at least 9.30 and I wasn't going to waste time with her guffawing friends when everyone was still sober. Their flat was on the fourth floor of a mansion block with views over the park. The building was beautiful, with marble steps and an original lift with brass gates. I never saw anyone else in the lobby or hallways. Rich people owned these flats. Rich people who have several homes around the world which they call 'bases'. None of them homes which have overflowing junk drawers or old bicycles clogging up hallways.

The party was loosening up when I walked in the door. A smallish group of Jimmy's mates congregated in the kitchen – a few school friends that I liked well enough, and some dull blokes from university that he refused to shrug off completely. But mainly, the flat was full of Caro's friends. Girls who were nervous level thin, dressed in muted silk dresses. They all had posh-girl hair – you know the kind – thick, shiny, long, looks careless but the highlights alone cost £500 and are anything but. The men were all in identikit chinos and blue shirts. Occasionally there was a loafer on display, but mainly it was trainers in an attempt to look more relaxed than they really were. Pretty much everyone was white. The music was turned up loud but nobody was dancing.

I nodded at a few faces I recognised but kept moving towards the drinks table, grabbed a glass of wine and headed out onto the balcony. I've never been someone who enjoys parties. The amount of small talk involved depletes my energy and makes my whole body tense up. Not because I'm shy, but because it's so boring it makes me want to die. Life is so short, and we spend so much of it talking to terrible people about the minutiae of their nothing lives. I cannot do it with any enthusiasm. It's no better in prison, you know. You might think that there would be less bullshit filler chat. You're in jail, you don't need to talk about the weather, or your commute or your kid's art project. But prison makes people even smaller than usual, desperate to cling on to reassuring normality. That means there's a lot of chat about breakfast options or discussion about what's on TV that night. And unlike in normal life, I cannot escape it.

* * *

I light a cigarette on the balcony, slotting myself in between two groups of people I don't know, and turn away so that it's clear that I'm not trying to join in the conversation. I smoke my cigarette (I aim for one a week, like Gwyneth Paltrow does – and that is the limit of our shared experience) and listen to the conversation going on around me. Someone called Archie is going skiing at Easter with his new girlfriend and someone called Laura is pretending to find it sweet but her increasingly shrill cooing suggests that she hopes said girlfriend falls off the mountain. Someone on my right is telling a story about how he once met our dreadful Prime Minister at a bar off the Kings Road, and thought he was 'genuinely a very funny bloke'. The conversations all come to a stop when Caro emerges onto the balcony. Her tiny body is sheathed in an emerald green slip dress, which requires no bra (posh girls don't need bras), her hair is loose, and she's barefoot. That suggests a sort of next-level nonchalance, doesn't it? As though you're usually holidaying in villas where maids sweep the floors constantly and someone comes to give you regular pedicures. Everyone cheers when she steps into the group, quick to proffer fags and wine. She spots me, and draws me towards her with a slim wrist.

'Hello, darling, so good of you to come. I see you've got a drink. Jimmy is inside panicking about glasses but I'm sure he'll be thrilled to see you – go and find him. I know he'll be so relieved that everything is . . . OK.' She looks at me with a tiny raise of an eyebrow, just the hint of a smile. He told her. Of course.

I go inside, not wishing to talk to Jim but desperate to get away from Archie and Laura and some guy called Phillip who's now loudly suggesting that someone bust out the Charlie. It's not 1989, Phil, you fucking embarrassment.

I find Jimmy on the sofa with a nice girl called Iris who he works with. I am given a bear hug, the kind that only a big man can give, and I know that he's determined to forget our conversation and he's very physically trying to tell me to do the same. So I do. Tonight he pats me on the back and grins with relief that everything is well between us. The flat fills up, booze is consumed until the only bottles left are the kind of chardonnays you find in Tesco so I switch to vodka. By 1 a.m., I can tell most of the people still here are high. I've never taken drugs – a classic need to stay in control – and I'm never offered them. But I can see the signs, the glassy pupils, the inner gum chewing, the fucking inane conversation (though frankly, that could just be the company). Caro is swaying in the middle of the room, rubbing her own arm. Jim walks over to her and takes her hand. She pulls away abruptly, says something and turns away. He tries again and she shoves him. Not hard, but sloppily, visibly.

'Let's all wake up a bit, you guys are getting sleepy,' she says, and heads to the kitchen. I look across at Jimmy and make a face – trying to convey that I'm here and also less obviously that his fiancée is a nightmare – but he looks at me with something veering on contempt and sits down. Caro emerges from the kitchen with a silver tray teeming with shot glasses and people assemble around her.

'To my betrothed,' she says, before downing her glass and slinging an arm around a brunette next to her. She doesn't offer Jimmy one. I can feel the rage build up again, at her for being a bitch, at Jimmy for letting her behave like this. Someone has brought a cake, covered in chocolate ganache and bearing the letters C and J in pink icing. It has been forgotten by the baker in the frantic desire to get drunk. I grab a knife and start carving it up into rough slices. Putting one on a napkin, I hold it aloft.

'Caro, have some cake. I know it's not your usual fare but you've got to keep your strength up, don't you? Don't want to lose that famous right hook of yours.'

The group huddling in the doorway titter. Caro looks at me, her mouth frozen in fury and stalks off. Jimmy, who was too far away to hear what I was saying, walks towards me with purpose and pulls me into the toilet.

'What are you doing?' he hisses, leaning on the sink and pushing me down onto the seat. 'Are you trying to pick a fight with her at our engagement party? I thought we'd agreed that you were going to at least try and be happy for us.'

'How can I do that when you've agreed to marry a narcissist who seems to actively dislike you?' I said, standing up. 'I want to respect you, not pander to you. Why do you expect me to be kind but you don't ask the same from Caro?' I push past him, and past the queue of people waiting for the bathroom to become available.

The night has ramped up now, it feels frantic and sharp. It's not a happy show of love, we aren't here to celebrate a union, we're here to indulge Caro. But in what? I want to leave, but I can't abandon Jimmy here with a drunk fiancée and a group of people who probably don't even know his full name. I sit in a corner of the sitting room and pretend to be on the edge of whatever group is nearest. I pretend to check emails, I break my strict limit and smoke more cigarettes. The party thins out, people stumbling into the bedroom to get their coats, pulling away from Caro as she entreats them to stay. She keeps pace only with herself, her small body unable to stay still. Jimmy hasn't even attempted to try to engage her again, but he won't look at me. Eventually, at 3 a.m., it's just the three of us and one other woman left in the flat. The woman is talking earnestly to Jimmy, and over the music (which Caro has cranked up) I catch some words: 'Worried . . .', 'Eaten?', 'Again . . .' I imagine they've both seen this version of Caro before and are waiting to intervene and get her into bed. But Caro is in her own world, changing songs every minute or so, pouring another drink, numbing herself. I sit and watch, wondering whether to call a cab and leave them to sort her out, but abruptly, she stops dancing and looks at me.

'Have you got any tobacco? I need a fag, it's so hot in here.' Jimmy gets up and starts to suggest we all call it a night but she cuts him off and I pull out my cigarettes and tell her I'll come with her. Jimmy finally looks at me.

'It's fine. Stay here. I'll sort this,' I say as I usher her down the corridor and onto the balcony.

Caro stumbles outside and leans against the balustrade. I produce cigarettes and light her one. I stand over her, aware of how tiny she seems.

'You are behaving like a lunatic,' I say, as I drag on my fag. She doesn't look at me. 'You have made this night a nightmare. I can only assume you're desperately unhappy to behave like this. Why are you marrying Jim? Break it off and find someone who has a nice family estate and will let you starve yourself to your heart's content as long as you look nice on his arm. It'll be easy. You'll be happier, Jim won't be gradually destroyed. I won't have to pretend to tolerate you. Go on, Caro, you know I'm right.'

She pulls herself up onto the lip of the balcony so that she's sitting astride it and throws her head back. She's laughing. It's the most natural she's been all night. Caro coughs, sits up straight and tucks her hair behind her ear.

'You are so stupid,' she drawls. 'You are SO STUPID. I don't want to marry some bonehead with a trust fund. Of course it's what I *should* do, but I'd die of boredom. I want to marry Jimmy – he's kind and he adores me – not like some fusty banker who'd treat me with disdain and fuck his secretary at any opportunity. I want Jimmy.'

I can't help but roll my eyes. 'Such a cliché, Caro. Wouldn't therapy have been cheaper? At least it might help with some of your other issues. They're not going away, no matter how hard Jim tries to help. Why make him a wreck too?'

There is no point to this, I think. She hates me, we are trying to wound each other with words and neither of us will really land a fatal blow. Caro's pupils are enormous, black and boring into me.

'Oh stop it. You don't get to have an opinion here, you fucking single white female. Wearing green to upstage me at my own engagement party. Christ, I shouldn't even have to indulge your jealousy and delusions. Everyone's a wreck, Grace, you should understand that. But we're adults. We'll work out a good understanding. I'll earn the money and he'll be an upstanding chap and our life will be nice. Simple. Normal. I *want* normal. He won't be like Lionel, never there, never warm, always desperate for the next thing.' She draws on her cigarette. 'It'll all be just grand. But for that to happen, it's becoming increasingly obvious that you probably need to not be

A. THING.' She emphasises those last two words, looking at me, not laughing now.

'Jimmy loves you, you're like a weird sister wife, aren't you? Always around, but not quite his. Part of the family, but you're not – not really. Sophie is obsessed with a good deed. You were just one of them. Why didn't you take the hint when you hit 18 and slink off? A grown adult with a boring job isn't quite the prize that a child with a dead mother is. You're no use.'

She's almost shouting, flailing her cigarette in the air. My hands are curled into tight little balls, and I can feel the urge to pull at my throat welling up in me. I move towards her and she leans back, her eyes widening just a little. My head is boiling hot now, and I take one useless deep breath, trying to dispel the adrenaline I can feel flooding my entire body.

* * *

What might I have done differently in that moment? Would I have pushed her violently, right in the chest, forcing her backwards over the balcony? Would I have grabbed at her foot as she fell, realising my impulsive rage and trying to rectify it – all in the space of a second? Or would I have loomed over her and said something equally as devastating in the hope that I would somehow gain a valuable point or two off her? It's something I've mulled over many times, an interesting little 'choose your own adventure' where the path you take leads to dramatically different end scenarios. In all my revised scenarios, I deal with it less impulsively, with a little more style. But then, that's hindsight for you. In reality, I did nothing. Caro fell off that balcony all by herself, her thin little body unable to cushion her fall. She was dead within seconds. I told you I won. That is, of course, until I didn't.

CHAPTER ELEVEN

George Thorpe runs through every development surrounding my appeal. He's meticulous, I'll give him that. So meticulous that I'm nodding along silently wanting him to hurry up and just give me the highlights. The man seems to think he has to recap every single part of the case before we can get to the part which hopefully gets me out of this place. Am I bored by my own wrongful conviction? Now there's a thing.

Once he leaves, curtailed by the buzzer which signals the end of visiting time here at Limehouse, we're escorted back to our cells in silence. I want to write down what he's said and absorb it all in my own time, but prison doesn't recognise the need to be alone. Sure, you can be incredibly lonely here, but you're never actually given any time to just be by yourself. And for me, that usually means that Kelly will be hovering nearby. In this case, she's sitting on my bunk when I get back.

I don't believe in God, but I swear sometimes I think that Kelly was sent by some vengeful angel to piss me off. If an all-seeing deity really does live in the sky, then bravo for conjuring up a suitable punishment for my actions in the shape of Kelly McIntosh as a cellmate. Kelly is bent over her foot, filing her toenails on my mattress. There are nail clippings on my bed.

'Wotcha!' she says, without looking up. 'How was the brief?'

As far as I know, Kelly has never attempted to appeal her sentence, nor met with a lawyer, nor protested her innocence like so many others do in here. As if anyone else cares about your situation when they have their own to contend with. It's like hearing about other people's children – or worse – hearing about other people's tiresome mental health problems. She's been in here before. This time it's for blackmailing men over sexy photos, when she was younger it was for robbing people on the Caledonian Road. She likes to say that the crime rate in N1 dropped by 80 per cent when she was put away. Kelly is a woman who doesn't like change. Her crime works, she says, blithely ignoring her repeated incarcerations, why change your modus operandi? Except she doesn't say modus operandi because Kelly would undoubtedly think that was a Latin American soap opera.

'Oh the usual,' I say as I hover over her and look pointedly at the toenail shavings with what I hope is a suitable amount of withering disgust. Nothing gets to Kelly though. You cannot shame her, upset her, embarrass her. It would be fascinating, if she weren't such an empty vessel. A psychologist could spend hours with her before reluctantly concluding that maybe there's not always something hidden in the depths of the psyche. Some people inhabit shallower pools. Kelly spent most of her time in the paddling variety.

'So are you getting out or what? Did your fella find what he was looking for? I suppose you need a witness, huh? Is your mate still not talking to ya?' It bothers me that Kelly takes such an interest. I'm sure she's looked up my case, since I barely tell her anything and yet she asks me questions that make it obvious that she knows more than she should. The story is out there, the *Daily Mail* practically had a reporter assigned to my trial, I can't expect other people not to want to know more. But I don't want anyone in here gleaning anything that they can embellish and giving it to a journalist when I get out. I want to disappear back into my old life. Or not so much old life but the life I planned to start before this hiccup.

I give her a bland run-through of my meeting, how we're hoping that there will be a decision soon, how I feel confident in my appeal. She moves off my bed and sits cross-legged on the floor like a little girl as I shake down my sheet and smooth out the pillow, desperately hoping her feet haven't been on it.

'Isn't it mad,' she says as she starts painting her toenails a lurid shade of coral, 'how I've done so much bad shit and nobody knows my name, and you ended up, like, a celebrity for something you didn't even do?'

Kelly is obviously annoyed that I've fascinated so many, as though I don't deserve the dubious attention I've received. As though it'll springboard me onto a reality dance programme and get me a hair-care deal and a photo spread in *OK!* magazine to tearfully talk about my ordeal. After months of living cheek by jowl with the woman, I know this to be exactly Kelly's dream.

I don't know how to explain that women like her are a dime a dozen. She's not going to end up on the front page of the tabloids because there's nothing really salacious in her story. Sure, she's attractive to a point, and there's a sex angle to her crimes (it always helps), but there's nothing unique about someone hustling for money after a bad start in life. Nell Gwyn did it centuries ago, and she did it with more style than Kelly can ever hope to have.

'I guess I just got lucky,' I say, rolling my eyes.

'But did you never do anything bad before? Not even the odd shoplift? We was mad for a bit of that down at the local Sassy Girl, I used to shove tonnes of stuff down my trackie bottoms and sell it on at the local car boot on Saturdays. My mum couldn't believe how well I saved my pocket money. That shop got a bit fancy later on though, started sticking tags on things and we had to move on.' She smiles at this memory, as if it's as wholesome as something Enid Blyton might've conjured up. I smile too, well practised in making it look real. A fake smile takes work – it doesn't quite reach your eyes, and your facial muscles seem to sense that they're only going through the motions so it feels like you're dragging them along. And yet it can't look sarcastic, as half-hearted smiles so often do.

'Nope,' I say. 'Nothing really. I've lived a pretty dull life.'

I know it's just a coincidence. I know she's only saying Sassy Girl because there was one on every high street. I'm certain she doesn't know that Simon Artemis is my father. She wouldn't know who Simon Artemis was. She doesn't know who owns that shop, whose stuff she was shoving down her pants to flog on a Saturday morning. I look back at Kelly, but she's lost interest, immersed in applying a top coat to her newly painted toes. I grab my notepad and head to the computer room to go over my meeting with Thorpe. But I find that my fingers are already lightly pulling at the skin on my throat. I don't like coincidences.

* * *

I find a space in the so-called computer room as far away from other people as possible and sit down. The room has three chunky monitors which look like they were donated by Amstrad back in the early Eighties. Supposedly, computers are being slowly allowed into cells in some places, but Limehouse seems to be low down on the list of prisons to receive such privileges. There are computer literacy courses available here, as if anyone wants to learn how to send emails and write a word document, when really most of us are just here to browse

Facebook and search for that ex who dumped you for the girl who worked in HR, to see if they're happy.

I write down everything my lawyer said in bullet points and go over them again and again, until I think I've got it all. Isn't it absurd? Everything that I've done in the past few years, all the plans and all the death. The tunnel vision ambition I'd cherished, fuelled and successfully achieved and then . . . this.

She fell and I was arrested, charged, and tried with murder. She fell like the drunken emaciated mess she was and I ended up here in a tracksuit paying a man in tortoiseshell glasses hundreds of pounds an hour to try and find proof of my innocence. How can you prove something didn't happen when the only witness is you? Caro will never be able to tell the truth about that night, and I suspect she wouldn't even if she could. She'd find this amusing.

I've been in close proximity to death, if you forgive the perverse brag. I've found that seeing death happen in real time often panics people, makes them nut out – scream and cry and faint and run in circles. Thankfully, it's never had that effect on me. I've always known it was coming, perhaps that's the difference? But with Caro, I had no idea. She wobbled sure, but the suggestion that she might actually fall never entered my head. Perhaps it just felt too obvious – people fall off balconies drunk in Magaluf, not in Clapham. And it was amazingly sudden – and so quiet. She didn't shriek or wail. There was no hand to grab onto as in a movie. One minute she was there, the next she wasn't. If I hadn't been watching her, been inches away from her face, I wouldn't have believed it. And so I panicked. My usual detached approach to witnessing the end of a life deserted me and my vision went blurry. I sank to my knees, holding onto the stone spindles, looking between them to see if I could spot her. But all I saw was the well-clipped hedge which surrounded the flats. I didn't yell, or run to fetch someone. I didn't even notice my phone in my hand. Nobody really knows how long I sat there, but it can't have been more than a couple of minutes. Jimmy told the police that he came to find out why we were still outside long after the time it would take to smoke a cigarette. He told them that I hated her. Jimmy told the police a lot of things.

* * *

I heard footsteps and turned towards the French windows. He stood there and I looked up, suddenly aware of reality.

'Where is Caro, Grace?' He didn't wait for a response. I pointed (I think I pointed) towards the balcony and he stepped over me and looked down. I never saw what he saw. I didn't look. And by the time we were allowed to leave the flat later that morning, she was gone. But Jimmy saw her. And he didn't scream or moan or let out a guttural wail like you'd imagine. He just turned back towards me, crouched down and grabbed at my hands like he wanted to rip my arms from their sockets.

'What have you done?' he whispered, his face screwed up in confusion and shock. 'What the fuck have you DONE?'

I just looked at him. He lurched to his feet, crashed back through the French doors and I heard the flat door slam. The girl inside whose face I have completely forgotten must have called the police. I was still sitting on the balcony when they arrived, wailing sirens and three uniformed officers. They were quickly followed by an ambulance, which seemed strangely funny to me, a true triumph of hope over experience. She *was* dead, wasn't she? Such a performance.

I was given a blanket, helped to my feet, led back to the sitting room and left with the female officer, who insisted that I drink some water. She told me her name was Asha, and explained that I was in shock. That felt ridiculous to me. I didn't like Caro, this had solved a huge problem for me and besides, I hadn't really *seen* anything. But looking back, she was probably right. I felt achingly cold, I couldn't stop shaking and I needed to pee every fifteen minutes. Jimmy didn't come back upstairs, and I kept asking where he was. The other girl had vanished by then, and I felt too tired to protest when Asha said that I wouldn't be able to go downstairs and find them. In my head, I replayed the moment that Caro fell as calmly as possible. How close was I? Did she look scared? Could I have done anything?

As I went over it all, my body started to relax and I could feel the anxiety slipping away. I was wrestling control back by working through the chain of events. To have a moment of panic was acceptable – it's not every day a woman you had sort of wished might die actually does just that right in front of your eyes – but any more than a moment would be indulgent and worse, damaging. Even though it was an obvious accident, I'd have to answer questions. I'd come under scrutiny from the police, something which could be potentially catastrophic. If I didn't hold it together I might make this situation worse for myself.

By the time a detective came upstairs, I had warmed up, sobered up, and firmed up my story. The man introduced himself as Greg Barker, but didn't need to ask mine, calling me Grace the moment he sat down on the blue velvet sofa and pulled up his trousers so that I could see his yellow socks. They had little hot dogs on them. I hope his kids bought him those for Father's Day. I hope he pulled them on in the dark when he was getting ready. There's no excuse for comedy socks on a grown man. Especially one investigating a tragic death at 5 a.m.

Detective Barker was fairly brusque, but not in an unkind way. I appreciated it, actually; I was fed up with Asha's hushed tones and arm stroking. I sometimes wish I could wear a badge like some rescue dogs do when they've had a rough life: 'Aggressive, do not pet'.

'I'm sorry to inform you that Caroline Morton was declared dead by my paramedic colleagues earlier this morning. Obviously you've had a terrible shock, Ms Bernard, but it's imperative that we get a clear sense of what happened here tonight and for that to happen, we really would like to question you sooner rather than later.'

He fixed me with his grey eyes, and I considered pushing back, demanding to go home, have a shower, and take off this outfit which felt absurdly flimsy in the morning light. I wanted to put on a thick jumper and high-waisted trousers. I wanted a structured blazer enclosing my body before I talked to the police. But Greg Barker was still staring at me. And I wondered if it said anything to the police when witnesses stalled. The police aren't exactly known for their open-mindedness and staunch refusal to make assumptions, so I imagine any reluctance on my part to follow protocol would mean a big black mark being levelled against me.

'It's just so fucking awful,' I said, pushing my left eyebrow up with my palm. 'So needless. Poor Caro. Poor Jim. Can I see him before we talk?'

At this, Barker tilted his gaze just a fraction. 'I'm afraid that won't be possible today. But Mr Latimer's family have been called and he's in good hands, so don't worry too much.'

I'm his fucking family. His mother will be a ghoul, weeping and repeatedly talking about how terrible it all is. His sister will become increasingly anxious and retreat into herself. And John will try to be practical. Help arrange things. Family friends will turn up as if they're needed and not just there to signpost their own goodness by making their presence known early on. The kind of people who get to funerals early so they can sit near the front and signal to those sitting further back that they are important. But Jimmy needs someone to scream at. Or be silent with. Or sit in his old bedroom and watch old episodes of *The Sopranos* with because sometimes that's all that helps.

Again, to push or accede? This time, I thought it would only make me look caring to insist.

'Sir' (men always like being called sir), 'I want to make sure my friend is OK. He's just lost his fiancée, surely I can just see him for five minutes – if his family haven't arrived yet I think he'll need me.'

Again, Barker settled his gaze somewhere just below my ear and let out a tiny grunt. 'I'm afraid it won't be possible today. I assure you my officers will look after him.'

Right. Did that mean that Jimmy had left already? Or did that really mean that the police didn't want us to talk before they'd taken our statements separately? Or worse. Much worse. Did it mean that Jimmy didn't want to speak to me?

'What the fuck have you DONE?' The last thing he had said to me. I'd assumed it was said in panic, in disbelief. In that specific momentary madness that the brain foists on you when something happens that you cannot process normally. But what if it wasn't just of the moment? Could that thought have taken hold? Could it even now have laid down roots in Jimmy's trusting brain, burrowing deep so that when the first shock wore off and he'd managed to get some sleep, he'd wake up and believe it?

Jimmy wasn't the kind of person to not trust his own thoughts. Me, I had thoughts all the time that I dismissed, knowing them to be warped, self-defeating, treacherous. Intrusive thoughts which feel like your own, but they aren't, not really. They've muscled their way into your brain and dressed up as your thoughts. 'Your mother was a whore', 'you want to fuck that old man until he collapses', you know the kind of thing. Jimmy won't know not to trust his thoughts because when has he ever had a thought so scary or perverse that he's come to understand that his brain isn't always his ally? If he wondered whether I somehow played a part in Caro's death, then why would he question it? His brain had come up with the seed, would that be enough for him to run with it?

I hoped I hadn't betrayed myself in front of the policeman. He was still watching me, waiting for my answer. Outside, the sun was rising ever higher in the sky.

'OK,' I said. 'How can I help everyone?'

* * *

I was taken to the police station in Battersea, and made a mental note not to cross the river again any time soon. Drunk men stumbled about in red chinos, drunk girls fell off balconies. Nothing good happens there.

Despite the carefully curated oatmeal atmosphere – constant offerings of tea, a cheery woman behind the desk offering to get me a jumper – everything suddenly felt like a trap. Why weren't me, Jimmy, and that bland friend of Caro's huddled together, sharing our shock, explaining the night and then being released to go and recover together? I was led into an interview room that looked exactly like it might have been hastily built for a mediocre ITV crime drama and left there for fifteen minutes. I looked around for a mirrored wall where someone would potentially be observing me, or an obvious microphone designed to catch out a weak criminal prone to blurting out his deeds when given five minutes alone, but there was nothing. Just me and the weak tea I was pretty much forced to accept. Why offer tea when you're facing prison? Give me some vodka and at least I could have some fun when the questions get going.

When the door finally opened it wasn't Detective Barker but a young woman wearing a polo neck and a silk skirt. Both her gender and her outfit exposed the internalised misogyny that I would normally give myself a pass on because how does anyone grow up not absorbing it at least a little? I do wince at the sight of a female pilot though. Not sure I can let myself off for that.

The detective, upon closer inspection wasn't so young, but she wasn't exactly a grizzled Jane Tennison type either. No wedding ring. Nice nails. I wondered what red that is, Crimson Tide? I was always on the lookout for the perfect red.

'Hello, Grace. I'm so sorry to keep you waiting, we've been a bit all over the shop this morning, Sundays aren't normally as busy as today. All our cells are full and we're playing catch up. I'm Gemma Adebayo and my colleague joining us is Sandra Chisholm.' As she talked, a dumpy blonde woman in regulation police garb slipped into the room and sat down next to Adebayo. She smiled tightly.

'We're just here to have a chat about the sad events of this morning. It's not under caution or anything like that, Grace, it's just to get a statement so that we understand the chain of events and hopefully get some peace for Caroline's family.' Gemma raised her eyebrows in what I took to be an encouraging gesture and started the tape recorder, stating the date, time, and people present.

I spoke slowly, explaining everything that had happened at the party. I told the officers that Caro was drinking heavily, taking drugs, and that she'd seemed edgy, wound up and nervous. I didn't tell them anything we talked about, instead I said that we had a drunken chat about weddings and dresses, as though we were mates bonding over her special day. That seemed like something a bride would do at her engagement party with the best friend of her betrothed. That is, if the bride was a normal basic girl excited to have invites designed featuring love birds and gold embossed lettering and not an entitled mess marrying my best friend just because she wanted someone to love her who wasn't her father. Christ, what is wrong with women that they demand so little? 'Not your father' seemed like a low fucking bar. Does anyone have a father that doesn't disappoint in some low level but ultimately incredibly damaging way? Oscar Wilde (him again) once said, 'All women become like their mothers. That is their tragedy. No man does, and that is his.' There's too much that's wrong with this to unpack but just to say, he'd have been better off looking at the men who end up like their fathers. You'd come closer to fixing the problems of society if you focused your search there.

I expressed my utter (and genuine) shock that Caro had fallen in the middle of our cosy chat. 'I'd only been to their flat twice and I'd not clocked the balcony before. I don't really do heights so I wasn't too clear on how high the drop was or how precarious her position was, but I certainly don't remember thinking that she was in any danger. It's just . . . so awful.'

It was their turn to say something now. I put my hands over my face and breathed in through my nose, shuddering slightly as I exhaled. Suitably traumatised, I imagine, even for these women who've seen it all. The older blonde nodded, clearly warming to me. I was a sympathetic figure here, a shaken, tired girl worried about her friend, finding it all overwhelming. And some of that was true. Adebayo smiled quickly, but didn't rush to reassure.

'Thank you, Grace, I know you must be tired. I'm just going to run through some questions and then we'll let you go. You must be longing to get home.'

CHAPTER TWELVE

Bryony died before Caro's accident. Looking back, it's funny to think of Caro's family gossiping about Bryony's tragic demise, just weeks before her own unhappy end. I wonder if Caro's death hit them as hard as Bryony's hit Simon. I suspected (correctly) that Bryony would be the kicker for him. You could always marry again, and a man like my father, well, he wouldn't wait long. A new squeeze half his age would emerge before the headstone had time to be engraved, I was sure of that. But Bryony was his only child and, unlike his wife who spent her time shuffling between plastic surgery offices and stuffy restaurants in Monaco, Bryony actually chose to live with Simon. I thought her death might well tip him into some kind of action. So Janine would go first.

I'd decided how to kill Janine before I'd even thought about anyone else in the family. That seems ridiculous really, but there it is. A lot of these plans have come down to luck, despite the constant plotting I did as a teenager, coming up with meticulous and ingenious ways to kill these people. It turns out that as with everything, the reality is always slightly more given over to chance, or an idea that pops into your head at 3 a.m. Janine's murder was a bit of both. I read an article in some Sunday supplement three years ago about the rise in 'the internet of things', a term which gets bandied around a lot by excited nerds but basically means a bunch of devices connected to the internet which can communicate with each other. They have automated systems and can gather information and carry out tasks – collate a shopping list when you run out of cleaning products for example, or turn on your heating when you're set to come back from holiday. It's hardly the vision we had of the near future, this isn't *The Jetsons* and we still don't have flying skateboards – but we can now expect our houses to do more of the work. No keys needed for the front door when it just takes a fingerprint, no time spent vacuuming when a robot can do it for you while you're out. At the moment, the most normal people come to having a smart house is by buying an Alexa or something like it, which they smugly instruct to play music or google something. Mainly in front of bored friends who dread coming over. But for the uber-wealthy, it can mean linking up your entire house and everything in it.

Guess what Janine had done with her penthouse in Monaco? That's what I mean about chance. I read that piece with a slight hangover and only a vague interest one morning, and three weeks later, Janine was featured in the magazine *Lifestyle!*, a monthly glossy which mainly featured interviews with very rich women photographed on plump sofas and let them talk about whatever they wanted. Normally that was a charity lunch or a renovation project which involved a lot of glass and marble and an overuse of the word 'authentic'. I think the only people that actually bought this magazine were other rich women who wanted to hate-read pieces about their society rivals, but they ran a lot of adverts for exclusive interior design companies and craftsmen and so the serpent ate the tail and the magazine stayed in business.

Janine's feature focused on her new terrace, something she'd added on a whim when she realised that she wanted somewhere to do yoga in the morning sun. The roof garden was at a slightly tilted angle, she explained, and was much better suited to the evening light. I wondered how the interviewer reacted to this, presumably with genuine sympathy for such a terrible burden. But she didn't stop at the terrace, which seemed to have been modelled on some kind of Grecian vision, with large terracotta pots and an honest-to-God white marble fountain twice the size of anything else in the space. There was a tour of the rest of the penthouse, which spanned three floors and housed nine bedrooms, six bathrooms, and a, wait for it, 'serenity room' which seemed serene only in that it didn't contain any furniture apart from one cream sofa and a floor-to-ceiling mirror. Janine explained that she retreated to it when 'life gets overwhelming and I need to recentre', which didn't explain the mirror but perhaps sometimes it's better not to ask. The reason she moved to Monaco, she explained, was for her health. A heart scare made her 'reassess how she lived'. There must be an awful lot of health benefits in the principality. The tax loopholes? Not mentioned.

As the interview spread out over 5,000 words, the interviewer clearly got slightly desperate for something new and original and prompted Janine to talk about her clever wardrobe. 'Tell us about your dream closet, it's got some special features I can imagine every woman reading this will be dying to hear about.' Accompanied by a photo of an enormous walk-in wardrobe, Janine explained that every item in her cupboards was itemised, photographed from every angle, and stored in a database which she could access from an iPad. It made dressing in the mornings a dream, she told the magazine, because the system could tell her which item to match with what. 'It reminds me of clothes I'd forgotten about. Just last week I bought a beautiful Chanel bouclé jacket in royal blue, only to find, when I added it to the database, that I had two exactly the same!' Those jackets retail for £5,000. How we all laughed. The technology didn't stop with the wardrobes though. That was just the start. Everything in the home had been connected to the internet, Janine explained. The lights were no longer turned on with switches, the oven did not have buttons ('Not that I've cooked in a while,' she trilled) and even her morning sauna was temperature-controlled by the smart hub. Every room was able to be locked remotely, in case of a security breach, and it gave her so much comfort to know that, she confided, 'I don't completely understand how it all works really, but our wonderful housekeeper has really mastered it and I barely have to do a thing.' That was the motto of Janine's life really.

It was her mention of the sauna which really piqued my interest. It seemed like the set-up in a crime novel and I had visions of infiltrating her house, perhaps as a maid, before shutting her in the sauna and watching her beg for mercy. Perhaps this wasn't exactly feasible. But the remote element appealed, and it felt like a house connected to the internet would be worth at least a little research. Could you use this technology to nefarious ends? Was it completely secure or could it be hacked with little effort?

The web was full of stories about smart devices breaking down, malfunctioning and messing up. Couples who'd split up when their AI gadgets accidentally mentioned the name of a mistress, children exposed to swear words, kettles boiling for hours on end and heating systems which were impossible to work. But the really interesting flaws in this kind of intelligent design were in the security element. There was a spate of scare stories online about people breaking into baby monitor streams and parents hearing strangers talking to their children at night through the devices. There were reports of burglar alarms being easily hacked into and silenced well before intruders even entered the house. Frazzled families claimed that their smart devices had been taken over by criminals who demanded ransoms to stop tampering with the temperature and playing music at all times of the day and night. In most cases, this was because the system which these devices ran on was not encrypted nor updated. Sure, some of these companies took it a little more seriously, but most businesses just sold you the kit and told you to make sure you had a good password.

I had to find out whether it would be possible to hack into the system Janine had, but where to start? I couldn't just type 'how to find a hacker' into Google and take my chances (I actually did do this initially, and felt incredibly foolish for days afterwards). Moving on, I searched for academics who were doing research on smart devices, and found a woman who'd written a paper on the future implications for home security in the era of smart houses. She worked at UCL and, God bless our higher education system, her email address was right below her name on the website for anyone to find. I emailed Kiran Singh from the mailbox of sarah.summers@journo.com and asked her if she'd have some time for an interview. I told her I was hoping to place a piece with the *Evening Standard* on the dangers of inviting this kind of technology into our homes.

Everyone always wants their name in print. Even though print is dying on its arse, people still get excited to see themselves mentioned. Online, you disappear within minutes mostly. But your gran can tear out the page of a newspaper and show her mates. Perhaps frame your achievement in the downstairs loo, where you'll see the paper yellowing and curling every time you go in there to pee. Academics are no different. Kiran emailed me back within an hour to say that she'd be happy to speak to me and was the coming Friday any good?

We met at the café in the British Museum. Her idea, and a nice change from the normal banality of grabbing lunch from one of eight million Pret A Mangers in this city. I went armed with a notebook and a tape recorder, bought that morning from a tech shop on Tottenham Court Road, in the hopes that it made me look somewhat like a journalist. The recorder was guaranteed to be simple to use, I was told by the slightly desperate man selling it to me from his empty shop, nestled between two furniture megastores displaying identikit pale pink velvet sofas in the window displays. I switched it on and hoped for the best.

Kiran was a nice woman, if a little earnest, sitting at a table sipping green tea when I got there, but easily identifiable as an academic. Normal people don't wear cords. They think about it, perhaps even try some on in the near permanent half-price sale at Gap. But ultimately they realise that they cling to you, collect fluff like no other fabric on earth and worse still, they make you look like an academic. After some small talk, she was happy to get down to the topic in hand, and gave me a ton of helpful information on whether it was possible to use this technology to hurt someone. Kiran thought there was one obvious way she could see a hacker using these smart home devices maliciously. If you could obtain access to the owner's hub, then all bets were off.

The hub, she patiently told me once I'd asked her to go back and explain it again, was the brain box running all the gadgets in a smart home. It sends out commands and they obey. The hub can instruct the thermostat to increase the temperature in a home, or tell the TV to update the channels. Once a device is marked as 'trusted' by the hub, it's in the network and can converse with all the other gadgets.

Some of these smart devices run on end to end encryption. 'Amazon is generally pretty good with cloud security, but I wouldn't touch Ergos devices with a bargepole,' she said, sliding a finger across her neck. A lot of them didn't though, given that the companies are smaller and the resources limited. There were easy ways to get access to the hub, Kiran told me – if you can obtain the serial number from the owner, then it's a piece of cake.

'I see people post it online all the time,' she said, rolling her eyes. 'Even if it's not handed to you on a plate, there are ways of getting it by force if you've got basic hacking skills.'

Once a hacker gains control of the smart hub and the devices connected to it, the smart home can become a weapon for the person in charge.

'You could use the homeowner's cameras to spy on them,' she said, 'or gaslight someone by turning on music at certain times of day, opening doors, closing blinds.' I suppressed a smile, she wasn't to know how wonderful her hypothesis was. 'But mostly, we're not at that stage yet. Most people buy an Alexa or a Google device and use it to order milk. Sure, those devices are hackable, but the real danger is when everything in your house is connected, and we're not there yet. That technology is still in its infancy, the preserve of the very rich.'

I asked her who was doing this kind of hacking and she looked around the café quickly, as though we might be surrounded by people eager to know where to start. In actual fact, we were sitting between an elderly woman in a floral coat eating blueberry cake on one side, a Japanese couple who were busy taking selfies on the other, and a young guy with dark hair and a well-cut coat engrossed in a book sitting three tables in front of us.

'The big stuff is done by nation states – China, Russia, the US – though they deny it. Second-tier hacking tends to be groups focused on extortion – using webcams to blackmail LGBT people in the Middle East, for example. Then you've got isolated teens in their bedrooms who are totally self-taught and do it for laughs, because they're bored, who knows? They have time to mess with someone's head by interfering with their doorbell or turning off their heating, and then boast about it on Reddit or 4Chan or Babel . . .'

After a few more questions and a promise to get in touch when the article was done, I made my exit, careful to avoid the couple still determined to get that perfect selfie, and headed back to work. I walked briskly through the back streets behind Oxford Street, mulling over whether I could risk recruiting an accomplice to help me hack Janine's house or not. I'd been loath to outsource any part of my plan from the outset, unwilling to add any obvious tripwires when there would be so many already. But I was sure that I couldn't do it alone – my understanding of technology began and ended when I had to update my phone software – and I was already completely enamoured with the idea of Janine's own home turning on her. Could I find someone I trusted enough to help me do it?

* * *

That weekend, I spent twenty-eight hours online, rubbing at my eyes every five minutes and alternating between coffee and wine depending on my energy levels. I looked at the sites Kiran had mentioned, reading thousands of posts by amateur hackers who boasted of their successes, crowing about infiltrating clouds, hubs, phones, and cameras in language that was almost completely alien to me. Was it lazy to imagine they were all scrawny 16-year-olds who'd not seen daylight for weeks? Perhaps, but I have no doubt it was accurate nonetheless. There were many posts from people asking hackers to help them, mainly to spy on partners suspected of cheating. 'Girl (22) needs help to prove BF (28) is carrying on with co-worker. Help!' was typical of such a plea. Normally the replies offered to take the conversation private, so I didn't get to see what the result was, and whether a helpful hacker stepped up to the job.

But I was exhausted and tanked up on caffeine, so I posted a message. It didn't matter if it failed to attract anyone, but it was worth a shot. It was vague and short, explaining that I was female (16, I figured that might appeal to some white-knight nerd), and wanted help to mess with my horrible stepmother. I won't go into the details of some of the messages I received in the days that followed. Suffice to say, my plea was like honey to a bee. If the honey was a young vulnerable girl and the bee was a fucking swarm of old gross blokes. I replied to the least disgusting messages and blocked everyone else. I spent the next week drip-feeding further details to three users, seeing how they'd react, what they knew about hacking and what they'd want in return. The one I held out least hope for was ColdStoner17, who seemed not to be able to use proper words and replied at the most random times of day, often with gifs which I didn't understand. I was about to cut him loose when he messaged me at 7 a.m. one day as I was getting ready for work.

Yo, he typed, *when we freaking out the old lady then? I fucking hate my stepmom too. This can be like the therapy my dad won't pay for.* The language was basic but the full sentences were a start. I discovered that he was 17 (hence the username), lived in Iowa with his dad and the aforementioned evil stepmother, and spent a lot of time messing around on the internet when he should be doing his school work. I told him bluntly that it seemed unlikely he'd be a superstar hacker, but apparently I didn't understand 17-year-olds very well at all. He spent the entire morning bombarding me with all the ways he could infiltrate laptop cameras, mess with baby monitors, and turn off people's heating. It was mild stuff, but it still sounded more impressive than anything I could attempt, and so instead of binning him off, I engaged with him.

We talked a lot into the night on an encrypted instant messenger, as he told me how lonely he was and I told him fabricated stories about how much I hated my parents. The more we spoke, the more he relaxed and used proper spelling. He told me how much he loved reading, and we bonded over a love of Jack Kerouac (I have never read any Kerouac but Google kept me just about up to speed). I deliberately held off on any proper details about my plan, happy to form a relationship with him first, albeit one based on lies and sexist fairy-tale stepmother tropes.

This went on for a few weeks, as I attempted to act like the fictitious 16-year-old he thought I was, while also giving him a confidence boost that I reckoned would help him feel indebted to me. He confided in me about being bullied when he was younger because his parents had got a divorce (I guess Iowa wasn't the most progressive of places) and he told me about his fears that he'd never get a girlfriend. Despite my attempts to keep it entirely chaste, sometimes I'd wake up to voice notes where he'd sing me little songs about how much I cheered him up, and I'd bat them away with smiley emojis. He was becoming infatuated. I'd forgotten how easy it was to manipulate teenage boys, but it came back to me pretty fast. I felt like I was on the right track with Pete (he told me his real name on day four, I told him that my name was Eve) and decided to press ahead and tell him a little bit more about what I wanted to do to Janine, my terrible stepmother.

I explained that she lived in Monaco (kind of like France, yes) and that she'd turned my dad against me over the years so that we were almost entirely estranged (not a complete lie). I wanted to freak her out and teach her a lesson. Did he know anything about smart houses? He knew a little, he said, but came back to me a day later fully clued up on the different methods used by companies who offered smart technology. The kid must have been up all night reading about all the ways you could infiltrate a home like Janine's, and he was confident that we could get into her hub. *The best way would be if we could get a new device into the house – if you can add another item to the system, we can take control of the whole thing. Are you planning a visit any time soon?* This threw me. I had hoped that we'd be able to access the home hub without ever having to set foot inside the property and I had no clue as to how I might be able to get into Janine's apartment without risking everything. I wasn't a cat burglar and I had no illusions about how well secured it would be. But then, I'd never actually been to Monaco to see how Janine lived for myself. I had some holiday to take, there was no harm in seeing the lie of the land, even if it meant knowing for sure that there was no way to carry out this particular plan.

I told Pete that I was going to be out there in a couple of weeks but wasn't sure if I'd actually be invited in. *She hates me lol,* I wrote, *and I usually stay with my mum at a hotel and see my dad when she's not around.* It was weak, but if Pete thought this was a weird familial set-up, he didn't say. Despite nearly being an adult, his family made him go to church twice a week and every day during the holidays, so I guess he didn't have a great yardstick for what was healthy.

I booked a week off work and sorted out a hotel in Monaco, which hit my finances hard. This entire project had drained a large amount of the savings I'd diligently gathered, and it pained me to see my hard-earned funds being depleted like this. I'd been putting a little bit aside every month since I started getting an allowance from Sophie and John (they obviously felt as though they had to treat me like one of their own in this respect. I felt uncomfortable about it, but I still took the money) and it gave me a sense of security that I didn't get from anything else. Every time I checked my savings account I felt a fresh sense of fury at the imbalance between the Artemis financial landscape and my own. I accept that this is ridiculous, given that I was spending my money in order to kill them, but not every emotion is rational.

Still, a week in the sunshine wasn't something to entirely despair about, and Monaco was tiny, roughly the size of Central Park, so deliberately bumping into Janine wouldn't be a problem as long as she was in town. Unfortunately, there were no guarantees for this, given the propensity of the super-rich to jet off at a moment's notice. Her Instagram was private, but she'd accepted a request to follow her from the handle 'Monaco deluxe', which was an account I'd made with pictures stolen from society sites. They showed the rich and powerful at parties and charity events – it was easy to repost them with gushing tributes to 'Mrs Daphne Baptiste, generously donating a beautiful mink coat to the Children's care fund' or 'Mrs Lorna Gold, who hosted an elegant evening soiree at her beautiful penthouse for the street dog society.' If these women ever even looked at my page, they would just accept the praise at face value. They were pillars of Monaco society, of course people wished to show some thanks. From that page I could see a little of what she was doing, but Janine wasn't a frequent poster, nor was she a talented photographer. Apart from a few posed pictures taken by professionals, the images on her account were mainly blurry photos of sunsets from private jet windows, the odd snap of a lunch table with a caption like, 'Great time catching up with Bob and Lily at Cafe Flore', and a few photos of family events. Bryony lived her life in real time on Instagram and it was invaluable. Janine was old school. Her last picture was three days ago, and was a close up of her slightly chubby bejewelled hands, showing off a dark red manicure. The caption said, 'Thanks again to @MonacoManis for a good job', so at least she was there for now.

I flew out on a Monday, and as soon as I'd showered off the sadness of a budget flight and a shuttle bus, I went out to explore. Of course, I knew where Janine's flat was. It's remarkable how easy it is to find out where people live. Even if they're not on the electoral roll, so many people geotag their locations, or follow accounts on social media from their area. If you follow eight different accounts with 'Islington' in their name, nobody gets a prize for figuring out where you get your morning paper. Even worse, people are so trusting that they post photos of the view from their bedroom windows, or of their own front doors. And for celebrities, it's even easier. A lot of the time, the media will report on the exact location of someone's home. If they're involved in something truly scandalous, they might even fly a helicopter over it, or mock up a floor plan. Janine gave me her address directly. She gave it to every reader of *Hello!* two years ago when she opened her doors for a reception to honour a Turkish businesswoman who was winning much praise for inventing a possible cure for eczema. The piece literally opened with 'Janine Artemis welcomes us to her beautiful penthouse in the Exodora building in Monaco's gilded playground.' The businesswoman by the way, was later sentenced to eight years in jail for taking close to £100 million in funding and fabricating research. The fight to eradicate eczema goes on.

It was a lovely warm day and I used the map on my phone to take me to the Exodora building, walking past cafés stuffed with feline-faced women and tubby men in shirts with contrasting collars, all of whom could have used some factor 50 earlier in their lives. The building was only ten minutes from my hotel, which was a relief because the heat was rising now and the hope of a nice walk was slightly marred by the supercars which left a trail of fetid petrol fumes in their wake every time they whizzed by me. It's said that one in three people who live in Monaco is a millionaire. I understand that rich people mainly stay alive in order to keep hold of their money, and that a tax haven like this one helps them to do that, but it felt like one big gated community where there's no need for open space or fresh air because the helicopter can take off in twenty minutes and zip you over to Switzerland or Provence if you find yourself craving it.

The building Janine lived in was stunning, in a sort of McMansion type of way. It was a cream stucco house, though house is a misnomer. I'd wondered why the Artemises had chosen a flat instead of a secluded villa somewhere, but now I'd seen the place, I understood. The building was vast, stretching the length of at least six houses, and as it rose, balconies appeared, getting larger and larger. Roses bloomed off the sides of them, tumbling down as though they were allowed to grow wild, but retaining a very symmetrical appearance. Carefully arranged to look casual. The windows were floor to ceiling but all blocked out by blinds, and the top of the building had a large flag pole from which hung the principality's colours. I stood back and counted the floors. Eight in total, and I knew from the design magazine that the Artemis property took up three. Craning my neck, I could just see the glass balcony at the very top where Janine liked to do her yoga in the morning sun. I walked around to the back of the property, but it was shut off with a large and imposing wall and a gate which presumably led to the car park. There was a big metal entrance door to one side, which suggested the presence of a goods lift.

Naturally, CCTV cameras were dotted about, I could see them in at least five places. For all that, the main door was remarkably easy to access, only a wrought-iron gate and a big gold knocker stood between me and the intercom. Oh, and a man standing guard at the door. I was fucked if I thought I could just walk in though. Security was almost certainly why they'd chosen this place. It was fortified and presumably had porters on call 24/7 on high alert.

Disheartened, I walked down the street and found a coffee shop where I ordered a café creme and messaged Pete. *Had a huge fight with Dad and can't stay here, no chance of getting into wicked SM's.*

Guess it's all off. I added a crying emoji for full effect and lit a cigarette. He pinged back immediately: *oh no, that sucks. Can you give ur dad something to take home?* Now there was a thought. Maybe I couldn't get into the flat, but there must be staff coming and going all day. Janine clearly hadn't lifted a finger in several decades apart from to point and click at hired helpers. There must be someone who would be open to taking a small device into the property in return for suitable compensation.

I spent the next two days watching the people who entered the building through the side entrance. At first it was hard to tell which flats they were going to, but I built up a profile of them, using my eagle eyes and my perceptive acumen to figure out who worked where. Of course I didn't. It turned out that the staff at Janine's all had to wear white hospitality uniforms with Artemis sewn in italics on the breast. Nothing says 'I've lost my humanity' like making underpaid migrant workers wear your name across their hearts so it was very on brand for this family. Slightly nervous-looking women would emerge carrying laundry bags and handing them over to drivers of dry-cleaning vans, or they would sign for parcels from delivery men and head back indoors quickly, as though they were being timed. I never had the chance to talk to any of them, such was their rush. But there was also a lady who emerged every day at 8 a.m., 2 p.m., and 6 p.m. on the dot with a fluffy little Bichon Frise, and marched off down the street to the promenade. I hate fluffy dogs. They're always so fucking yappy and up themselves. I assume they're that way because their owners make them so. You never see a nice calm person with a Bichon Frise. It's always permanently discontented middle-aged women who communicate their disappointments through the dog. 'Betty can't sit here, it's too hot and she's getting anxious.' Betty is fine. You, on the other hand, might want to contact a therapist.

On the second day of surveillance, I went to get a coffee and headed down to the promenade prepared for the 6 p.m. dog walk. Sure enough, the lady in the humanity-free uniform came into view, dragging the unwilling fluffy bundle. I waited for her to pass me, and I followed her for a few minutes before coming to walk beside her.

'Cute dog,' I said and smiled. She was tiny this woman, with dark black hair pulled into a low bun. She barely reacted, and would've kept walking if the dog had not jumped up at me, leaving faint dirt marks on my pale trousers.

'No, Henry!' she cried, bending down to admonish the dog, who looked remarkably uncontrite. I assured her that it was fine but she stopped by a wall and pulled a handkerchief out of her pocket and attempted to brush my legs vigorously.

'Is he your dog?' I asked, even though it was obvious from her expression that she didn't have any affection for the animal. She told me she walked it for her employer, and I expressed sympathy, telling her that it was boring to walk a dog every day – especially such a rude one. She smiled at that, before quickly looking around as though Janine was going to jump out in front of us and berate her for not praising the little fellow.

I kept pace beside her as she carried on walking, asking how she found Monaco and telling her that I'd only recently arrived and was finding it all a bit overwhelming.

'The people are rude,' she said abruptly. 'Everyone thinks money is everything and nobody is kind.' Well what about your employer, I asked, were they not kind? And then it all came out. How Janine harangued her about the smallest things, how she worked six days a week and only got Thursdays off and even then she was called if needed. 'She took money from my wages last week because a shirt had shrunk at the dry cleaners!' she exclaimed, shaking her head. Lacey, for that was her name, sent money home and supported three teenage children. She had worked here for three years, before that she'd been in Dubai for another family. They'd not been much better but at least there she'd had her own accommodation. We walked the length of the promenade before she turned around, the dog whining in protest.

I expressed sympathy, and told her that Janine sounded like a total monster, careful not to say her name or give any hint that I knew her. And like that, I suddenly felt I had an in.

'I work for a newspaper back in the UK. I'm thinking that there's a story in rich women like this exploiting their hardworking housekeepers. We could expose these people, and shame them into behaving properly.'

She shook her head. 'No, I need this job. I can't speak to you no more.'

Lacey increased her pace but I stayed beside her.

'I would never ever use your name or say who you worked for. But we could hold a mirror up to this behaviour. The newspaper is famous and these women would read it. If they all knew that society thought it was unacceptable, they'd be better – if not for you, at least so that people thought they were good employers.' This was total bollocks of course. A hundred articles had been written about the way the uber-rich treat their staff and nothing had ever changed. If anything, it was getting worse, with stories coming out constantly about maids who'd escaped terrible and inhumane conditions while their former bosses suffered little to no consequences. I was exploiting her too, I know that. But needs must, and at least I could offer her something for her cooperation.

She shook her head again, more vehemently. 'I can't do it. I need this job.' We were nearly back at the house.

'OK, I respect that. But I'd barely need anything from you and of course we would pay you for your trouble. That would be cash in hand for your family, Lacey.' She slowed down but didn't look at me. 'Think about it?' I said. 'If you're interested, I'll wait here at 2 p.m. tomorrow. You'd help so many people in the same situation.' With one last tug on the leash, she and Henry headed back to the penthouse. She'd do it, I thought, as I saw her look back at me. If Janine had treated her with a fraction of decency I'd have no way in here. Lucky for me, she hadn't.

I took myself out for dinner that night, and dressed up for the occasion. Even in my knee-length black dress and neon pink heels, I still looked pretty casual by Monaco standards. Despite the heat, fur wraps were in abundance, PETA clearly hadn't made it to the principality recently. There were diamonds the size of quail eggs stuck to earlobes and fingers at every turn, and watches that I couldn't identify but knew would be worth more than enough to ensure the downpayment on a flat. Would I be like this when I had money? It was hard to think of a super-rich person who had taken a different path. Bill Gates perhaps, but who wants to wear ugly trainers with chinos and be that earnest? None of these people looked happy. It's a cliché that money doesn't buy happiness – tell that to someone struggling on the minimum wage – but it's clearly true that it breeds dissatisfaction for many. Perhaps the difference for me would be that the money would be mine. So many of these women were wealthy because of their husbands, and that must make for a lifetime of insecurity. Because rich men don't tend to stick to one wife, do they? They exchange and upgrade, and very rarely do they say, 'Thank you for being by my side, darling. Thank you for raising our children and running our house and taking care of all the emotional labour, which enabled me to work without distraction. It's time for something new now but here is 50 per cent of everything we built together.' No. They lawyer up and try to shaft you, hiding their money offshore, pleading poverty, arguing that you never contributed in any way, protesting that the kids don't need that much. Or they do what my dad did, and relinquish all responsibility as quickly as possible.

On my way to Monaco, I saw two women looking at a cabinet of rings in duty-free. I heard one of them say to the other, 'Just once I'd like to be able to buy myself something like that without asking my husband if I can.' I would never have that problem. I would never be beholden, timid or lassoed to someone else like that. And if I ended up with a partner, I would be magnanimous about the money. We would be equals in it, and enjoy what it could give us. Not diamond rings which made you afraid of being robbed in the street, but experiences and comfort. A life with endless possibility. Perhaps I didn't know how it would affect me until I had it, but looking at the people around me in the restaurant, I felt certain that I would try to remember how not to do it. And having the Artemis family at the back of my mind would help. Every now and then I would chuck a lot of their cash at charities I felt sure that they'd have hated. It wouldn't ameliorate their mark on the world, but it would be a small pleasure to start a fund with their name attached to help squatters fight eviction notices.

Back at the hotel, I messaged Pete to tell him that I thought I could get my dad to take something to the house, and asked him what would work best, before turning off my phone and falling into a deep sleep.

The next morning I woke early. Pete had replied with a stream of messages about hubs, unencrypted devices, and routers, which was all written out in techy language I couldn't quite decipher. I sent back a fairly terse message asking him to be clearer and went for a run. An hour later, I grabbed a book, headed for the promenade, and settled down at a café to wait for Lacey. It was nice to do absolutely nothing for an entire morning, and it almost felt like I was really on holiday – if you discounted the fizzy feeling in my stomach which told me I was slightly on edge. I read a few chapters of *Israel Rank: The Autobiography of a Criminal*, which I'd come across years ago when I was still considering what to do about the Artemis family. It had been sitting on my bookshelf for a while, but I'd noticed it again when I was packing for Monaco and shoved it in my bag. It's a book about a man in Edwardian England who kills his family for revenge. I wonder if you can possibly decipher the appeal? At 1.45 p.m., I paid for my three cups of coffee and one mini doughnut, trying not to kick off at the waitress when I saw I had been stiffed for 26 euros, and walked towards Janine's flat.

Just after 2 p.m., I saw Lacey and Henry hove into view. As she got closer, I gave a small wave and fell into step with her. We exchanged brief greetings and I talked lightly about the heat for a few minutes until the dog forced us to stop so that he could relieve himself.

'What would you need from me?' Lacey asked anxiously, as she rummaged in her pocket for a plastic bag. I wanted to hug her, and I'm not one for spontaneous physical contact.

'I think the easiest way would be to put a little microphone in the flat and record how she talks to you. That way, we have hard proof for a story but we still won't use your name or implicate you in any way. After that, me and you could just have a chat about the industry and what needs to change. How does that sound?'

Lacey bent down to pick up the dog shit and said something I didn't quite hear. 'I said how much,' she repeated when I asked her to say it again. I thought fast. I had to go low for financial reasons, but how much did she really expect? If I went too high, she might assume there was more to come.

'A thousand,' I said. 'You can have it in any currency you like, cash in hand. But my editor won't sign off on more. Would that help your family, Lacey?' I couldn't tell from her expression whether or not this was a decent amount in her eyes, and we kept walking.

'OK,' she said finally. 'But the money upfront and you promise not to use my name or the name of Madame or mention anything about Henry.' I was puzzled, and it clearly showed in my face. 'He is a rude dog but I love him,' she said simply.

'OK, nothing about Henry,' I promised, trying not to look incredulous. She was going to let a stranger put a recording device in the house of her terrible employer and she was worried about the ratty dog who clearly hated her. Other people are truly a mystery.

I explained that I would meet her the next day at the same time and give her a device, which she would have to connect to the main hub – did she know how to do that? She did. It turned out that she was the person who had to learn how to use the smart house technology.

'Madame doesn't understand but she can use voice commands now.' Fine, good. Once it was connected, she didn't need to do anything else, the device would pick up conversation and feed it back to me for the article. We could have a chat on her day off and that would be that. Lacey nodded and made to leave for home.

'Bring the money tomorrow – in euros. I won't do it without the money first.' Canny. I respected that.

'Of course,' I said and wished her a good afternoon. Henry flashed his tiny teeth at me and they took their leave.

I spent the next hour messaging Pete, who had finally woken up, about what device would work best. I'd told him that it had to be something I could plausibly give my dad as a gift, and we worked through things we thought were appropriate. I emphasised that it should be small, so that evil SM didn't notice it and ask what it was. Really I just wanted it to be easy for Lacey to get into the house without any worries. The cordless hoover was too big, the lightbulb too random. Eventually Pete disappeared for a few minutes and came back with a link to a Wi-Fi controlled power strip. This, in English, was just a double plug socket and would fit easily into a pocket.

You're a genius! I told him, as I began to google where the hell to find such a thing in Monaco. Pete wanted to talk more, he had a test coming up and he was anxious about it, but I swerved it, saying that my battery was dying, and signed off. No wonder he was worried about never getting a girlfriend if that's the chat he was offering.

Turns out in Monaco there's not an Argos to be found, so I ordered the power strip on next-day delivery at considerable expense. Then I checked Janine's Instagram, which had a new post. It was a photo of two dresses hanging up beside each other. One was a full-length pale gold number with sequinned long sleeves and the other was a similar shape but dark red, and instead of sequins, there was a thin trim of fluff around the bosom. Janine had clearly never met an embellishment she didn't like. The caption read 'getting ready for dinner, which beauty do I choose?' The comments were gushing, all exclaiming that it was hard to pick between them, and assuring her that she would look amazing in either. Dolly Parton would've approved. As she famously said: 'It takes a lot of money to look this cheap.'

I decided to chance it. I threw on a black suit with a white T-shirt and added the neon heels of the night before. A cab took me to Janine's at 7.30 p.m., and I asked the driver to wait across the road for my friend. At 7.45, Janine stepped out of the front door (she'd plumped for the gold dress), accompanied by a flamboyant man in a silver blazer, and headed down the steps to a waiting Mercedes. As the car pulled out, I gave a theatrical sigh and told the driver that my friend must have forgotten that I would pick her up. We followed the car for about eight minutes, pulling up outside a restaurant with a large red canopy and bouquets of flowers in stands around the door. Janine was helped out of the car by her young friend and they walked into the restaurant, a doorman bowing slightly as they passed him without acknowledgement. I gave it a minute, and followed. A woman in a tight polo neck greeted me without a smile. When people like this try to intimidate you, the only thing to do is mirror their behaviour. Without saying hello, I asked for a table.

'Have you booked?' she said, looking me up and down.

'No? I can't imagine it's necessary for just one,' I replied, making a show of checking my phone. She sniffed and walked over to the maître d'. A few minutes later I was given a seat at the bar and left alone. Janine was sitting in a red velvet booth, the colour and fabric conspiring with her dress to give her an unfortunately festive look. Her gaudy companion sat beside her, and two other women completed the party. I was too far away to hear much of their conversation, but I was content to watch. They were hardly likely to talk of anything interesting, but it was nice to see her up close properly. It would have felt sloppy not to see her in the waxy flesh before I killed her, this way I got to feel like I'd given her a proper send-off.

I had a mildly disgusting chicken dish and two glasses of wine, occasionally watching the young man adjust Janine's hair or offer her a bite of his food. It was weirdly flirtatious, even though he was obviously gay and at least twenty years younger than her. Perhaps the arrangement was that he accompanied her around town and gave her attention that Simon clearly did not. In return, she paid for his dinner and bought him little gifts? How retro. Occasionally they'd all break into tinkly laughter and Janine would stretch her face into a smile. When I saw her signal for the bill I did the same, and followed them out into the night air. The man lit a cigarette as the women chatted, one of them telling Janine that she'd pop over on Thursday for coffee. Janine shook her head 'No, come tomorrow. The maid is off Thursdays and I'm going to sleep all day. I'm off to Morocco on Friday and need to relax before the early flight.'

I walked back to my hotel. Could Pete set it all up for Thursday? Perhaps that was a rush job, and I knew that rushing led to mistakes. But the thought of being here when she died appealed to me, it would give me a sense of control I was lacking with this plan. And I had no idea how long she was going away for, which might mean weeks of waiting for the next opportunity – who knew if Lacey would get cold feet in the meantime? At the ATM next door to the hotel, I took out 500 euros, the most my bank would allow me to take out in one go. The residents of Monaco would be appalled by such a rule – the initial options for withdrawal *started* at 500, the kind of petty cash you need on you to tip waiters on yachts, I guess.

Pete was annoyed I'd been offline all evening, and I had to endure twenty minutes of him complaining about his dad not letting him have a lock on his bedroom door before I could move him back to the business in hand. Teenagers are extraordinarily self-absorbed, all during the stage in their lives when they are at their most uninteresting. It took all the restraint I could muster not to tell him that freedom to masturbate at all hours wasn't a basic human right and that not being allowed a lock on his door was not privacy violation, no matter how much he talked about the Fourteenth Amendment. I told him about the plug I'd ordered, and said that it would be in the house tomorrow. Then I explained that I wanted to freak out my stepmother before I left on Saturday. I thought a little basic reverse psychology might work well on Pete, and assured him that if he wasn't up to the technological challenge of it all, then that was fine.

It's just nice to have made a friend in u, I wrote, *I can probs find someone else who can help now.*

That got his head back in the game. It was too predictable really. He replied with a broken heart emoji, telling me that he was definitely up to it, and would stay up all night to work on the plan. I'd told him what I wanted to do – up to a point. He knew that I planned to lock Janine in her sauna and turn up the heat, but he didn't know that I wanted to keep her in there until she was overwhelmed by it. And he didn't know that she had a heart condition that might speed up that process. For all his teenage bravado, I didn't think he'd fully embrace my real intentions, no matter how much he wanted to impress me. I figured it was better just to pretend I'd pushed it too far, and then place the burden of responsibility on him later if he panicked.

We need access to the CCTV in order to know her whereabouts, he said, launching into action. *It should be on the same network but we'll only know for sure when the plug is patched in. Then we control the place from our phones – you can tell me what you want to do and I'll make it happen. You can even speak to her if you like, that would really shit her up huh?*

We went back and forth into the small hours, Pete telling me how it would work, and me asking him to speak in plain English over and over. By 3 a.m., he was trying to veer the conversation into a more personal one, sending the dreaded voice notes again, so I turned off the Wi-Fi and went to sleep without saying goodnight.

I woke up to the sun streaming through my windows and lay in bed for a bit, feeling positive about my progress. Janine would be a big scalp to take down. Simon might not be a faithful or devoted husband, but they had been married for decades and she was his gatekeeper in many ways. His parents would have been a loss, his brother probably less so. I doubt he'd registered the death of his nephew in any profound way. But losing his wife would knock him sideways. Would he begin to see a pattern, to question the string of deaths? He didn't strike me as someone who'd buy into any idea of a curse, but would he think that he had an enemy somewhere out there, cutting down his family but never making themselves known? I hoped these notions started to seed. Not enough for him to take any action, but enough that they wormed their way into his brain and made it hard for him to think about anything else. He'd made enemies in business, people he'd fucked over on deals, companies he'd bought and restructured – a polite way of saying that he'd fired a lot of people. He'd had mistresses since my mother, the papers hinted as much. Would he look back and wonder whether any of them hated him enough to take such dramatic revenge? Rich people are paranoid at the best of times, with their security systems and their armoured cars. Perhaps he'd beef up security, hire a private investigator to look into possible enemies. Maybe he'd even go to the police. All sensible tactics, but ultimately pointless. Jeremy and Kathleen were long buried, and their car accident would never be shown to be anything but down to their own carelessness. Andrew was a troubled weirdo in the family's eyes, his death was a tragedy but hardly suspicious. Lee, well, the less the authorities dredged up about his messy end the better. And Janine had long-established heart problems, she really shouldn't even have been in the sauna. Let the question linger on people's lips. 'But wasn't she supposed to . . . ?' Always nice to add a little victim-blaming.

I checked my mobile. One message from Jimmy, asking if I wanted a drink tonight, one from my neighbour telling me there was a parcel waiting at her flat for me. Two emails from work that I ignored. Then I turned on the Wi-Fi on my other phone – the one I used for Artemis-related business, and was alerted to new messages with a string of beeps. Nine from Pete. Scrolling down, one was a message telling me that I had to find out what system the hub was on. I could ask Lacey to get that information. The next few were links to articles about smart doorbells which had been hacked and then there was a message asking where I'd gone and a photo, which when I clicked on it, showed Pete in front of a mirror. His head was cropped out of shot, but his tracksuit bottoms were pulled down and I could see his penis, held up to the camera like a special offering. Why do men send unsolicited pictures of their dicks? I am not friendly with many women, but I feel confident that I could answer for most of my sex when I say that nobody wants to wake up to that. Especially from a barely legal teenager with too much pubic hair and a sad case of chest acne. I felt simultaneously depressed by having to see it and sorry for Pete, who obviously thought it was an obligatory rite of passage when talking to a girl. I saved the photo, and sent it to my real phone. Might as well keep it in case Pete had a crisis of conscience. I messaged him back gently asking if we could take this all a bit slower. I hope I struck a note which made him feel more than a little self-conscious, while still giving him hope that there'd be some sort of reciprocation at a later date. He'd never get anything back from me of course, but I wouldn't feel too bad for the lonely teen. If you strike up a friendship based on hacking, you deserve to get scammed. In fact, you should expect it.

* * *

As soon as my package had arrived, I took it up to my room, unboxed it and read the instructions. I wrote them down in an abbreviated form on a small piece of paper, and then rolled up the plug and put it in a small toiletry bag along with the money. It was pretty compact now, and would fit in Lacey's pocket without causing any concern if Janine saw her coming back from the walk. Next door, I took out another 500 euros, added it to the bag and walked down to the promenade, seeing Lacey appear in the distance. She was in a better mood today, clearly she'd spent time planning how she'd use the money. Or perhaps Janine had been extra vile that morning and Lacey just wanted to take back some agency. Probably it was a little of both.

I gave her the money and told her what she had to do. 'There are instructions in the bag too, if you need them. And my number, so please text me when it's installed and give me the brand of the hub, and the serial number on the side. It'll be sixteen digits.' She nodded, and told me that Janine would be going away on Friday. I reassured her that we'd turn off the listening mode while she was gone, and only activate it again on her return. I wondered whether Lacey kicked back when Janine was out of town, painted her toenails in the cushion-stuffed lounge, smoked in the kitchen, had long baths in Janine's tub. I hoped so, but she was probably too scared in reality.

'We only need a week or so of audio – that should give us enough examples of this kind of shoddy behaviour. Then you can remove the plug and throw it away OK?' She nodded again, and bent down to stroke Henry under one ear.

'I do this for my family, and so that other women don't suffer like I do with a bad boss. It makes me feel good to help someone.' Henry was busy trying to bite her fingers, and I suddenly felt a tiny pang of guilt. She wasn't helping anyone except me. And she'd be out of a job too, soon enough.

'What's your surname, Lacey?' I said suddenly. She looked up at me, deeply suspicious. Henry looked suspicious too, but that was normal for the little fucker. 'I promise it's not for anything but my records – I won't use it anywhere.' She still looked uncomfortable. 'If the story gets sold globally, you'd get a cut of it,' I said, trying to think on my feet. That worked, money usually does.

'It's Phan,' she told me, spelling it out. I thanked her, and made her promise again to send me a text later that day when she'd installed the plug. She looked solemn and told me she would. We parted, and I walked back to my hotel to wait.

Four hours later, after I'd completed an online workout, had a bath and spent an hour going through Bryony's back catalogue of videos on Instagram, my phone pinged. *All done,* the message read. *It's installed, blue light blinking. Make on box is Henbarg. Code is 1365448449412564.*

I rolled around on the bed, punching the pillows for thirty seconds, before sitting up and breathing deeply. I messaged Pete, who'd been quiet all day. Even with the time difference, it was unlike him. Normally he was awake half the night, bouncing around his playground, the internet. The blue ticks on my last message indicated that he'd read it. Possibly he was embarrassed, or hurt, or angry. Nothing like a polite knock back to make a man angry. I wrote that the plug was installed, and gave him the hub information. I finished up with, *Can we make some fuss tomorrow then? It'll be soooo funny to get her panicking lol.*

It was close to 7 p.m., and I was full of adrenaline, despite the punishing jump workout, so I got back into my gym gear and went for another run. I managed 10 km, running through the clean streets, lined with their neat cobbles and well looked after plants. It was like a toy town really, a place you could feel as though the rest of the world was far away and unable to sully you. I bought myself an ice cream and walked back to the hotel, enjoying the sugar hit as I cooled down.

There was still no word from Pete, but he'd seen the last message. Two blue ticks showed on my screen again. Had his dad taken his phone off him? Was he just busy working out how to hack the system? Or was there a darker reason for his silence? Had he used the serial number to find out who Janine was. If so, he'd have done his research, and he'd surely find out that I was lying about who I was and what I wanted from him.

I'd known it was always going to be a possibility. He was the one with the technology expertise, if you can call a 17-year-old boy an expert on anything except disgusting bodily excretions. That meant I was giving up the control here, and not totally knowing how deeply he'd look into what we were doing. I hoped that he'd help me hack Janine's house, be shocked when she dropped dead and back away from the entire thing. That was the best-case scenario. But I wasn't naive, and I knew it was completely possible he'd figure out I was pushing for more than 'a little shock' and that he'd want answers from me. Or worse, want to go to the authorities.

That was the trouble with asking someone else for help. On balance, I still felt that it was better asking an idiotic kid for help, using some light manipulation to get what I wanted and claiming ignorance about the eventual outcome than it would have been to hire someone 'professional' who would be able to hold it over me forever. That kind of person would have researched everything they could've about me, and used it against me forever. Probably to demand an exorbitant amount of money. If Pete was the bored and slightly sad teenager I thought he was, then it shouldn't be too hard to keep him quiet.

But where the fuck was he? It was 9 p.m. by the time I'd showered and got ready to go and eat and still nothing. I messaged again, asking if I'd upset him, and saying that I missed him. *Message me back, I'm sooo bored here and need you xx.*

I ate dinner at a touristy bar with photos of the food on the menu. Always a fatal mistake, but I was distracted and in a hurry to get the night over and done with. A wilted salad and two glasses of wine later, I paid the bill and went back to my hotel. On the way, I texted Lacey asking who'd be in the house tomorrow, explaining that it would be good to identify who was speaking so that we could understand the audio we got. She replied quickly, saying that she'd be off from 9 a.m. until 6 p.m., when she'd be back at the flat. When she was off, a girl came in the morning to make Janine's breakfast and quickly tidy the house, but there shouldn't be anyone else around until the evening. *Madame likes to spend Thursdays at home relaxing. She says it's nice to have her house to herself. Sometimes she gets her nails done, or her hairdresser comes. I tidy everything up again when I get back.*

It didn't seem like Janine needed to designate a full day every week to relax when her entire life revolved around that singular pursuit, but it kept her at home where I wanted her, so I was glad that she prioritised self-care so rigorously.

I got into bed at 11 p.m., which was ridiculously early for me. The morning people won the battle long ago, but I still resisted their pull, normally going to bed at 2 a.m. and rising no earlier than 11 a.m. whenever possible. But I was keen to get the night over and done with, like a child who is waiting for Santa and forces sleep only so that they can wake up to presents. But I couldn't sleep. Pete hadn't sent me a message in sixteen hours, and I lay in bed with the dawning realisation that if he didn't get in touch soon, I would have no chance to kill Janine tomorrow. And after tomorrow, this particular plan would be unworkable and I'd have to start at the beginning. I tried listening to a calming soundtrack of waves hitting a beach, but it only made me need to pee. I did the breathing exercises I'd taught myself years before, but they couldn't quash the butterflies bouncing around somewhere below my ribcage. At 2 a.m., I got up and recorded a voice message for Pete. I went up an octave, in order to sound younger than I was, and adopted a suitably shaky tone.

'I don't know where you are, or if you're OK. I've been crying for hours, worried that I've hurt you or fucked things up. I'm scared of my feelings for you babe, and that made me push you away but I didn't mean to make you sad. Please get in touch. I don't care about our plans for evil stepmother, I just want to know you're OK. I'm here whenever, just please reply.'

Five minutes later, he messaged back. *I was fucked up when you told me to go slower lol. Thought you were disgusted by me and felt exposed. Got angry – fell down an incel hole, fuck girls fuck being a nice guy. People are fake, you know? Thought you were fake and wanted you to feel punished. Lol I'm so messed up. I care about you 2 bb. Sorry for taking it too far, when I heard your voice I realised what a fucking idiot I am. But I'm working on making it up to you.*

Genuinely disturbing, that insight into his mind. His willingness to punish a girl for not immediately embracing a photo of his penis was chilling, and I say that as someone who has killed six people. I'd be glad when this was all over and I could vanish from his life, retaining his pathetic dick pic as collateral.

We talked for an hour, me playing the part of an injured and shy teenage girl, him puffed up by my display of affection and keen to be my protector once more. I let Pete come around to the subject of hacking, keen for him to be the one to feel in control. As we spoke, he was telling me how he was working on the smart system, always using language I didn't fully understand. I must have drifted off at some point. He'd left long gaps in the conversation as he figured out how to access the system controlling Janine's house and, despite the importance of the task, the wait got boring.

I woke up at 9 a.m. with a start, my brain scrabbling around to remember what was so important about the day. I reached for my action phone and saw twenty-two new messages from Pete. Would they be about the plan or would they be penises? The first message was a photo of a naked cartoon figure, complete with a six-pack, holding up a gold cup. Typical teenager, Pete chose to communicate through memes rather than language. I hoped the image meant success and not an incomprehensible way for him to further expose his incel tendencies. The next message was a video, the thumbnail image blurred. I braced myself, and clicked play. The video was dark, and hard to make out. I squinted my eyes, trying to figure out the pale shape in the middle of the screen. There was a movement, a jerk across the object and then a small noise. That was it. I played it again. It was . . . yes, it was. It was a bed. And that movement was a person. It was easier to see the outline of the mattress this time, and the jerk had been an arm, or a leg maybe? Was Pete sending me videos of him sleeping now? Christ, this was not ideal.

Slightly alarmed, I opened the third message, which was an audio-file. 'If you're going, make the bed before, please. I don't want to have to see crumpled sheets all day. Oh, and call the manicurist and tell them not to come until midday now. No, I don't know who I booked with, probably Monaco Manicures – just find out, it's not hard, Lacey! I'm going for a shower, tell the porter to ring when the delivery arrives.'

I sat there completely still, the imperious voice still echoing in my ears. It was Janine. No question. I scrolled back and watched the video again. That must be her asleep – I checked the time Pete sent it over – 6 a.m. And the voice recording at 8 a.m. Only an hour ago. The next few messages were photos of the flat taken from CCTV footage. The beige lounge with its ill-advised gold accents, like a DFS version of Versailles, the hallways, with their gilt-framed paintings of things that people who don't care about art buy in an attempt to look cultured. Landscapes, horses, a few twee sketches of ballerinas. The kitchen was the only sleek space in the flat, with white cupboards and a marble floor. It looked like it had never been used. The dining room was an assault on the eyes – dark red walls, a fluffy rug underneath an enormous mahogany wooden table which was laid with a full dinner set. Is there anything more tragic than thinking a permanently laid table is the height of sophistication? As though a minor royal might pop in at any moment and be disappointed in the lack of dinner plates.

The photo of the walk-in shower was the prize for me. It showed a vast white marble room, almost the size of my flat, with a huge round shower head, a freestanding bath and two sinks under an ornate mirror. Behind the mirror was a wall which had been decked out in mosaic tiles showing nymphs bathing in a freshwater pool. A glass door from the shower led into the sauna, which was traditionally clad in wood.

Pete had sent a few more messages, where he expressed great pride in his work through the medium of gifs, and then a final comment, which read, *And for my masterpiece . . .*

I clicked the last video. It was a shot of the bedroom again, the curtains open this time, Lacey had made the bed. I watched the screen as the door opened, then closed, then opened again. Pete was showing off what he could do. He had control of the house. And I had control of Janine's life.

I replied to Pete in the most grateful way that I could. I sent him a gif of a sexy cheerleader throwing her pom poms into the air. He was online immediately, and told me that he hadn't slept.

It's mad, Eve, I can literally do anything I want in this house. The system has no end to end encryption. I did some digging into the company and knew I was onto a winner. It's run by some old dude in Germany who only sells it to crazy rich people but he doesn't bother to run any updates on the tech or secure the data. These fools are paying 100 grand for something with less security than a fucking Fitbit.

I asked him if it was possible to speak to Janine through the system and he mocked me for my terrible grasp of it all. *Lol at 'through the system', you sound like my mom. But yeah, you can shit her up a little when she's locked in the shower room – did you see that mural by the way. Sum sexy nymphs for sure. Will your step-mom be naked in our plan?*

I ignored this, and we messaged some more about how I'd be able to access the system from my phone too. He sent me a link to a file, and told me to download it. The little icon turned green and I clicked it and it opened up a webpage showing me a live image of the hallway in Janine's house. Pete walked me through what I could see, and how I could access the cameras in different rooms.

I'll control the other stuff from here and you can speak through the phone and I'll link it up with the house whenever you like.

Is she in the house now? I asked, clicking around the apartment in wonder.

Nah she left about ten minutes ago. You didn't tell me just how fucking rich your dad was. This place is insane.

It's her money, I wrote back, keen to disabuse him of the idea that I was some kind of heiress.

Well lucky Dad then. Wanna see some cool tricks while the house is empty?

I watched as the blinds started zooming up and down in the lounge, while loud house music blared out from an unseen speaker. He really could do this, it wasn't some teenage brag. I told him to stop, not wanting neighbours to notice and alert Janine when she got home. I suspected Janine rarely played house music at full blast in the mornings. Really nobody should play house music full stop.

I told Pete to keep exploring and to message me the moment Janine came back to the flat. I showered and dressed in under five minutes, and grabbed my phone, a charging pack and some headphones and went down to the beach, where I chose the nicest looking café and sat outside under an umbrella, watching the waves lap the shore. I turned my attention back to the footage of Janine's flat, and looked through the rooms to see if there was any sign of her again. Still nothing. Pete hadn't messaged either, so I ordered a coffee and a croissant and sat gazing out at the beach, forcing myself not to check my phone every ten seconds. I didn't have to hold this discipline for too long. My phone pinged just as I finished the last few flakes of the croissant, and I hurriedly wiped my buttery hands on a napkin before opening the message.

She's baaackkk, Pete wrote.

* * *

I click back to the camera view, and see Janine walking into her bedroom. She puts her large orange Hermès bag down on the bed, alongside a small paper shopping bag, and takes out a gold-rimmed candle which she places on the table next to her bed. She walks around the room for a few minutes, plumping up a throw pillow with gold tassels, inspecting her finger for dust after running it along the windowsill. She's bored, I think. Not the boredom of a rare free day when you feel like you're wasting time. This is years of built-up ennui, a life filled with lunches and organising staff and too much time spent on physical maintenance. Buy a candle, have a blow-dry, take a yoga class, fly to your other house and repeat the routine again and again. She filled her hours with activities, but none of them really amounted to anything. It was just a carousel of banality. So here she is on a day with no staff and no friends around, wandering through her apartment and trying to find things to complain about to Lacey later on. If she'd had any insight into the depressing reality of her life, she might have jumped off her yoga balcony.

Pete pings me a message, *Incoming: woman holding bag – can see on door camera.*

Janine walks down the hallway, Henry suddenly appearing behind her, yapping ferociously. She bats the dog away and opens the door. A young woman in a black T-shirt and jeans comes in and follows her to the lounge in silence. As she unpacks her bag, I see it it's the manicurist, come to fill up an hour of Janine's day.

Pete and I chat while she has her nails done, mocking the decor in the sitting room and exchanging opinions on what was the worst thing there. I plump for the small neon sign on the wall which says 'Love' in italics, a knock-off of a Tracey Emin design from a few years ago and the only concession to modernity in the space. Come to think of it, it might well have been an Emin. Doesn't make it any less hideous. Pete is adamant that the glass coffee table is the winner, telling me to zoom in on the legs, which show tiny cherubs working hard to hold up the load. I order another coffee, and we wait and watch, two strangers breaking into a house without having to move a muscle.

Eventually, the manicurist finishes her job and leaves, but not before Henry lunges at her, knocking over a bottle of red varnish which leaves a few drops of polish on the woman's top. Janine scolds the girl for flinching when Henry jumped up, and tells her not to come again if she's scared of dogs. 'You really should be more professional, that could've gone on the rug,' she says as she leads the girl out.

As she shuts the door on the chastened manicurist, Janine lets out a sigh and heads for the bathroom. She begins to run the bath, and carefully pins up her hair in the mirror.

Can you turn on the sauna now, without alerting her with lights?

I message Pete. I switch back to the camera. Janine is applying a gloopy cream to her face.

Done and done, Pete replies.

Good. When she's finished in the bath, make the lights go on in the sauna – she should go in to turn them off and then we'll shut the door. He messages straight back with a thumbs up.

I decide not to watch Janine take her bath, feeling as though she's allowed a little privacy in her last moments. But Pete has no such qualms, narrating her ablutions and laughing at the way she sings Celine Dion songs as she lies back and soaks. Some people love to linger in baths, calling it self-care and pretending it's got nothing to do with wanting to escape your family for a precious hour or so. Janine is one of them, despite having nobody to escape, unless you count the arsehole of a dog. She spends nearly an hour in the tub, topping up the hot water and adding various oils. While I wait, I find I'm becoming jittery from the coffee so I order a glass of rosé to offset the caffeine.

Eventually, Pete alerts me that she's getting out of the bath, and he makes a crude joke about her breasts which nearly makes me shoot back a choice comment about his dick pic, but I refrain. Pete makes me want to stick up for Janine, a sign that they both need to get out of my life pronto.

The sauna will be baking hot now. I take a deep breath and tell Pete to turn the lights on. I watch the camera footage, and see the sauna suddenly clear in the frame. Janine hasn't noticed. She's wrapped in a towel and is cleaning her face with a cloth over the sink.

Make them flicker, I type. The lights duly turn on and off in rapid succession. Janine stops cleaning and frowns. She walks towards the sauna with a look of annoyance on her face. *Be ready to shut the door, Pete, please be ready.*

I am, jeez, I'm the king of this place babe, comes the reply.

She walks into the sauna, and I hold my breath and scratch at my neck. The door closes silently behind her. At first, she doesn't appear to notice. I can see the top of her head as she reaches to turn off the lights, fanning herself as she realises that the heat is on full blast. I watch as she pulls the door, the glass wobbling slightly but not giving way.

LOL, she's realising she's stuck, messages Pete, but I ignore him, transfixed by an increasingly panicked Janine, who is now pressing a button repeatedly. *That's the alarm huh,* says Pete. *I've deactivated it obviously. Nobody can hear you scream, lady.*

Janine has sat down now, and hidden by an angle I can no longer see her, but she's banging on the glass, and Henry runs into the bathroom, alerted by the noise. She can hear him, and stands up, her eyes peering over the frosted strip on the door. She tells him to get help, an absurd order which shows me that she's getting frantic now. Henry looks up at her, his ears pinned back and his little body quivering with excitement. Then he tilts his head, turns around and walks out of the bathroom. I flick images, and see him lie down in his little bed in the hallway and promptly fall asleep. Perhaps Henry is a better judge of character than I'd thought.

I check the time on my phone. She's been in the sauna for fifteen minutes. *What's the temp in there?* I ask Pete.

Lemme check. He comes back two minutes later. *Sorry I had to convert it into your weird degrees. It's 110 degrees. Want it higher? She might pass out.*

I consider. We don't have hours to let her sit and slowly cook to death. But I'm reluctant to let it get to a point where she gets badly burnt – a sign that might suggest she wasn't able to get out. *Crank it up a little, I don't care if she faints. Would do the cow some good.*

I sip my wine and savour the breeze anew, knowing that Janine's entire body will be crying out for it. I distract Pete from watching the CCTV too closely by talking about a potential trip to Iowa, and he rises to the bait immediately, telling me how cool it would be to hang out in real life. We go back and forth on what we'd do together, him getting increasingly flirtatious and me suggesting wholesome activities that his church leader would have approved of.

All the while, I keep an eye on Janine, stuck in that little hot cupboard. There's no movement that I can see, and I realise that if I want to talk to her, I'd have to do it now. I tell Pete to patch me in, aware that what I was about to say would throw up some questions later.

There's a short pause and then Pete tells me I can speak. I take a sip of wine and look around to make sure that nobody is within earshot. I lift the phone to my chin and speak quietly but clearly.

'You're probably not in the mood for a big heart-to-heart right now.' Her head shoots up above the frosted glass and she wipes the steam away with one hand. 'But I just wanted you to know why this is happening to you. It's not an accident. You've probably realised that by now. But I'm not a criminal mastermind who wants to steal your diamonds. There's nothing you can give me that will stop this.'

She starts to yell something, frantically banging on the glass door.

'Be quiet. You don't have the energy for a fuss. Your husband left my mother with a baby. He abandoned her. He rejected me. And your family have lived a life of complete pleasure and comfort ever since. Is that fair? It didn't seem so to me, watching my mother take a series of shit jobs and get weaker and weaker with every day she worked. Is it fair that your daughter had everything she could ever have wanted and that I was raised by people who only did it so that they could feel good about themselves?'

She looks wild now, one hand clawing at her neck.

'It's getting harder and harder to breathe, huh? Well it won't be a problem much longer so do try to keep calm, it's worse if you panic, I imagine. I'll be honest, I considered not explaining any of this, but I wanted you to know the backstory as a courtesy more than anything. My father. Your husband. That's why you're in there. It's good to know who to blame, isn't it?'

Pete messages me. *Mega funny but it's been ages now. I think she's really struggling bb, shall we let her out? I don't care if she stacks it but it's your call.*

One minute. She's fine. Turn it up a notch and give it a bit longer. I reply, staring at Janine, who's tracing something with her finger on the glass. I strain my eyes, trying to make it out. She makes a noise, but it's muffled.

'Did you want to say something?' I say. She whispers again. I feel irritation rise. 'Louder please, you've probably not got long so if you want to say something, speak UP.'

But she's not listening now, intently moving her finger up the glass again. She's barely able to move more than a millimetre before stopping. We watch in silence, until the first shape becomes clearer. A letter G, wobbly and small but clear enough. I feel a tiny pang of nausea. Pete is engrossed. *What is she doing, an SOS message?* The next letter starts to take shape, a long line, and then, as she tries to prop herself up against the door, a circle stuck to it. She's drawn an R. The waves crash onto the beach as my vision goes a little blurry. She is going to write Grace. She knows. She knows everything. She'd probably always known – about me, about my mother, happy to let us live in poverty while her daughter had it all. And now she's going to expose me. When Simon finds the message, he'll know. Maybe not immediately, but he'll put two and two together, think back over the other deaths and realise what was happening. He and Bryony would be safe and I would be in jail for the rest of my life.

TURN IT UP, I message Pete. *All the way. The bitch deserves it.*

God you really hate her huh? That story was mad, makes my stepmom sound like a fucking angel. Cranking now.

Janine is trying to finish the R. Her perfectly coiffed hair is stuck to her face, which is mottled, parts turning a weird purpley blue. I sit there in the sun, one hand clenched around the phone, the other holding my neck so hard I can feel my eyes bulging. And then, as I watch, her finger slips down the glass, her head disappears from sight and there's a loud thump. Silence. I down a glass of water. No movement.

My phone beeps. *That was DRAMATIC. I think she's fainted now. Want me to release the doors?*

I signal to the waiter to bring me another glass of wine. *Let's do it.*

That thump wasn't just her body falling to the floor. It was too loud. She'd hit her head. I check my watch, Lacey isn't due back for another two hours. Enough time for her to suffer irreversible damage, if she wasn't already dead. The door to the sauna opens, and steam pours out, obscuring the view for a minute. As the waiter brings me a fresh glass, I can see the bathroom slowly come back into focus. Janine's feet are lying by the door to the sauna, her body slightly out of sight, inert and small. The shaky G was already fading away into nothing.

Henry has slept through the whole thing. Truly, we don't deserve dogs.

* * *

Well she died. The heat and the shock and the burns would have got to her, even if she hadn't had a mild heart complaint. I guess no heart complaint is mild when you're stuck in a furnace. God bless Lacey, who never asked a single question of me when I waited outside the promenade the next day. Did she suspect anything? Hard to say. I feigned shock and sympathy at the news. But Lacey seemed completely untroubled by the scene of horror that had greeted her. If anything, she was walking taller, no longer in her uniform but in jeans and a T-shirt, with gold flip flops showing off remarkably jazzy orange toenails. She picked up Henry and stroked his silky little ears.

'I'm going to give you some money, Lacey, it's the least I can do during this difficult time,' I said, looking concerned. 'Will you be going home now? Or will the family keep you on?'

'Mr Artemis has given me a month's pay and told me I can stay for a week, but it's OK. Madame Janine's best friend Susan called last night to ask me to come and work for her. She has a much bigger house up in the hills and she's offering me more money. She told me she's been planning to ask me to leave for a while.' She smiled brightly. 'And she's not a bitch like the dead lady. And I'm taking Henry. Nobody will stop me.' I waved her off, marvelling at the incredible chutzpah of Susan, a woman who hired her best friend's housekeeper less than twenty-four hours after she had died. In another life we might have been friends.

* * *

Pete was a slightly trickier task. He didn't go to pieces and panic about what we'd done as I worried might happen. Instead he was euphoric, wanting to go over and over the day's events, sending me memes about barbecues and asking who we could target next.

This could be a business baby, he texted me a week later, as I was drinking a glass of wine and contemplating what colour to paint my toenails. The hormones of a teenage boy are not to be messed with so I didn't throw the phone in a river and disconnect from him entirely. The boy was infatuated and I didn't want to test his tech limits so I handled it delicately. Mainly by finding God. A sudden flurry of bible passages every time he messaged me something flirtatious really slowed down the frequency of his contact. Nothing like a bit of smiting to get rid of a horny teenager's spontaneous erection. But three months later and he wasn't giving up entirely. He was still getting a trace high off the fumes of our adventure together and wouldn't leave me be completely. So I took a rougher route. I pretended to have catfished him. I mean, I *had* catfished him, but I doubled down. Aware that a reverse image search would be easy for him, I joined an online chat forum where you could video chat with anyone on the planet and I clicked through until I found the gnarliest bloke who spoke basic English. I endured five minutes of his company, which mostly consisted of him gesturing at me to show him my breasts. I asked him to send me a selfie first, saved it to my phone and then deleted my account. With the resulting photo, which showed a bald man-mountain grinning and waving, I waited for the next suggestive (read – masturbating) video message from Pete. As sure as the sun rises, there was a wanking video within time. Immediately, I sent back the photo.

'We are a collective. We have your pathetic videos and we have proof of what you did. Unless you want these files sent to your family you will cease contact and go back to your normal life. And be grateful every day that we allow this.' He called twenty-two times that evening, but I did not pick up, sending the message again with a FINAL WARNING addendum. He replied saying that he would never tell a soul and begging me not to send his dad the videos. I guess for all his braggadocio, the kid couldn't bear the idea of his dad thinking he had sent a twenty-stone middle-aged man jerk-off clips. He might have helped kill a stranger, but some things never change. The idea of a parent finding out you have a sex life was still much worse. And that was the last time I ever heard from ColdStoner17. That's how teenage relationships should be. They burn short, but boy do they burn bright.

CHAPTER THIRTEEN

Kelly has a phone. She has been crowing about this for weeks now but only to me, the first time she's been able to keep something quiet in her entire life I would imagine. Rightly, since if the other women here knew they'd do anything to get their hands on it. Kelly guards it fiercely, like a terrier with a bone. She hunches over it and types constantly, her long nails clacking away and the glow of the little screen just visible from under the covers. I don't ask where or how she got it. I imagine the gormless Clint managed to get it to her somehow, but I can't think what they have to say to each other that would require quite so much back and forth. I fervently hope it's not sexual. I cannot stomach sharing a tiny space with someone having text sex with a man who gels his fringe. Normally Kelly is quite generous with her things but she hasn't offered to let me borrow her new prized possession once. I wouldn't ask even if I had anyone to call. You don't want to be in hock to someone like Kelly. She might be a prize fluff-head but she wouldn't hesitate to call in a favour. I try to block out the sound with a pillow over my head, wishing fervently that I could do the same to her.

* * *

Do you want to hear something funny? The first time I met my sister was in a nail salon. There was no planning, no carefully orchestrated scheme conjured up so that I could bump into her in an unsuspicious way. It was a completely random encounter, if such a thing exists. I don't believe in fate, it's not weird that two women of roughly the same age would cross paths in central London. Chance meetings don't *mean* anything – there's nothing intrinsically interesting to them, despite what your mate Sarah who's really into horoscopes and tarot might insist. But it was funny. It was nice to have the work done for me for once. She belonged to a family who travelled in chauffeured cars and private planes, who had security gates and security dogs and a security detail. They lived ten feet above the rest of us. Unable to colonise another planet quite yet, the ultra-rich might be forced to inhabit the same vicinity as everyone else, but they are never quite within our grasp. They might be on the same street as you (only if that street is the Kings Road) but they are not experiencing it in the same way. Shop doors silently spring open for them in nanoseconds, pavements are merely a runway towards waiting cars, restaurants reveal private rooms, museums open at any time. The way you see a place is not the way they do. They are already moving on to the next thing by the time you've shaken the rain off your umbrella and begged the maître d' for a table. You cannot touch them. And yet here she was, sitting next to me, asking for a gel manicure. Not saying please.

Bryony Artemis has one of those faces you've seen before. I don't mean that she looks like a girl you know – she absolutely doesn't – but she's got a look that social media has made ubiquitous. Pillowy lips, a bundle of glossy, wavy hair, a body encased in athleisure wear – far too thin, but one that the owner would go out of their way to say was strong, emphasising their biceps, their 'booty'. The kind of skinny that some women profess not to think about as if it's not all they think about. Women like Bryony look startlingly beautiful in photos but a bit 'uncanny valley' in real life. I love that description – the roboticist Masahiro Mori coined it in 1970 to describe our revulsion towards robots or computer-generated images that look almost like human beings . . . but not quite. The Bryonys of the world are flawless, their features plumped and filled and smoothed. In photos it works. In real life it's deadening. It makes me long for the days of wonky breast implants and terrible facelifts when at least the insecurities that made women mutilate themselves were visible in their appearance. You could laugh at the Bride of Wildenstein or be sad that she did that to herself. This tribe can't show anything with their faces, nothing that would drive you to feel empathy, pity, or even derision.

She was wearing the kind of expensive trainers that have never seen the inside of a gym, skin-tight leggings with electric blue stripes down the side, and her tiny top half was swaddled in an enormous puffer jacket, not zipped up but wrapped around her and held in place by a giant cross-body bag. She looked like every other girl on Instagram. Except that the bag was Chanel, and she'd embellished the look with gold rings, diamond studs, and a small Rolex. The markers which show you that you'll never be able to 'shop the look' because the look costs more than you earn in a year. The look costs more than your parents paid for their house. The look costs more than you'll ever scrape together to buy your own house. I'm kidding, you won't ever be able to buy a house.

I knew it was her in seconds. I didn't spend years watching her grow up online without knowing innately what she looked like from every angle. What a depressing waste of brain space. 'What did you spend your twenties doing, Grace?' 'Well I watched an entitled airhead make vlogs about lip balm and I learnt all about her top five sunglasses shapes.' Maybe I should off myself too.

She was looking down and typing intently on her phone, with

one hand stretched out in front of the manicurist as though she were giving her a gift. I wonder what the women who work in salons like this say about their clients at the end of the day. Do they rage about the rude customers who never make eye contact? Do they laugh at them? Or do they become so numb to it that it barely gets mentioned?

I leant over and asked to borrow the varnish colour wheel, and she handed it over without looking up. One headphone dangled from her ear, signalling that she wasn't available for conversation, a tactic I won't judge since I use it myself. God bless the man (I'm guessing) who designed headphones not imagining that women the world over would use them to signal that they were unavailable to men who would try to engage us. The salon was buzzy in the way that women-only spaces always are, but I blocked it out and focused entirely on her. Watching Bryony was easy, she was like a dog who slows down for every passing stranger they meet, expecting that they will want to pet them. She was used to people looking admiringly at her, expected it, welcomed it. To be ignored would have been more disconcerting, I imagine. That didn't mean she would look back of course. It simply meant that I had carte blanche to observe without being noticed. The adrenaline was whooshing around my body at this opportunity. I felt like I was wasting every second, I had to make something happen. Soon she'd glide out of the salon and hop straight into a warm car, while I sat here waiting for my nails to dry.

This was my half-sister! What is meeting your long-lost sibling supposed to be like? I imagine you might examine each other nervously, make some stupid joke, tentatively reach for a hand. All preamble until you can eventually fall into each other's arms – allowing yourself to acknowledge that this person's existence was the missing piece of your life's puzzle finally slotting into place.

'OUCH!' Bryony angrily pulled her hand away from the manicurist, looking down at her cuticle and rubbing it. 'You've cut me,

FFS. Can you be careful?' The lady lowered her head and said sorry, though I couldn't see any sign of blood. Bryony sighed and stretched out her hand again, as another lady hurried over from the reception desk. This woman, who I assume was the manager, bent over and looked at her fingers, examining the damage. 'Sorry, miss, so sorry. I'll get you some water, yes?'

My sister didn't look up again, but nodded in assent. She was scrolling through her Instagram feed, hitting like on several photos of blonde girls standing on leather banquettes in darkened night-clubs. Then she opened up the camera app, raised it towards her face and arranged her features into an expression of composed disdain. I watched as she took photo after photo, before finally appearing to settle on one, her slim fingers quickly flicking and swiping. Bryony sighed again, and set her phone down. She didn't stop though, using her free hand to refresh the app again and again. I pulled my own phone out and opened up my own Instagram app. I use a pseudonym on it, a generic photo of a youngish mum with two small boys. My bio reads, 'Wifey of one big fella and mum of two small terrors, living in Hertfordshire and always up for a (insert banal wine emoji here).' I was fairly proud of the base level I got to here. Nobody will ever notice Jane Field watching their live videos more than once. Nobody will ever want to follow her back. I click on Bryony's Instagram stories and it loads to reveal the photo I just watched her take – eyebrow raised in disgust, lip curled, heavily filtered to make her skin look almost shimmery. The message written over the top of the image reads, *when you go for a much-needed relaxing manicure and the clumsy woman nearly slices your finger off. #badservice #moron.*

I tell you this just so it's more obvious why the falling into each other's arms reunion scenario was never going to be likely. I didn't have any feelings towards her other than a complete, but detached, fascination. Would I have been like her had I grown up within the monied bosom of her family? Probably. How many fantastically rich people do you know that you admire? I mean the ones born into it, not Oprah. I don't kid myself that I'd have done anything differently. Her cousin tried, bless him, but he wasn't really carving out his own life with those frogs. He was just rejecting the life that he was given, a life that was powerful and all encompassing – one that he'd have had to battle to stave off for the rest of his life. And that fight would have been exhausting. One day, when he was tired of living in a series of grim flat-shares and helping hideous animals that showed him no thanks, his father would have asked him for dinner. And worn down, he'd have revealed a chink in the armour he'd developed to protect him from the evils of his previous life. A little help would've been offered – nothing too much you understand – his family would have known how far they could push it. Perhaps just covering the rent that month, for example. And he'd have taken it, wrestling with it but just wanting a break. From there, the door would have been opened. The Artemis family would have pulled him back in – his chosen path was an affront to theirs after all – and he'd have given up his resistance. Maybe he wouldn't have sworn at staff and dated a succession of younger and younger models – he'd developed some moral compass despite his background – but he'd have ended up running an arm of the company, perhaps throwing regular charity fundraisers to make the process less crushing.

Andrew couldn't fully escape it and Bryony had fully embraced it. I'm sure I'd have ended up somewhere in between.

The manicurist painted my nails a deep red, the same colour my sister was having applied. There's nothing frivolous about these small rituals that women all around the world indulge in – they're a brief escape from the labour we take on. A tiny respite from a society which forces us to carry the emotional labour and carve out a professional path, while showing that we're not *too* emotional. Nail varnish is not vapid. It's a lacquer, a protective layer.

I was being useless. I wasn't gaining anything from this chance encounter. I was just sitting there like a lump, dumbly watching Bryony focus on her phone, occasionally sigh, and constantly smooth down her hair. But then I realised that maybe the problem was not with me, perhaps there was just nothing really to learn about this girl. Maybe it's like when women drive themselves insane wondering why a man they're dating hasn't called, ascribing reason after reason until they land upon something completely labyrinthian like, 'He likes you so much but after losing his father at an early age he's got complex issues with emotional intimacy and not calling is a sign that he's actually falling in love with you and probably just needs space but not too much space – you should send him a gift of your own hair,' when actually, he's just completely forgotten all about you.

I guess I didn't really need to learn anything about her. With some of the family, I've sought to understand them better in order to get near enough to kill them. With Bryony, her entire life is lived online. I can see it all, there's just not much to it. Normally the wealthiest people, I have learnt, don't want to be on any annual rich lists. They don't want to live in a spotlight where normal people know what they have and where they go. If the Artemis clan were like that my job would have been infinitely harder. That awful phrase 'money talks, wealth whispers' comes to mind. Happily, Bryony doesn't just want to talk, she wants to scream. Specifically, on Instagram, all the time. Those dreary predictions everyone makes as though it's original and not just an episode of some dystopian Netflix series about the bleak future where we're all just existing through our phones? That's actually Bryony's life.

As the manicurist rubbed oil into her hands and signalled that she was all done, Bryony lifted her head as though it were a tremendous effort and inspected her nails. She took an inordinate amount of time checking each individual finger before sitting up straight in her chair and laughing. Not a cheerful laugh, but one meant to signal absolute derision. She crinkled her eyebrows and fixed a stare on the woman sitting across from her.

'You've ripped my cuticles. All. Of. Them. Are you qualified to do this? No really, I mean it, how did you manage to damage every single cuticle? Did you use a crowbar?' The manicurist frantically gestured to her manager, either stunned into silence, or lacking the right vocabulary to respond in kind. The salon had hushed in seconds, everyone deliberately not looking at Bryony, but staying stock-still in order to hear what was happening. Normally this kind of attention might make someone pull back, but Bryony clearly had very little sense of embarrassment. There's a theory about Eton, that it doesn't produce the cleverest boys, but it does produce the most confident. That's why all these mediocre Pillsbury Doughboys with a nervous system feel as though they're more than capable of giving being prime minister a shot. That's what you pay for. Bryony had that kind of confidence. She could behave terribly and not give a flying fuck.

The manager came over, and ushered Bryony to the reception desk, clearly aware that this was a customer ready to *make a scene* and eager to get her away from other paying clients. But it was no use. Bryony had a voice that carried and she used it to full effect.

'This is just embarrassing – are you telling me that you're happy to let customers leave your salon with ragged nails? I was told that this place was good but my friend must have been drunk as per because I've never had such a terrible manicure. I have a video to shoot later – am I expected to show my hands on camera like this?' The manager was making calming sounds, I imagine offers were being made, apologies given. I shouldn't have to tell you that there was nothing wrong with her nails, now should I? They looked fine, good even. This was just a bored young woman wielding power because dissatisfaction is currency in a way that kindness is not. 'It goes without saying that I'm not paying for this.' Bryony wasn't even looking at the woman, she was browsing the nail varnishes on display. 'And I'll take this colour home with me for when my nails inevitably chip within hours. You're lucky I'm not going to put this all on my social channels,' and with that she grabbed a bottle of varnish and walked out, the door slamming behind her.

Reader, she did put it on her social media channels.

* * *

I've told you that there wasn't much to know about Bryony. And that's true. Waters didn't run deep with that one. As far as I can tell, she wasn't exactly stupid, she just never had to be smart. She lived a very nice life with everything she ever wanted and as a result, she wasn't very nice. I'd go further, actually. She appeared to be a total cunt. A great word, it can be enunciated in several different ways to convey varying ferocity and it perfectly encapsulates so many people. I can't dance around the truth calling people disagreeable or unbecoming. Jane Austen could conjure up a put-down withering enough to leave you breathless without resorting to profanity but then, she didn't end up in Limehouse. If she had, I imagine Wickham might have been called worse than merely 'idle and frivolous'.

Perhaps I should've got to know her better. Some people might wonder why I judged her almost entirely on her online presence, when it's pretty universally understood that nobody is their true selves on the internet. This murder, more than the others, might make one feel increasingly uneasy. 'I understand killing the rotten old grandparents but this girl is so young, they probably have more in common than that which divides them.' But this is not a story about reconnecting with family. This is not a tale where anyone finds out that they have a whole bunch of relatives waiting to embrace them. And I am not a damaged bird, who desperately wants such shelter. What I want is these people gone. With apologies to Elizabeth I, I have no interest at all in making windows into these people's souls. Or exploring the lack of them.

* * *

Bryony still lived at home. I guess when you live in a house that has sixteen bedrooms and two staircases you can pretend to yourself that you're living alone in some way – I assume she occupied a floor, or a wing, if the Artemis McMansion has such pretensions. But still. She lived at home, as an adult. Since she had done a jewellery design course in London and turned down the experience of a true uni life, she never moved out. Not once. Her parents bought her a Chelsea mews house when she turned 21, but she never spent more than a couple of nights there. Instead, she held parties there for the young and beautiful, but always returned to the family enclave. Does that say anything about her character to you? Again, maybe I'm looking for meaning where there is none, but rejecting all the potential that the adult world offers seems like a waste. And staying near your parents when your parents are Janine and Simon Artemis seems like a real personality red flag.

Bryony did not have a partner, or at least, not one that she talked about. I took this to mean she was single, since her previous love interests were featured heavily on her social media and also in the society pages. She referred to herself as pansexual but only seemed to have dated men. Sure.

There was a small dog which featured heavily in her life at one point and then, well, didn't. Much was made of this, and the hashtag

#WHEREISFENDI trended for a while on Twitter, forcing her to admit that she'd given the dog to her personal trainer because of unforeseen anger issues (the dog's, not hers).

She had a million friends but no friends. There were photographs of her out on the town with other rich, nothing-eyed women – cheek to cheek but never actually touching – but most of her images were of her alone, looking in the mirror, pretending to react to an imaginary photographer.

Bryony didn't have a job. Sure, she'd dabbled in modelling (I don't mean high fashion, I mean one season being a brand ambassador for an old British design house grown fusty and desperately looking to get a profile boost on the society pages. The other ambassadors included the son of an ageing rock star and a minor royal – one minor enough not to look anything like Prince Andrew) but she never did a job that would surprise you. That daughter of a multi-millionaire? Oh, she works in her local estate agent, really knuckling down trying to work her way up. No. Of course not. She had a singular low moment when it was announced that she was going to design an exclusive range of embellished headbands for Sassy Girl, and someone in the PR department, clearly desperate not to get fired, took the bold step of describing her as a 'gemstone artiste' in the promo material. Do you blame the newspapers for digging up her brief stint (read six weeks) on a jewellery design course and christening her 'Daddy's diamanté'?

Still, Bryony is nothing if not completely immune to criticism. You cannot keep an overly privileged white girl down. She might not need a full-time job, but in a world where women are constantly exhorted to be a 'girl boss', she had to do something to justify her life of handbags and back to back exercise classes (she briefly went to a members-only studio in Mayfair called The SS Collective, which stood for 'the slim, strong collective' but really served to show us all that history is not adequately taught in our schools). So Bryony did what any less than self-respecting person does in the modern age – she became an influencer.

A lot of people might not know what that is. There's no reason to be smugly proud about such a lack of knowledge. The only thing worse than someone who enthusiastically devours all pop culture and spews it up (wearing a T-shirt that says 'We should all be feminists' while queuing up for forty-five minutes to buy the latest trainers made by women in a sweatshop) is someone who takes pride in not understanding new trends. You're not better than that. You don't get points for deliberately trying to avoid learning about what's happening around you. And you've almost certainly looked at the Mail Online in the past month, so cut the smug. An influencer is someone who has a large social media presence and uses that to endorse brands for money. No different from the heady days of the Nineties when big name actors would hawk toothpastes in other countries for mega bucks. Well, except that this new group isn't famous for anything but their influencing. There is no talent that lies behind it, no singing or art or writing that gave them a springboard to start flogging stuff. It's usually just thin white women (or bulky white men) who have preternaturally bright smiles and unnervingly beige homes (all the better to photograph tat in) and who try to convince the minions that they possess a lifestyle that others should desperately try to emulate. Usually the influencer also bangs on about gratitude, or living in the moment, and pretends they've suffered from mild anxiety or struggle with some unspecified hardship in order to present as more relatable. The platitudes that gush from these people could overpower the Thames barrier. Watching some of this stuff will make you wish that it would.

So it was a perfect job for Bryony. Job is possibly a stretch. It was a perfect fit for Bryony. She made video diaries which detailed her day to day activities (one video, with 180,000 views, revolved entirely around a trip to the osteopath) and posted photographs of herself in various bored-looking poses, using a variety of props and backgrounds. By props, I mean her stupidly fluffy carpet, her mirror wall and her walk-in wardrobe. By backgrounds, I'm talking about exclusive holiday locations, often accompanied by hashtags which suggest that she's desperately in need of a break – #neededthis – as if the carousel of facials, gym classes, and nightclubs was leaving her dangerously close to burn out. I can only imagine that her loyal followers, many of them presumably earning crappy wages and on zero hours contracts, would nod in sympathy and praise her sensible prioritising of self-care.

She interspersed photos of such holidays with sponsored posts which looked just like the rest of her feed. These adverts were supposed to show you how to be a bit more Bryony – tooth-whitening kits, flimsy dresses available for next day delivery, a plated ring with her initials that she described as 'a must have'. This stuff is gobbled up by the Instagram herd, keen to fit in, desperate to be told what's good, what works, what will distract them from their lives. But it's all a trick. Bryony was laughing at them. Or she would have, had she been able to take joy from anything in her life. Perhaps not laughing but sneering. Because if my half-sister wanted her teeth whitened, she'd go to the best dentist on Harley Street. And if she wanted a new dress, she'd put down a grand and have it delivered in a tissue-lined box by courier within the hour. Her jewellery would never leave a green mark on her finger, it's all from Cartier. The stuff she promotes is photographed, uploaded, and then discarded. I could just about imagine that she gives it to the family housekeeper, but could equally believe that it goes straight in the bin.

Her lifestyle disgusted me and fascinated me in equal measure. Well no, that's not quite true. It fascinated me more. I have spent hours of my life scrolling through her curated online life, watching her boring makeup videos and logging on for her live Q&A sessions where she spends fifteen minutes at 7 p.m., nightly answering hard-hitting questions from fans like 'how is your hair so shiny' which she answers with the intensity and seriousness of someone testifying at a war crimes tribunal. While the internet is a place to get closer to your heroes, it's also a place to obsessively hate-watch people you would try your best to avoid in real life. I always told myself that it was valuable research, but engaging with it for so long leaves you feeling demoralised and dirty. It's like repeatedly picking at a scab and wondering why you end up with an ugly scar.

Bryony's openness on social media had provided me with a lot of options. I had *too* many – I fell down scenarios of such complexity that at one point I was researching how quickly I could get a helicopter pilot licence. I had to reassess. While not all of my plans had been elegant, they had been effective. Sometimes the lack of style bothered me somewhat. Who doesn't want to dispatch someone with a bit of wit after all? But it would be the height of vanity to centre all my fragile plans around the visuals of the situation. And vanity can get you caught – just ask the many killers who end up in jail because they hang around the crime scene to admire their handiwork and attract obvious attention.

As it happens, the plan I settled on did have an element of humour to it. There's one other thing I knew about Bryony, and initially, I almost wrote it off as something she'd exaggerated for effect. All social media influencers try to show some minor vulnerability. It helps the brand. Some pretend they have a palatable mental illness as I mentioned – anxiety often works, never psychosis. Some bang on about ailments like Lyme disease or a chronic pain so vague that nobody can disprove it. Bryony cast her net for something new. A while back, she did a very personal (you knew it was serious because she was wearing a plain black jumper and minimal makeup) video about a recent diagnosis that had shaken her world. Trembling, she spoke directly to camera, explaining that after an evening at Vardo (a restaurant that had recently opened to much fanfare in Chelsea), she'd collapsed and stopped breathing. After extensive tests, the culprit had been revealed and she could never eat a peach again. There were tears, for peaches were her very favourite. When I watched this tale of tragedy, I rolled my eyes and moved on. But she didn't stop with her PSAs about the dangers of stone fruits. The national food allergy trust got in touch with her, and Bryony found a little cause that would make her look civic-minded and serious. She held a gala evening to raise money for research, roping in fashion designers to donate looks to a catwalk event where she and her friends sashayed through a room in the British Museum, draping themselves around marble statues and posing next to ancient sarcophagi (if there wasn't a Pharaoh's curse before there damn well is now). Every so often she'd tell her followers to be mindful of friends with allergies, a service only slightly undermined by the fact that she'd teamed up with a private allergy testing company and recommended their £79 testing kit so that you too could see if a seemingly innocent fruit trifle might kill you. #AD.

Her feed soon filled up with photos of couture and sunsets, and I'd half-forgotten her stone fruit crusade until one night when she live-streamed an A&E visit. To be fair, even with a filter she did look dreadful, eyes swollen up, blotchy skin, rasping as she whispered to camera about how she'd had to have three shots of adrenaline after she'd stopped breathing in a nightclub. Someone had given her a cocktail, blithely assuring her that it was peach-free, and she'd gulped it down, before immediately recognising that tangy taste and running for the exit in a wild panic. Because her friends were idiots, or more tragically, perhaps because they didn't really know her, nobody put two and two together and realised that she was having a serious allergic reaction. Instead, one bouncer assumed she was having a panic attack and the other suspected she was just drunk. It was only when she turned purple and hit the floor that an ambulance was called. I wonder if the experience of an NHS A&E was almost more traumatic for Bryony than the episode itself. She was on a public ward, with only a curtain for privacy, as she whispered into the camera about how scared she felt. Not because she nearly died, but because a drunk man covered in blood in the bed next to her wouldn't stop singing a Bowie song. She didn't know it was a Bowie song, I imagine she'd have written Bowie off as a weirdo. Always with the priorities that one.

You know where I'm going now, don't you? You should, it's incredibly obvious. I don't want to have to be holding your hand as you read this. Fucking inspired, if I do say so. Not that the idea wasn't handed to me on a plate. God sent me a boat and all that. About ten people a year die from food-induced anaphylaxis each year. Even with all the money and privilege, why wouldn't she be one of them? And it's hard to pin a deadly peach intolerance on an unseen enemy.

But why shouldn't this one be easy? Some of these kills took proper planning – let's not forget the weeks of frog drudgery, and the deep dive into London's sex party scene. I spent months figuring out just how much I could manipulate a kid on the internet so I could get to Janine. Hard when you have a full-time job, an increasingly obsessive long-distance running habit (Lady Macbeth sleepwalks, trying to scrub imaginary blood from her hands, I run for miles in any direction away from my crimes, yeah it doesn't take a therapist thank you) and a dispensation towards anxiety that isn't so much a character flaw, but doesn't help when you're juggling responsibilities.

I never knew quite how close Bryony was to her parents. For all that I studied the family and befriended their staff, they were set apart, living in a world I would never gain access to – no matter how high I climbed or how much I stalked. What I knew for sure – that she was an only child, that she still lived at the family home, that she never mentioned her parents on social media – was mixed in with other titbits. Her mother had spent most of her time in Monaco (nobody does this unless they're very keen on avoiding tax), living there for at least eight months of the year for five full years. Simon would fly in and out, but seemed to be based here full-time. Bryony, like all the other girls in her world, frequented St Tropez but didn't seem to show up chez Maman very often. The last official visit (official as in she posted it on Instagram) was two years before Janine had her unfortunate accident. Even after Janine died, there was no direct mention of her on Bryony's social media. She took a three-week break from posting, and then came back with an image of her silhouette against a disappearing sun, complete with a heart emoji, and was posting sponsored content two days later. Janine was buried in England, and the house she owned in Monaco had sat empty ever since. I don't imagine that was for any sentimental reasons, but because the house was where the business was registered.

Then there was just total supposition based on all of this information. I suspected that Simon and Janine had lived completely separate lives, probably for a long time. This wasn't just because of the Monaco situation (though it obviously bolstered the theory – who spends most of the year away from their partner if they don't need to?), the gossip had long been that Janine had grown tired of Simon's constant infidelities and had finally taken action to protect herself and her stake in the business. The rumour (backed up by Tina, who reiterated it in an excited whisper one day when I met her for a drink after work) was that the kicker came when Simon was discovered to have kept another yacht for his mistress and had been using a speedboat to ferry him between the two when the family were on holiday.

Threatening to divorce him and take half his money, Janine played a blinder and somehow managed (with the help of a truckload of accountants who she must've been paying handsomely) to persuade Simon that there was another option. No divorce or loss of assets, but he had to sign the business over to her. Simon must've done the maths, realised that this deal kept him Janine's prisoner, and still signed the papers. Better to be a rich prisoner than suffer the indignity of the tabloids raking over your private life and having to hand over a hefty chunk of cash to boot. There was an upside – Janine living in Monaco meant that he would no longer pay tax. Rich people see tax the way some people see climate change – it's a social justice issue worth taking to the streets for. The very rich mainly live under the impression that they earned their money. They have no time for any theoretical argument about whether it's truly possible for anyone to deserve such an individual accumulation of wealth – once they have it, they turn Gollum-like, ferocious in their protection of their goods and wealth.

So Janine had lived a nice life in Monaco, where lunches took weeks of planning and there was much complaining to be done about the responsibilities of staff, and Simon was free to do whatever he wanted back in London. Bryony wasn't involved in the equation at all really. She was their daughter, in that she held the family name and provided the bridge between her parents, but it didn't seem like she was playing Monopoly round the fire at Christmas with them. It didn't feel like the kind of family you would recognise – either functional or dysfunctional. Instead their unit felt like one which had all the bearings of something enviable, with none of the emotions which would actually make it so.

Maybe I was wrong. The problem with doing all of this from a distance was that I could never really know these people and their innermost thoughts. Then again, I thought I understood Jimmy inside and out and he'd surprised me. His betrayal made him 5 per cent more interesting at least. Maybe Janine and Simon really did love Bryony in a very deep and real sense. I could only go on what I glimpsed. Not that it mattered, I wasn't trying to absolve myself or hope that it wouldn't hurt Simon to lose his daughter. I'd have killed him first if I wanted to spare him that pain. No, obviously the sequence in which I murdered his loved ones was crucial. That's why he came last. He had to experience it all. The reveal would be the thing that broke him.

* * *

I knew it was a long shot – I couldn't rely on such a sloppy approach – and yet something in me couldn't shut it down without even trying it out, albeit from a slightly different tack. I wouldn't waste any time on it – it was a one-time attempt and it had to be done fast, without too much thought. I took myself off at lunchtime to buy six luxury beauty products in cash from a few different department stores. I bought a range of face creams, one with peach seed extract. When I got back to the office, I locked myself in the disabled toilet, spread them out on the floor and got to work. The most expensive bottle contained a facemask made from pearls (is there anything now that brands won't add to a beauty product to make it more desirable? At some point, a clever marketing manager will suggest using antimatter in a night serum and the rich women of London, Moscow and New York will lap it up) and I hazarded a guess that Bryony would, if she bothered even to open the box, have an eye for the most high-end product. This was the bottle I was staking it all on. It was a tree to be hidden in a forest – hence the other products ready to be packed beside it in a fancy box. All nice stuff, but she'd have tried most of it already. And there's nothing as alluring to a vain Instagrammer as a new product promising a level of luminosity not seen before.

The facemask and the cream which contained the peach-seed extract were made by the same company. That was important for any future investigation. The other products were a mishmash of brands. I decanted four drops of the cream into the facemask bottle using a pipette I'd bought at a veterinary surgery a few weeks back (for my poor dog's eye condition. Animal lovers are always mad to talk about ailments, and I had to work hard on my feet to explain the fictitious dog's weepy eye to the weedy-looking nurse who seemed to find this condition completely fascinating) and shook the bottle vigorously. Opening it again, I sniffed the liquid. If it smelt like peach I'd be in trouble. It pretty much smelt like any generic face lotion. Sweet, but not identifiably fruity. I needed a little more reassurance though, and added one drop of the almond essence you add to cakes to be certain. That stuff overpowers anything else in a recipe. One more shake and I sniffed it again. Success. The liquid now reminded me of a bakery, warm and reassuring, which, given my intent, felt pleasingly inappropriate.

I carefully cleaned the bottle with a baby wipe, and threw the peach extract cream in the bin. The products then went into a plain white cardboard box lined with tissue paper. A card attached simply read 'Bryony, we hope you enjoy these goodies – the pearl facemask is a dream! XX.' I desperately wanted to say it was to DIE for but I couldn't allow myself to be quite so on the nose. All wrapped up, I stashed the box in a bag under my desk and tried to forget about it as the working day dragged on.

I wasn't normally someone to leave on the dot of 5.30 p.m., people who do that are usually the dullest and most aggravating colleagues – the kind that go on and on in inconsequential meetings and insist on a proper system for the communal fridge but refuse to engage in meaningful work. They are also the least fireable employees, since they have normally read their contract requirements thoroughly and know exactly what they can get away with. And not that it matters, but this particular kind of colleague is never the attractive charismatic one. They're not leaving in order to go and get changed for an exciting party.

But bang on 5.30 p.m., I packed up my stuff and headed out, vaguely mentioning a doctor's appointment in case anyone raised an eyebrow. Nobody did. People swanned in and out for appointments all the time, and it wasn't uncommon for some members of staff to take 'pamper hours' where they'd duck out of the office for a teeth-whitening session or an eyebrow tint. 'It's great for customer interface,' my boss would say, which meant nothing but let her go and get Botox on company time.

I managed to get to the parcel shop five minutes before closing. I sent it recorded delivery, assuming the Artemis housekeeper would sign for it, and gave no sender details. She wouldn't look for them – people like Bryony receive a hundred gift boxes a week. As I stepped out into the fading autumn light, the shop bell tinkled as the door slammed shut. I took it as a sign. I would not check Bryony's social media accounts in the hope that she'd succumbed. I'd given it a shot, and it was out of my hands now.

* * *

I spent the next month busy at work. Sale season was approaching, and I was organising the social media campaigns and making sure that discount emails were sent out to customers who'd signed up to receive them. I knew from research that 95 per cent of these went unread, dropped in spam boxes the moment they landed. It was a pointless exercise, but data was invaluable, we were told. The tone of the messages we sent out was enough to make even the most ardent shopper a card-carrying anti-consumerist. The word 'Fri-yay' was used in one email before I shut it down. When I wasn't trying to preserve the English language and my own dignity in the office, I was looking at new ways to kill Bryony.

As with all the previous deaths, it felt important that this one should take place while Bryony was doing something normal for *her*. It lent more credibility to the accident scenario and required less elaborate planning. I want these killings done – done well, yes, but I'm not an enthusiastic fan of homicide, researching the most fascinating and gruesome ways to kill. There's a certain art to a good murder. I will admit to being impressed by the lengths that some people will go to, but I don't want to get caught up in more and more extreme plans which eventually result in me hanging off a zip line through central London, decapitating someone with a samurai sword just for theatrics.

After a lot of false starts, I came across a potential opportunity. There is a man, some of you might know of him, who has become a mainstay in the wellbeing industry. His name is Russell Chan, and he has made millions off a nutrition programme called 'Manifest and Maintain'. If you've not heard of this nonsense, then you could spend a thousand years trying to guess what his company does from the name alone, so I'll break it down. His brand, or 'innovation' as he called it in his TED talk which I watched three minutes of before deciding that death was preferable, consists of two main elements. The first is making you copy down positive affirmations that you stick around the house on special pastel-coloured Post-it notes that he sends you once you've signed up. The second is telling you to exercise for eighty-five minutes a day and giving you juicing recipes every morning. The creativity that goes into coming up with different blends of fruit and vegetables 365 days a year (you absolutely do not get Christmas Day off) is stunning. And by stunning I mean a waste of some poor nutritionist's degree. The Post-it notes conceal the fact that this is a diet plan. The MM app is £8.99 to download and costs a further £4 a month for the rest of your life. People have tried to cancel their subscriptions but I've never met anyone who's managed it. But most people don't, because idiots LOVE Russell Chan. They seem incredulous when they lose weight, as though it were a secret science they've discovered and not a meal replacement offering which cuts out all calorific options. They bang on about the confidence they've got from (I assume) computer-generated inspirational quotes that they stick around their bookless homes, where they presumably fight for space between the reclaimed wooden sign that says 'Love' and the rose gold plant baskets.

I admire Chan. He's a terrible monster but he's only rinsing the willing. He got out of finance before the huge crash a few years ago, and he tapped straight into the wellness market – using that banker's brain to speculate on what the masses would want in a time of financial insecurity. And he has made millions from it – correctly guessing that the herd would want to treat themselves in small but comforting ways, find peace of mind in platitudes and crucially, look better. You can't get a mortgage anymore, but you can wear shiny leggings with that new-found confidence.

So the MM ideology is available to the masses, but it relies on looking exclusive. Chan knew from the beginning that the scheme would only work if the beautiful people repped it for him. Every year around May, he invites 100 of the most influential 'movers and shakers' to come to his private retreat in Ibiza where he hosts a weekend of exercise classes, juice workshops, and positivity seminars. Every year without fail, the *Daily Mail* and other celeb sniffing publications breathlessly scour the Instagram accounts of said movers, grabbing screenshots of the beautiful people doing sun salutations by an infinity pool, hugging each other in a tangled mass of undernourished bronzed limbs and generally gushing about how much they've learnt about their soul from the three-day trip. There is a party on the last night, where, according to a girl I know who works in beauty PR, copious amounts of alcohol and drugs get mixed into the fruit smoothies, everyone gets completely off their faces and all phones are banned. I suppose this last-night blow-out acts as an apology for all the dull hikes they've been forced to do over the previous two days.

Guess who was going on the next retreat?

I found out about Bryony's plans because my boring mum Instagram account follows nearly everyone that she does and I keep tabs. Months ahead and Chan was already busy teasing his 8 million followers with photos of the planned Ibiza weekend, using the dubious hashtag #cleanhedonism below photos of yoga mats neatly aligned on the sundeck and video clips of white linen clad staff mowing lawns. Below an image of neon balloons tied to a tree, Bryony had posted a comment. *Can't wait to join my soul tribe.*

I got busy. The weekend itself would be off limits but the party sounded like something I could work with. I looked around to find out who organised the last-night party – not an impossible task, since everyone tags everyone on social media as a way of getting discounts for genuine work. Sure enough, the event was run by a company based in Watford called Bespoke Bangers. Such genuine Balearic vibes. I'd wait-staffed many events in my early twenties and felt confident that I'd be in with a shot at serving a bunch of coked-up models. There was an application form on their website and I filled it out, emphasising the many exclusive (and imagined) parties I'd worked at. I stressed that I'd be working in Ibiza around the dates of the party, and explained that I'd heard that they had clients on the island and I was looking for extra shifts. Someone called Sasha emailed back within twenty-four hours, asking for a video chat which I assumed was to make sure that I looked attractive enough for the gig. It was fine by me – a fake name covered me, and I wouldn't be stupid enough to send over a photo which could be easily retrieved.

I slapped on make-up for the chat, darkening my brows and applying red lipstick, two things which change the face subtly but effectively. Sasha called ninety minutes later than suggested, which meant I had to hop off a bus and dash into a coffee shop to take the call. She was brusque and decisive, asking me to do some London shifts over the next week to ensure that I was going to be a good match for the company. The whole call took less than five minutes, I'd been right about appearance being the main purpose of it. We agreed that I'd work an event at the Shard the following Tuesday. Details were vague but it was an event for a well-known YouTuber who was launching a self-tanning product. I was to get there at 5 p.m. and wear black trousers – a shirt would be provided.

'Don't look at the guests unless you're offering them a top-up – nobody wants a creepy waitress getting starry-eyed,' Sasha said as she typed on her keyboard, taking her own advice about eye contact.

The event went smoothly. I had to rush from work, another day knocking off early but what else could I do? The room was bathed in peachy light, with flower arrangements dotted about the space and goody bags stacked under tables weighed down with biscuits iced with the brand logo. It was far from packed, but everyone was eagerly taking selfies with the host, who seemed pleased with the guests busy livestreaming the wall of balloons. I poured champagne and kept my head suitably bowed. Not that I recognised a single one of these people. The Warhol prediction about the future of fame has been completely gazumped by the rise of online personalities. Fifteen minutes seems oddly quaint when you see these empty-headed kids desperately trying to make a video go viral every single day.

The feedback obviously satisfied Sasha, and I was booked for three more London events. They were cash in hand, which was a relief, and usually over within two hours – the youth of London don't large it up much, preferring to get home and apply a sheet mask while watching the latest Netflix drop.

A month later, I got a text from Sasha telling me that she had three events lined up in Ibiza that I could work. She enclosed the dates, and one of them landed on the last night of the wellness retreat. There was no further information, but I felt pretty confident that there wouldn't be two parties happening on the same night both covered by Bespoke Bangers. I replied immediately, confirming my availability, and booked flights and accommodation for my Ibiza stay that night. I wasn't going to veer too far from the original germ of an idea. Bryony liked her booze, and a party as hedonistic as the MM one would likely get messy fairly quickly. Nothing like a three-day juice fast to get you drunk after one cocktail. A few drops of peach purée in a glass and she'd be done on the dancefloor within minutes. A bunch of health obsessives surrounding her and yet I'd bet my life on none of them having any proper medical training to help her. I had six weeks to wait.

Except I didn't in the end. Because Bryony died later that very night.

* * *

I didn't even know about it until the next evening. For all we're bombarded with news all day long, it's remarkably easy to opt out of it all if you do something as basic as to forget to charge your phone. I was out of the office that Wednesday, on a training day designed to 'empower women in business'. It was mandatory, which suggested that it was more to do with ameliorating the recent sexual harassment allegations against a team leader than it was about promoting women in the business. After eight hours spent in workshops where fourteen of us sat around in a circle and role-played challenging office scenarios with each other, I ducked out of the coffee and cake option at the end and speedwalked for the Tube. My phone was dead, so I spent the journey watching a young couple having a fight about whether their success in keeping a houseplant alive meant that they were ready to get a dog yet. She rolled her eyes a lot, he looked away even more. I worried for this imaginary dog. I even felt a pang for the houseplant.

As I exited the Tube station, I grabbed an *Evening Standard* and rolled it up, stashing it in my bag. Twenty minutes later I was home, and I set about unpacking the food I'd grabbed from the local health food store and turning on the heating. It was only then that I took the paper and sat down at my kitchen table. The main story was something typically dull about a council house shortage which I skimmed over because everyone knows the *Standard* only lead with that stuff so that the rest of the paper can be filled with coverage of a new ten-quid ice cream shop in Kensington or a puff piece on a fitness class where you use gold weights. To the side was a small photo of a girl, a selfie taken from an angle, 75 per cent mouth. The familiar whoosh of adrenaline began snaking through my veins. Adrenaline punches your energy levels up to 100 while also freezing time. Everything slows down, becomes woolly, reactions get blunted. I knew instinctively who I was looking at, but the fog which had enveloped my brain prevented me from fully registering what was happening for a split second. 'Heiress dead at 27.' I opened the paper, and there, on page three, was another photo of her, this time much younger, standing between her parents at an event.

Bryony.

The details were scant. She'd been found unconscious in her

bedroom at 7.30 p.m., by a member of staff (read, maid). Paramedics were called, but she was pronounced dead at the scene. The article mentioned the tragic death of her mother just months before, intimating that suicide must be a possibility. I knew that was nonsense. Bryony wouldn't have killed herself in a fug of grief. She didn't dive down to those emotional levels, everything was boredom, mockery or desire for her. Base level stuff. The family spokesman had pleaded for privacy at this difficult time, and apart from the basic stuff about Simon and her gilded life, no more information was given.

I spent a frenzied hour checking Instagram, news sites and gossip blogs. Her last post was at 4 p.m., a photo of her on a rug looking at a sausage dog (hopefully this one was just on loan #WHEREISFENDI) which sat beside her. The caption read 'when bae wants love'. So no helpful pointers for the press which would help them with their tragic rich girl narrative. Elsewhere, a few Instagram friends professed their shock with prayer hand emojis and crying faces. RIP was floated around a lot, an expression I've always hated. Rest in peace. No matter how lively or funny or desperate to live you were. Just rest now. A generic, pointless comment. But there were no new details, nothing to grasp at. Where was Simon? Was he at home when it happened or was he out with some new fling, dining at a private members' bar, making a business deal? How did he find out – did the maid call him or did the police? Was he alone now, without his wife, without his daughter – his only recognised child, his parents gone? His brother dead. Did he have an inkling of what was happening yet? How could he. He'd managed away my existence just as he'd managed every other troublesome detail in his privileged life.

But I was alone too. With every other death I had made it happen, been there for the last breath, felt like I was in control. Here, I was just like everyone else who had picked up a paper. I knew nothing and could tell nobody. For the first time in a long while, I wanted my mum. I wanted her to know that her daughter was the one who was alive, that I was doing this for her, that I would never let her life have been discarded and forgotten by these people. But I wasn't going to be one of those people who thought that they could sense their dead loved ones smiling down on them, and I wouldn't be pulled into a maudlin pity party for myself. I opened a bottle of wine, and ran a bath. Bryony was dead, the details could wait. Her demise meant so much more than ticking another one off my list. It meant that the list was almost complete. One more to go. Daddy dearest, I was coming for you.

CHAPTER FOURTEEN

Writing all that down made me laugh. What a hammy cliffhanger to end on. But I'd finished the story of Bryony's demise at 2 a.m., in total silence and darkness. Even Kelly wasn't snoring. I was wired by the end of it, remembering the moment when I realised that I only had one target left. I'd been so close and it had felt so monumental. From the confines of this cell, I wish I'd enjoyed those moments a little more. I should have gone dancing after every murder, or bought myself precious jewellery for every target I'd crossed off the list. I had a list; did I mention that? A physical list, I mean. It was written down in pencil on the back of a photo of me and my mother. The Latimers had given it to me one Christmas, shortly after I'd moved into their house. It wasn't a huge surprise, given that it was my photo. But Sophie had found it in my desk drawer and taken it to the framers to be displayed properly.

'You must see this every day, my darling,' she said when I opened it. 'Your mother loved you so very much.' I knew this of course, and I didn't need Sophie to tell me how much. Besides, I'm not sure Sophie had spoken to my mother really, beyond brief arrangements about playdates which always took place at the Latimer house ('So much easier for the kids with all this space,' she'd tell Marie), so her insistence at constantly reminding me that I had been so loved used to get slightly irritating. Jimmy used to roll his eyes when Sophie would trill about how proud Marie would be of my exam results, or my 'excellent' fairy cakes. Thank fuck for Jimmy.

But it was a nice frame, and I'd hung it by my bed at the Latimers'. When I moved out, it was always displayed somewhere I could see it when I woke up. When I was planning how to kill Kathleen and Jeremy, I'd taken it off the wall and held it, looking at Marie's face a while, wondering what she'd make of my intentions. Probably she'd have been horrified and anguished, devastated that I'd decided to waste my life trying to avenge her own. But she wasn't here to tell me that, so I didn't have to give her opinion much weight. And besides, I was doing this for myself as well. Marie was dead and gone. In life, she'd never wanted to right the wrongs done to her. But she'd never wanted to right the wrongs done to me either. We both suffered because she was too weak to demand what was fair. I'd ended up as an extra in a family that wasn't my own, with no security or safety net. With the shot of losing my mother and the chaser of seeing my father parade his legitimate family all around town. If I wanted to redress the balance, she could hardly protest.

Before I'd put the photo back on the wall, I'd taken the pencil I was making notes with and scrawled the names of every Artemis I figured I'd have to kill on the back of the frame. The marks were light enough that you'd barely notice them unless you were really looking, but every time I'd drawn a line through a name, I'd held the pencil down, dragging it through every letter until they were completely obliterated. It was a small but important marker. But I could have bought some nice jewellery too.

After I'd finished recounting the tale of Bryony and her sad encounter with some peach serum, I'd fallen asleep, waking in a panic when the morning bell sounded. I was still holding my notepad, and Kelly was moving about the cell, singing a hideous rendition of a One Direction song. I assume the original was dire enough, but her pitch made it endlessly worse. I pushed the paper between the mattress and the bed frame and said good morning. Stupid, careless mistake to risk Kelly seeing my work. I watched as she brushed her teeth and applied foundation that was slightly too dark for her skin. I was surprised to see how many women made an effort to look nice while locked up when I first got here, but now I understand it better. Prison will try to dominate every part of you if you're not careful. From prosaic things like how many pairs of socks you can have to more intimate ones, like changing the things you dream about. Before I came here, I had vivid and surreal dreams almost every night. Now I dream about just one thing. Running down the river path, wind behind me and sky all around. Don't need Freud to analyse that. So if a bit of makeup helps ground you a little bit, I understand. But blend it better, Kelly, that's all it would take.

I felt fairly confident that she'd not seen the notepad. Her demeanour was as blandly cheerful as ever, and she wittered on about a visitor she had coming later that day. 'A friend,' she said, as she applied coat after coat of spidery mascara, 'but maybe he wants more. Couldn't blame him.' Kelly looked at me in the mirror, and I could see that the girl was desperate for me to ask her more about this visitor. But I wasn't in the mood to listen to a slightly delusional monologue about how desirable Kelly was to the opposite sex, and so I pulled on my tracksuit, told her I hoped it went well and headed off to the library.

I should finish off explaining what happened with Caro since it's why I'm in here, wearing a polyester tracksuit instead of something nice from MaxMara. It's why Kelly is the closest person to me, since

Jimmy won't reply to my letters and I've realised I have very few other friends. I knew that before really, I didn't exactly spend my time cultivating close relationships before all of this. I was possessed, I see that now. Only focusing on my plan to cut down the Artemis family and not even having the foresight to build up a life that would be waiting for me once it was all done. Stupid, of course. I relied on Jimmy to be there when I was finished, thinking that he'd be enough and that the rest would come easily. And most people are sort of terrible. Thick or dull or a hideous combination of both. I could never tolerate it, and so I never tried to. My current predicament has hardly disabused me of this notion.

But Jimmy wasn't the constant in my life that I presumed he would be. Two days after Gemma Adebayo had told me that I was free to go, I had been woken up early by a hammering at my front door. I opened it blearily, and was promptly arrested for the murder of Caro Morton. I was taken back to the police station, this time with less concern for my comfort or wellbeing, and charged. As I sat with the detectives for several hours that day, it all began to come out. Jimmy had told the police he thought it was a murder immediately, yelling about how much I hated Caro. My jealousy, it was suggested, led me to push her violently off the balcony and hope that it would look like a tragic accident. The other girl left at the party gave a signed statement saying that I'd argued with Jimmy about his engagement and then asked Caro to come and smoke with me outside. This mousy girl, who I later found out was called Angelica and who was decidedly less weedy than her appearance had suggested, was instrumental in the case against me. Who knew that the girl with a fulsome collection of Alice bands had it in her?

I was refused bail, after it was passionately argued that I was a risk to the public, which made me screw up my face in disbelief and swear loudly, something the judge didn't appreciate much. My appointed brief, a flailing graduate who hadn't even read my notes before he entered the courtroom, did nothing to push back on this and was fired the moment I exited the building and was remanded into custody.

It was then that I got my first taste of jail. It was a horrible shock initially. The centre I was sent to was a grim concrete block behind a huge wall in South London. I was strip-searched, relieved of my possessions and sent to a holding cell. It was freezing cold and I spent three days obsessing over what, if anything, I had left in my flat which might point the police towards my actual crimes. I visualised every corner of my home, mentally walking around the flat to try to remember anything I might have been sloppy enough to leave on display. I couldn't sleep, and my mind kept distorting the images I tried to conjure, making me start again and again until I wept with frustration. By day three I felt calmer, having forced myself to breathe deeply for an hour. By then, I was confident that nothing would point towards the Artemis deaths. This was bolstered by the knowledge that the police weren't looking for anything that wasn't connected to Caro, and nobody knew of my connection to the murders anyway. As far as they were concerned, I'd spontaneously pushed a love rival off a balcony in a fit of jealousy. Unless they were hoping that I was the kind of person who kept a deeply confessional diary, any evidence for that would be sparse. How ridiculous that I only decided to start a deeply confessional diary once I was actually in the bowels of the criminal justice system.

I hired a new lawyer, Victoria Herbert, and prayed that she would be the Rottweiler she promised to be. A Rottweiler in Hermès scarves and Louboutin heels. The way I liked it. Herbert was bullish about my chances at getting off. There was no forensic evidence, apart from some contact Caro and I had had during the course of the night, and the bulk of the case was based on testimony from Angelica

Saunders and Jimmy. Jimmy, giving evidence against me. Jimmy, the only person I truly cared about, telling the court that he believed I had pushed his fiancée off a balcony, not looking at me once during the trial. Jimmy, pictured in the *Sun* one Friday, walking hand in hand into court with Angelica. Her in a hideous tweed pencil skirt and ballet shoes looking proud. Jimmy might have left me in a bemused heap but I began to respect Angelica's hustle.

The jury deliberated for six hours. Victoria sat with me during that wait, which felt like a year. When we were told that the jury was ready to return a verdict, she was ebullient, assuring me that a quick turnaround was definitely a good sign. For all her bluster, she was completely wrong on that count. Guilty. Guilty. Guilty. The word echoed around the courtroom as people gasped and one man shouted something angrily from the gallery. I stood there, my hand reaching for my throat, trying to remember to breathe and failing. I looked towards Jimmy, who was sitting with his head on Sophie's shoulder as John patted his arm mechanically. Only Jimmy's sister, Annabelle looked at me, tilting her head as though she were sizing me up for the first time.

And that was that. I was sentenced to sixteen years and taken to Limehouse a week later. I missed the window for an appeal, stuck in shock and unable to know what to do next. But then George Thorpe came along, a middle-aged white man here to save the day as he imagined he was born to do. He had an appeal granted, arguing that there was further eyewitness testimony which was not sought out by police at the time.

I appointed Thorpe at considerable cost after I got here, realising that Victoria Herbert was much more interested in promoting herself as a glamorous attack dog than actually being one. She appeared in *Grazia* off the back of my case, barely pretending to bat away praise and using the word 'empowered' far too much. The staggering fee my new brief charged was made possible because he offered to do it on a buy now, pay later basis. I could see his rationale for this – he wanted some publicity and I could give it to him in spades. I imagine he was aiming for QC, and felt like a high-interest murder case might bolster his chances. He was quite the showman. At the many high-profile trials he'd worked on, the media slavishly reported on his arguments, his floral language, his habit of thumping the table when he was mid passionate defence of his clients. Thorpe had a stellar success rate which meant I felt relaxed about his final bill. Whatever happened, I'd have enough money to put him on a permanent retainer once I'd laid claim to the Artemis empire. Credit to Thorpe, he exposed every possible flaw in the trial, and he used the press to highlight those flaws, knowing that they'd run any story they could on the Morton murderer. During the trial, they'd painted me as a bitter and damaged girl in love with her step-brother (he wasn't of course, but the tabloids love them some incest-lite), but once I'd been sentenced a new angle was needed. Now I was damaged, but no longer bitter. My fragility was played up – 'She had nobody really, except for Jimmy' – and images of me were printed where I looked shy and vulnerable rather than hard and arrogant. These photos were provided by old workmates judging by the clothes I was wearing, and I'm only in them because they were mandatory. It's amazing what you can decide somebody is like simply from a photo. Thorpe had an old school friend who worked in PR seed some stories about Caro's mental health problems and hints were dropped about her eating disorder, her love of a good party (read: drugs) and her temper. Awful tactics really, but this isn't a discussion about media ethics and besides, I would've taken one hundred stories ripping Caro to shreds if it had helped my case. I'd have read them even if they hadn't helped my case.

I have been festering in Limehouse for fourteen months now,

and waiting on the appeal for nearly half that time. When I first appointed him, I would call George Thorpe daily, and write long letters to him urging him to explore the balcony again or to force Caro's therapist to testify to her mental state. I was desperate to be out in days, not weeks, and I was furious every time the lawyer told me to be patient. When it became clear that I would be here for a while, I fell into a depression of sorts. I'm not somebody who gets depressed. I sometimes feel a rising panic in my throat and a need to escape, but I'd never understood people who get so sad that they retreat from life. Perhaps prison makes us all more empathetic, or maybe it's just natural to get depressed in a place which has strip lighting and communal showers. I started to sleep more, and for a time it felt as though my brain were swimming in treacle. My thoughts slowed down, I stopped exercising and on one particularly low day, I watched the *Emmerdale* omnibus all the way through with Kelly constantly telling me who everyone was without wanting to slam her head against the wall once.

One day eight months in, I woke up and did 500 press-ups. I was fed up of this alien mood and scared that I would languish in it forever if I didn't force myself to climb out of it. So I started a strict regimen, waking up at the same time every day, pushing my body harder and harder with exercises in my cell and walks around the yard. I spent hours in the library reading anything that would give my head a break from this place, and I pestered my lawyer again, but this time with more focus.

And now I am near the appeal decision, and writing this all down to take my mind off it. I am confident that I will be freed, and have already written my speech to read out on the court steps. I think I've struck the right tone – injured but magnanimous – and I will wear just enough makeup to look attractive but not so much that I look like I've spent fourteen months having a nice time. I want you to be able to see the dark rings under my eyes, and immediately know that I have been nearly broken (but not quite!) by my ordeal. I will talk about how we must remember that despite the trauma of being incarcerated, there is another victim in all of this. Caro, I will say, looking straight at the cameras. I lost nearly two years of my life to this injustice, but Caro lost her whole life that night and we must never forget that. Perhaps I'll end neatly by announcing that I will be establishing a mentoring scheme for female prisoners with eating disorders in her name, in the hope that I can help even one vulnerable woman. She'd fucking hate being called vulnerable.

I don't think my confidence in being released is misplaced, by the way. The police, with help from the devious Angelica, really did just decide that it had been a murder and did little to test their supposition. I cannot claim to be the perfect innocent in all areas of my life, but in this I truly am the victim of a huge miscarriage of justice. What a tightrope to walk. George Thorpe saw immediately how badly the case had been handled, and has exposed flaws in practically every part of the process. This might all be enough, and it was certainly enough to ensure an appeal was granted, but it was no silver bullet. That came only a couple of weeks ago, but it's enough to almost guarantee my conviction is quashed. Thorpe had come to see me for a long-arranged update, and I wasn't expecting any major news. But I could tell the moment he walked in that something big had happened. His neck was red, and it was rising up towards his face as he strode purposefully towards me in the visiting room, brushing impatiently past other people, his long wool coat flying behind him. It was, he said, the result of two months relentless digging by his team.

'The night Ms Morton had her unfortunate tumble, the police made enquiries at every other flat in the mansion block.' He pulled out a list of the other properties in the building. 'There are five flats on each floor, arranged almost like a pentagon, but only three face the gardens while the other two face the road. Ms Morton's apartment was the middle of the three garden-facing properties. Her neighbours to the right are a couple in their mid-sixties who have been in the block for thirty years – long before the high-income professionals started buying in Clapham – and they were at home the night of the incident.' Thorpe never used the word death when a more polite description could be found.

'They were very used to Ms Morton's parties and showed a remarkable lack of sympathy about her tragic accident, perhaps as a result. They were very clear about not seeing or hearing a thing because they retired to bed at 10 p.m. armed with ear-plugs.' Thorpe raised his eyebrows here, but I could well understand how annoying it must have been living next door to that entitled girl. 'The police attempted to make enquiries at the flat on the left of Ms Morton's flat – number 22 – but there was no answer that morning or later that day. They did further investigate the flat and its owners, but were told by the building's management company that the owners lived abroad and were never in the country so the police left it there.' He used his gold fountain pen to stab at the paper in front of him. 'That was a HUGE oversight, but sadly typical of our police force. The reason we didn't look into this earlier is because the write-up suggested that contact had been made with the owners of number 22 and assurances had been given that they were out of the country. We had no reason to doubt that your previous brief had investigated this thoroughly, but a clever chap in my office went through the reports from the evening in question and found that she hadn't looked any further into the next-door flat.' I thought again about Victoria Herbert's vertiginous high heels and fervently hoped she would fall down an escalator in them. Perhaps I would help make that happen when I got out of this place. Thorpe looked at me quizzically and I snapped back to attention. 'This is where it got interesting. This fellow, one of my team as I say, did a bit of digging and found out that the flat is registered to a company based in the Cayman Islands. Do you know what an offshore company is, Grace?' I rolled my eyes and followed the action up quickly with a sweet smile as I assured him that I did in fact know what that was. Patronising fool. 'Well, under current UK law, foreign entities can buy property here without revealing who they are. It's scandalous of course and a system which allows for all sorts of dodgy dealings – mainly money laundering, of course. The government is planning to force these anonymous owners to reveal themselves but it's tricky and likely to take a while.'

I cut him off. 'Right well I think I've heard enough about land laws. What did he find, this man of yours?' He cleared his throat and looked suitably chastened, but that might just be the default expression of posh men so it was hard to tell.

'Well it's been hard work, as I say. A tangled web. David, that's my associate's name, he's spent two months on this, trying to make contact with the company, but a phone number in the Cayman Islands which doesn't work isn't much to go on. Often these companies don't even have a real office out there, just hiring a room so they have an address. Eventually, he hired an investigator who deals with this sort of thing to dig out who owns the company and where they are.'

I was getting impatient now, and visiting hour was whizzing by. 'With respect, George, I hired you to deal with all of this and it sounds like you're doing a marvellous job, but sometimes you don't need to know how the sausage was made, and I've got spa treatments lined up back to back this afternoon, you understand?'

'Right, yes, sorry. Well. *Well.* David finally, after a lot of misdirection and fobbing off, found the owners of the flat. They live in Moscow and are none too keen on replying to emails. So he went out there last week and made contact with them on Thursday. He explained your plight and asked if there was any way they could help

– a housekeeper who might have been in the flat for example, or a CCTV camera. It was a long shot, of course, but it was worth trying. And what do you know?' Thorpe was looking as jolly as a school boy now. 'They told David that they had CCTV cameras up the wazoo! Said it was standard at all their properties. David could hardly keep up the pretence of calm professionalism when they said they had one on their balcony, concealed by a small bush. And did they keep the tapes, asked David. Why yes, said the Russians. They kept everything on a database of course. It was best, though they didn't elaborate on exactly why it was best.' He stopped for breath as I held mine. 'David has a copy, Grace. He's watched them and they will be in the office as soon as the footage has been verified by an expert. It doesn't show the entire balcony, but it shows enough – you're not in scene when Caro takes her final bow.'

I nearly fell to the floor in relief. A feeling like the sun warming your body on the first day of summer enveloped my body and I grabbed Thorpe's hand without thinking about what I was doing.

'Thank you. Thank you. I don't know what I can say but thank you. And David. And the Russians. Thank you.' He looked pleased, the blush rushing up his face once more.

'Well, we've done our job and it's all very good news. I can't get you out today sadly, but you've only got a few more weeks in here and there can be no doubt that this footage will exonerate you completely.' A bell buzzed and he looked at his watch and gathered up his papers. 'I'll be in touch the moment we have news. In the meantime, hold tight. And keep this all quiet until it's official.' I thanked him again and shook his hand. As he turned to go, George Thorpe looked round at me and said, with some embarrassment, 'Do they really have a spa in here?'

* * *

And that, as they say, was that. I walked back to my cell, fists clenched in excitement, barely able to focus on where I was going or what I was doing. Kelly was sitting on the lower bunk, using a piece of string to thread her eyebrows and singing Beyoncé songs in a key I'm not sure the lady herself has ever been acquainted with.

'You look white as a ghost, mate,' she said, as she looked up at me. 'Bad news from the brief?'

I told her what Thorpe had revealed. I was too excited not to, all my usual front was gone. Stupid to tell Kelly anything, really, but what harm could it do now? She was genuinely sweet about it, grabbing my hand and offering to hook me up with a friend of hers in the Angel who rented rooms with no need for references. I'd managed to keep my flat on while I'd been in this place, it was a stretch but it was important for me to know that there was something waiting for me when I got out. Even though I knew it wouldn't be my home for much longer. Once the money came through, I'd be looking to upgrade as fast as possible. And even if I wasn't, there was no way I'd be renting a room off some dodgy mate of Kelly's. Nothing in life was that desperate. She pulled out her secret phone and started typing, presumably looking to alert her slum landlord friend to a possible new tenant before I talked her down. I hoped the offer didn't mean she thought we'd be continuing our relationship in the outside world. Kelly was a limpet I found it hard enough to detach in here, if she had the freedom to travel and the use of a mobile I'd be completely at her mercy. Visions of her turning up at my house with facemasks and a cheap bottle of wine loomed ominously in my mind. Not quite the new life I had envisaged.

Oh, I should go back a little bit. Time is strange in jail. It goes so slowly that I really thought I would go mad at the beginning, and then the appeal gained traction and suddenly I'm whizzing over things in my haste to finish this story off and start living a new life, one not dominated by nasty but necessary things like murder.

The moment my conviction was quashed, Jimmy got in touch. Well actually, the CPS had been in touch with him a week before the final decision to inform him of the new evidence. He'd written a letter for Thorpe to give to me almost immediately. I won't relay the entire thing, going on as it did for three full pages. Jimmy is not a natural writer. His continued, and I think wilful, misuse of grammar has always made it hard for me to read his emails and texts. I guess the *Guardian* is more relaxed about grammatical errors than some publications. A deluge of small mistakes littered a letter that otherwise might have been quite moving. As it was, I winced at every line. Suffice to say, he was full of remorse. He had let me down in the most monumental of ways, which was true, and he had barely slept since I was convicted, which I knew was bollocks. The man has a special gift for falling asleep in the most trying of times, but I appreciated the sentiment. After endless apologies, he told me that he had moved back in with the Latimers and had taken two months off work to grieve Caro. There was no mention of Angelica, who I assume had been cast off when it became obvious that she was a grifting snake trying to get into his pants. I assume she did, in fact, make it into that particular area before being unmasked, but then they do say that grief does funny things to people. And besides, Jim was channelling his sadness in a different direction. An upholstery course, as unlikely as it sounded. I suspect that means that we'll all be getting slightly wonky armchairs for Christmas. Caro's death wasn't for nothing then. Even without the free furniture, her death wasn't for nothing. It meant no Caro. That was a blessing in itself.

He ended the letter with a clichéd passage about how he didn't expect me to forgive him (why do people say this when just the mere fact that they've got in touch with you to say it means they clearly expect forgiveness?), but he would spend the rest of his life trying to make it up to me and would be at the prison come the day of my release. Love you, Gray, I'll help you sleep again soon, he signed off. I wondered if Sophie would insist on coming along, desperate to make my story her own for currency, just as she did when I was younger. Perhaps we'd all go to the local bakery for a celebratory breakfast. Jimmy would inevitably forget his wallet and Sophie would pay for us, shaking her head in exasperation and telling the long-suffering café owner that her kids were, to use her favourite phrase 'total rotters'. I'd been in jail too long, because even as I thought about it, I felt a tiny zap of warmth. It was a facsimile of a family, but it was what I had.

Since the letter, we have slotted back into our old relationship with a strange ease. I phoned him two days after I read it, letting him panic a little bit. We have talked at every opportunity since. I have been magnanimous. He has been wracked with guilt, and had come up with a plan to move me into his flat and nurse me back to life, as though I had been marooned on a leper colony for months and not in jail because he accused me of murdering his ghastly fiancée. I firmly shut that down. I wanted to be in my familiar place as I planned for my next move, and having Jimmy bringing me cups of tea would hamper that somewhat. There would be time for cohabitation later, when we could live in a house big enough to spend a pleasurable amount of time away from each other.

Thorpe was also fielding calls from the media, especially from the tabloids, who had done a 180-degree turn on my case with such speed that reporters must have sprained muscles. The narrative of 'The Morton murderer' was about to be replaced by something equally terrible, at least in my mind. I idly speculated about my new moniker. If I'd had access to a betting shop I'd have put money on 'Full of Grace' being at least one headline used upon my release, complete with an image of me reading out a statement. Composed, long-suffering, dignified. The playbook was too easy. I wouldn't speak to any of them immediately, of course. I wasn't some desperate novice who didn't understand how this stuff worked and took the first cheque she could. My narrative would be my own. Besides, press attention would wait until I revealed myself to be not only an innocent victim, but also a grieving daughter. That's high-class human interest, the kind that guarantees your name will be known for decades to come.

Once the dust has settled a little, I'll make some initial overtures to Thorpe regarding my father and his estate. Of course, I won't put it as bluntly as that. I'll just say that this experience has made me reassess my life and explain that I want to explore the connection with that side of the family. It's too late to know my father, I'll say as I dab my eyes with a tissue, but I want to know where I come from and who he was. There is nobody else left in that family, except Lara. And Lara isn't even a blood relative. She's an estranged wife, and one that I graciously spared at that. I knew from the moment I decided not to kill her that she would be my gateway. I will approach her with such charm and grace (ha!) that she will be on my side from the start. Two women wronged by Artemis men, both of us trying to lead lives away from their heavy presence. Women supporting women, that's what we like to see. Perhaps we'll even become friends, though a connection solely made because we were both damaged by brothers seems like an unhealthy foundation for lifelong kinship. But then again, forging a connection over hatred can be stronger than anything else. Stronger than bonding over a love of ceramics or a passion for avant garde opera. We would have a much tougher bond. The money is important, but the goal was always the annihilation of the family. But that didn't mean I would be content with nothing. And if she wouldn't play ball, there were other options. She'd been spared, but that was always negotiable. And now you're up to date.

I've spent a further eight days in Limehouse and I have one more to go. Today I was told by a bored-looking guard I'd not seen before (the turnover of staff is high, probably because who in their right mind wants to wrangle a bunch of angry women for twelve hours a day for minimum wage when you could work in a Starbucks and wrangle slightly less angry women but also get free lattes?) that I should expect to be released at 3 p.m. tomorrow on the dot. Since the guard had no care for my privacy, she told me this in front of Kelly, who has now insisted on having a party of sorts for me tonight, in the games room. As part of the preparation, she made me go to her friend Dionne's cell to have my makeup done, something I hotly protested but was bounced into anyway.

I finish this from my cell, unable to sleep. I faintly remember this excitement from childhood, when Marie would creep across the room on Christmas Eve with a stocking for me. Like all children, I would try to stay awake, waiting for Santa to bring me my loot. Unlike most children, I succeeded and realised the con early on. It didn't faze me much. I still got the presents, despite the subterfuge. Tomorrow I will spend the morning readying myself – staying calm and conserving my energy. But tonight I am all over the place, thoughts running wild, adrenaline surging. As I thought, my makeover was an experience I won't be repeating. I emerged from Dionne's cell after an intense twenty minutes with a face that vaguely resembled a blow-up sex doll and hair that had been backcombed within an inch of its life. The only excuse I have for allowing it is that I was high on the fumes of my freedom and knew that there could be no photographs of the night in question. Despite my complete success in making precisely no friends during my stay, a fair few women turned up to the party, lured by the distraction and the promise of soft drinks and cake. There was no cake as it turned out, but it limped on for forty-five minutes anyway, as Kelly told everyone how much she'd miss me and I took care not to return the compliment. I doubt it drove the message home, Kelly has the hide of a knock-off Birkin bag. When I retreated back to my cell, I got into bed, pretending to be asleep by 8.30 p.m. I'm writing this under the covers. Even with mere hours to go until I leave, I can't risk encouraging Kelly to attempt one last deep and meaningful. Tomorrow morning I shall pack up my meagre possessions and get ready to re-enter the world. A world which will be very different for me from now on.

CHAPTER FIFTEEN

I dreamt about my mother last night. It wasn't a nice dream; I don't often have nice dreams. I never have horrific nightmares either, normally I just get transported back to difficult or sad moments in my life and relive them until I wake up. I suppose I don't possess a huge amount of imagination, but I respect my practical brain for not diverting me with night-time adventures. I won't bore you with the memory my sleeping mind dredged up, but I woke missing Marie more intensely than I had in years and feeling further away from her than usual. Every plan and every murder kept me feeling connected to her, as though she were right beside me powering me on. But she's not in here with me. Not that I blame her. This is not a place for lingering souls. A ghost would take one look at Limehouse and apparate through a wall immediately. If Marie is hovering around, stuck between this world and another, I hope she's haunting Fortnum & Mason or flitting around Harvey Nichols rearranging the mannequins.

I don't believe all that nonsense, by the way. There are no ghosts stalking these corridors and my mother was not whispering in the wind while I avenged her. But her memory was fresh while my rage was stoked, and now that it's all over, I find myself thinking of her less. Her face is blurring and fading. Perhaps a therapist would call that closure. I suppose killing people and getting away with it *is* a kind of closure. But possibly not one that a medical professional can recommend in good conscience.

I have to explain how Simon died. I know that the final death is normally the icing on the cake in novels, the biggest and most dramatic. That's partly why I've been putting off writing it all down. Because this is not a novel. I didn't arrange it so that his death would be the most shocking. I didn't push him out of a hot-air balloon or throw him off Waterloo Bridge at sunset. Perhaps I should have tried for a plan like that, just for the added dramatic flair, but I've never been one for needless stunts.

Once the final important member of Simon's family had been dispatched, my need for urgency slackened. Like a marathon runner who knows there's only a mile to go, I decided to enjoy the route for a little bit. That meant scoping out how Simon was doing. And given the circumstances, Bryony's funeral felt like the best place to observe him. It was a risky one to try to attend, and I'd mulled it over for several days before deciding that there would be enough weeping women my age there for me to fit in OK. If there was ever a time to see Simon's grief raw and up close, it was there. I'd just have to make sure I looked the part. The day before the funeral, I raided the company clothing cupboard, which held clothes and accessories that were ready to be loaned out to important clients for events. The array of stuff we kept in this dingy space was eye-watering – designer shoes stuffed on top of each other, bags which cost upwards of two grand forlornly lying on the floor. Above them were sequinned dresses and colourful jumpsuits on a rack, next to a sign which said

'The higher the heel the closer to God.' If eyeballs were capable of bleeding, the signs I had to see in this office every day would be the main trigger.

I knew how to dress for this kind of event. I'd spent my adulthood learning how to blend in no matter the situation. At work that means wearing clothes which walk the line of dull but avoid active frump. In the wider world, it means regular trips to Zara like every other woman my age to acquire the regulation armour of jeans, oversized jumpers and chunky boots. But in a crowd of uber-wealthy Instagram airheads, fitting in meant something else entirely. These girls didn't just spend obscene amounts of money on clothes, anyone rich can do that. Walk down Bond Street and laugh at the idiots who think shearling-lined Gucci loafers and fur-trimmed puffer jackets are the epitome of style and you'll see what I mean. No, these women were beady-eyed and specific about what they wore, and woe betide you if you got it wrong. It wouldn't be enough to have just any Prada bag, it would have to be the one that a certain Italian Instagram star was gifted three months prior to it hitting the shops. I didn't care about their judgement, of course, but I didn't want to raise eyebrows or provoke any challenge about my presence. So I purloined a brand-new burgundy silk trouser suit made by an up-and-coming Italian designer I knew *Vogue* were currently championing, and boosted a snakeskin Celine clutch bag whose absence, if noticed, would certainly get me fired. For shoes, I went with a pair of yellow leather mules and spent the rest of the day fervently hoping that Bryony's funeral wouldn't be one where everybody wore solemn black.

The actual burial was a private event, and I didn't even allow myself to entertain gatecrashing that. But the service of remembrance was a free-for-all, trailed in the *Evening Standard* as though it was the opening of a new bar. Nothing like a sombre event mourning the loss of a young woman for some pap shots. And maybe a performative sob on camera for your followers to see at the end of the day. The venue was a huge old church off the Marylebone Road, but there was nothing holy about this space. Years ago it had been turned into a private members' space which could be rented out for tens of thousands of pounds and had seen everything from minor celebrity weddings to the twenty-first birthday party of a Ukrainian oligarch's daughter which had to be shut down after the organisers allowed her to ride into the event on a horse spray-painted a pale blush colour. Even our equine friends cannot escape the proliferation of millennial pink.

I walked into the church sandwiched by throngs of other people, their dark glasses reflecting other dark glasses, their diamonds glinting in the sun and casting jewel-shaped shadows on the stone floor. The service was interminable. Ninety minutes of readings, songs, and even a slideshow of Bryony's most memorable moments – if a bunch of fucking selfies can count as memories. The true low moment was when a very skinny girl wearing a transparent shift dress displaying her neon underwear walked up to the lectern and began to read an excerpt from Bryony's favourite book – *The Secret*. The quivering vocal fry almost sent me over the edge, not helped by the next reading, the poem 'i carry your heart with me (i carry it in my heart)' by e e cummings – the patron saint of girls who want to appear to be deep but don't know any other poets. Thankfully it wrapped up pretty quickly after that. A gospel choir sang 'Stand By Me' beautifully, as weeping mourners hugged each other. Not a lot of actual tears, I noticed. Carefully arranged expressions of sadness, dry faces.

Mainly I was looking for Simon. The compère (clearly not the right word for such a solemn occasion but the man was wearing a suit with gold braiding and looked like a bingo caller, so I'm sticking with it) announced at the start of the ceremony that if anyone felt overwhelmed they should feel free to go out into the garden for some air. As a result, there was a stream of people heading for the door throughout the ceremony, only to come back wafting tobacco down the aisle. The constant back and forth meant that Simon was visible only half the time. I got a good view of him during the playing of an Adele song, as he heaved his shoulders and grabbed the neck of a young man sitting next to him in a fairly aggressive way which made the other man look faintly uncomfortable. It's a huge cliché for sure, but grief is not good for the skin. He really did look ten years older. I can only see Simon in a detached way, there is no true human link between us, but it nearly made me feel a sliver of sympathy for him. Then again, seeing him fall apart over the loss of a loved one also provoked a new sense of fury. Men often say they are feminists only when they have a daughter of their own and are forced to see women as equal human beings. Simon could only experience sadness and vulnerability when someone he loved had been taken from him. My mother died and he knew I had been left alone in the world. For me, there was nothing. He had the luxury to pick and choose who he held close. Well, now he didn't.

A week later I was sitting at home reading the papers while picking at a Danish pastry. One a week, a stupid rule I initiated to test my limits of self-denial. I opened up the Saturday supplements to find a diary item about Simon, which spoke of worries from friends about his mental health. Ah, mental health. The get-out clause for all bad behaviour. The friends were unnamed of course, but the quotes were revealing. Simon was 'paranoid and reclusive, muttering about enemies who were out to get him'. Not wrong, but it made him sound satisfyingly unhinged. Apparently he kept telling people that his daughter had definitely been murdered, despite police assurances that they were satisfied it had been a tragic accident. How awful it must be to know in your bones that those around you were being picked off one by one and to realise that you must therefore be next. Even worse, it seemed like nobody was listening to him – a terrible thing for a powerful white man to experience. I hadn't thought far enough ahead to really savour the prospect that Simon would begin to fear for his own safety. All along, I had only concentrated on the sadness he would face when I killed his loved ones. This panicked paranoia was an added bonus. It made me wonder whether his innate selfishness meant that this fear was actually stronger than any grief he felt. Exploring it further, I decided that it was. A man like my father would feel the loss of his family, but he'd be absolutely shaken by the idea that he might be in danger. A wife and daughter could be replaced – he would hardly be the first 50-something man to start another family in middle age – but his sense of safety was being tested for the first time. I felt so cheered by this realisation that I ate a second pastry in celebration.

* * *

At the time I thought that this moment in my life was glorious. Now I look back and see only how terrible it was all about to get. I had scored six names off my little list. Six down, one to go. The pressure had lifted and I began to cultivate some form of a life. I upped my running, took time to read a few of the books I'd been piling up on my bedside table, and even went on a few dates. Nothing much was doing in that department, because really who wants to carry on seeing a man who has vintage *Playboy* posters in his living room? People think that buying something and calling it vintage puts them a cut above. But old *Playboys* are still wank mags, just in faded colour. And men who order dirty martinis are not men who'll be playboying anywhere near me.

Anyway, the dates were not the highlight of that period. The wonderful thing was the feeling of a load lifting. I am stubborn. It's good to admit one's flaws. And that stubbornness meant that a plan I conceived as a child was one I felt sworn to carry out well into adulthood – to the detriment of everything else. If I hadn't decided that revenge was a path I had to charge down, I know my life would have been unthinkably different. Unthinkable mainly because to really consider what it could have been like is painful. It feels a little weak to admit that, but it's true nonetheless. As a result, I've never thought about it much. I've never thought about the career I could have had. I wanted to be a journalist at one point, which I imagine would've ultimately meant a life similar to the one I have now – deceit and drinking. I've never thought about the possibility that Jimmy and I could've built a life together without me holding him at arm's length while I completed my own private quest. I've never thought about how deliberately small I'd made my life, always filled with anger directed at people who never thought of me at all.

Even though I knew this, the anger burned bright. It bubbled out of me every time I walked past Simon's enormous gated house (and I did it a lot as a teenager, it being just fifteen minutes and a whole world away from the Latimer enclave), every time I saw a Google alert tell me that Bryony was in the *Daily Mail* sidebar of shame, every time Janine threw a charity gala and one of the society pages featured it. Every time they were projected into my world I felt a new burst of it, like another tendril had suddenly sprung and uncoiled.

But during this interlude I felt the anger wilt. Not entirely, you understand, I wasn't suddenly going to call it quits and walk away. But Caro had just arrived on the scene, and I was dealing with that spiteful spanner in the works. The drain on my focus made me notice I was spending a lot less time thinking about the Artemis clan (perhaps that's rubbing it in since there was no clan to speak of anymore) and more time thinking about the wider world and what I might do in it.

The vague plan I'd always carried in my head was one which looked something like this:

Kill my family
Make a claim on said family fortunes (this was pretty blurry in my mind, I didn't want the whole toxic empire, just a few million quid to be able to live life in any way I chose)
Get together with Jimmy (obviously this was almost stymied by Caro, but her helpful demise and my wrongful conviction meant that this was very much back on the cards)
Buy a house, travel, make some friends, adopt a dog
Get away with all of the above.

It was the scheme of a child, a lofty and ridiculous one, with no specifics or safety nets tacked on. The money was an added extra that I increasingly believed was in reach. But the plan, which formed when I didn't understand the wealth just beyond my fingertips, was all about revenge. I kept it stoked even when there were moments where I admitted to myself that it was a damaging obsession. But somehow I'd followed it fairly faithfully – grandparents, a breeze. Andrew, painful but well executed. Lee, pffft. Janine and Bryony, a triumph – and I was now tentatively sure I'd be able to follow it to completion. That feeling, after years of adrenaline, was intoxicating. So instead of actually knuckling down and finishing it all, I spent hours on estate agent websites looking at houses. St John's Wood was too gaudy, full of beautiful houses lived in by greasy people who thought chrome banisters were the height of elegance. Primrose Hill was exactly the same, only the people who lived there bought expensive vintage knick-knacks and thought they were better than chrome. Kensington is a terrible place altogether and I would never consider living in Clapham or Dulwich or anywhere else buggies outnumber adults. It took me three days to settle on Bloomsbury for my fantasy new home and a further two days of teaching myself how to do lino cuts before I realised how fucking slack I'd become.

I'd fallen into the danger zone of complacency and I was gloriously wallowing in it, stretching out and wiggling my toes. I gave myself a stern talking to, deleted dating apps, packed away books, nail varnishes, and anything else which might entice me into distraction, and cleaned my flat until it was all in order. Then I stuck an A3 piece of paper up on my bedroom wall and got back to it.

An hour later, I had written down ten ideas and they were all ridiculous. This part of the plan suddenly felt like the most gruelling, when I'd always thought it would be the best bit. Kill the boring Z-list members of the family to get to Simon. Race through the starters to get to the main course. But instead, I just felt like I was trudging on. So I put on my running kit and set off for Hampstead, taking a route I knew like the back of my hand. I ended up outside the Artemis gates hoping for inspiration. The road was quiet, except for a private security contractor in a yellow bib who wandered past me smoking a cigarette. He barely glanced at me, which confirmed my long-held suspicion that private guards are just there to give a false sense of security to paranoid rich people but could no more disarm a burglar than your grandmother could. Depending on the grandmother, she might actually have a better chance.

I stood just beyond the reach of the CCTV camera attached to the gate and looked up at the house, set back from the road and almost concealed by a garden which wrapped around the property.

The blinds were drawn on every window, shutting out the world. The front door, partially obscured by an enormous Range Rover, was firmly shut. It wasn't just a house in mourning, the homes of the ultra-wealthy often look as though they are uninhabited. Which, a lot of the time they are. When you've got four or five houses, you're not in one place very much. If Simon decided to flee to his Barbadian bolt hole or spend months walking around the Monaco penthouse wailing for Janine, I'd be in trouble. That last option was less likely, since he didn't seem to have spent too much time grieving for his wife, and I can't imagine wanting to hang around in the place where she came to a fairly grotesque end. But then the gates whirred into motion, and a soft-top sports car hove into view, being driven by a young guy who I guessed was an assistant. That must mean Simon was at home and that gave me some hope.

Back at home I crossed off all the plans I'd held in my head for him over the years. Some of them were silly, fanciful, unworkable. An early plan to pose as cabin crew on his private plane made me particularly embarrassed. How long would I have had to train to get to that point? Stupid Grace. Some were more realistic and I didn't disregard the idea to send a condolence parcel to his office which might just happen to contain a substance which just potentially might kill him within seconds. But mainly I felt a sinking feeling, that I'd done it all wrong, that I should have killed him before the rest of his terrible family. I'd made him paranoid and prone to hide away. In my excitement and my insistence on build-up, I'd made the final target almost impossible to reach.

My gloom infected my confidence and made me pull back from every partial plan I had laid out. Then matters were made infinitely worse when Jimmy got engaged to Caro, darkening my mood and causing me to wake up in the night, pulling at the skin at my neck, breathing heavily, sweating through my T-shirt. I felt a looming sense of doom, as if things were rushing ahead of me, already out of my grasp. I could not get a handle on anything.

And I was sadly, horribly right. Did you look back to the beginning of this text and note that I killed six members of my family? Did you see that we seem to have already reached this magic number? Well, there are no prizes for such eagle eyes. Don't be smug, or think me too much of a fool. I have already spent months dealing with my failure, trying to shake off the feeling that it was all for nothing.

For those with a slower cognitive process, I will spell it out. I did not kill Simon Artemis. My one aim in life and I will never get to achieve it. And why not? Because he's dead. Dead but from a terrible accident and not by my hand. I'd rather he lived another 50 years in ignominy and sadness than to die by fucking accident. What a cruel joke.

Three days after I was arrested for the murder of Caro Morton, Simon was reported missing by *The Times* newspaper. It wasn't front-page news at first, taking up half of page three (my initial arrest only made page six). But the next day, his face was on the front of every paper. Why would it not be? The story had everything, money, power, death, scandal, and an intriguing mystery. The media revisited their reporting on the tragic year in the Artemis family. Lee, whose death had been hushed up somewhat successfully at the time, was outed as a sexual deviant. A tabloid reporter managed to get into Janine's empty apartment and take photos of the sauna, sombrely accompanied by a caption which read 'Burned alive, did Simon take his own life after tragic wife's gruesome death?' Before there was any real certainty that he was dead, friends of Bryony used the story as an excuse to post photos of her with the hashtag #reunitedinheaven. If Heaven welcomed in sleazy moguls and spiteful posers, then something had gone horribly wrong in Elysium's HR department.

Simon had disappeared at sea. This makes him sound like an ancient mariner when in reality he'd started off on his speedboat while drunk, despite warnings from the crew. He'd fled to his villa in St Tropez, apparently. I didn't even know he had a house there, given that it's just round the coast from Monaco, but perhaps Janine wanted a country house for much-needed rest. The rich are slippery. None of these properties are ever in the name of millionaires. That's what anonymous offshore trusts are for. An assistant went with him, out of concern that he might do himself harm, which was pretty prescient as it happened.

According to the assistant, Simon was driving too fast, pushing the boat up onto its side. Alarmed, the assistant went to take control, and as he pushed past him, my sozzled father tumbled over the edge. The boat was travelling fast, and the assistant took a while to figure out how to get it under control. By the time he'd managed to slow it down and turn back, Simon was under the waves. The other man circled around for thirty minutes, searching in vain for any sign of his employer before returning to the yacht to call for help. The coastguard was called and a search took place but the dark sky and the expanse of water proved too much, and Simon Artemis was presumed dead. Presumed dead just means dead, doesn't it? They hadn't found his bloated corpse nibbled on by sea creatures, but perhaps it was only a matter of time. Or maybe his body sank to the bottom, quickly disintegrating, never to reemerge. It all amounted to the same thing. And as I write this, the authorities have yet to find any trace of him. Not even a monogrammed cufflink remains. He is gone. He never got to know what I had done.

I wept. I wept for two full days. The sorrow I felt was worse than when my mother died. Not for Simon but for all I had pinned on killing him myself. That it would make my life mean something. I would avenge Marie and prove that I could rise above my circumstances.

I would make things fair. Now all I had for my troubles was the knowledge that I successfully killed some pensioners, drowned a nice boy who wanted to help amphibians, enticed my uncle into a deathly sex club, and bumped off two spoilt women the world would never miss. Not quite the glorious victory I had envisaged for myself.

I didn't even have the opportunity to drink wine from the bottle and walk around my flat listening to The Cure in the bowels of sorrow. No such fun. I was charged with the murder of Caro Morton and arraigned. That I now had to face a trial for a murder I didn't commit felt like a surreal joke. I had been bested by the universe and if you believed in karma, which I do not, given that it's for people who also set store by crystals, then you would think I'd been whacked in the face with a suitcase full of it.

I've mentioned that I fell into some sort of depression early on in my prison stay. Perhaps it's a bit more obvious why it hit me so hard now. I didn't feel as though there was any point in bothering to fight the case because I didn't know what kind of life was now on offer to me that would be worth raising my hopes again for. I look back and see a shambling, vacant-stared husk of myself. I was being completely pathetic. Happily, the shock lifted. Partly the routine became less unbearable, you really do become institutionalised at a startling speed. I began to find it less scary and more boring and as my brain lowered the threat level, I started to think about things other than how to breathe normally when the doors locked at night. That meant taking an interest in my case and waking up to the weaknesses in it. I'd gone through the trial like a zombie, barely engaging with the process at all, weighed down by my own failures. But I began to see how my verdict could be challenged. That's when I brought in George Thorpe. As with so many parts of British life, if you want to be listened to, taken seriously and treated with respect, employ a posh white man to speak on your behalf. Even better if he's middle-aged. That's the privilege jackpot right there.

Thorpe made me see that I didn't have to take a jury decision as final.

'Grace, jurors are, let us say, not always the type of people we necessarily have to listen to. They are often wrong, largely motivated by their own small personal animuses and have a remarkably basic grasp of actual facts. There are many options open to us so let's see their verdict as a mere opening offer, shall we?' I could have kissed the man, had he not been wearing actual braces under his suit jacket.

The thing that really changed my attitude was reading that Lara had announced that she'd be opening the Artemis Foundation to help migrant children. I enjoyed this immensely, imagining this to be her final *fuck you* to a family only slightly less likely to care about the plight of vulnerable minors than the witch who lived in the gingerbread house. But it also panicked me. Just how good was Lara intent on being? If the money was about to be tied up in charitable trusts, I'd have a hard time accessing any of it. It's perhaps not a great endorsement of my character that I was boosted into action by the worry that my money would be given to scared refugees, but we are who we are. I've killed six people, there's very little point in panicking about my moral fibre now. I got to work then, any lingering depression fading away remarkably fast. I've even managed to reframe my failures. I didn't get to kill Simon, no point trying to soften that blow, but I did dispatch six members of his family in pretty quick succession, causing him great fear, confusion and grief which followed him all the way to his final moments. I comfort myself with the knowledge that he would never have been drunk and manic on a speedboat without my actions, so I did play a vital role in his death, even if I couldn't be there to witness his glorious demise. I don't like boats much, so perhaps it all worked out for the best in some strange way. I had a good hand, even if it wasn't quite the royal flush I'd hoped for.

CHAPTER SIXTEEN

I suppose I should start by introducing myself, otherwise this will be even odder for you than it already is. My name is Harry and I am your brother. Gosh that sounds silly, doesn't it, like I'm doing a terrible Darth Vader impression. But nevertheless, it's true. Not the same mother, of course, that would be nonsense. Same father, but that's probably obvious. Sorry, I'm no good at explaining all this.

Perhaps I'll just start at the beginning. I didn't find out who my father was until I was 23 years old. Well, that's not quite right actually. I spent that time with a lovely father. Christopher was a fantastic chap, always ready to drive me to rugby practice, taught me how to shoot when I was barely old enough to hold a gun. He used to come upstairs when Nanny had bathed me and put me in my pyjamas. Holding a glass of whisky, he'd perch on the side of my bed and read me a story every night. He wasn't a fan of modern children's books, preferring Arthur Ransom and John Buchan stories. He had a low, deep voice and used to gesticulate with his hands as he read to me, his drink swilling about so that the ice clinked together. It's a sound I enjoy to this day.

My parents had two daughters after me. There was a fairly solid age gap, five years between me and Molly, and another two between Molly and Belle. I was always told that it was because they were devoting all their attention to me that they'd waited. That was something I held over my sisters' heads a lot, let me tell you. It's fun having siblings, even with such an age gap. You were an only child, weren't you? I can't imagine not having co-conspirators around all the time.

Always someone to gang up on. Always somebody to play with. Mum has always been a nervous sort really, but a lovely woman despite it all. She worked before she had me, she was a primary school teacher, but I think what she really wanted to do was raise a family and live in the countryside. I know that's not a fashionable thing to say anymore, but it worked very well for our family. And Dad was happy enough to make that happen. I don't think Mum was strong enough for work. You'd probably think that was ridiculous. I know how tough you are. You probably also think that's ridiculous, since we've never met properly. But I'm right, aren't I?

Oh dash, I've rambled on, haven't I? As I said, I didn't find out who my real father was until I was an adult. I'd graduated from Exeter with a degree in PPE, and I'd made the move to London to work in the city and have some fun. Growing up in Surrey meant that London felt raw and exciting to me. Still does actually. You were born there, weren't you? I imagine you're jaded about the city, too used to it. Lucky you! Mainly though, I wanted to make money. We were well off, certainly. But I saw what the other lads had at my school, and I always felt a real desire to get that for myself. Christopher was the director of a mid-sized accountancy firm, and he earned a good-sized whack. It was always enough. Until, one day, it wasn't. That day was when a boy in my class came over for tea during half term when I was about eight, and asked if the driver could take him home later on. Mum smiled and said that she'd get him back safely, but he looked bemused. That's when I knew what I was missing. Funny that, realising at eight that you want a driver. I imagine most eight-year-olds want an Xbox.

Training to be a stockbroker was gruelling. About eighteen months in, I got a phone call one lunchtime when I was shovelling a sandwich into my mouth while trying to speed read that day's figures. It was Mum; her name is Charlotte, by the way – everyone in the family calls her Lottie. Dad had had a heart attack and she was at the Royal Surrey Hospital with my sisters. I hailed a cab on Liverpool Street and told the driver to get me there as fast as possible. But it was too late. He died before I arrived. I know you'll understand how I felt that day, having lost your mother so young. We were all inconsolable. I took three days off work to be with my mother and sisters, though Mum took to her bed and refused to speak much during that time. But I had to get back to work, and arranged for Granny to come down from York to stay with them. The funeral took place a week later. The church was stuffed full of Christopher's friends – those he'd had from school days at Eton, those he made from work and everyone in between. The choir sang 'Jerusalem' and everyone said what a true gent my dad was. Mum took a mild sedative to get through it, and my sisters wept a lot. But it was a proper send-off, a lovely day, despite the sadness. Or at least it was, right up until 5 p.m. The wake was back at our house. We'd had it catered, Mum was evidently not up to laying out a spread. So all there was to do was go around and accept as many sympathetic words as we could from the people in attendance. Mum had retired to her room half an hour before, and I was trying to speak to as many people as I could. The girls were sitting in the living room with Granny. They looked worn out. It was my duty now. As

I extricated myself from a dull man in a grey checked suit who'd worked for Dad and headed for the lav, I felt a tap on my shoulder. It was my aunt Jean. I call her my aunt, but really she was just my mother's oldest friend. As close as sisters though, and a fixture of my childhood, though I'd not seen much of her in the last few years. She looked old now, big hollowed-out rings under her eyes and a weird bony hand which grasped mine.

'I am so sorry about dear Christopher,' she sniffed. I murmured thanks and we made some small talk about the day. 'He always treated you just like a son. Always. He was a wonderful man.' You'll think me a fool, but I would absolutely not have realised what she'd said there, if it hadn't been for the fact that as soon as the words came out, she flinched, dropped my hand and her eyes bulged. Just for a second, you understand. But I saw that she'd frightened herself. Jean started to say her goodbyes, she had to go, it was a long drive. I nodded, gave her a hug and told her that I'd say goodbye to Mum for her. I dived into the downstairs loo and rummaged in my jacket pocket for the packet of fags I'd made sure to keep on me in case I needed a minute to myself that day. I know you do that too, don't you? Not all the time, not a morning coffee and a cigarette kind of girl. Just sometimes, when you need a break from the world. I borrowed your lighter once at the pub around the corner from your office. It's a good tactic if you want to spend a second or two looking at someone without them minding, or getting creeped out. I went out the side door and into the kitchen garden, where guests weren't congregating. Crouching over, with my back against the wall, I replayed Jean's comment in my mind again and again. A comment made by a sad woman that normally I'd have put down to mild battiness. But she looked so panic-stricken when she'd said it. There was no mistaking that. I think I'm a rational person, Grace. I pride myself on cutting through mumbo jumbo and quashing any self-denial. So the only sensible conclusion, as painful as it might be, was that somehow Christopher was not my real father.

I waited until the last guest had gone, made sure that my sisters were safely ensconced in front of the TV, and headed up the narrow staircase to my mother's bedroom. Was your mother weak, Grace? I imagine she was. I bet she was very similar to mine in many ways. The only difference is that my mother had a husband to protect her from the world and yours did not. I didn't want to land a harsh blow on her, that day of all days. But I suddenly felt so tired of tiptoeing around her, making sure that she wouldn't face any stress or unpleasantness as she often called it. I wanted to be blunt for once. And so I was.

Lottie wasn't asleep. She was just lying in semi-darkness, a cushion hugged to her as though it was a sleeping pet. She looked tiny, her wispy blonde hair spread over the pillows like a child's. I sat down on the other side of the bed and told her that I knew that Christopher wasn't my real dad. No point in letting her have even a tiny opportunity to lie. If I was expecting her to crumple and beg forgiveness, I was wrong. She ducked and weaved with an energy I'd not seen in her before. It was energy I didn't know she had in her, to be honest.

It took us ten minutes to get past the outraged stage, where she couldn't believe that I'd make such an allegation. It was twenty minutes to move on from the weeping and repeated insistence that we couldn't talk about such things today of all days. At the half an hour point, Lottie was hugging me, telling me that Christopher *was* my father, no matter what anyone said. Ten minutes later, she began to tell me the truth.

My mother had a fairly sheltered upbringing in Somerset, with a family who had a nice little ancestral home and a respected name. Not too much money for her when the first child was a prized son, but she was happy enough. She went to London aged 20, ostensibly to work at an art gallery off Savile Row, but mainly, she told me, to have an adventure. For my mother, this meant a lot of parties, nightclubs and jaunts to the south of France with rich pals. I knew she'd lived in London before she'd had me, but I was a little surprised at the freewheeling life she was telling me about now. My mother has worn cardigans and wellies every day of my life. It's still hard to imagine her going to some of the clubs that I frequent in town. She already knew Christopher, she told me, but they were just friends. He was shy, something I knew he had been all his life, and she didn't notice him much when out in a group.

One night, at the nightclub Vanessa's, she was sitting in a booth with a group of girlfriends when a waiter brought over a glass of champagne and told her that it was from the gentleman at the bar. When she looked over, she saw a dark-haired man in a T-shirt and black trousers, staring at her intently. Between quivering breaths, my mother explained that she was intrigued. Most of the men she knew were already facsimiles of their fathers. Proper and reserved, looking for the right kind of wife. This man was different, and her girlfriends made a huge fuss about the approach, urging her to go and talk to him. So she did. My anxious mother, who takes to her bed whenever life overwhelms her, walked over to this stranger and struck up a conversation.

I don't need to tell you the rest really do I, Grace? Because you know. It's not your story, and yet it is. By the time Lottie found out that she was pregnant, this man had moved on. And she wasn't strong like your mother. Terrified by what her parents would think, she carried on working in a state of denial. Until one day, my father turned up at the flat she shared with a couple of friends just off the Kings Road and told her that he knew what had happened. I don't know whether he'd guessed or what, Lottie was crying at that point and I didn't want to push it, but he was very kind and told her that they should get married. That makes me smile to think of. Such an act of Victorian heroism from the old man. It was the Nineties, for chrissakes! But my grandparents were old fashioned, and I'm sure would've hated any society gossip. As would my mother, for that matter. There is a section of the British upper class which enjoys scandal, or at least finds it all a hoot. My family, despite our good fortune, weren't quite at that level. She smiled as she remembered her reaction to this proposal, still hugging the cushion to her body.

I don't know whether Lottie loved Christopher with a romantic passion back then. Maybe she never did. But they were happy, Grace. Really happy. And that seems like it might mean more than the fireworks and passion that men are always being told women want. Prince Charles, who seems like a decent guy, got in a whole heap of trouble when he answered a reporter who asked if he was in love with Diana by saying 'whatever "in love" means'.

I didn't know what to do that night. Watching Mum cry was an awful thing. So I hugged her and gave her a sedative that our family doctor had prescribed for her and left her to sleep. The rest of it came out over the next few weeks. I went back to work and travelled to my mother's house every Friday night, walking the dog for miles with my sisters and making sure Mum ate (she has a tendency to forget when she's anxious). Occasionally I'd ask a question or two about my dad, and she'd flush and sag. Sometimes she'd answer, sometimes she wouldn't, or couldn't. But I couldn't let it go. I'd look at my sisters and suddenly see the ways in which their features weren't like mine. I'd wonder which bits of me were from my mum and which bits were not. My temper was always a source of conversation in my family – I can explode in a way that nobody else does. Christopher was far too mellow, Lottie far too meek. Now I knew it was given to me by someone else. Breeding matters to me, Grace.

Not in some stuffy blueblood way, like some of the chaps I went to school with who sought to know what land your family owned in the 1500s, but because it tells you things about yourself that nothing else can. I thought I was the son of Christopher and Lottie Hawthorne and I knew what that meant. I knew who I was, and who I would be. And now I had to figure out the ways in which I was wrong about it all.

She gave me my father's name on a Sunday, just as I was loading my car up to go back to London. As I lifted the last bag from the boot room, she came over to me, wrapping her arms around her body as though she was protecting herself from me, and kissed my cheek.

'Simon. Simon Artemis,' she whispered, as she pulled away from me and walked purposefully back towards the kitchen where my sisters were making cakes.

I am not *au fait* with the world of celebrity. Ask me about the Kardashians and I will proudly tell you that I thought they were a Middle Eastern dynasty until two years ago. But I know the world of business and that name hit me right between the bollocks. The whole drive home I scoured my brain for every detail I had on him. His parents were bog-standard comfortable middle class – and proud of their recently attained status – but Simon wanted much more for himself. He had that aggressive business mind from the start. He started a market stall selling second-hand electronics down his local high street, but moved on to selling vintage clothes in a poncey West London neighbourhood, when he realised the resale value was higher on a grubby old poncho if you could spin a line about how Jane Birkin might have worn it in the Sixties. He bought his first shop aged 19, which he stocked with old tat bulk-bought from flea markets. It didn't look so grubby when modelled on stick thin mannequins and bathed in cool neon lighting. Buffered by his family's own financial security, Simon ran this mini empire all while attending university. Much of his 'self-made image' is just that. Image. But it's helped his reputation immensely.

Clothing wasn't Simon's main business interest, though. His real money came from investment and property, but the fashion brand kicked it all off. Since then the Artemis empire had only grown, making him a permanent fixture on the rich list. Simon Artemis was a government adviser on trade and commerce, a token role really but it gave him a sheen of respectability that, to be honest, he didn't earn.

I don't know how much you know (or care) about his businesses, but he was a wheeler-dealer from the start and not much changed over the decades. His fashion business worked when so many others failed because he kept a fierce eye on margins and exploited every loophole available to him. He bought Sassy Girl with money from private investors and then paid them back with assets he drew from the business. It didn't cost him a fucking penny! He pivoted to churning out new clothes when he discovered factories in faraway countries where labour laws were non-existent. This changed when there was an outcry over factory conditions in the mid-Nineties, but he just moved operations to another country more eager to turn a blind eye and more able to keep journalists and activists at arm's length. Simon employed a team of lawyers and accountants to ensure he paid the minimum UK tax possible, and he kept staff on very dubious contracts which often ended before he'd have been liable to pay benefits. NDAs were rife at his company – God only knows what they covered. There were at least eight cases of women dismissed when they got pregnant, and though his representatives were able to successfully argue that there had been legitimate reasons for the firings, everyone knew that the Artemis company was run by sharks.

I don't have a problem with any of this, by the way. I believe that business should regulate itself, and that legislation designed to protect workers exponentially stifles innovation and growth. Tie the hands of a corporation too tightly and it will have no choice but to move its headquarters somewhere else – a disaster for the UK economy. Simon played within the law, and I don't blame him for exploring the limits of it.

I found it hard to accept who my father was for a different reason, and I'm aware that it may paint me in a bit of a bad light to you, Grace. But I'm being totally honest here, and it's not like you can do anything with this so I have the freedom to be blunt. My main reaction when I found out who my real father was after twenty-three years was one of enormous embarrassment. Christopher was a man who knew which Wellington boot was just the right shade of green so as not to be flashy. He wore subdued wool suits and would never have countenanced a gold card for fear of looking gauche. I grew up in a family where taste and etiquette were innate, bred into us, never discussed because we never needed to articulate any of it. But this man was the opposite of everything I understood. I spent a couple of days searching the internet for every bit of information I could find on him and every single page I clicked on horrified me. Simon owned a fleet of cars with personalised number plates. He wore a ring on his pinkie finger with a coat of arms he'd had designed for his family by a jeweller who sold mainly to Russians. There were various *Hello!* spreads which showed off the Artemis family home and the amount of cream and gold on display made me groan out loud. It was all indescribably tacky. It was new money, new furniture, *arriviste*. Everything I knew I wasn't, without ever having to articulate why.

I just couldn't get my head around how Lottie could've been seduced by such a chap. She was weak and young, sure, but Christ this man was antithetical to everything she'd ever known. It disgusted me, truth be told. My sisters were born into a happy family where convention and tradition meant a lot. I thought that I was too. But instead, I had landed here after my mother was foolish enough to give herself up for one night with a playboy who holidayed in Marbella and occasionally featured on a TV show about new business ideas called *Mogul Wars*.

Class matters, Grace. I know it's not the done thing to say that, but I think it's utter madness to deny a truth just because it's uncomfortable. I don't know what you thought of Simon's background or his fondness for watches so large they could be a bedside alarm clock, but I imagine you had similar reservations. I don't want to say that it was worse for me, but come on, it was worse for me. I grew up bang slap in the middle of the rigid class system the British skilfully created a thousand years ago. It's always worse for those of us who are teetering precariously between the categories – at least you knew where you were in the order.

I spent a few months bouncing between work and Lottie's house, trying to give my sisters a sense of normality, and if I'm honest, trying to give myself the same. In London, I was progressing in the office and earning a decent whack, but back in Surrey it became increasingly obvious that Christopher hadn't been quite as comfortable as we'd assumed. His will left everything to Lottie – the house, the car, his investments, and pension – but he'd remortgaged without any of us knowing just three years ago, and he'd been dipping into his pension to pay the girls' school fees and cover lifestyle expenses. Nothing too fancy – Christopher wasn't a spendthrift – but as I say, our social circle had pretty exacting standards and Dad was clearly as keen to keep up with the Joneses as anyone. Only in our case, it was the Guinnesses, the Montefiores, the Ascots.

Lottie preferred to bury her head in the sand, distracting herself from any immediate issues that her husband's death had thrown up by gardening almost obsessively from dusk until dawn. Every time I tried to broach the subject with her, bulbs would be shoved in my hands or weeds lobbed at my person. Once she walked through a spiky hedge just to get away from the conversation. But I had pored over the numbers and I knew that we needed a cash injection and fast. Losing the house would be an indignity that none of us would easily bounce back from. Our family is traditional, and I was now the head of the house, regardless of modern norms. Lottie couldn't or wouldn't face up to the facts, so I took on the mantle.

I'm practical, Grace. I was often berated by my English teacher for lacking the imagination necessary to understand great fiction. I couldn't see the point in most of it myself; if I'm going to read a book, I want it to be an autobiography. Sports focused if possible. I've never felt it held me back in life. I'm not a dreamer. I know what I want and what I need for a good life, and I'll work my arse off to get it. But I didn't have enough time to secure my family's future while holding a junior position in the City. So I took a different course of action.

Can you see what's coming a mile off? I guess it's fairly obvious. I decided that Simon would be our lifeline. The thought first came to me one night in my bedroom, as I went over the accountant's notes on the mortgage, the school fees, the running of the house. The outgoings were enormous and there was no future income large enough to knit it together. *Just ask your real father*, a voice inside my brain whispered. I almost laughed. Me, contacting that man out of the blue, and asking him to fund a family he knew nothing about. Nonsense. And even if I could, I certainly didn't want to get involved with that man. Not from any moral qualms – money is money and he certainly had plenty – but because it was all so tasteless and grubby. A newfound father, a man who was photographed with oligarchs at slightly seedy private members' clubs. A Bentley driver.

I dismissed the thought, but it kept coming back. Every time I looked at the finances, his name danced around my mind. Finally, after a slightly harried conversation with the accountant, who explained bluntly that the girls would have to leave their school at the end of the year unless something was done, my resolve crumbled.

You don't email a man like Simon Artemis. I've learnt that from a few short months in the finance world. People like that are too important. They have five assistants and their inbox is monitored, sieved, messages prioritised and actioned in minutes. Anything I sent would be assigned to the 'bonkers' pile and left well alone. So I turned up at his office. It was a risky move, but I felt the direct approach suited me well. From reading the financial pages every day, I knew that the Artemis company was eyeing up a smaller clothing company called 'Re'belle' with choice real estate in Soho and Kensington. The ancient owner wasn't budging, insisting that the business would always be a family-run one. I used the name of his son at reception, and said I was there to open up a new channel of communication. It could've all gone tits up, but the assistant seemed to know who I professed to be (I suppose Benny Fairstein is a fairly memorable name if you're in the fashion business) and got on the phone immediately. I only had to wait for ten minutes before I was shown into Simon's office. His eyes narrowed as I entered, and I knew I only had a moment to explain who I really was.

Grace, you're the only other person in the world who I care to share this with. I know you'll find it fascinating, without being interested solely in the gossipy element of it. I was direct, I did not apologise for the false pretences. I sat down in an armchair across from him and looked him dead in the eye, and I told him that I was his son. Even before I explained further, I have to say he didn't seem very surprised. Perhaps he'd been waiting for a stray child or two to appear. Sensible, if so.

I told him about Lottie, I asked him to cast his memory back. I waited. He examined my face with his eyes, and I examined his right back. We alighted upon our identical noses at the same moment. I guess in a film that moment would have cued up some soaring background music. But we sat in silence. Then he asked what I wanted. Now in business there are two ways of approaching this question. You can obfuscate, flatter, and throw up vague and unfinished ideas, or you go direct. I have no time for the first option. I told him that I had no intention of embarrassing him, that I didn't want to be the long-lost son eager to join his new empire. I respected him, I assured him, but I had a family to support now and he was the only person who could help me out. I proposed a one-time deal, slid a figure tucked in an envelope across the table, and sat back. He opened it, and he laughed. I'm not sure what I was expecting but laughter wouldn't have been my top guess. Looking back, I think it impressed him. Maybe he thought it was a power play. It wasn't – I just wanted money plain and simple – but perhaps the leverage I had was enough to make me bold.

The strange thing was, it broke the ice. I guess when you're that rich you spend your life assuming and suspecting that everyone wants something from you. If a person just confirms that outright, you can move on together. Instead of addressing my request, he stretched back in his chair and pressed the intercom, telling his PA to cancel his next meeting. Then he asked me about my life – where I lived, what I did, which football team I supported. It felt a bit weird initially, but I went along with it. He nodded when I told him about Christopher, and smiled when I said I was working in the City. It turned out that we both supported QPR, and we swapped opinions about the manager for a bit, him ribbing me for missing their last big game. To an outsider, it might have looked like a standard father–son encounter. I kept thinking that. I kept remembering that this man was my dad. This tanned, gym fit man in a steel grey suit who was wearing a gold watch which flicked sunshine into my eyes when he moved his arm.

God, I'm boring on, Grace, I'm sorry. But this whole situation has been truly bonkers for me, and I'm not the sort to let it all out to a therapist. Best to crack on, I always think. And I've got very little to complain about really. A nice family, a good job, financial stability. Ah yes – I should get to that. Simon gave me the money. It took some wrangling, which was surprisingly good-natured. My initial figure was rejected out of hand, but we eventually settled on a nice six-figure sum to tide Mum over until I was in a more senior position to shoulder the burden. It came on the proviso of a DNA test, which I understood, but still silently seethed about. I felt like Lottie's honour was being called into question. But there's little honour with businessmen like Simon, is there? We both know that.

In the six weeks it took to negotiate the settlement, I met with Simon a few times. Often at his office, but once in a while at a private members' club off Berkeley Square. On one occasion, we went to a match together, eschewing his private box for the stands – I suspect he didn't want to introduce me to his friends, which I understood. How do you introduce your secret son to a bunch of property tycoons who would love to tap that kind of vulnerability while eating food from a buffet you've paid for? QPR won 2–1 and our relationship stepped up a gear. It didn't take a genius to see that Simon enjoyed having a son. I might not have been a son he raised, or even a son he knew very well, but he got a kick out of it anyway. He bantered with me, mocked my blazer, offered to introduce me to his City mates. Sometimes he'd arrange to meet me under the pretence of going over the terms of our little arrangement, only never to mention it when we were face to face, preferring to buy me a drink, tell me about his latest deal, challenge me to a game of cards.

There was a swagger to our dear old dad. Not exactly charm, but a teeth-baring grin, a confidence that overwhelmed others, a feeling that things could go well for you but only if he wanted them to. His handshake conveyed a serious strength, but it felt a little contrived – like he'd read a manual on how to show dominance with physical contact. He knew the names of doormen, valets, the cleaner in his office, and more than once I saw him press money into their palms with a sort of aggressive gallantry. And still everyone who passed him looked faintly scared of the man. It felt pretty good to be the one in his company, truth be told. Respect, that's what it felt like to me. People nodded at me as though I must be someone too, if I was part of Simon Artemis's inner circle.

But when I wasn't being dazzled by the power he exuded in the flesh, I would remember that he wasn't wholly respected in the way he'd have liked to imagine he was. People in the City took a dim view of his bully boy tactics – it looked pretty grim when the *Evening Standard* did another splash on him double parking his latest supercar outside a hospital entrance so he could go get a massage, or berating a waiter for failing to clear plates at the speed he felt it warranted. A table was turned over on that occasion, if I remember correctly. The worst of his behaviour was his propensity to take a piss off the top of his office building, no matter which unfortunate might happen to be walking the pavement below. Luckily the press never picked up on that delightful titbit. Simon would call journalists who wrote such pieces, haranguing them for writing 'bollocks', and dismissing the stories as jealousy. Once, after he held a fiftieth birthday for his wife at the Colosseum (he actually hired out the bloody Colosseum, Grace), a tabloid ran a story sniffing at the reported £500,000 price tag, and he sent the journalist a first-class ticket to Rome with a note which read 'Sorry you'll have to queue with the rest of the great unwashed fuckers. Bet you'd have liked to see it at dusk with a glass of champagne in hand like we did.' I wonder if she took him up on the offer?

He wanted to be part of the establishment, but he couldn't quite conceal his provenance. I once looked down at his hands as he was talking and noticed that his nails were buffed shiny, almost as if he'd had a manicure. I suppose he might well have. I'm no metro-sexual, but I know there are chaps who go in for that. But it's never going to sit exactly right with the old guard, is it? But then he'd have known that and he still retained those gaudy edges. It was like he understood he'd never quite fit and so he doubled down. He'd drive up to a charity dinner in a car so flashy it would make people actually grimace, but then he'd spend more money than anyone else at the after-dinner auction, knowing that that way, high society would be forced to talk to him. To thank him. To engrave his name on a gallery wall.

Christ, I'm rambling again. All of this is to try and sum up how conflicted I was about the whole thing. He was charming and interested in me and I'll admit I was a bit swept up in that. But I never felt totally comfortable in his company and was relieved when negotiations were wrapping up. The way I saw it, he'd pony up for eighteen years of my upkeep, and I'd be able to look after my family. Done and done. I'd never have blackmailed him or anything sordid. If he'd rejected my request I'd have walked away. I'm pretty proud and I wouldn't have begged for it. I hoped that he'd be a gentleman about it all, and to an extent, he was. But there had to be something in it for Simon. You don't get to be that rich without a constant *quid pro quo*, I guess. I'd thought my silence was the leverage, but I was completely wrong.

After he'd done the bank transfer (from his accountant to mine, complete with an NDA so tight it'd make your eyes water), he shook my hand and ordered a round of drinks. That night we spent nearly six hours together, in a private room at one of Soho's finest restaurants where the steak he ordered for me cost £68 and the waiters didn't make eye contact. It was like a date, and every time he ordered another bottle I blinked at the absurdity of it all. I kept trying to leave but Simon would brush my attempts away with irritation. 'We're getting to know each other, son of mine! What could be more important?' Then he'd plunge into another story about his clever business strategy, or explain how he fucked over a rival by being more ruthless. I got home and rolled into bed at 3 a.m., knowing that I'd have to be up again in three hours. I woke up at 6 a.m., my head screaming in pain and my hands shaking. I picked up my phone and saw he'd already texted me. *Football this weekend. See you for breakfast before.* Even though my mind was cloaked in fog, I understood then that there would be no clean break here. Simon had paid up and now he wanted me in the fold. Was it because he liked me and was glad to have found this long-lost son? Could have been. More likely though, he just wanted to control the situation, control me. If he had to endure being put in a vulnerable position, he was going to extract something, anything from it. Even if I didn't want to play ball. Especially if I didn't.

I don't know what I'd have done if I'd had to go on like this for years, playing the version of a son he wanted. Within just a few weeks of handing over the money, it was already pretty unbearable, Grace. The fascination with me wore off pretty quickly, and Simon started to treat me like he treated everyone else. That meant I was expected to jump to it when called. He'd call when I was at the office, and if I didn't pick up, he'd just call again. One day I put my phone on flight mode for eight hours just so I could avoid the blinking light out of the corner of my eye. When I turned it off, I had three text messages from him, one which called me a 'lazy cunt'. The message was wrapped up in his usual banter, but it was obvious that he meant it.

I continued to go home as much as possible. My mother was doing a little better, though still gardening obsessively. I didn't tell Lottie that I was spending so much time with Simon, of course. I didn't tell her anything. The school fees were paid and the mortgage settled. Lottie didn't ask how I'd managed it all. It made me feel angry for a minute, she'd always had everything handled for her and never stopped to consider what it took. But it was ungenerous of me. Mum couldn't be expected to know what I'd done to secure our family. She wasn't strong enough. She might never be strong enough.

Simon only mentioned my mother once in my presence. After our first meeting I had wondered whether he really remembered her. It was clear she wasn't exactly the only woman to have received the full Artemis treatment. It would have been understandable if she was just a vague blur in his mind. But he glanced down at my phone one day, as it lit up with a text alert and noticed my screen saver.

'That your mum?' he asked, his eyes focused on a photo of Lottie hugging my sisters on the lawn outside our home. I nodded, but tensed up slightly, not wanting him to see my family or pollute our space. 'Christ, time isn't kind to women,' he said. 'You shack up with a firecracker at 25 and you wake up at 50 with your nan.' A white-hot rage swept up my body, heat flooding my face. I tipped over the small bar stool with rather too much drama, and stormed out. Simon sent me a case of wine later that night, my housemate Ben bringing it up to my room and asking who was buying me £5,000 worth of plonk. At least it was good wine and not the filth he served up under his own label. Anyway, wine or no wine, it was too late. I'd decided that I was done with this late-in-life dad. I was going to write him a letter explaining that I was grateful for his help but emphasising that I had spent twenty-three years with a wonderful father and wasn't looking for a replacement. I felt rather an astonishing amount of relief as I typed it out that night. His world was overwhelming and I wanted to go back to mine.

And that might've been that. He would've kicked off a bit, but really what could he do? My existence was a potential grenade in his life and I couldn't see that changing. He would never tell his wife or daughter about me. And I didn't want him to. Better to shake hands and go our separate ways – I felt confident that he'd see that eventually.

But that night Simon's parents were killed in a car crash. I found out when he called me sobbing the next morning. I had the letter in my bag, ready to send on my way to the office. Instead I found myself leaving work (I pleaded a family emergency, which wasn't a total lie) and heading for Simon's house in Hampstead. His wife and daughter were in Monaco, he had said. Could I come over? I'm not a monster, I couldn't leave the man crying alone. So I sat in his lurid mansion as a small Vietnamese woman served us iced tea and offered up an endless amount of biscuits. The biscuits sat uneaten, even though I was starving. The iced tea was rejected in favour of a bottle of whisky that Simon kept reaching for, topping up a gold glass on the floor by his feet. Simon himself sat slumped on a sofa surrounded by huge tasselled cushions that threatened to envelop him. I positioned myself across from him, perched on a large pouffe, wishing fervently that I was almost anywhere else on earth.

In between phone calls to his brother, a lawyer, and his assistant, he talked in my general direction about how Kathleen and Jeremy were 'diamonds'. I offered him up some words of condolence, and told him I knew how hard it was to lose a parent. He didn't much like that, slurring that I was trying to make him feel bad about not taking on his responsibilities. So then I apologised, trying to downplay my own loss and then being annoyed with myself for doing it.

The day dragged on, and I was mainly left on my own in the sitting room as Simon took more phone calls and drank more whisky. At 4 p.m., he muttered something about Bryony being on her way home, which I gratefully took as my cue to leave. As I made obvious moves towards the door, Simon grabbed my arm and pulled me down onto a peach chaise longue in the hallway. And then, in a slightly garbled and not entirely coherent way, he told me something which changed the course of my life. He told me about you, Grace.

Until that moment, I don't think I'd really examined the idea of having a whole other family. Simon was a means to an end – I had my family and I didn't have any desire to know Bryony or her ghastly mother. I didn't want much to do with the way they lived and I suspected that they'd feel the same about me, had they had any idea of my existence. But you were different. You were an outsider, someone who had no choice in the matter either. And as Simon rambled about how he'd failed to live up to the standards set by his own parents, I saw the similarities in our stories. Both born to young and silly women dazzled by this big man, and then cast aside when he was bored and it became inconvenient. Though I do think that two illegitimate kids by two different women stretches the word 'inconvenient' somewhat.

I don't know why he told me about you, Grace. He was drunk, but he must've been drunk a thousand times and not told people about his secret daughter. I can only suppose it was the grief. It's supposed to do funny things to people, isn't it? Like my old aunt Jean, toeing the party line on my parentage for twenty-three years and blurting it out at a funeral as though she couldn't hold it in any longer. He told me that he was young, that his parents had told him to sort the problem and that he'd been afraid of losing everything. It was all bollocks, of course. A real gentleman wouldn't abandon one child, let alone two, but I couldn't say that while he sat there drunk and weeping. I just told him he'd done what he thought was best while I asked questions about you as gently as I could.

In his slightly broken state, his guard was down just enough to give me enough to go on. I'll be frank with you. He didn't know much. His sadness about it all was pretty performative and I don't imagine he'd kept up with your life. I hope that doesn't upset you. From what I know of you, I imagine it won't. He knew your name, and where you'd grown up. He even knew that you worked in fashion, which meant that 'the apple didn't fall far from the old tree' apparently. I stayed poker-faced, not showing that this information meant a thing to me, and I extricated myself half an hour later, at which point he was on the phone shouting at his brother about the family house in St John's Wood. He'd forgotten everything we'd discussed.

But I hadn't. I spent the next two hours in a pub trying to find out as much as I could about you from Google. I must say, Grace, you've got a remarkably minimal online presence. It's so small as to make one suspicious actually. It's almost as if you're trying to hide from the world. Still, you can't avoid it entirely, can you? There's always going to be a footprint, even if you have sworn off social media and seemingly never so much as looked at LinkedIn. Well done you for that, by the way, it's a cesspit of braying estate agents and other bullshit merchants.

It took a little while, because Simon hadn't given me your surname and asking for it would've been too direct, despite his drunken fog. But I found you eventually, after spending hours sifting through girls called Grace who worked in fashion PR. I worked by digging up info on the other girls, most of whom gave enough information about their lives on social media to make it easy to eliminate them. Happy photos of their families? Off the list. Wrong age, wrong ethnicity, lived somewhere else? Crossed off. Eventually I came across Grace Bernard. There was no photo on the company website, which felt like a sign since everyone else was happy to pose away. With the surname, I went down a few wrong lanes before I landed on a tiny article about you in the *Islington Gazette* from well over a decade ago. Well, it wasn't actually about you at all. A woman called Sophie was protesting about a spate of muggings near the local school. A grainy photograph showed her holding up a sign which said 'safe streets!', and behind her was a surly-looking teenage girl and a slightly bemused-looking boy of the same age. The photo, well that's when my heart started pounding. The caption gave your name. The boy was called Jimmy. The angry woman referred to you both as her children, which confused me for a minute. Simon had said that your mum died. Sorry, I'm being nosey. But there were gaps I couldn't fill in and the mind wants answers! No matter, I got them later.

Anyway, I came to your office. I'm sure that probably sounds frightfully creepy but I felt more nervous than you'd have been had you known! I waited around from 5 p.m. one Friday, suspecting that PR girls, like us City boys, knock off early for drinks. A gaggle of women came out at 5.15, forming a human chain as they swept down the street. You came out at 5.32. I knew it was you straight away, you looked like me. Well maybe that's not very fair to you. My nose has been broken twice in rugby scrums and I've got hands the size of dinner plates according to my mum. But I just knew your face. It was like I'd seen it before a million times. You're petite and have much darker colouring than me, and you've got eyes a shade of green that neither me nor my sisters share. Mine are a slate grey, which I've always rather liked. But you were undeniably the right Grace Bernard. I almost ran across the road to say hello, like the duffer I am, but I restrained myself. Difficult to make an introduction like that on the street!

I don't know what I wanted from you back then. Perhaps just to see you in the flesh? I think I had a deep need for information. Not knowing about my parentage had shaken me up, and I firmly believe that knowledge is power. Knowing everything about you would help me be more in control, something I'd not really felt since Christopher died. So I followed you. I'm not proud of that, by the way. It's not nice for men to tail women around. I felt grubby really. You sat on the Tube across from me, gazing over my shoulder at nothing very much. I tried not to stare at your face for too long, but I took in as much as I could. Black trousers, a cropped leather jacket, and a weird fluffy top that I assume was fashiony. Chunky buckled loafers which I imagine you wore to make men like me feel intimidated, and it worked. I walked behind you from the station to your flat, and gazed up to the first floor as the light went on. Then I had a stern word with myself and went home. Madness really. I'm a man who doesn't even go to North London for a hot date.

I couldn't leave it there. I wanted to. But over the next few weeks I found myself walking down your road every spare moment I got, hoping to catch you on your way out. Seeing if you'd lead me somewhere that would tell me more about who you were. A couple of times I saw you go out running, which meant I had to wear trainers just in case. Once I followed you to a local café where you ordered a ridiculously specific coffee. Not a big socialiser, are you, Grace? One visitor in two weeks – a man who looked a lot like the teenager in the local paper.

I was getting sort of bored of it all by then. I was ready to stop following you around and weighing up whether I should send you an email explaining who I was. I wasn't sure I even wanted to open Pandora's box really. But it was surely saner than skulking around, not learning anything about you. Then one evening flipped everything on its head. And if I'd ever assumed that you were a bit dull Grace, I never would again.

You went to a pub and had drinks with a fairly motley crew. A young guy who looked like a total hippy cliché. An old man, and a plain-looking girl who wasn't his daughter but definitely wasn't his girlfriend. You didn't seem like you were too attached to the hippy either. But you spent most of the evening talking to him. I nursed my pint and tried to sit near enough to pick up the conversation. Not that it was worth hearing. Newts, Grace? I really wondered about how you'd turned out when I heard that passionate discussion about amphibians.

You left alone, shortly followed by the crusty, and I was intrigued. When you wandered down the road and went into a wildlife centre, I was completely bemused, but followed your lead and jumped the fence a few minutes after you'd gone in. I began to suspect that you were looking for a place to be alone with the chap, and I worried that I might catch you both *in flagrante*, as it were – something a brother should never see a sister engaged in. So I stayed well away as you both went down to the deck by the water. Not quite near enough to hear what was said, but transfixed all the same. Something odd happened where he held a match to your foot, but I couldn't make out much in the dark. And then, just as my legs started to seize up from crouching and I started to think about whether I could order an Uber to a remote wildlife centre, you pushed him into the water. I stood up in shock, Grace. You looked round quickly but I was protected by the dark. I didn't know what to do. My brain was screaming at me to rush to the water and pull the fellow out, but my legs didn't move. It all seemed so utterly mad. You were sharing a bottle of wine with this harmless-looking man, and then you were killing him. Why? As you tidied up around you (impressively calmly when I think back to it), I dialled 999 but I didn't press call. I told myself I would when you left, but by the time you actually did, my mind was calmer and I knew I couldn't. How to explain what I was doing? Ah yes, officer, it's all fairly simple, I was following my sister (who doesn't know she's my sister) and I lurked behind this lovely bush while she drowned a fellow. Then I watched as she washed up some mugs and hopped into a cab. That would never do. However good my intentions, I'd be dragged into a sordid story and Lottie and the girls would be marked by it too. Whatever you'd done was your business. But it did make me realise that perhaps the vague notion I'd had about forging a relationship with you was doomed to fail. You can't be too close with a woman who goes around pushing people into ponds really, whatever the blood ties.

Simon let me know who you killed two days later. Less whisky and regret this time around, he obviously wasn't that fond of his nephew. But it was still a shock. An accident, he said. Andrew was troubled and had tried to seek a new life, but he was always floundering. The family were keeping it as private as possible, and I knew that the potential scandal was the reason for such privacy. That only made me feel like I'd made the right choice to stay schtum.

So you'd killed our cousin. But why? As far as I could tell, he was a nice man with no connection to you. You wouldn't benefit from his death financially, and I couldn't see what you got out of it emotionally. It buzzed around my head, getting worse and worse because I couldn't tell anyone about what I knew.

I guess a therapist looking at me around that time would say I was still processing Christopher's death, and for all I don't hold with that stuff, they'd probably be spot on. On top of that I was bombarded by Simon, who had stepped up his demand for contact, plus I had Lottie asking me to come home every time she called. I felt quite bonkers. As a deflection from it all, I kept on following you, desperate to figure it out, to know why you'd done it. I became a man slightly possessed. For a while, things went quiet and I scratched my head wondering why you'd kill our cousin and then blend back into the background. I started running, following your routes, but you never did anything out of the ordinary. But a few months later, you started to go to nightclubs and bars alone. I started going too, always sitting a little way away, careful to try to blend in. It's not hard to do that, Grace, when you're a fairly average-looking white guy in a smart establishment. I seem to blend in well, you've never seemed to remember my face, though I was by your side for months. Besides, you weren't looking for me. You were on the hunt. For our uncle, it turned out. That's when I started to figure out what was going on. I suppose you'd think I was a bit slow at the uptake really. But my feelings towards Simon were nothing like yours, and it took me a while to try to put myself in your shoes. Even when I did, I couldn't muster up the burning hatred it would take to carry out such a plan. Watching you spend hours waiting in bars only for your eyes to light up when Lee walked in, that could only be something you'd planned.

I still wasn't entirely certain, mind you. For a while, I thought you were playing out some kind of mad fetish where you were actually going to sleep with your own uncle. I'm sorry for thinking that, but you've got to admit it's weird to watch someone walk into a sex club with a relative. I enjoyed that night actually. It's not something I'd normally go in for but I thought I'd better get in character. At an orgy, a man in chinos would probably stick out more than a bloke in assless chaps would at an annual budget meeting. I wore a mask which made me feel like I was playing a role and I was sad I had to leave the fun early when you took Lee down the hall to a private room.

Anyway, when I saw what happened, I knew exactly what was going on. I waited for you to leave the room, of course, loitering in the dimly lit corridor. Do you remember me looking you up and down, our hands brushing? I was both impressed by the boldness of killing a man in a busy nightclub and slightly horrified that you'd left him to be found by someone else. Me, as it happened. I left him too, of course. But I suspect that bulging face won't leave my brain for a long time yet.

You were killing our family. I had no proof you'd got to Kathleen and Jeremy, but it didn't take much to imagine you flying out to Spain, hiring a car and ramming them off the road. You took a much more rough and ready approach as a beginner, didn't you? But I guess you were intent on making each death look like an accident, and two old people driving off a cliff in the dark is an easy initial win.

Now I had to decide what to do with this information. The Artemis family wasn't big – and the only ones (that you hadn't bumped off) connected with the money were Simon's wife and daughter, and his sister-in-law. That's if it *was* the money that was driving you. If I had to guess, I'd say there was more to it though. From the little I saw of your life, you lived a pretty boring existence. Not many friends, no big career (I hope that's not offensive to you) and a small flat in a dingy street. Almost like you were treading water until . . . until what? Until you rid the world of your toxic family and could then go forth and prosper? I harbour very little resentment towards Simon because I had a wonderful life with Lottie and Christopher and my sisters. Had it not been for Jean, I would have gone on happily because I had that foundation. I still will. But you didn't. And maybe that made you obsessed with the unfairness of it all. It *is* unfair, Grace. Out of all of us entangled in this mess, you got the short straw, didn't you?

After a few days turning it over in my mind, and a bracing conversation with Simon which involved him shouting at me for not being able to come to his office at 11 a.m. one Wednesday, I decided that I would let whatever you were doing play out. Partly, I felt that you should be allowed to right the wrongs done to you. And partly, since I'm being honest, because I weighed up what was best for me and realised that you might be doing me a favour. Two things made my decision. One is that I wanted Simon out of my life. I could now see the future, and it involved spending time with him whenever he demanded it. The money he'd given me had made him feel like he'd earned it, and I could not bear the idea of being absorbed into his family, driving around in his Bentley and spending summers in Marbella. The other thing was, if you did succeed in cutting down the lot of them, I'd be in line for some of the fortune. You see, Grace, I'm a happy hypocrite. I didn't want much to do with dear old Dad, but I would be completely at ease with taking some of the spoils. Money is money, no matter how you come by it. And I would use it in a different way to Simon. No brash displays of excess, no gold taps. I was meant to have money, or so I've always thought. I'd be rather good at it I think. And your plan could get me there faster than toiling away trying to work my way up the ladder.

I'd never have even considered doing what you did if I'd not watched it play out. Even if I'd been wronged in the way you felt you'd been wronged. But that didn't mean I couldn't make something good out of it. I guess on a sliding scale of morality I'd be somewhere in the middle. I reckon most people would look at my situation and come to the same decision as me if they were being honest. Hard thing to be honest about though – that's why telling you all this has been so freeing. I know you can never show anyone this. It's enforced trust, which is probably better than the normal kind.

I'm getting tired of writing all this down though, so I'm going to try and wrap it up. You know the majority of my story now. Or as much as you need to know. I watched you continue on with your course of action. Janine went a bit far, if you don't mind me saying – the description of her death really made me feel queasy. Again, I wasn't there (you took off abruptly and I couldn't get the time off work at such short notice), but I found out pretty sharpish from Simon's PA. I still don't fully understand why you let Lara off – did she just seem like small fry? I wasn't there for Bryony of course, but I very much enjoyed how you executed that (well, her). Funny and effective. But that's when Simon really started to unravel. He loved Bryony. I think he was bored of Janine – had been for years. We're the result of that, I suppose. But Bryony was his only child. His only *true* child. He's oddly old fashioned, for a product of the modern world. Marriage, kids, a reputation, that all mattered immensely to Simon. And no matter how ghastly she might have seemed to you or me, he loved his daughter. Beyond the pain of losing her, he also began to get paranoid. Though I guess it's not paranoia if someone is actually out to get you. He would summon me to his house, and sit on the sofa with the curtains closed, occasionally getting up to pace the room manically. He'd tell me repeatedly that someone was killing off his family. He'd been to the police, hired security, the works. Nobody really believed him, which I guess you can take as a compliment. Everyone thought it was just a series of unlucky coincidences – the *Daily Mail* ran a double-page spread on 'the mogul's misfortune' listing all the bad luck that had fallen on the Artemis family. But the fact that nobody seemed to take him seriously made Simon even more insistent. He thought it was someone he'd crossed paths with in business. He didn't say who, but he clearly had someone in mind because he was frightened.

I stepped into the role of dutiful son at this time. I slept at the Hampstead house, often woken up several times a night by Simon, who would want to point out more ways in which someone was trying to kill him. These were always nonsense – a man he thought was loitering outside the front gates, or a car parked too near his office entrance. He was just looking for signs. Every time a window rattled, the man would fall apart. Not that the windows at his house rattled, the originals had long been ripped out and replaced with sturdy double glazing.

We became close, as I leant into my new position as closest relative and confidant, hopeful that it would be short-lived with your assistance. I helped organise all the grim things that need doing when someone dies. And I listened when he wanted to scream and shout about it all, which was often. He became more and more unbearable as the weeks went on and from what I could see, you weren't doing much. I occasionally saw you lingering outside his gates, you know. It wasn't very subtle, Grace, I must say. Even if you did have some big plan in the works, I was beginning to despair of you being able to get near Simon. His security detail was immense by now, he was surrounded by burly men who would have snapped you like a twig if you'd got within five feet of him.

I began to feel furious with you, which is bonkers, isn't it? But I felt like I had finally figured out how to extricate myself from this appalling situation and I'd come to imagine that we were working in tandem and to a schedule. But you weren't playing ball. I barely had time to follow you much back then, since Simon was growing more aggressive, more erratic, more dependent on me. But when I did, I saw you going for dinners and heading off on long runs, carrying on as if you'd not got one more target to tick off, and I was confused by your lack of momentum.

I was barely able to function at work because he called every five minutes, crying or drunk or both. I'd turn my phone off and he'd email me. I began to flinch whenever I looked at my inbox. I pride myself on being a hard worker, I really do think that work makes a man and I was furious with myself for doing a half-arsed job when I was meant to be attacking this opportunity and rising up through the company. Bonus time was looming and I could just see mine shrinking every time my boss saw me on the phone.

Looking back, my mental health was plummeting, something I'd never even considered before. My sleep was shot to pieces, my weight dropped alarmingly, no matter what I ate. I just felt completely trapped, like a fox in a hole. It's rather put me off hunting now that I see the analogy actually. Another thing Simon has ruined for me. But he wouldn't leave me alone and his will was overwhelming. Eventually, I marched round there and told him that I couldn't do it anymore. I was firm but I was calm. I told him he was behaving appallingly and couldn't treat me like one of his assistants. I went on and on until he started crying again, but I wasn't swayed this time. The tears dried up pretty fast when he realised I wasn't going to comfort him, and he walked over to his desk and sat down. I carried on listing the ways I felt he wasn't being a gent, getting so worked up that I wasn't paying attention to what he was doing until he came back over to me and presented me with a cheque. It was made out for £500,000. That stopped me in my tracks, I can tell you. My mouth hung open for a few seconds as he pushed it into my face and told me that if I went with him to St Tropez for a week, he'd make sure it was worth my while.

'I need to be out of the country for a few days, just keep my head down, son. And I don't want to go alone. Don't tell me this wouldn't help your mum. What about those girls, Harry? They need this. It's just a week or so.' I stayed silent, weighing it all up in my mind, and he watched me, eyes narrow. 'You're bargaining with me, is that it? Well there's no clearer sign that you're my son. I'll make it official. I'll make over an inheritance. That's what you want, isn't it? That's what everyone wants in the end.' He wasn't wrong there. But he couldn't see that he made his money the only currency he had in life all by himself.

Simon wasn't clear about why he needed to leave the country initially, but for all he fudged it, it became clear that there was some kind of investigation into his company going on and his advisers had strongly suggested he not be available for a while. I wondered which part of the company was likely the most dodgy (the airline seemed a prime contender) but to be honest, Grace, having seen how he worked, it could have been any of them. It was clear that shit was about to hit the proverbial but I couldn't concern myself with that. I wouldn't get more enmeshed in his villainous world. That's how I saw it by now. A seedy and nasty life that I was ashamed to have gone looking for. But that kind of money was impossible to ignore, and I would have been a fool to do so. And that is why, not six hours later, I stepped off a private jet and out into the warm French air. If I'd known what would happen I might have asked for that cheque to have a few more zeros on the end.

CHAPTER SEVENTEEN

12 p.m.

It's all over. The past fourteen months are about to become a strange footnote in my life story. Kelly wished me luck before I left for the decision.

'I'll miss you, Gracie, come visit me sometime. I'll make *you* a spoon in the next class, haha.' She hugged me tightly, digging her nails into my back. I allowed her to stay like this for five seconds, before striding through the door without looking back. George Thorpe came through, his face ruddy with pride as he met me in a visitors' room at Limehouse after he'd been to court and seen my case successfully overturned. I'd watched via video-link, which deprived me of the chance to have a dramatic moment in front of the judge and meant I missed out on the inevitable media scrum outside the court. Better this way, despite the slight anticlimax, I can work at my own pace now. Instead, I received an awkward embrace from my lawyer, a pledge to catch up in a few weeks to go over everything and an invitation to dinner, which I will certainly not take up. I even got a congratulations from the officer supervising our meeting. Not exactly a cinematic climax, but momentous nonetheless. I did what I set out to do for Marie. Now I am free.

4 p.m.

I am home! I was released at great speed, which took me by surprise since I'd become used to a system that took months to make even the smallest decisions. I guess they were desperate for my cell. Even now I imagine Kelly will be telling her new roomie all about the last occupant, sitting an inch too close on the thin bunk. I had to scramble to get my stuff together and get out by midday, which meant Jimmy wasn't there to meet me. I didn't mind though, not when I realised it was to avoid any hopeful photographers. I was grateful for it, since fourteen months in prison doesn't exactly help you look camera ready. I took a cab home, weaving through London streets bathed in rare bright sunshine, staring out of the window and smiling the whole way. The flat was quiet and warm when I opened the door, everything in its rightful place. Sophie had even sent her cleaner over, and there was a bottle of Brunello and some tiramisu from the local deli waiting for me on the table. I took both into the bath, and soaked in Le Labo oil for two hours. A glorious experience, I was half hysterical with glee. I'm going to go through all my mail and then meet Jimmy for what I hope will be a suitably indulgent dinner at Brasserie du Balon. Life feels like it's finally unfurling and showing itself to me.

CHAPTER EIGHTEEN

God what a mess, Grace. What a godawful mess. It all turned into a sort of hideous farce, except nobody remembered to laugh. On our first day in France, Simon crashed out on a sofa in the games room and I escaped to the veranda and asked a timid member of staff to get me a coffee. I stretched out in the sun and tried to shake off the dreaded chance that he'd wake up and find me. For a couple of minutes I stared out towards the sea, marvelling at how little I could enjoy this beautiful place. This sunny place for shady people, as someone once said. Then, out of habit, I picked up my phone and scrolled through the BBC news site. Flicking past war and news about some minor Tory MP shagging his PA, my eye was drawn to a photo of a beautiful woman, 'tributes were still pouring in for'. She'd been pushed off a balcony and you'd been the one to push her. My face went cold, despite the humming heat, and a roaring sound rushed through my ears and into my head. I felt like I didn't understand you at all, despite all the time I'd spent trying. You were a cold-blooded revenge-seeker, not an impulsive crime-of-passion killer. Why would you waste all your hard work to throw a love rival off a balcony? What a moment of stupidity. I don't want to risk being called sexist, but this emotional reaction was hard to see through any other lens. How would you get to Simon now?

After a few hours spent trying to find out more about your arrest, I heard Simon yelling at me from the sitting room and had to give up the quest. I wasn't too worried about him seeing your news, since he was by now practically living on another planet of paranoia and rage. In his state, he was more likely to be found watching YouTube videos about aliens than checking the headlines. I spent two hideous days with our father in his villa, where he shoved a frankly astonishing amount of cocaine up his nose and refused to open the curtains in case someone was watching the house. His security detail stayed outside, wary of his outbursts, and the poor housekeeper, who hadn't been told we were coming, fled to her room after he threw a vase at her head when he discovered the beds weren't made. It was just me and him. Every time I tried to retreat to another part of the house he would follow me, ranting about how there was a conspiracy and insisting that 'we have to stop the bastards'. I kept telling myself, 'Come on, Harry, a few more days and there's half a million quid for the family,' but it felt pretty far away, I can tell you. On the third morning, I awoke to find Simon standing over my bed, eyes bloodshot and shirt ripped. He'd clearly been up all night, and he stank of whisky.

'We're out of here. There's cameras. The yacht awaits, get your shit together, son.' I bridled at being called son, thinking of my dear old Christopher with sorrow, but he was already off, grabbing his suitcase and slamming doors.

The yacht was a monstrosity. I've never seen anything like it in my life and hope never to again. A fancy floating caravan, that's what it looked like, all chrome and glass and nothing like a real boat at all. Thankfully, once on board, Simon seemed to relax and he passed out on the sofa for the entire day, only to wake up when dinner was served. We ate in semi-silence, as he downed glass after glass of wine – 'Chic Chablis' from his own vineyard, he told me as I tried to keep the disgust from my face. As if anything could tell you more about a person, right, Grace? My hand started twitching as we ate dessert, and I tried to steady it, alarmed at this new development. Simon noticed, and he laughed. He laughed and told me I was too delicate for a big chap. I said nothing, my heart beating and my ears humming. When it was all over and he was pretty steaming, he yelled for the captain and told him to prepare the speedboat. The man, clearly sensing that Simon wasn't in a mood to argue, hurried off with no word of warning, but a steward clearing the table raised his eyes in my direction. I tried to distract our father, telling him that I was in no mood for an excursion, but he waved me away in irritation. 'You're here on my dime, young Harry. We're going for a ride.'

And so we did. He took a fresh bottle of Chic Chablis under his arm and staggered down the stairs to the speedboat, as I trailed behind him feeling a bit sick. We roared off into the dark black distance, me holding the seat for dear life, him yelling into the wind as he held the bottle between his knees. After about fifteen minutes, he slowed the boat down and came to a stop. He fumbled his way back towards me and laughed at my expression. I admit I felt queasy. Boats have never really been my thing and his ducking and weaving through an empty ocean had me feeling all kinds of green. Mainly I was just fed up. Of him, of this boat, of my life every day since I had met him.

Simon sat down and thrust his face into mine with a leer.

'Man up, Harry, this is bonding right here. Act like you're enjoying it, for fuck's sake.'

'I'm not though,' I said with as much dignity as I could muster while trying not to throw up. 'I'm not enjoying it. I want to go back to the yacht.'

He screwed up his face and mimicked me. 'I want to go back to the yacht, Daddy, I'm bored of this. How quickly you've grown used to my lifestyle and my money, son. You could at least pretend you're here for the company.' He belched in my face, and roared with laughter. 'But you can't, can you? You're just like your mother. She pretended to be all pure of heart too, but she was just looking for some rich mark to spread her legs for.'

I stood, pulling him up with me by his shirt, and I grabbed the disgusting wine bottle which sat next to him. I had but one thought in my head: I desperately wanted him to shut up. I smashed the bottle over his head with a strength I can only imagine came from all the pent-up rage I had. A familiar buzzing sound rushed through my ears before being replaced with a loud splash. I could make out an arm in the water and a loud, sickening gurgle. I put the torch on my phone and shone it down by the side of the boat. Simon was holding the side of the boat with two fingers, but the rest of him wasn't moving. He had blood streaming down his head, pooling below his nose and flowing into his mouth. That was the sound, a wretched sound I can still hear when I think about it. He was trying to stay afloat as he choked on his own blood. I stood there watching him, readying myself to reach down and pull him out. But then an odd thing happened. You came into my mind, Grace. I thought of all you'd been up to, how hard you'd tried to get to this man. I knew how unlikely it was that you'd ever succeed now. I thought about our mothers and what they suffered at the hands of Simon Artemis. And then I thought of how much I was suffering now. If I pulled him out and took him back to the safety of the yacht, he might have me prosecuted. Or worse, he might hold what I'd done over my head for the next twenty years, keeping me close by forever.

It had been an accident. I would never be able to plan something so hideous or carry out violence in cold blood. But I'd been sorely provoked and we all have a breaking point, don't we? I didn't know that I was going to let him die, truly I didn't. It all just sort of happened, as though I was watching it from a slight distance. I bent down towards him and prised his fingers off the side of the boat, before giving him a tiny push so that he bobbed away a few inches. His eyes widened but he couldn't speak. Then I sat down.

'If you try to touch the boat again, I'm going to drive off. So don't. Just sit there for a few more minutes and I'll pull you out. You need to learn how to treat people properly. Maybe this is what it takes,' I told him as I rubbed a tiny speck of blood off my knuckles. He was in no position even to attempt a lunge towards the side by now anyway. It took three minutes for him to disappear, his sandy hair slowly dipping below the water. I sat in silence and stared up at the stars. When I saw that he was completely submerged, I cracked the bottle against the side and dumped it into the water, which was surely a suitable fate for Artemis wine. Then I waited for thirty minutes to be sure he wouldn't suddenly burst from the water. You'll remember doing something similar with our dear cousin Andrew, no doubt, it's tricky to know how long is long enough, isn't it? When I was satisfied there was no chance, I took the speedboat back to the yacht. I'm a shockingly poor navigator and it took me almost an hour to get back and raise the crew. I explained that he'd lost control as he sped up, and fallen overboard. With no signal, I'd been forced to search the area alone for an hour in the desperate hope of finding him alive but I'd failed. The captain didn't seem that surprised; it helped my case that Simon had been absolutely sloshed when we'd set off. Search and rescue found no trace of him over the next twenty-four hours but I held my breath every time they radioed over an update.

And that was that really. My story was accepted as gospel, why wouldn't it be? I was referred to as an assistant in the papers but I went unnamed, which was a huge relief. I wouldn't like to upset Mum or make trouble for the girls at school. But Lara Artemis got in touch with me to thank me for being so discreet, and she was so nice about it that I told her my true connection to Simon. She wasn't surprised, I must say. I supposed she'd known him long enough to greet an illegitimate child without so much as a raised eyebrow. And Simon's DNA test was all the proof I needed. Lara is a lovely woman, Grace, I'm sorry you'll never meet her. She's in charge of the family fortune now and she's been incredibly generous to me. More than I could ever ask for really. I cashed that cheque of course, and my family are all doing much better now. Lara has even been down to lunch a few times. It's never mentioned explicitly, but I think she and Mum recognise the bond they share. Part of a select group of women who survived the Artemis brothers.

So why am I telling you all of this? You must be wondering. Well, partly it's because I wanted you to know how he really died. I thought it might help you feel less of a failure to know that I took on the mantle and finished off what you started. In a funny old way, we were a team. The timing couldn't have been more perfect really – given all your recent problems, you'd have had less opportunity to kill him yourself anyway. And if we're being entirely honest, you would never have managed it. I know you gave it a good old go with the rest of them, and well done on that. But Simon was a different matter entirely. And it would've needed more than vague plans and luck. It didn't really look to me like you were working with anything else. Am I wrong, Grace?

So that's the gallant part. I hope it pleases you. But mainly I write this to let you know that you need to leave it there now. The revenge was your motivation, I understand that, I really do. And you've got it now, with a little help from yours truly. Expand your life, shack up with your old pal Jimmy – there are people in the world who want to love you, Grace, if you decide to let them. Write a book about your harrowing incarceration – publishers will be champing at the bit to sign you up. But all the other stuff stops here. I need to protect my new life. Along with a sizeable chunk of the family fortune, Lara has graciously made me CFO of the new foundation and we'll be running it together. It's not been announced yet, we've been building up to that, but it won't be long now. She's lost interest in the wildlife stuff and I'm glad, it's not quite as grabby as the new endeavour. I won't say I know much about refugee kids but I'm relishing the opportunity to hold gala dinners and invite the great and the good from the banking world to open up their wallets. There will be amazing corporate tie-ins and we'll work closely with the financial world to make the foundation as big as that of the Rothschilds and the Guinnesses. It will be prestigious, a world away from Simon really. Certainly no Chic Chablis up for auction under Lara's new reign.

Just to make sure you won't come for me (I respect you too much to think you wouldn't), I set up a little scheme while you were in prison. I hope you'll forgive the slightly dirty tactics, but I'm sure you'll understand the need for collateral here. When I found out you'd been sent to Limehouse I paid a fairly low-rent investigator to find out who you shared a cell with. It wasn't hard as it turns out. Kelly had somehow told half of Islington that she was the lucky one chosen to bunk up with the notorious Grace Bernard. I wrote to her, asking to visit and explaining that there was money in it, and she agreed. Of course she did. I saw you at that first visit as it happens, sitting with your lawyer. You glanced over several times, perhaps surprised to see Kelly with someone like me. I must say I'm still surprised you didn't find me familiar. Off the top of my head, I've been within three feet of you several times. Outside the Wildlife

Centre, on the steps of St Paul's, in the strange sex club (I'll let you off there since I was in a mask), grabbing a lighter in Soho, in the British Museum café, in the visiting room. I guess having a slightly generic face works in my favour here. You looked a little thin, if you don't mind me saying. I hope you make the most of your newfound freedom and enjoy some slap-up meals. Sorry, where was I?

Yes, Kelly. Not the kind of woman I'd come across much in my everyday life – I couldn't stop staring at her astonishingly bright nails when we met – but I found her to be a lovely girl. Very helpful. I explained that I worked for a firm investigating your crimes for a private benefactor and wondered if she'd be open to keeping an eye out for certain things. I'll say this for Kelly, it was refreshing to see how little detail she needed on me once financial remuneration was dangled. Through a contact of hers, which took me to a fairly insalubrious part of East London, I managed to get a phone to her. It had the all-important camera feature – what did we do before that innovation, eh? And Kelly, fair play to her, took to her new role like a duck to water. She watched you much more closely than you probably imagined, and texted me with much excitement when she realised that you were writing down your life story. She read it of course, I'm surprised you were so careless. And she photographed every single page with an enthusiasm I was in awe of. Then, just to be sure, she took a few choice pages for fingerprints and the like. I hadn't even thought of that, but I guess when you've been blackmailing as long as she has, you learn to keep hard copies too. I have to say, you underestimated her.

So you see, this must be where your journey ends. You cannot kill me, because the history of your crimes will be released immediately along with a letter my legal chaps have detailing that any accident which might befall me would be nothing of the sort. You must not contact Lara, or said information will be handed to the police. We've both been through a lot at the hands of the Artemis family but between us, we're free now. And it might not look exactly how you'd hoped, but you still won. We won. Tomorrow you'll likely be released, so Kelly says. This email will be in your inbox by the time you get back to your little flat. Good sense keeping that on, well done you. Oh, and the message expires after it's been read. A nifty bit of tech recommended by our mutual friend actually. Blackmailers keep on top of this stuff it seems. Now that I've told you that I'd better stop writing. It might initially feel as if a man has swooped in and taken your victory away from you, but that's not it at all. I just had better cards. I encourage you to enjoy your life. Money isn't everything, and you're lucky to be walking free. Good luck, Grace, I will think of you often.

Your brother

PS

Don't worry about Kelly, I've paid her handsomely, so I'm confident she'll leave you well alone.

POSTSCRIPT

Hey roomie! It's Kel. Hope the outside world is treating you well. Call me, there's things we need to discuss. Don't even think about ignoring this, I know where u live, LOL. PS – my mum loved the spoon but she was confused by the marks on it. I wasn't though! I'll keep it safe. Miss u! Xxx

ACKNOWLEDGEMENTS

Thank you to everyone at The Borough Press for taking a chance on my first novel. Most importantly, my editor Ann Bissell for picking up the draft when it was already halfway done and fully embracing it, meticulously editing it and for knowing and understanding the characters as well as I did. Ann tolerated my casual approach to deadlines and handled my occasional panic flare-ups with supreme kindness and grace. She made writing during a pandemic enjoyable, and she made the book infinitely better. I really couldn't have asked for a nicer editor.

Thank you Fliss for actually getting the book out to people, for showing it off so well, and for working so hard to give it a good launch – not easy during the weirdest moment in our history.

Thank you also to Abbie Salter, Caroline Young, Sarah Munro, Margot Gray, Lucy Stewart and Suzie Dooré. What a team of women.

Thank you to my agent Charlie Campbell who steadfastly ignores office hours and has been there to help me at any time of day or night since I came up with the idea for this book. I can't imagine anyone being more invested, more patient and more by my side throughout it all.

Thank you Aoife Rice, who has brilliantly handled all my other work, while knowing the book had to come first.

Thank you Nicki Kennedy, Sam Edenborough, Jenny Robson, Katherine West and their colleagues at ILA for selling the book in other countries. Hopefully this means I get to attend wine fuelled book festivals in hotter climes sometime soon.

Emily Hayward-Whitlock and Fern McCauley, thank you so much for all your hard work on the rights side of things. I know how much you've put into it all.

Huge thanks to Owen O'Rorke, Nigel Urwin, David Hooper and Anthony Mosawi for all the gracious advice and guidance.

Thank you to my neighbour Robert, who gave me the benefit of his immensely detailed legal knowledge to help me through some of the novel's plot points. You're also a lovely neighbour, lucky us.

Thank you Max Van Cleek for helping me figure out smart homes and for taking my ludicrous questions about whether I could kill someone with a remote control seriously.

Josh Berger, you're a true pal. Thanks for your counsel.

Pandora Sykes, thank you for being the first person to read a proof of the novel and provide a quote, it was immensely kind of you.

Janine Gibson, you read my first few chapters and laughed. Making you laugh was the encouragement I needed to carry on.

Archie, Maya, Miranda, Nesrine, Ben, Benji, you're the best people. I love you all.

Lizzie, my dearest sister. Thank you for reading the book. Thank you for your notes, which helped me more than I can say. You are my en.

Linds and Alan, thanks for literally everything. You inspired this book (in all the best ways).

Finally, Greg. All the men in my book are complete bastards and you are the total opposite. You told me I was a writer long before I ever called myself one. I am so very lucky to have you by my side.

If you loved How to Kill Your Family, *look out for another deliciously dark novel from Bella Mackie in 2023!*

Available to pre-order now